Weathercock

Glen Duncan

Scribner

First published in Great Britain by Scribner, 2003
An imprint of Simon & Schuster UK Ltd
A Viacom Company

1 3 5 7 9 10 8 6 4 2

Simon & Schuster UK Ltd
Africa House
64–78 Kingsway
London WC2B 6AH

Simon & Schuster Australia
Sydney

www.simonsays.co.uk

A CIP catalogue record for this book
is available from the British Library

ISBN 0–7432–2014–5

Typeset by M Rules
Printed and bound in Great Britain by
The Bath Press, Bath

Praise for Glen Duncan

'One of the hottest literary properties of the new century' *Independent*

I, Lucifer

'Duncan is a sharp, sometimes savage observer of the human condition, whose talents are as many as the legions of Hell'
Matthew Baylis

'Lucifer is charming and sexy and very very funny. Glen Duncan knows way too much and says it far too well. I fear for his soul'
Stella Duffy

'Clever and challenging . . . sizzling with mephitic energy'
Independent

'The devil gets all the best tunes and on the strength of this fiendishly funny, wickedly eloquent little number, it would seem he gets all the best books as well' *Big Issue*

'Devilishly clever . . . a suitably sulphurous take on London and humanity' *Time Out*

'A wicked, impish conceit, ably orchestrated with Duncan's playful intelligence and sizzling wit' *Arena*

Love Remains

'If good writers are those who make the ordinary remarkable, Duncan is a very good writer indeed' *The Times*

'His use of language is so precise, his dissection of male and female emotions so spot-on, it almost takes your breath away. His plausibility rating on the gender bending scale is up there with Tolstoy' *Time Out*

'Duncan takes you down paths of the heart you had forgotten existed, and others you fear to tread' *Sunday Times*

'A graphic, shocking account of the physical and mental horrors that overtake people whose lives have exploded . . . intense, perceptive and brutal' *Sunday Telegraph*

For
Stephen Coates

whose friendship
has remained constant
through every change
in the weather

Acknowledgements

My thanks to: Jonny Geller at Curtis Brown, Ben Ball, Rochelle Venables and all at Scribner, Carol Anderson and Helen Simpson.

Contents

There are people for whom evil means only a maladjustment with *things*, a wrong correspondence of one's life with the environment. Such evil as this is curable, in principle at least, upon the natural plane, for merely by modifying the self or the things, or both at once, the two terms may be made to fit, and all go merry as a marriage bell again. But there are others for whom evil is no mere relation of the subject to particular outer things, but something more radical and general, a wrongness or vice in his essential nature, which no alteration of the environment, or any superficial arrangement of the inner self, can cure, and which requires a supernatural remedy.

William James, *The Varieties of Religious Experience*

By a Papal enactment made in the middle of the 9th century, the figure of a cock was set up on every church steeple as the emblem of St Peter. The emblem is an allusion to his denial of our Lord thrice before the cock crew twice . . . A person who is always changing his mind is, figuratively, a *weathercock*.

Brewer's Concise Dictionary of Phrase & Fable

PROLOGUE

The Ghost

Kelp's ghost came again tonight, after a thunderstorm that drenched the skyscrapers and cooled Manhattan's malarial streets. Didn't say a word. Just hovered in the open window six floors up, smiling. Death hasn't changed him. Still the epicene glamour, the bespectacled green eyes and ravenous grin, still the halo of white-blond hair, the tantalizing look of knowing something you don't. Still everything as when alive, in fact, except the crucial thing, except life.

Didn't say a word (never does, contrary bugger), but I know what he wants, now that Deborah's gone, now that I've turned my back once and for all on the Devil's work.

I had what I'm sure was my last laughing fit today, on Broadway, in the afternoon sun. Just below Canal a small crowd had gathered round a long-fingernailed man with dark skin and an oily head of hair, who, standing behind a fold-out table draped with a felt cloth, was going through his version of find-the-lady. Three silver cups and a cherry. A hundred dollars on offer, a dollar to try your luck.

Light bounced off the flanks of passing cars. I stood and watched for more than half an hour. Every time I knew exactly where the cherry was. Increasing amazement as punter after punter selected the wrong cup.

The hundred rose to two hundred. I watched on. Another half-dozen saps, another half-dozen wrong guesses. Me bang-on another half-dozen times.

Unable to bear it any longer, I paid my dollar. Watched the moves. Knew exactly where the cherry was. Nominated my cup. Wrong. The audience's unsurprised murmur, my mouth popping open. *Oh that's too bad*, said the huckster, then swung back into his pitch. *It's real simple, folks, just keep your eye on the cherry. No magic needed, no trickery involved. Just keep your eye on the cherry. A buck wins you two hundred.*

I looked up and found that a small, brown, wizened man in Nehru jacket and baggy silk trousers was observing my disappointment with a look of sympathy. I hesitated, catching his eye. Then with a slight comedy-Asian head-waggle he shrugged, showing his palms – *that's where I thought it was, too* – and that was me gone. A chortle, a giggle, a wheeze – then full capitulation. Every detail colluded: the head-waggler, the crowd, the fire hydrant, the giant buildings, the blue sky and glittering asphalt; everything conspired to make me laugh my head off for perhaps three minutes, bent, shaking, hands gripping knees, helpless, remembering among other things the shape and weight of the gun and the shape and weight of the empty spaces around me.

When it was over, I had the feeling it might be the last time.

★

Some facts are not in dispute. My name is Dominic Hood. (Surname suspiciously apposite, given the criminality and the cloaked self, but life does after all sometimes play into the hands of art, and in any case I spent too long in publishing to think autobiography an ingenuous enterprise.) I'm thirty-five years old, and a Roman Catholic, Dominic *Francis* Hood in full, five eight on my collapsed arches, small-skulled, with Oxo-coloured eyes and the very beginnings of a pot belly; the overall look, as my sister Julia once said, of a degenerate and shifty chimpanzee. In spite of which some women still seem willing to sleep with me, thank God.

I left London and publishing for New York on the trail of an exorcist. (Laughing fits, ghosts, exorcists – I know. There are miracles, too. *Two* of them.)

Of most recent significance, I've said my third and final good-bye to the great and monstrous Deborah Black — that *is* a fact – and am holed up now with quiet and damaged Holly the waitress, who herself ran away from London three years ago and about whom, despite a winter and spring of coitus and cohabitation, I know next to nothing.

Wordless and generally awkward copulation with Holly, whose damage has driven her a long way from her body. For the first couple of months she didn't look at me. Then she did look at me, with an intense animal detachment, and I realized we'd moved up a gear, albeit inarticulately. I've no idea how many gears there are. Not talking seems to be the best way of going about whatever it is we've got. Neither of us is sure we've got *anything*. We let other sounds fill our silences: television; music; rain; the brownstone's voluble plumbing; 13th Street's murmurs and honks. Tonight (very articulate), the thunder. I lay with my cheek sweat-stuck to her thigh, close to the pulse in her groin. She had looked at me – *looked* at me, I mean – when I'd come, after which there was less to say than ever. So we lay gently throbbing in silence, lightning-strobed, the big thunder detonating bits of my childhood, and, I imagined, hers. When it was finished (the air relieved of its pith, the streets surprised at their sudden ability to breathe), she said, 'Your head's too heavy there,' and I said, 'Sorry,' and we sweatily disengaged, and she rolled onto her left side, closed her eyes and fell asleep. Therefore missed the appearance of Kelp's ghost – by his design, no doubt. In the after-storm quiet it was just me and him, me with backache and foully smouldering American Spirit, him with incorporeal arms folded and grin like a moonlit knife. Even the dark-rimmed specs have passed over, apparently.

I know what he wants. *Some are born to leave, some achieve leaving, and some have leaving thrust upon them.* Well, we'll see.

Holly woke after the thunder, the lightning, the visitation, to find me sitting on the edge of the bed, trembling.

'Was it him?'

'Yes.'

'What did he say?'

'Nothing. He never says anything.'

It's buying me time with her, this supernatural nonsense. It distracts her from self-loathing and all those frail questions – floating like motes in the apartment – of who and what we are to each other. It's not that she believes in ghosts. It's that she believes I believe. This makes me someone against whom it would be perverse to judge herself. That, in the end, is why I'm still here: I'm a relief from her judgement of herself. Her judgement of herself, otherwise, attends her life in an ambient scream.

'Did you have any laughing fits today?' she asked, after it was apparent that both of us were past sleep.

'Yes. But it felt like the last.'

'What makes you say that?'

'I'm not sure.'

'You're not sure?'

'No. But I feel like I'm past something.'

At which distant thunder rumbled, and subsided, and we went quiet together. In the moments when we go quiet together I know what it is I want to give Holly. But there's a long way to go before I can offer it to her. And when I do, I'll find out it's the last thing on earth she wants. Nonetheless.

Poetically, there was thunder and lightning (along with the first of the great laughing fits) the day I said my third and final good-bye to Deborah Black, nine months ago. Good-bye. *God be with ye.* I thought of the uncontracted original, and how *inapposite.* Possibly she thought the same, since it provoked her last three words to me in reply: 'You fucking idiot.'

I looked at the dark eyes in the cold little face, unlipsticked mouth the colour of raw steak. Then the electric window hummed up between us and she drove away.

She's gone. (That, too, is a fact.) Drawn away like the sea from the strand; and like the sea she's left behind her the smashed shells, the glass fragments, the homesick litter and the brazenly dead things exposed at last to the rub of wind and sunshine. Now I'm trotting along the salt line with my bucket and gloves (and my disturbed female assistant), my magnifying glass and tweezers, bent at ninety degrees, with all the time in the world to figure out what such violently left leavings (thrust upon me or achieved – I'm not sure which) might mean.

★

I know what it is I want to give Holly. But there's a long way to go before I can offer it to her. And when I do, I'll find out it's the last thing on earth she wants.

Nonetheless.

CHAPTER ONE

◆

The First Miracle

I first met Father Ignatius Malone the day Callum Burke did for me with the cricket bat. Burke was a meaty and freckled Irish boy-thug with tight shorts and a habit of burping sourly. Loathing was mutual, immediate, and without reason or question. Our first exchange set the tone. We sat opposite each other across one of the dining hall's long tables, me staring at the ugliness of him eating: indecorously large spoonfuls of pineapple sponge and custard shovelled into the chomping and not properly closed mouth.

'What the fock're yew lookin' at, anniewayz?'

'Not much.'

'I'll kick yer fock'n face in.'

'Try it.'

And so on.

Cut, therefore, to a wet afternoon two years later, St Edmund's RC Primary School, the medical room, September 1972, me going on eight years old. Not much of a medical room, differing from an office only by virtue of the small bed, set of archaic weighing scales, First Aid kit and laminated poster showing a man reduced to his circulatory system. Nurse Maggie in sole charge, a buxom, soft-spoken woman with green eyeshadow and a helmet of back-combed auburn hair, who chewed Juicy Fruit and wore Charlie perfume, excessively. Burke had whacked me between the legs with a cricket bat, from behind, as I stood clutching my kneecaps and catching my breath after a cross-yard sprint. I had gone straight down, first onto all fours, then onto my side. Burke had run off, giggling, and I, after the dinner lady's solicitations had elicited nothing but a single gout of vomit, had been carried up for treatment.

No objection to that. Nurse Maggie's brand of healthcare was a stick of Juicy Fruit and melodious first-person-plural rhetoric until it was established, via taken pulse and temperature, that there was nothing serious wrong with us, after which, as long as we were content to read a book or pretend to be asleep, we could stay on the starchy cot till Home Time.

I must have genuinely fallen asleep, however. When I woke, Nurse Maggie wasn't there. The window showed turbid sky and silver rain darkening the playground. One out-of-sync street lamp had come on, prematurely, in glamorous scarlet. In a few moments, I would be afraid. The supernatural's horde would perceive me and the fact of my aloneness, and I would have to deal with them, somehow. The first prickles of sweat. Blood tuning up. Hold on to that street lamp. They're coming. Oh God. Hail Mary, full of grace, the Lord is—

'Ah, there's a boy here.'

I started, and turned.

'Don't be afraid,' he said, ducking his head for the lintel

and entering the room with a long stride. He sat on the cot's edge and looked at me. The wind threw a prodigal broadcast of rain at the window, then subsided.

'Not too good?' he asked. A softly gravelled voice, and the English had fornicated with foreign parts. Not that he looked English, with the long, worn face the colour of a Spanish saddle, the grey-green eyes and old Injun cheek-bones, the white thatch of hair and glimmer of stubble. A terrible mish-mash to one of my tender years, compounded by the worse-for-wear collar and greasy cassock: the first priest I'd seen who wasn't white. Certainly the first priest – the first *human* – I'd seen who had to duck his head to get through a doorway.

'Sick?' he asked, leaning forward to examine me. I opened my mouth to answer, then caught the whiff of him: sand, herbs, perfume, evoking deserts, distance, the Bible. These perceptual extravagances, yes, but overriding them – gentle tingling in scalp and bowels – the conviction that he knew about the Things.

He smiled out of the cross-hatched face. Straight white teeth. Eyes over-alive, fierce when they settled on you.

'Skiving?' he asked. The slang and the accent a porno-graphic conjunction, like a woman and a dog (one *of* the Things, seen on a sodden scrap in Logan Street's flooded gutter, now touched by his gentle clairvoyance). I sat up against the stacked pillows.

'What happened to you?' he asked.

'Callum Burke hit me with a bat, Father.'

'Did he?'

'Yes.'

'And why would he do a thing like that?'

'I don't know.'

Eyebrows raised, slightly.

'We hate each other,' I explained.

'I see,' he said. He sat up and stretched, to the sound of ticking elbows and scapulae. Then one by one began cracking his knuckles. He looked out of the window. His profile made me think of him standing stone still, sea-sprayed at the prow of a plunging ship. 'Well, it's to be expected,' he said. 'I notice you're not complaining about it, which is just as well, because, you know, if two people hate each other, chances are they're going to go after each other with bats and such things. Are you planning revenge?'

'No, Father.'

Another look. Indulgent omniscience. The Things glowing, heated by his knowing. I imagined a panel in his chest, openable, behind which another universe of swirling galaxies and pink nebulae. Correlative with my own panel, behind which the Things like a thieved stash.

'I don't know, Father. Yes.'

He stood up and went to the window and leaned forward, so that his nose touched the glass. *Thinking of lost adventures.* Raindrops shadow-freckled his face. His hands disappeared into the cassock pockets, from the left of which a red-beaded rosary hung.

'What's your name?' he asked, breath fogging the pane.

'Dominic Hood, Father.'

'Mine's Ignatius Malone,' he said, looking out, seeing, I supposed, not drizzle and playground but lowering thunderheads and roiling waters. 'Hard to believe, I know, but true, nonetheless. Ever heard of such a name, Dominic?'

'No, Father.'

'Do you say your prayers every night?'

'Yes, Father.'

'What prayers do you say?'

'I say the one about my soul.'

'What's that one? Say it for me now.'

'It goes: "Now I lay me down to sleep, I pray the Lord my soul to keep. If I should die before I wake, I pray the Lord my soul to take."'

He rested his forehead against the glass, blinking, slowly. Another handful of rain. I had a nauseous glimpse – his, from the prow, surely – of the fleshy sea, upheaving in a squall. Then an image of my father's head, my point of view receding from it at incredible speed, taking in not just our living room and house, but Logan Street, Begshall, fields, coastlines, oceans, deserts, the blue and white globe in space.

'Do you know what that is, Dominic?' Malone said, still leaning, half reflected.

'What what is, Father?'

'That prayer.' He straightened and turned. I shook my head. 'That prayer,' he said, 'is the perfect prayer.'

We stayed like that for a moment, him at the speckled window, me hugging my knees, both of us breathing the medical room's camphorous fug. I had never before encountered an adult who behaved spontaneously, without concern for whether such behaviour might alarm a child.

His left hand came out of the cassock pocket and up to stroke with a rasp the silver stubble, then over the front of his face to slow-rake the white hair, once, twice, the third time ending with him gripping the back of his skull and giving it a gentle twist, to crack the neck. He gasped with relief. 'That's better. Terrible joints, Dominic. Now, here's Nurse Maggie.'

Before she had quite appeared in the doorway. Then she did appear. 'Oh – Father Malone,' she said, the initial start giving way to a dimpled smile and a cobra-like movement of the head. '*You're* here. When did you come in? Does Miss Warburton know?'

He gave me a conspiratorial look, a precise measurement of my soul — *those Things, yes, I see* — then turned and beamed at her. 'Hello, Margaret,' he said. 'No, she doesn't know. I'm on my way to interrupt her work just now. It's been quite a while, hasn't it?'

'Seven years if it's a day, I should think,' Nurse Maggie said, indulging in a series of slight, indecipherable movements of hands, lips, shoulders and hips, not breathing properly.

At the doorway, Malone paused. 'I'll see you again, Dominic,' he said. A saucy eye-flash, then he turned, ducked his head for the lintel, and was gone.

We, the Hoods, lived on Logan Street in Begshall, a littered and generally drizzled-on ex-cotton town not far from Manchester. Two rows of terraces facing each other, with a strip of moss-grouted cobblestones in between. Clanking and stygian repairs garage at one end of the block, pre-war corner shop at the other. My world, until medical room, Malone and the intimation of bible lands.

It had taken mass, *The Greatest Story Ever Told*, Christmas carols and my mother's *Illustrated Bible for Children* the proverbial seven years to seize infancy's lawless phantasmagoria and bring it under Roman Catholic rule. In the pre-school years, carpets and skies had been prone to abstract hallucinogenic misbehaviour; now they signed God and the Devil, Heaven and Hell, caverns of burning torment or the dental brilliance of infinity. The Trinity was supposed to be a mystery. Not to me. The Holy Ghost blew in with gusts of rain, or the smell of burning rubbish. God the Father (as opposed to the Son, who hovered in the stratosphere with gently tilted head and hands parting the robes to reveal the pink and thorn-crowned Sacred Heart, dripping blood) lived in deep space but squeezed himself on Sundays into the tabernacle, shrouded in Cadbury's purple or tinsel green, the gigantic octogenarian who loved, infinitely, and sent to Hell for ever. I wanted to return the love, but the fear of Hell got in the way.

'I've heard of him,' my sister Julia said to me that evening, after my report of Malone. 'But I've never seen him.' She lay on her bed with her chin in her hand and her big book of *100 Great Paintings* open in front of her. (I was allowed to look at this, subject to good behaviour or outright bribes. Our chief interest was nudity and gore, for which our religion was hard to beat: Christ after bloodied Christ with flogged ribs and nailed appendages, half-naked Salomes with their gleaming platters and hacked Baptist heads. Our favourite was Caravaggio's Doubting Thomas, whose sceptical finger entered the wound in the resurrected Jesus's side with a sort of gynaecological realism.) I lay on my back on the floor next to the bed, the warm spot above the hot-water pipes. Outside, Begshall's dark autumn. Wraiths of cloud. The wind every now and then hurling itself at the house, sash windows rattling.

'He's an exorcist,' Julia said, in a sudden silence as the wind dropped.

'What's that?'

'God, you're a bladder-head. Don't you know what an exorcist is?'

'No. He was brown, though, with totally white hair.'

'Shut up. People, right, they get possessed. That means that the Devil, or some of his demons, *take control* of a human being. Then that human starts speaking in weird voices and doing obscene and evil things.'

'What things?'

'Sex things. Maria Blaskovitch's sister saw the film. She

said this girl who's possessed by the Devil, right, sticks a *crucifix* in her *fanny*.'

To which there was no answer. Jules, warming to her theme, put the cap on her fountain pen.

'*And*,' she continued, 'her head spins round on her neck, completely round, and she smacks her mother in the face and grabs her head and makes her *lick* her fanny.'

Me stilled by this, receiving, inside, intimate explosions.

'Anyway,' Julia said, 'the person who's possessed by the Devil has to be exorcised. Ex*or*cised, right? Not ex*er*cised, not *jogg*ing.'

'Ex*or*cised,' I said.

'The priest comes and throws holy water over them and says all these prayers, and by the power of God forces the Devil to go out of them. It takes ages, because the Devil *loves* being in a human body.'

'Why?'

'Because he can do all those evil sex things, stupid. And because he can kill people and desecrate holy objects like crucifixes and statues of the Virgin Mary and stuff.'

My mother's voice from downstairs: 'There's tea and toast here. And almond slices.'

'I don't believe you,' I said to Julia.

She rolled towards me, swung her legs over the edge of the bed, stood up. 'What do I care whether you believe me, you verruca?'

'What's that?'

She stomped past me in her stockinged feet. 'It's what your farting head is, Dommie,' she said.

That night's dream replayed the medical room *tête-à-tête* with an added special effect: out from his mouth with words came glittering particles which on closer examination turned out to be tiny images of all the sights he'd seen: camels, trumpets, carpets, spires, butterflies, orchids, faces, goblets, horses . . .

I'll see you again, he had said. But at school the next day I learned that he had gone. After me he had spent an hour with Miss Warburton (his old teacher, it was said, which I found hard to believe, since the two of them looked the same age) then left Begshall, destination unknown.

It deadened the day, let school's joyless details in again, unmediated. I scuffed around the yard at dinner time, kicking a deflated football, theatrically unapproachable.

Nonetheless high hopes of inside information when irredeemably local Father Feeney housecalled the following week. 'In my opinion, Mrs Hood, yev done your duty. I can't say fairer than that now can I?'

The predictable conversational terminus. I didn't understand the particulars at the time (subtextual Dr Durex like some lewd clown or adult balloon artist was inferred later), but the gist was plain: my parents' mix of penitence and bile, Feeney's equivocation. At Communion, Julia and I shuffled to the rail while my parents remained on their knees in the pew. It had never been explained to us why they didn't go; furnished with childhood's sixth sense, we had known not to ask.

'So my conscience should be clear then, Father?' my mother wanted to know.

Feeney sat in what at all other times was my dad's armchair. My dad stood by the window, half looking out, only occasionally chipping in, topping up Feeney's Teacher's with facetious regularity, a sardonic smile on his normally generous mouth. Meanwhile receding Feeney like a holy but threadbare rag-doll with legs not merely crossed but *plaited*, smoked Embassy filters, scratched his flaking forehead with a nicotine-stained index, and put up mighty and ingenuine resistance every time the bottle came out.

'Ah, but I can't dictate your conscience, now, y'see. As a human being, Mrs Hood, as a flawed, confused creation, I can tell you plainly that I believe yev done your duty. But— ah sure Mr Hood I'll be *staggerin'* with another of . . . No, now . . . Oh, well, thanks to you' – while my dad tightened his smile and returned the Teacher's to the mantelpiece, where it glowed like amber in a shaft of cigarette-smoked winter sun – 'But as a representative,' Feeney continued, 'however humble, of the Holy Roman Catholic Chorch—'

'In other words, don't quote you at the next Inquisition,' my dad said.

'Do you know Father Malone, Father?' I asked, from the floor, amid Lego. Feeney smiled, showing equine, smoker's teeth, and glanced briefly at my mum, then my dad, to see if either was going to veto my presence in the conversation.

'Heh heh, little fella, now, is it?' he said, when it became obvious that they weren't. 'Now, why would you want to know about Father Malone, umm?'

'Julia says he's an exorcist,' I said, at which my dad snorted into his Scotch. Father Feeney jumped, and unplaited his legs. 'What the—heavens above now. And what does Julia say an exorcist *does*?'

'Drives out devils,' I said.

'That's right, Dommie,' my dad said. 'That's quite right.'

'Would ya *listen* to the little fella now,' Feeney said. 'Would ya *listen* to the cool of him!'

'I just wondered if you knew him,' I said. My dad was loving this. And Julia, at the dining table, smirking behind her cup of tea.

'Well, now,' Feeney said, having passed through the aphasia the cool of me had caused him. 'No, I don't actually know Father Malone, personally, although I do know *of* him.'

'And is he an exorcist?' my dad asked, holding his Scotch up to the light for brief amdram effect before turning and looking fidgeting Feeney straight in the eye.

'Ehh . . . that I couldn't tell you, Mr Hood. That's not something I'd have . . . That I couldn't say. I do know that Father Malone *travels* a great deal. He was, for a while, at a mission in Africa, I believe. But as to the – ah – the other . . . that I couldn't tell you.'

Feeney's visits left tarnished air, an hour or two in which my mum and dad would go quiet and precise, dispelled eventually by *The Two Ronnies* or *Morecambe and Wise*, occasionally by turning the television off altogether, the two of them sloping off to the front room, my dad with a large and tinkling Teacher's, my mum with a slender sweet sherry, where they would play Glenn Miller records and – to my and Julia's astonishment – dance, fully visible from the street, should anyone care to glance through the bay window.

That night, however, my father went out to play snooker and my mother settled down in front of the television. I spent the evening with Julia in her room watching her do her homework, longhand and the smell of ink irresistible, as were Jules's *shits*, *fucks*, *buggers*, and ribald anecdotes of secondary-school life. 'Angela Stoppard saw Miss Carlisle and Mr Greaves at it under the stage. She said their tongues were out and she had his knob in her hand.'

But when I went downstairs for a drink of water, my mother looked up from the screen, her face strangely tight. 'Don't dawdle,' she said.

The living room's air weirdly annealed, the television at the centre. A programme with a bleak absence of background music. She got up and changed the channel while I was in the kitchen. Changed it back when I was halfway up the stairs.

'Mr Kilcoyne's only got one ball,' Julia said, when I returned. 'He was shot in the goolies in the Second World War. That's why he squeaks.'

Much later that night, coming back from the toilet, I overheard my mother and father talking in bed.

'They made tapes,' my mother said.

'I know,' my father said.

'So they could listen—'

'I know all about it.'

'While they were—'

'I *know*.'

A long pause. Pyjama'd and moonlit me frozen on tiptoe, staring at the landing's threadbare rug, seeing nothing.

'How can people *do* these things?' my mother asked. 'I mean what makes someone . . .? Where's the pleasure in . . .?'

'It's pure evil,' my father said. 'Pure evil. Should've hanged the filthy bastards.'

Another long pause. I waited. Nothing. I crept back to bed, not having a clue what they were talking about, except that it felt (distant clairvoyant nod of affirmation from Malone) like a Thing.

The Things were inarticulable. (Then. Now, I suppose, not – or at any rate since I've taken this upon myself – to be treated as if not, to be treated as if their mysteries have been exploded, by language, time, the indefatigable god of ordinariness.) In any case they belonged to me. They had been there as long as I could remember. They had arrived from odd angles, coalesced, enamelled and welded themselves in. You must read what follows and understand:

18

Malone knew. The sky had rained and my testicles had throbbed and he had stretched out his consciousness over the place inside me I thought of as my soul and seen there the Things, my seven years' hoard of dark and imperishable jewels . . .

A warm afternoon at my uncle Terry's house. Adults in living-room conclave. The smells of sweet sherry, whisky, coffee, cigarette smoke, a finished-with Sunday roast; me warm-faced and sated, fingers still gleaming with meat fat. Jules, irritated, lolling on my dad's lap, trying to cadge a sip, though she'll only make a face of disgust if she gets one. A bay window showing the facing terrace and, above, a cloud-packed sky. The feeling of having slipped from my mother's even peripheral awareness. A stack of magazines under the sound-down television. One, *Weird Crimes*, having been teased from the pile, sparks recognition via knucklish movement in my gut; I crawl away under the table to look at it. On one page is a grainy black-and-white photograph of a walrus-moustached man in a fur hat and coat holding up a severed human head, like an angler with a prize catch. His foot is on the headless corpse, and he and the friends around him are all laughing and clapping. I have the suspicion that if I lean towards it in the right way the image will let me pass – as through *Star Trek* vortex – into it. Then my mother, with sherry breath and tinily cracking knees, down on her haunches and blocking out the light to ask me if I want to go to the toilet (what my retreat under a table usually means), her seeing the magazine, frowning, confiscating. Some clipped words at adult head height and my uncle Terry's dark eyebrows up in surprise, and my dad tilting the whisky's gold and Julia, irritation forgotten, fox-sharp on the scent of it, the Thing, whatever it is. Whatever it is, it has called upon me to remember something giantly true from the time before I could remember. Whatever it is, it has opened pleasure in me like a flower, a queer, time-lapse-photography bloom. My mother seems to know what it is I can't remember, but there is a look in her face of resistance to it . . .

Samson, as played by Victor Mature, betrayed by Hedy Lamarr's Delilah and imprisoned by Hollywood's version of the Philistines. Julia and I curled up on the couch, my father in his armchair, my mother ironing nearby. Living-room curtains half drawn to cut the day's reflection on the television screen. Delilah brought to visit Samson in prison, where, blinded and in chains, he must spend his days turning a huge millstone. Loinclothed and manifestly suffering Victor Mature, manifestly pampered Hedy Lamarr in gratuitous décolletage – but, more importantly, sitting on top of the millstone an obese and bone-gnawing Philistine jailer, sweating bubs and oiled gut gleaming in the torchlight. My mother, between shirts, disgusted. *Look at that dirty fat pig.* A lash from the whip. Samson's flinch. Delilah's untouched midriff. *See the bitch*! – my father's happily outraged pronouncement on Hedy Lamarr. Julia's bare feet hot against my thigh . . .

In an oblong of sunlight on the bed tawny Julia with open and liquorice-browned mouth asleep on her belly with her dress ridden up to reveal downily aura'd buttocks and pink cotton knickers skewed into their cleft. The same call from somewhere deeply familiar to remember something fiercely true. Creeping, knowing and not knowing what, I climb up, delicately raise and peel back my sister's underwear. A little brown apostrophe in the pink cotton. Julia dough-soft and smelling of the street. She mumbles, grumbles, frowns, but doesn't wake. I cheek-part, very gently, draw closer, see the anus like a signal of refined contempt or insolence. I bend for closer scrutiny – but then horror: my mother in the doorway in her lemon cardie, arms bearing folded bedsheets. Her face's strange sequence: incomprehension; angry recognition; cold resistance (to what she has recognized); then – to my surprise and not surprise – sadness. The flower of pleasure. At her sadness. There is something to remember about this, from the time before time; the anus like a rudely stitched-up socket where an eyeball used to be, and the sadness. *Dominic Hood. Go downstairs at once.* Scalp tightened in readiness for the clout, but she lets me past her hip without moving . . .

Which is enough, and never enough. *That is all I can remember, Father,* I'm tempted to say, old habits dying hard. Of course there were others, but memory is fair to me: these were the Things. I remember what matters. What matters is that Malone, in the little room above the wet yard, had known. *I pray the Lord my soul to keep.* At 'my soul' my soul had shivered. (Sudden sensuous empathy with the skinless circulatory man.) He had seen me – *seen* me – offered understanding (or at least an absence of horror), but also, it had seemed, a warning.

'I don't know what else to do with you two. I've made it absolutely clear that I will not tolerate violence in the playground, the classroom, or any other part of my school. You've been warned, haven't you?'

'Yes, sir.' Side by side in Mr Halliday's office, Burke and I answered in approximate unison. That afternoon break the whole of the Juniors had gathered in a circle around us, such the animal intensity of our scrap. Miss Tyldesley (young,

pretty, new, with long eyelashes, knee boots and a smell of apricots) had struggled to fight her way through the cheering throng. As she dragged me off (me the smaller and safer bet), Burke had high-kicked and caught me under the chin. Restrained, I had had no option but to spit – bloodily, thanks to bitten lip – in his face. Miss Tyldesley, appalled, marched us both straight to the headmaster's office, where Halliday, after whipping his spectacles off, sat back and heard her out in awful stillness.

'Hold out your hand.'

The cane had been apocryphal until now. Halliday's office was low-ceilinged and lit by a shaft of strong sun, redolent of industrial carpet, new paper, the corner's elephantine Xerox, his alpine aftershave. These and a lingering trace of apricots, though Miss Tyldesley had left us to our fate. Halliday, with hairy nostrils and crisp white cuffs, was not quite able to look at me (nor at Burke, who stood to one side in his own aura, rapt, lips parted, eyes heavy); this thing he had to do was ugly, ugly and unpredictable, likely to pounce and mean something he didn't want it to. It must be done with consciousness slightly averted. Two or three times he looked up and out of the window, eyes narrowed against the sun.

'Hold it higher, please.' The room's weight pressed his voice into a quiet, rich, essence. Burke had so forgotten himself that he had put his hands in his pockets.

Two whacks – the switch's sigh, hum and crack – on each palm, pain for which the preceding minute's compressed imagination could never have prepared me. A third, I knew, and reflexes would have snatched my hand away, Halliday or no. Perhaps he knew this, too, from prior experience. Either way, two on each it remained. Halliday, as if not sure what to do next, stood for a moment breathing through his nostrils.

Aside from or beneath or above the pain (very gingerly I stepped back a pace, slotting a wrecked palm into each armpit) an acute sense of him as a man; images of him flitted, modelled on ones I had of my father: waking from an afternoon sleep with hair askew; opening a tighly screwed jam jar with a curious grimace of effort; sitting in shirt and tie but with trousers down, on the toilet. I received these with a strange deflation, a slight dismal tenderness for him, the man, not Mr Halliday, who must *be* Mr Halliday, and skulkingly do this, against himself.

I watched Burke get his two, and two. Eyes welling, bottom lip tucked under top, he replicated my pace back and palms-in-armpits move as if careful to get every detail right. Whereafter the three of us stood like menhirs; silence, and the low-ceilinged room filled with something, as if an angel had come with a message we were determined to resist. Then Mr Halliday rolled his head, quickly, as to remove a cramp.

'Off you go, then,' he said, as if he'd just given us each an ice-cream.

His office and the school secretary's faced each other across a narrow corridor which was a dead end. Both doors closed, Burke and I stood with faces thick and palms singing in gloom that was almost darkness. It occurred to me, then, that I had never been alone with him. Presumably occurred to him, too, since for the first time in our filthy history we simply stood, existing in each other's presence. The angel had followed us outside with its message undelivered. Or not angel, but something less personal; and not urgent, but impartial and with patience to wait out infinity.

Then Burke did a curious thing. Getting up on tiptoe, he flared his nostrils, opened his eyes wide, and *leaned*, as if about to fall, towards me. Our foreheads bumped, once, then he settled back on his heels. Throughout which our palms remained firmly clutched in our armpits. It lasted just a moment, but when it passed it left me with the feeling of detonated identity and lost history I'd only known before on sudden waking from deep sleep. Even now, looking back, I have no idea what I would have said or done next had the secretary's door not suddenly opened to let in light and, in it, her, Mrs Roe, silhouetted, clutching a quartet of coffee cups with one set of fingers and a biscuit tin with the other.

'Christ,' forgetting herself. Then recovering. 'Get a*way* from here, you two boys.'

I didn't look at Burke, and I daresay he didn't look at me. Four or five paces (Mrs Roe resettling her mugs, muttering), then he stomped on my foot with his heel and ran.

Malone sent subliminals from afar. In October the *Sun* had a picture of the Shroud of Turin on its front page. I had never seen or heard of it before. Someone had broken into Turin's Royal Chapel and set fire to the place, in an attempt, according to my dad, to destroy *hard evidence* of the existence of Jesus Christ and the miracle of His resurrection. The shroud, thanks to a protective layer of asbestos in its housing, had remained unharmed.

'Come and look at this, Dominic,' my dad said. 'This is a picture of Jesus – a *photograph* of Jesus. The actual cloth they wrapped His body in. The *actual cloth* of His *actual body*.'

I climbed up onto the arm of his chair. My mother was in the kitchen, cooking breakfast. The smell of frying bacon filled the house. Julia was still in the bathroom. The living-room window showed our dark back yard, glimmering under the morning's drizzle.

'There,' my dad said, making room for me, 'what do you think of *that*?'

It took me a few moments to make it out. Then, suddenly, the figure emerged. It was the negative image, the long face in cobalt, the silvery hair and mouth; the look of a most delicate brass rubbing.

'How does it feel to see a *photo* of Jesus?' my dad said.

I couldn't answer, pinned as I was by two other forces. The first was the look of the Page Three Girl alongside (pushed back by the shroud story to page five); head down, lips tightly pouting, eyes staring straight at me, with, incontrovertibly, her own piercing knowledge of the Things.

The second was negative: Jesus's overwhelming resemblance to Father Ignatius Malone.

'It's him,' I said.

'That's right,' my dad said. 'Let's see what the buggers are going to say about *that.*'

I thought I saw him on television, too, that Christmas. A programme about an ancient dwarfish woman in Spain, notorious for an alleged visionary relationship with the Virgin Mary, there was cracked footage of her walking backwards at speed – except when one looked closely one saw that she wasn't walking at all, but *floating* an inch or two above the ground, feet dragging, eyes closed, mouth open. A cult had formed, expanded, taken over the whole town. The woman had been recorded on a number of occasions speaking in tongues – a sound like a retarded monster, deeply disturbing. The Vatican had declared her a heretic and excommunicated her. The programme climaxed with the rebellious celebration of a mass (the town's priest on the verge of excommunication himself) during which the eucharistic wafer appeared on the old woman's gargoylishly stuck-out tongue seemingly from nowhere. The camera crew had been told to clear off; this footage shot on an eyewitness's archaic standard-8, hand-held, the smuggled–out film much damaged. In the crowd, like a black mantis, a white-haired head taller than everyone else, I thought . . . surely that was—but a woman in the congregation fell down in a fit and the camera panned left, away from him.

It snowed in February, and, after the first forty-eight hours of magic, rained, heavily, leaving a residue of freezing slush with which nothing could be done. Evenings, it was dark by the time Julia and I had walked home from school.

'Who was it made tapes?' I asked her on Ash Wednesday. She was in the front room with her friend Kelly Saunders, a stocky and knowing blond girl only three years my senior (a *right* lickle slag, according to Logan Street's mums, slippered and curlered in the doorways) who had not long before burst my nose with a tubular section of her mother's vacuum cleaner, and to whom Jules represented the model of sophistication. Kelly always took her shoes off and folded her legs under her on the couch, during which manoeuvre – timing was everything – I might glimpse the fat white feet and exotically painted toenails: magenta; ruby; chocolate; puce. All three of us still had our ashes on our foreheads, Julia's and Kelly's intact, mine fading, having been fiddled with too much.

'Who was it made tapes?' I repeated.

'Piss off, Dommie, will you?'

'Mum said they made tapes. Who was it?'

'What's he on about?' Kelly said.

'Christ only knows,' Julia said. 'Go on, Dominic, will you for fuck's sake?'

Malone would have known. *He was, for a while, at a mission in Africa, I believe*, Feeney had said. In my mind his backdrops were always exotic: sprawling banyan trees or wind-sculpted dunes, birdless blue skies or gory sunsets. I pictured him, hands in pockets, crossing a sunblasted waste in patient strides, the frayed cassock flapping, the unravelled shadow rippling at his heels. These were the images, now, when I prayed. Sometimes he looked up at me and grinned or waved – at which terrible inner jabs from the Things – at which *he* stopped and momentarily shook his fist. What did I know about the Things except that I should never have taken possession of them? That they were deeply precious, deeply wrong.

My hands were tied and I was forced to perform an obscene act. Titbits from the *Sun* and *News of the World* with danger words spelled out letter by letter over our heads, but occasionally my dad would forget; therefore my mum, lips clamped, making *not in front of* gestures and Jules shooting her eyebrows up and down like a panto villain; me, as with *they made tapes*, prickled by the nearness of meaning.

There had been (since Malone) startling erections, and an insistence from somewhere that something must be thought about to accompany them. Out of the slew, slyly, Julia's anus like a puckered bruise and my mother's face resolving from shock and anger into sadness. A faint signal from the place before birth that I was on the right lines. Therefore, tentatively (but with immediate confirmation), Samson and the glistening belly of the Philistine glutton; Salome's gemmed navel and oiled cleavage; *Spartacus*'s bejewelled and grape-nibbling Roman ladies, thumbing-down, bored; the moustached head-holder and his happy comrades . . .

◆

I'm tempted to sell the gun. Not for profit, but because any day now Holly's going to stumble on it, rootling, and then –

haunted or not – I'll be out. A gun and Holly's opinion of herself make bad housemates. This evening I sat on the fire escape after yet another thunderstorm (13th Street's reek of rubbish freshened by the rain), holding the weapon in my hand. A Smith & Wesson revolver, according to my research. To be precise, a .38 Special, six rounds, single and double action, .265 semi-target hammer, .312" smooth target trigger, K-medium frame, serrated ramp front sight and fixed notch rear, weight 36 ounces, carbon steel with a blue finish and Uncle Mike's combat grip. All marks of identification gone. Untraceable. Illegal. Worth something in Brixton, maybe, here, peanuts. Holly would give me a hundred for it, in her worst moments.

Down in the basement, the day Deborah Black and I said good-bye, my hand holding the gun had seemed the centre of everything, Laplace's fixed point from which the rest of the universe could be understood.

◆

If I'd had the gun in 1973, things might have been different. In an ideal world – one in which one could select the consequences of one's actions – I would have killed Burke and selected consequences like *getting presents* or *going on holiday*. But by the time Malone returned to St Edmund's, on the last day of the Lent term, I was eight years old and well aware that I didn't live in such a world. The consequences would have been things like *going to jail* and *breaking my mother's heart*, not to mention *dying and going to Hell for eternity*.

'Pull his pants down. Go on, I dare yez. Pull his fock'n pants down.'

Dinner break. A steely day of swift-moving cloud. By

turns drizzle and blinding sunshine bouncing off the wet. Boys' and girls' bare legs ravished by the scuttling wind.

'I've got his erms. Go on, pull 'em down.'

Burke, naturally, and his henchman for the day, large-headed Darren McGuinness who had an old-butter smell and a big, clownish mouth of waxy teeth. I was down on the playground's damp concrete out of sight of the on-duty teacher, netball markings sweeping away in cold geometry under my head. Burke sat astride me, pinning my arms with his knees. McGuinness draped giggling hysterically across my shins. Neo-Gothic St Edmund's red brick towering under a dunnish March sky. The only warmth the weight of Burke's body on mine. Since the day of the cane – and his bizarre *lean* in the corridor – our opposition had acquired a new urgency.

I went still, in preparation for the unimaginable discharge of energy that would be required to shake them off – and in the stillness suddenly thought of Kelly. Burke's white legs were the same colour as hers. I had a mental flash of the gooseflesh and the painted toenails, and for a moment the feeling that it was her on top of me. It called up an all but overwhelming desire to surrender, to dissolve altogether into his–her will.

Then McGuinness was socked in the face – the sound a precise *pock* – by a bald and sodden tennis ball; with my legs free, such was the violence of my convulsion and twist, I toppled Burke.

The bell rang and we traipsed inside, me unavenged, but on fire more from the glimpse of Burke–Kelly. Unspeakable images sprouted: me kissing Burke's knees; Burke with blue-berry toenails; me pulling *his* pants down; him astride me with genitals rubberishly jiggling and sourly burping mouth triumphantly agape. All stirring in spite of *six sevens forty-two, seven sevens forty-nine, eight sevens fifty-six* visceral warmth and the familiar Thingish flower-bloom of pleasure. I stopped off en route to Miss Warburton's and splashed my face with cold water, not looking in the mirror. I would not think of it. I *would* not.

An afternoon of sun-slats and silvered motes followed. The classroom's torpor and tea-breathed Miss Warburton asking us to *really think* about what life might be like in the year 2000. I had no numerical sense of the year 2000. It was science fiction. Nonetheless I knew the sort of thing *really thinking* was supposed to reveal. *Mashines will do so much of Man's work*, I wrote, *that people will have gastronomical amounts of leshure time.* (It would come back, eventually, crossed through with a red line and the crippling correction Astronomical, *but good try!*) *Peeple will jet around with jet packs. Food will be in small capsyuls. Many diseeses will have been defeeted by sience. By the year 2000 Man will be living on space stations – or perhaps even on other planets*! I paused here, considering whether the world might not have ended altogether by the year 2000, as Julia had often predicted. If that was so, Jesus would have come again. Judgement Day would have happened. The dead would have risen. Food – in capsyuls or otherwise – would have been made redundant.

The door opened and Mrs Sharpe poked her head in.

'Miss Warburton?' she said. 'Could I have a word?'

Miss Warburton looked at us, index finger raised. 'I will be *right outside* this door,' she said.

The door swung shut behind her and the room's volume rose. *Dolfins and wales may have learned to talk*, I had written (on the strength of a half-watched natural history documentary), but decided on reflection to cross it out. *Sientists will have—*

'Dominic?'

I don't know why I looked up, since I knew it was Burke. Perhaps because he'd said it without discernible malice.

So I did look up, and saw the fat-fingered hands in front of my face, the rubber band primed and loaded.

The maths begins – the escape calculations, the avoidance equations – because one doesn't have a choice, though the brain knows it's futile. I flinched – then took my enemy's pellet straight in the left eye.

Laughter. His and a dozen others. My eyes began watering, instantly.

'You soft get,' Burke said, giggling. 'You fock'n soft little baby *get*.'

I wasn't strong, but I was a filthy fighter. Having left my body, I watched from a position just below the ceiling. Burke was on the floor, curling and opening like a dug-up worm, and I was stomping on his face. There was blood on his teeth – of no concern to me, waltzing with my own liberated self. Sound drained away. I was beatified, hair follicles to fingertips. I pulled my foot back (as in preparation for chipping the goalie), felt the blameless potential in muscle and joint, sighed, then kicked Burke in the head.

He screamed, crawled a few paces on his hands and knees, got up, lurched for the door, and fled. The yellows and pale blues of the classroom tilted, swirled. The windows' light liquefied, reared and plunged silently into the mix. I went after him.

Rage had dissolved my boundaries, fear Burke's. He ran down the corridor (Miss Warburton and Mrs Sharpe passed in a blur of tweed and floral print), out of the Infants' main doors, down the steps, across the gleaming yard, over the rinsed playing fields and on into the woods that bordered them. I tore after him. The field passed under my hoofbeats and the sun opened everything up around me. Under the first trees Burke abandoned the path and cut away left through the undergrowth.

He was heading for home, I realized afterwards, Burnside Council Estate, which backed onto the woods. What would've happened had he made it? Would I have dogged him to his own front door? His hall? His living room – an abrupt introduction to his frayed mother and booze-breathed dad?

As it was I found his body in the brick pit.

Fifteen feet deep, twenty across, containing a scatter of large industrial concrete slabs. The path crossed the pit on a wooden bridge. But Burke hadn't been on the path. He'd been running to the left of it, looking over his shoulder for me in pursuit. For me. And now here I was, and there he was.

Julia had once found a way of making our Alba reel-to-reel play backwards. We had recorded and played back for hours, experimenting. Then she had taped a scream and played that backwards, and the silence at the end of it (which was the silence at the beginning) had startled both of us with its solidity, like something from before creation. The sound of God, Jules had said.

This silence the same.

I stood on the pit edge and looked down at him. He was lying on his front with his head turned to one side, one leg and one arm bent, like the drawing of the recovery position. His one visible blue eye was open. While I watched, his mouth begin to speak a small, dark bubble of blood onto the stone. It spread unevenly and irregularly, as in a primitive animated cartoon.

The sound of God. I sat down on the lip of the pit with my suddenly swollen feet dangling over. All the day's details had been moving to this composition: the green shadows; the bluebells; the body. Now there was no going back.

Holding on to two fistfuls of damp grass (convinced that if I didn't I'd float up into the air), I took another look at him. No change, except that now the blood bubble was the size of an inflated party balloon.

What had happened settled on my skin, became intimate with me, joined me beyond doubt or separation. The world, on the other hand, revealed itself terminally discrete, a disinterested *thing* now that it had orchestrated my arrival here. My body throbbed. Little images: the planet seen from space; bearded God milkily surrounded by creation's first swarm of stars; the *Weird Crimes* head-holder in his bored landscape. My mother and father whizzed away from me, became tiny in a curved distance, disappeared. I sat and held on to my fists of grass, deafened by my own careful breathing. In one of Julia's schoolbooks there was a poem that said *You don't want madhouse and the whole thing there,* which, since she had taken to using it herself, non-sequiturially, had become a mantric bruise on my brain. Burke's body and dark balloon set it off now. *You don't want madhouse and the whole thing there.* My own body felt anachronistic, now that the leaking blood had put me in touch with eternity. I felt awkward in it and terrified of leaving it.

'I thought it was you,' Malone's voice said, behind me. His shadow approached, cooled my back. I looked up.

'I wonder if you'd do something for me?' he said, smiling, one hand pocketed, the other caressing his stubble. 'I think I dropped my rosary on the path back there. Would you go and look for it?'

I stood up, unsteadily, horribly light without my bunches

of grass. Malone wasn't looking at me. He was looking at Callum Burke on his darkening tablet of stone. The trees revolved, slowly, around us.

'Would you go back along there and see if you can find it?' he asked.

Still without having uttered a word, I turned and headed towards the path.

◆

'No testimony is sufficient to establish a miracle,' said David Hume, 'unless the testimony be of such a kind that its false-hood would be more miraculous than the fact which it endeavours to establish.'

Now, in the small hours (Kelp's been again tonight, five minutes grinning then the Cheshire-Cattish dissolve) sky-scraping Manhattan twinkles and beeps, criss-crossed by airliners, bluntly uninterested in miracles. The city's hard facts — its *matters* of fact, as David Hume would have said — stand tall, wearing a look of impersonal endurance.

◆

I met them walking back from the pit. Burke fat-lipped and shivering in the sunlight, holding the side of his head, Malone by his side, smoking a cigarette.

In the shade of a maidenly silver birch, I stopped and stared.

Malone, white hair just caught by a shaft of sun, wolf-grinned and held up his red-beaded rosary. 'In my pocket the whole time,' he said. 'Must be losing my marbles, boys.'

★

He didn't explain anything. Either the mystery was my punishment or he had a misplaced faith in my powers of
understanding. He did, however, give me the rosary, ceremo-
nially. When groaning Burke was being cold-compressed and
coddled by Nurse Maggie the two of us slunk off to the car-
cinogenic staff room, deserted at that hour. Setting his
cigarette in the lip of a Tetley's ashtray he opened my grass-
stained palm and from above let the chain of beads coil down
into it, then with his own dark fingers closed my fist. 'We've
forgotten the power of prayer,' he said with a chuckle, as if
confiding a practical joke to which some poor sap was soon to
fall victim. 'I want you to have this, Dominic. Life is so
strange, don't you think? It's never too late to seek God. That's
the crux of it. That, you see, is the absolutely amazing crux of
it.' He laughed again – a long wheeze followed by silent
shakes – then sat back in his chair and put his feet up on the
mug-ringed table. In the laugh I'd spotted for the first time a
gold premolar. 'Probably,' he said, having calmed down, 'you
should go back to your classroom. Don't you think?'

It was Easter. The coverings came off things and I saw into
their hearts: flies; flowers; dog turds; clouds; eyes; fingernails.
God was loudly silent behind the show, blossoming and
exploding at will: in the back yard's square of sun; in Logan
Street's mossed cobbles and bacchanalian drains; in Julia's
expanding and contracting shadow, playing solo tennis
against the gable-end wall. I went about in a throb. My
mother kept testing my forehead for fever.

Malone frequented my dreams after that, aureoled in gold
leaf, chatting with blue-eyed Jesus among plump clouds and
fat-buttocked cherubim. Mary arriving (as if her bus had
been late), then shared smiles, pecks on the cheek, *dear*
Ignatius.

Julia had new information.

'He's only fifty,' she told me. 'He was born in Begshall, too. His mother was Irish, but the father nobody knows about. Some foreigner, possibly a Pakistani. Anyway she brought him up a Malone, but when he was seven she died in a fire and he went to an orphanage. Then they came and took him away.'

'Who did?'

'The Church bigwigs. The Vatican's got scouts and spies all over the place. They spot a holy child, they take him off the orphanage's hands, pay for clothes and education and all that. They train them up to be exorcists. I read about it. Doing the exorcisms makes them age prematurely. Lots of them have white hair.'

'How do you know all this?'

'I heard.'

'Who from?'

'People who know.'

'I don't believe you.'

Julia lay on her bed, flicking through a magazine devoted entirely to David Bowie. She had breasts now, grown-up undies, an arrowhead of dark hair pointing to her privates. These days, she locked the bathroom door.

'Actually, Dommie, you're a fraenulum. Did you know that?'

'What's that?'

'It's a type of astronaut.'

'Is it?'

'Yes.'

'I don't believe you about Father Malone,' I said.

Julia wet her finger and flipped another page. 'Like I care,' she said.

★

He said mass at St Joseph's on Easter Sunday, much to Feeney's ineffectual chagrin.

'We lose sight of the fundamentals of our religion so easily,' he said. It was a bright, still day, the church full. Sunlight tinctured by the stained glass flecked him with emerald, gold and rose. I sat with my mother and father and Julia four rows from the front. 'We forget the essentials and get distracted by details, by conversation. If I wish for you to take anything away with you today it is this: that you are soldiers in a war against evil.'

St Joe's parishioners shifting in their seats.

'The Devil is out of fashion,' Malone said 'Hell is no longer de rigueur.'

Feeney (and everyone else) mentally rifling his lexicon.

'But I tell you this: the Devil is a reality. Nothing to be embarrassed about, for all the space rockets and oil refineries and wonder drugs and psychoanalysis in the world. Our religion is based on a reality which transcends all that. There is an underlying spiritual fabric to this universe, created by Almighty God, perverted and fouled by the Father of Lies, redeemed by our Lord Jesus Christ, in accordance with which *each and every one of you should be living*. Do you understand? When you are tempted to do wrong – be the wrong mighty or be the wrong small – have no illusions: you are tempted by a real spiritual entity, an entity wholly corrupt, an entity whose very *raison d'être* is to wrest your souls away from God. Don't you understand that this is a war? A war on the most epic scale? Do you think there's no relation between the sins you commit and the sins that drove six million to their horrific deaths in the last war? Is that what you think?'

Silence.

'Then you think as fools. That war, perhaps more clearly

than any we have yet seen, was the earthly representation of the war that proceeds in the unseen realm. Do you not understand that the unseen realm is made manifest in all your choices and actions? Do you not understand that each moral choice you make marks an allegiance either to Christ or to Satan? Do you not *believe* in your own capacity for evil?'

All very confused now. Some heads bowed, offering a posture of accepted responsibility, but all thinking: What the bloody hell . . .?

'Freedom,' Malone went on, 'is not merely the ability to choose to do the right thing; it is the ability to choose that thing we know to be profoundly *wrong*. And we *do* choose that, time after time. We choose wrong knowingly, and in so doing we emulate and join with the original apostate. Do you hear? *We freely embrace the most corrupt force in the universe.* What does St Paul tell us in the letter to the Ephesians? "Put on the full armour of God so that you can take your stand against the Devil's schemes. For our struggle is not against flesh and blood, but against the rulers, against the authorities, against the powers of this dark world *and against the spiritual forces of evil in the heavenly realms.*"'

Images, for me, four rows back: the moustached head-holder from *Weird Crimes*; Julia's arsehole; Salome's jewelled naval and shimmying puppy-fat; Samson turning the mill-stone, powdered Delilah and the oiled Philistine glutton looking on.

They were the images I had, back then. I have others, now.

'Lastly know this,' Malone said (looking, I believed, directly at me). 'Evil is a doomed attempt to reverse life. It's only a coincidence that the English word "live", when reversed, gives us the word "evil", but it is illuminating, for such indeed is evil, the attempt to invert life, to drive the forces of life backwards. The Devil is doomed to failure in the end, as are his subjects. Truly, the Devil's defeat has already taken place. He knows this, and in the realm where time is – our realm – he rages. But he cannot triumph. He cannot triumph because God is the triumph of life. Never forget it.'

It's been a long time. I haven't forgotten it. Most of the time I've just ignored it.

CHAPTER TWO

The Old Disease

'I'm not going to leave her,' I said. 'So you might as well pack it in.'

Kelp had come early tonight, before Holly was home from her evening shift at McLusky's, a bar restaurant on Church Street, popular with Wall Streeters after work. The air had thickened and the hairs on my nape had lifted. I looked up and there he was in the window, green non-eyes framed in the non-glasses' black non-rims, non-arms folded, non-weight on one non-leg. Behind him the dark front of the opposite brownstone, and above that a dusk sky of lemony blue, one or two stars out.

'You can keep it,' I said. 'All the *Some achieve leaving* bollocks. I'm not leaving her.' Then, with a pang of realism: 'Not until she tells me to go, anyway.'

He didn't say anything.

'What you fail to appreciate,' I said to him, 'is that I'm not going along with this sort of thing any more.' I lit a cigarette, *almost* tossed him the pack — at which he grinned. 'Yeah, well, force of habit,' I said, then, after the first deep drag and exhalation: 'I'm not *doing this sort of thing any more.*'

No response.

'And what about the lottery numbers?' I said. 'Have you given any thought to those?'

In the street below a car buzz-thudding with rap pulled up at the lights. He looked down, then back at me, smiled, adjusted his specs, and dissolved into nothing.

❖

Children will assimilate anything, they say. Reality had ripped, then been dragged and roughly stitched by breakfast and the weather and fractions and come on get a move on will you into a sore-seamed version of itself. I suffered flashbacks, warps and dints in time in which brick pit and blood bubble swung across my sight. Woke up with Burke's corpse on top of me like a spent lover. Screams — then the bliss of Jules's voice and hands: *Shshsh, Dommie, it's all right, it's a dream.*

Malone disappeared immediately after his sermon. The Burkes had a premium bonds win and moved south. Nothing happened. Dead. Alive. Dead. Alive. *Must be losing my marbles, boys.* The welter of vampires, werewolves, ghosts and under-the-bed monsters indignant: *We told you.* God remained active — in cloud-shadows, thunderstorms, obelisks of silence in my room — but without Malone to intercede frightened me. In the incensed air of St Joseph's, God shared Malone's clairvoyance, but not, it seemed, his lack of horror at what I did. *Those Things, yes, I see.* Which still skulked like stray dogs around the bins of myself, wormy, bad-breathed, wise. But beyond intuition I had nothing with which to approach them.

Until the Sunday afternoon, almost a year later, when I found myself at the house of Kelly Saunders.

Memory of the vacuum cleaner was vivid, but these were the days of mercurial loyalties and protean fascinations. I had remained leery (not just of the violence but of the sock smell and lardy thighs); nonetheless a glimpse of her tongue plumb-lined into a sherbet fountain could make me weak and urgent, in an abstract, objectless way. Her family was a local totem. Legion, allegedly inbred, with a clan stink of cigarette smoke, chip fat, farts and dog licks left to set, the Saunderses had the pull of a pile-up, as did their tall and slovenly end terrace, which stood, room upon cluttered room, on the corner of Logan Street and Gower Croft. There *fuck-off*s and *cunt*s and *bastard*s and *twat*s slung around intergenerationally, without much consequence. There the attic, Shangri-La to us, with its cobwebbed skylights of bottle-green glass, through which light gasped to reveal the mystery of the chimney breast just before it reached out above the roof.

'Stay outer thar attic,' Doreen had wheezed, between carks. 'An don't come grizzlin' if yurt yerselfs.'

Therefore to the attic we'd gone, four of us: me, Kelly, Stew Fletcher and Elaine Sharples.

Elaine – a thin, raw-elbowed girl with scoliosis and a perpetual look of surprise – was terrified of Kelly to the point of imbecility. Sometimes Kelly would slap Elaine, hard, across the face, without warning, as if she'd suddenly reached the end of her patience with Elaine's mere existence. Elaine would rub the smarting spot, tears would well and drop, she would say nothing. Some minutes would pass. Then one of them would break the silence with a joke or a question, and the day would flow again as if nothing had happened.

In the attic, Kelly bullied with Caligulan caprice. 'Oi, Stew, Dominic's a right spaz, innee?'

'Yeah, a *right* spaz.'

'Oh yeah? You think ee'z a spaz? Worrabout you, you soft twat? Dominic, Stew's a *right* soft twat, innee?'

Stew found a tin of coloured chalk, with which he amused himself for a while, drawing armies on the chimney's unsullied brick, hands and face dashed and swiped with colour. One area of bright green below his eyebrow transformed his right eye into a thing of beauty which captivated me every time he looked at me. 'Stick it up your hairs,' he said, whenever he did look at me, this being his phrase for the day. 'Stick it up your hairs. Any objection?'

Then I found the matches.

A whole box, in the leg of a wellington boot, cook's matches, two inches long with plump blue heads. For a moment, after having slid the inner section of the box from the outer to reveal struck and unstruck matches lying alongside each other like the living and the dead, I sat and stared in disbelief. Live matches. Strike us. Go on, *strike* us.

'Right,' said Kelly reaching down over my shoulder. 'I'll have those, thank you.'

Stew looked up from a tin of oxblood shoe polish. 'What is it?' he asked.

'Kelly . . .?' Elaine said.

'Shuddup, Elaine. Come 'ere, Stew.'

Stew, multicoloured, came forward, hands in pockets. Kelly stood up, took a match from the box, and held it poised to strike.

'D'you know I can make this match burn twice?' she said.

Stew looked at me. I shrugged. He looked back at Kelly, who had gone very calm.

'Ten pee I can make this match burn twice.'

Stew took his hands out of his pockets and folded his arms. 'Ten pee,' he said. 'Yer on.'

Kelly struck the match, which flared, instantly.

'That's once,' she said, then she drew the little flame to her lips, pursed them, and extinguished it with a puff; thread of smoke, stink of sulphur. Stew opened his mouth to say something, but in a swift movement, Kelly stuck the burned end of the match to his cheek and took her hand away. The match stayed put, protruding like a solitary quill. A second of Stew's mute shock, then he screamed and clawed it from his skin.

'That's twice,' Kelly said. 'You owe me ten pee.'

Stew stood with his hand up to his face, breathing heavily through his mouth.

'I ant goddit,' he said. 'Anyway, what about them two? They aff do it an all, else they're soft. Go on, Kelly, meckum do it. See if they're soft. Go on, I *dur* yer.'

Kelly looked over my shoulder to where Elaine was almost at the attic's open trap door.

'Where the fuckin ell d'you think *you're* goin?' she said.

Elaine froze, then turned, slowly. 'I've got go home, Kelly. Me mam'll be geddin worried. Honest, I've got go home. Me mam'll—'

'Get back 'ere, soft-arse,' Kelly said. 'I'm not goin't do *you*, am I? What d'y'think I am? Schewpid?'

Elaine licked her chapped lips, having detected the lie. 'Thing is, Kell, I've reely got go. It's coz me mam'll start lookin round an askin and—'

'Shshsh,' Kelly said. 'Come on. Come on, yer all right. I won't do nowt to yer, honest. Come on. Sit down and don't be a soft-arse. Come on.'

They smiled at each other. Kelly put her arm round Elaine, gave her a sisterly cuddle, then stood up.

'Right, Dominic. You're next.'

Fear, and the recognition of necessity. I stood and faced Kelly.

'Ready?' she said.

I nodded.

Closing her eyes, she raised her chin for a moment, as if suddenly alive to a presence. 'I make this match burn once,' she said, drawing it firmly against the sandpaper until flame scurried up into being. She held it between us, opened her eyes, grinned, blew it out. 'And I make this match burn twice!' she trilled, then stuck the hot head to the side of my face.

The second of shock in which the brain computed its simple data, 'the flesh is melting', then the yelp like a stood-on dog, and I reproduced Stew's reflex hand-to-cheek swipe down to the last detail. I jammed my teeth together, but tears still swelled and fell, accompanied by a feminine whine and three knee-knocks of agony.

We laughed for a few moments, in idiotic and largely forced giggles, then fell silent, a trinity of intuition, until Kelly said, simply, 'Get her!'

Elaine's struggles were perfunctory. One or two surreal moments when she did fight (Stew and I with an ankle each, Kelly with both wrists), writhing as if with sudden voltage, but then the little charge would die and she'd go limp again, whimpering.

But at last things were as the day required: Elaine on her back, Kelly sitting comfortably astride her, Stew and I each redundantly pinning one of Elaine's arms. One of her shoes had come off – had been taken off, by Kelly, with an air of Masonic prescription (but in fact simply because it had dawned on Kelly that she could take it off) – so there was Elaine's bare foot exposed to add to her humiliation.

Meanwhile Kelly in unquestioned sovereignty sat astride Elaine and stared at her subject, blankly.

'Give us them matches,' Kelly said. I handed them to her. A pause, then she shook the box in Elaine's face. Elaine groaned, and wrenched her head from side to side in vigorous denial. Kelly bent down and rubbed noses with her, Eskimo style.

'Don't!' Elaine wailed. 'Pleeeze!'

'Don't!' Kelly parodied. 'Pleeeeeze!'

'Stick it up your hairs,' Stew said, frowning. 'Any objection?'

I, dry-mouthed, had swallowed a lump of lava, some warm bolus struggling through my gullet towards my groin. Kelly's ridden-up dress revealed substantial goosefleshed thighs. She bounced up and down a few times on Elaine, Elaine's face crumpling and opening. I thought of Kelly's weight going up and coming down on Elaine and felt the radial heat of a great mystery. It warmed me, this proximal revelation. Any moment it would enter me and fill me with wisdom. This was what happened with a Thing. You half remembered something huge from the time before you were here. Malone knew. It was what had passed between us in the medical room.

Another lit and extinguished match, Kelly giggling at Elaine's horror the instant the match was struck, and at her relief as soon as it was blown out. Another, and another, and another.

Eventually, after half a dozen struck and blown-out matches, Kelly's shoulders slumped.

'Norra fuckin sound,' she said to Elaine. 'Norra fuckin *word*.'

No response. Kelly cleared her throat and said, 'Now, let's 'ave a look up 'ere,' tugging Elaine's shirt up and out of her jeans. The thin-skinned belly with its faint blue matrix. An ivory whorl of navel.

I looked up Kelly's skirt to where the yellow triangle of her knickers glimmered, felt a cavernous space in my chest, my wet heart jumping like a landed fish.

Stew and I walked home through the oily heat half drugged, his face still flecked with polish and chalk, mine like an open rose. In the bathroom at home I went down onto my knees in a state of sleepy beatification and pressed my forehead against the sink's thorax for a salve. Then a dreary feeling of sickness. I got to my feet, ran scalding water, soaped and scrubbed my hands as if in preparation for surgery, then crawled with heavy limbs to my bedroom and took the rosary from under my pillow. *Don't you understand that this is a war?*

That night I woke with not just a prodigious erection but also sudden insight into what, practically, mechanically, to do with it. The room's darkness approved. Samson and Delilah, Julia, my mother's sad face, even the moustached head-holder stood aside in a ring of images to make room for my recreation of Kelly, and Elaine, and the matches, and the attic.

Don't, pleeeeze!

Don't, pleeeeeze!

Afterwards, I lay still, conscious of every hair and finger-print, wealthy with shame. Lips thick, nostrils hot. *The eyes of them both were opened, and they knew that they were naked.* Strands of guess and suspicion plaited. The skulking dogs weren't strays after all.

Malone had been with us in the attic. From Zanzibar or Bora Bora or Timbuktu he had tuned in, telepathically, to watch in silent anger as Dominic Hood, loins confusedly aflame and soul seductively curdling, had approached it, the Thing, and felt the warmth of its hidden core, out from which spun hints of infinite illumination.

I went on tender bare feet to the bathroom and quietly sponge-washed myself. I was shaking. I sensed the house's sleepers − my mother, my father, Julia − monoliths of love from which, now, I had turned away. I stood in front of the mirror and looked at myself. My eyes were big in my face, different, having made contact with the Devil. *For God doth know that in the day ye eat thereof, then your eyes shall be opened, and ye shall be as gods, knowing good and evil.* Kelly had laughed. Elaine had cried and Kelly had laughed. The Devil didn't insist on anything, merely showed you things, and you recognized them. You just had to let him show you. If you let him, there was no limit to what he would show you. There had been a time when I had seen these things before − hadn't there? A time before this life when I had known what there was to know? How else was it possible that I recognized it now? To recognize something, you had to have seen it before, didn't you?

I stood there for a long time, promising: I won't do that again. I won't. I *won't*.

'What sins have you to confess, my son?' Feeney said, from behind the gauze at St Joe's.

'Sins of the flesh, Father,' I answered, surprised by a sudden squirt from my salivary glands.

'With another person, my son, or by yourself?'

'By myself, Father.'

'How many times?' He sounded bored.

'Every day, Father. Hundreds of times.'

'*Hundreds of times a day*?'

'No, no − I mean, hundreds of times *altogether*. Sometimes a few times a day, though.'

A pause in which I heard him trying to yawn silently. 'And don't you feel ashamed to be abusing the body that God gave you?'

'Yes, Father. It's the Devil.'

'For your penance, I want you to—What did you say?'

'It's the Devil, Father. He's got inside me. Like in *The Exorcist.*'

'Now look—'

'I haven't done any of the things he tries to get me to do, though, Father, honestly.'

'Is that Dominic Hood?'

Sheepishly: 'Yes, Father.'

A heavily expelled sherry-flavoured breath reached me through the gauze. 'All right now, young fella, listen to me. First, for your penance, I want you to say five Hail Marys and five Our Fathers. Understood?'

'Yes, Father.'

'And second, stop all this nonsense about the Devil. Have you *seen* that dreadful fillum?'

'No, Father.'

'Good. Well, make sure it stays that way. Yev nothing to do with the Devil, young man, any more than I have.'

'But Father Malone said—'

'Never mind Father Malone. This is Father Feeney. You leave the Devil to the likes of Father Malone and make a good, clean confession to me. That'll be quite sufficient for God. Yev an unhealthy fascination with the Devil, Dominic. Truly, son, it's not good for you. Everything all right at home, then?'

'Yes, Father.'

'Good, good. Now then, make a sincere Act of Contrition, and try'n do better in future.'

I heard him absolving in quiet Latin while I read off my

Act from the plaque in front of me. The Latin almost convinced — but still, it was just Brylcreemed Father Feeney babbling in there.

'Good-bye, Dominic,' he said, after we'd both finished and I'd shown no sign of leaving.

'Er . . . yes, Father. Is that it?'

'Yes. Is there something else?'

'Am I forgiven?'

'For pity's sake, now, I've just given yez absolution. What're ya wantin'? A sip from the Holy Grail? G'wan now, away with yez.'

Seasons came and went: the sun's low-lying conflagrations; burly wind and thin rain; the scuttle and rasp of Begshall's dead leaves. I grew swiftly into a haggard and doleful addict. In the past I'd had secrets, a handful of discrete psychic objects as precious as golden eggs. Now I had an entire secret *version* of myself, for ever invisible to those who loved me best. The sin of Onan, yes, but compounded infinitely by what the Things had been hinting at all along. Hints no longer — now bald statement, into the truth of which I swooned like a silver-screen lady into the arms of a mascara'd sheik. Kelly had laughed and Elaine had cried. I was never the solo villain; there was always a woman (Kelly the totemic blueprint, one might be tempted to argue) in punitive charge.

Frequently, having come, I'd shuffle to the bathroom and try to make myself sick by sticking my fingers down my throat. Malone had known, and warned, and raised the dead for proof. (*Thomas, because thou hast seen me, thou hast believed. And now here I was, without doubt.) The Things had congealed, had become the Thing — or, as I found myself mentally referring to it, *It*.

'Do you want some Swiss roll, sweetheart?' my mother called upstairs to me.

Yes, but sweetheart had just filled his navel with seed courtesy of Mrs Walker (a hennaed, high-cheekboned, whorishly cosmeticized woman in her mid-forties, who lived on Escrick Street) beating her ten-year-old daughter black and blue while he (and beyond the tableau's perimeter Malone, shouting at the Devil) looked on.

In the bathroom, my skin having put forth its roses of heat, I stuffed a towel in my mouth to muffle my sobs. Not for sin, but for the distance I had travelled from my mother, and father, and Julia.

How can people do these things? my mother had asked, in strict resistance, though her resistance itself was an admission, as her sadness had been, discovering me crouched over Jules's anus like a miser over a guinea. My father I'm not sure; some ash-mouthed acknowledgement – *Should've hanged the filthy bastards* – some disgusted recognition . . .

'Jules?' I said, in the dark.

'What?'

'Am I adopted?'

'What?'

'Was I an adopted child?'

A snort; then a pause, seeing that, for whatever bizarre reason, I was serious.

'For God's sake, Dommie,' she said. 'Why do you think you're adopted?'

'Just tell me.'

'Of course you're not bloody adopted, you *moron*.'

'But I could be,' I said. 'I mean, did you actually see me born?'

I crawled to her bed and sat on the edge. Her eyes glittered in the dark.

'Dominic,' she said. 'Mum was *visibly pregnant* with you for months. Whether I was at the birth is irrelevant.'

'But they could have switched.'

'Could have switched what?'

'Babies. I mean, how do you know I'm not somebody else's baby they switched?'

'Can I ask you something?'

'What?'

'Who are "they"?'

I wasn't sure. 'That's not the point,' I said. 'The point is how do you know? How do you actually *know* I'm your brother?'

'Dear God,' Julia said, bored. 'Take a look in the *mirror*, fig-brain.'

Pollution refined my vision of Hell. Still the blood-red, Boschean place of infancy, but now the blood-red was of stripped muscle or a boundlessly complex organ. Writhing in the tissue, naked bodies, screaming, vomiting, defecating, and, naturally, having sex. Everyone in Hell was having sex, but you could tell it hurt, as my dad would have said, like hell.

'The woman was dressed in purple and scarlet,' said John in Revelation,

> and was glittering with gold, precious stones and pearls. She held a golden cup in her hand, filled with abominable things and the filth of her adulteries. This title was written on her forehead: MYSTERY BABYLON THE GREAT THE MOTHER OF PROSTITUTES AND THE ABOMINATIONS OF THE EARTH. I saw that the woman was drunk with the blood of the saints, the blood of those who bore testimony to Jesus . . .

I'd gone to Revelation pragmatically, reasoning that it was best to know the worst. A day of apocalyptic dread had followed. Then, the next night, further apnoeal and balletic self-abuse, Mrs Walker this time cradling in her phthisic and cerise-nailed free hand (the other occupied with poker, whip, truncheon), a golden cup, filled with abominable things and the filth of her adulteries, whatever they were.

And so again to Feeney, the sweat- and serge-scented confessional, contrition in English; simultaneously, absolution in Latin, with two deflating consequences. First, I realized (after morose masturbation in the bath two hours later) that I'd wasted my time. Halfway through the sincere Act of Contrition I'd already got a new version of the Mrs Walker-and-her-daughter story brewing. Second, Feeney's absolution might as well have been tips for the afternoon's steeplechase for all they convinced me he was acting on God's behalf. It was *Father Feeney* in there: Old Spice, tannic teeth, violet nose of yawning pores. Malone would have been a different proposition. His soul would have reached out, hovered over me, seen — through skin, bone, circulatory system — and understood what we were up against. The Things — the Thing — *It* — offered glimpses through the door that led to the Truth. If I could only walk through. If I could only walk through! Unimaginable enlightenment. Feeney's absolution was undermined less by flatulence and flaking scalp than by his manifest blindness to what was at stake. But Malone had known. The knowledge had surrounded him in a coronal glow. *Don't you understand that this is a war?*

In which he, patently, delighted. I remembered the eye-flash and wolfish grin as he walked towards me with Burke fresh from death. If it was a war, it was one which allowed for joy in battle. He had riled the Devil by returning Burke's soul to its body. Satan believed in an eye for an eye — my soul weregild for Burke's. He *would* have it. Thus I was tempted, time after time. And time after time I failed. In the most abject post-ejaculatory moments (sobbing, fingers down throat) I comforted myself with the theory that it was Malone's fault. I, Dominic Francis Hood, was nothing but a pawn.

My last year at St Edmund's dragged by with me in a state of nauseous duality of ecstasy and shame. That Easter we had *Jesus of Nazareth* on television. 'On the cross,' Mrs Sharpe told us in RE, the week the series ended, 'Jesus had to take upon Himself *all the sins of the world.*' Some of us must have looked puzzled: 'That means that every time you commit a sin – at the Devil's tempting – you're adding, yes, you, each of you, is *actually adding* to the horrific, agonizing load of sin Our Lord had to bear on the Cross.' She had perhaps expected more visible signs of our discomfort. Therefore: 'Every time you commit a sin . . .' (pause, looking around; me sitting in a hot aura of shame) . . . 'you're actually *pressing the thorns deeper into His head.*' Protracted and grotesquely ornamented masturbation that night, allowing for an extraordinary traffic jam of images. In *Jesus of Nazareth* Mary Magdalene had been played by Anne Bancroft. Anne Bancroft was also Mrs Robinson in *The Graduate*, which film, under Jules's lax babysitting, I had been allowed to watch, and which I remembered chiefly for the scene in which Benjamin (Dustin Hoffman) takes Elaine (Catherine Ross) to a strip club, where she's humiliated by a stripper rotating her nipple-tassles directly above her, Elaine's, head. Both stripper and Mrs Robinson/Mary Magdalene joined myself and Kelly in the attic, where *both* Elaines (Sharples and Catherine Ross) suffered horribly at our hands. The matches had long since been dispensed with in favour of harsher chastisements, but Kelly's bouncing up and down remained, with this time immediate thorn-pressing effect on crucified Jesus's head.

No amount of baths or showers sufficed. Even fantasies I began harmlessly (affectionate lesbian nurses, for example – television, the *Sun* and my mother's mail-order catalogues having helped with uniforms and lingerie) turned to reveal their true value.

'Wha – what are you *doing*?'

'Shut up, pig-slut! Get on your knees. You're going to be whipped like the dirty little bitch you are!' *Look at that dirty fat pig. See the bitch.* (The antennae pick up the fragments; the Devil's grammar claims them, quick.) A complete idiom revealed as by diabolical decree. I surprised myself, having not been precocious before.

Easter, summer term, summer holidays. The tidal wave of secondary school reared up and cast its shadow. Julia got all her O levels and a place on a foundation course at Begshall's College of Art. For long parts of the days and nights I went quiet, thinking of the backwards-played scream, the sound before sound, the endless noise of God. It was the sound of the picture in *Weird Crimes*. Pubescence had given me a dark twin invisible to the world, with four exceptions: myself, Ignatius Malone, the Devil, and God.

But the world was about to get larger.

◆

Infant peccadilloes, she'll say. Childhood's a barrel every monster sooner or later scrapes. But having reached the ugly conclusion of ourselves (I reached mine in the basement, with my beloved Deborah Black) we want the causes, the explanation, the story, the *plot*. We search for the well springs, as Matthew Arnold says, of the buried life.

'I've had it.'

'And?'

'And nothing. I tried it. I found it disgusting.'

Therapy, she meant. This morning Holly sat in the bath up to her neck in too-hot water that had turned her red. I sat on the floor with my knees up to my chest, just managing not to blurt out that she has the loveliest-shaped head of any woman I've ever known. She takes compliments like insults. I've learned. I'm learning.

A colleague to whom she has hitherto attributed a sound mind has recently begun having therapy.

'Why disgusting?' I asked her.

She lifted her left leg and began shaving it. She's businesslike with her body, indifferent, sometimes rough. She's afraid of letting its significance back in, of remembering that she might be gentle with it.

'The idea of entitlement,' she said. 'An entitlement to happiness. Sitting in a chair talking about your childhood to a complete stranger to cash in your entitlement to happiness. It's fucking disgusting. The whole idea of therapy's disgusting.'

She shaved on, briskly, nicked her shin, ignored the little leaf of blood. *Your beautiful legs*, I nearly said, battened it down just in time.

'Therapy just says nothing's your fault,' she said, her hoarse voice bouncing off the tiles. 'If you're unhappy it's somebody else's fault, not yours. That's what makes me puke.'

I watched the leg lowered again, the other one raised. Her limbs glimmered. Her scrubbed face looked tight and tired.

'You're the only person I've ever met who never does anything for effect,' I said.

The right leg done in silence, then. Her sharp face turned in closed profile. The thing in my chest went through some infinitessimally small motions.

She finished and lowered her leg, sat for a moment in the crackling foam, then stood up.

'I'd like a bit of privacy if you don't mind,' she said.

◆

Not much was required of you on your first day at St Dymphna's RC Secondary Grammar and High, but what was required was dinner money – and I forgot mine. (St Dymphna? Patron saint of the mentally ill, no joke. Pupils from 'the High' kicked in the ribs, skulls and pelvises of pupils from 'the Grammar'. Pupils from the Grammar dis-covered the uselessness of eloquence and the solace of scars.) I stood in the ammoniacal entrance hall filling up with gentle dread. It was raining. Every time the doors opened a wet draught blew in. High boys stomped up the drive with their hands ramrodded into their blazer pockets. Brollied or coat-tented High girls came linked in trios or quartets, with animated faces, gossip, shrieks. Properly dressed Grammar boys and Grammar girls trudged towards the main doors (combed hair, brand-new bags, dinner money) having been launched by their parents down at the main gate. I was a Grammar boy who had insisted his parents stay at home, which was a sign of intelligence. But I had forgotten my dinner money on my first day, which testified to deep stu-pidity. It was a miserable time for me there in the puddled vestibule, swarmed around and bypassed by hundreds of people who (execrable bastards that they were) weren't in trouble.

'I've forgotten my dinner money,' I said. 'What'll happen?'

I'd selected an older pupil to ask, a third-year with sandy hair, a slender, hircine face, and eyes of yellowish green. He'd looked friendly.

'Are you even fucking *talking* to me, you little menstrual blob?' he said. I took a step backwards. 'Are you even *alive*?'

'Sorry,' I said. 'Forget it. Sorry.'

'Come here. Come *here*.' (Very delicately pronounced, that second 'here'.)

'Really, I—'

'Get your miserable fucking menstrual blob of a head *right* here, *right* now.'

I stepped forward. A florid fourth-year girl with dark hair and conical breasts passed close by in a whiff of doublemint and patchouli, saying: 'Leave 'im alone, Dunleavey, you sorry queer.'

Dunleavey ignored her. 'Now,' he said. 'Let's have that tie.'

The only teacher I could see was standing in a far corner of the hall, bellowing into the face of a boy even smaller than me, who was snivelling, but with arms defiantly folded. Eyes welling, I unfastened my tie and handed it to Dunleavey, who, nostrils flared, trebled it into a soft cosh, thwacked me across the face with it, pocketed it, then waltzed off down a corridor.

I wandered away in search of somewhere to hide.

By the time I found the ground-floor toilets, two bells had rung: one short, constipated ring, and a second, protracted, soulless ring. They had meant something, that I should be somewhere, being accounted for. I didn't care. Hot-faced from the tie-thwack, resigned to the the day's cruelty, I pushed open the toilets' swing door and entered.

Silence, at first. Then the conviction that I wasn't alone. I stood with glowing face and tingling hands, listening.

Suddenly a string of clenched vowels and unattached

fricatives. Some scuffling, clanking and a couple of thuds. Last cubicle on the left.

Courtesy of Jules's liberal babysitting, I'd seen the film *Scum* on television. I knew boys got buggered, then slashed their wrists. I imagined him, whoever he was, a girlish eleven-year-old with long eyelashes and cherubic mouth, bent double, whimpering, bullishly covered by one of the fifth year's grunting hormonal grotesques.

I stepped up and pushed the cubicle door, gently. It wasn't locked. It swung open, slowly, to reveal a skinny, green-eyed boy with dark-rimmed spectacles and a nest of white-blond hair standing on the toilet seat with his hands tied to the cistern and his trousers and underpants around his ankles. They'd tied a string round his penis ('they'; self-evidently a 'they') with a small weight attached to the end; it clanked against the toilet bowl as he struggled. The penis itself was circumcised and the colour of a button mushroom except for the strangled glans, which, bloodlocked, was the colour of Father Feeney's nose.

I could help him; he was at my mercy. We looked at each other for what felt like a long time, understanding this.

Another bell rang. I reached in and picked the weight up. He gasped with relief. 'What's your name?' he said – this social fragment chipped off and thrown out by his wrecked dignity. We weren't ready for names, in my judgement, with his penis dumbly questing between us (the compression and chill had given him – in the perverse way of these things – the beginnings of an erection), so I slipped the weight into his blazer pocket and addressed myself to his other problems.

The simplest antidote to imminent hysteria would have been, I now see, to pull his pants up – but I couldn't do it. The maternity of the gesture forbade it.

'Can you untie my hands?' he said, face flushed, voice

hoarse. I felt disgust for their cruelty (whoever they were, the lousy fuckers), an unexpected, adult perspective in which the comedy of it, the success of the *prank*, disappeared. (It would return, later, for both of us.) Compassion sprouted like a new floret of the brain – then it was done.

We stood toe to toe on the toilet seat in a tense flamenco, my arms reaching round him to get at the knots, his penis nudging my trousers, our breaths embracing to form an intimacy which would otherwise have insisted on a decade. He smelled of cigarette smoke and the morning's ablutions; also, seductively, of Begshall wind and rain. An unexpected glimpse over the precipice, then: I could kiss him. Grab his penis. Suck him off. Wild and suddenly unforbidden possibilities struck me like soft sparks from a firework, then vanished.

I worked fast at the knots (tied, serendipitously for me, with a school tie: I sensed Dunleavey's hand), and after half a minute's puffing and blowing – the odd '*Fuck*ing thing' lobbed in to shore up heterosexual cavities – had him free. I got myself out of the cubicle to give him a moment.

After five minutes he still hadn't emerged.

'Shall I go?' I said.

'No. Wait.'

The quiet around us spoke of school going on. They'd be coming to look for us about now.

He came out, trousers up, presumably with penis unbound, and went to the basin to wash his hands. I leaned against the tiles, hands in pockets, looking at the floor.

'Bastards,' I said, shaking my head.

He sniffed. The green eyes flashed at me in the mirror, then he ducked and splashed water on his face. Kept his hands there for a moment. He was short, like me, but thin, ignited by the mineral eyes and white shriek of hair.

60

Androgynously striking. He'd come up, no doubt, in the enervated staff room, the first year's curio. I felt hot in the nose, chin and fingertips. That shallow navel and those miserable thighs. That shame naked in his face.

Having dried himself with a fistful of paper towels, he leaned back against the basin, sighed, and reached into his blazer pocket. 'Dominic,' he said—

At which the door burst open and a snuffling first-year boy stormed in with his hand clasped over his forehead. Clearly he had been much cuffed and yanked. His hair was full of static. One shirt-tail was out, and his tie was missing. Sobbing, rosy with the injustice of whatever had been done to him, he went straight to a basin and began running the hot tap.

Suddenly, he turned from the steaming sink and shoved his dark fringe back from his forehead.

'In case you're fucking wondering,' he said. 'Eh? In case you're fucking *wondering*.'

We looked. 'CUNT' it said, in pungent black marker, just above his raised eyebrows.

'Fucking funny, isn't it?' he said. 'Fucking' – he leaped to one side and kicked the metal wastepaper bin with all his might; it skidded across the floor and crashed into the urinal, chipping the ceramic – 'fucking hilfucking*arious*.'

A surreal few minutes of his forehead scrubbing and our vague fraternal support followed. All to little effect: 'CUNT' remained, slightly faded, surrounded now by a raw red perimeter. He turned from the sink, small-eyed with new tears, and palmed his forehead like a misunderstood actor. Reluctantly, recognizing a need greater than my own, I gave him the tie – just broad enough, when worn headband fashion, to cover all four letters.

The three of us filed out of the toilets, down the corridor, and through the nearest exit into the yard. It had stopped raining. Presumably, if anyone was looking out of the tower block's windows, we were visible. Once again the blond boy reached into his blazer's inside pocket, this time bringing out a pack of ten No. 6. He offered, and we took, me very dreamily, having never smoked a cigarette in my life. Then a worn brass Zippo, his hands professional, nonchalant, the first brain-bashing drag – and the knowledge despite all immediate sensory objections (searing pain in the bronchioles, one ferocious wheeze) that smoking was right up my street.

CUNT inhaled unproblematically, closed his eyes, blew out through his nose with the veteran's well-earned ecstasy. His cheeks were still flushed, but the static had dropped his dark hair in a soft mop on his head. The school around us was in deep silence. I looked at my watch: 9.23am. First period in two minutes, us unaccounted for. Somewhere, an irritated form teacher; somewhere a bad-tempered search party. The nicotine had begun its dizzying magic. Over the playing fields to our right a small vent in the cloud let in a shaft of light.

Exhausted, my habitual self had collapsed; now a new, insouciant, post-modern pilot had the helm. I took another drag.

'I've made a decision,' the blond boy said.

We looked at him.

'I'm taking the day off.'

He gave us a look, then turned and headed across the yard in the direction of the playing fields and the woods' shadow of freedom. CUNT and I looked at each other. Agreed, silently, with resignation to higher powers, then followed him like a pair of brainless dogs.

By which time, courtesy of abuse, confusion, intimations

of homosexuality and the loss of my smoking virginity, I'd stopped wondering how, back there in the toilets, he'd known my name.

◆

I make excuses to pause in this story when it tests my own credulity. The excuse an hour ago was that Holly would be home soon and the kitchen was a mess. Now the dishes are done and the white counter tops gleam. No Holly, though. It's understood between us that she doesn't always come straight home, that she's not accountable.

Where'd you get to?

Just went for a drink.

What did you have?

A huge Tom Collins.

Three huge Tom Collinses, it'll have been, by the sheen and stretch of her face. But I won't say anything. It would end the mystery of what exactly it is we've got here – it would disgust her with its predictability. As it'll disgust her, eventually, if I *don't* say anything – but in the meantime there's a narrow margin between the two disgusts into which I've steered and where I hope to stay until the job I've set myself is done.

The job I've set myself. Or that God has set me. He's never been averse to explicit sleights-of-hand, nor belief-beggaring irony. Dominic *Hood*. Deborah *Black*. A little divine insurance policy taken out against my scepticism. A design argument in two surnames. Holly's surname is, merely, Jones, so I'm entitled to think there's been some lightening of the formerly heavy hand. But let's not be hasty: there remains *Holly*, from a plant with its own clutter of omens: cure for chilblains, prevention of fever and whooping cough, protection from lightning, a defence (grown in churchyards) against witches and, as Chatterton has it, *foul fiends*. My favourite (I've taken to saying it to myself, watching her sleep) is a fifteenth-century carol — anonymous, naturally — which warns: *Whosoeuer ageynst Holly do crye, In a lepe shall he hang full hye . . . Whosoeuer ageynst Holly do syng, He may weep and hands wryng . . .*

No let-up, then. The dishes are done and the counter tops gleam.

◆

His name was Gregory Bernard Alexander Kelp. 'Call me anything other than Kelp,' he instructed, in his quiet voice 'and I'll ram your fucking head into Joshua Nkomo's buttock-slush.'

CUNT was Gwyn Holt — Welsh mother, English father — and was called (even by these parents) Penguin, or more often Pen. After that first day (hell to pay, come last bell: parents phoned and summoned; the head of year foaming; two porcine and excessively aftershaved young police constables; Kelp's mother conspicuously absent) the allegiance between us was set.

Kelp was slightly — but *only* slightly — odd from the outset. It was difficult to make him laugh, beyond a giggle, but when one did the results were spectacular: he laughed silently, doubled up, tears streaming. A joy to observe — up to a point — beyond which one thought he might go completely mad and start screaming and tearing his hair out.

He did all the things Pen and I did (except the things I did in private, I supposed), smoked, drank, burped creatively, farted with nuance, perused shoplifted pornography, told sick jokes and so on; but much of the time with a detatchment bordering indifference, as if giantly preoccupied; some elusive and insinuating real business of his life. You talked to him, he looked at you, nodded, *yes*ed and *umm*ed as if with full attention. Then, when you paused for his reply: 'Sorry, Dum' – I was Dum or Dummie, from Dommie, from Dominic – 'could you say that again? I wasn't listening.'

On the other hand there were moments when he seemed to see with an assaultive or Maloneish clarity. Some innocuous question – 'Oi, bastard, do you want a cup of tea?' – and the bespectacled green eyes would look up from the page (he read omnivorously, with a permanent frown) and fix their object, me, with a look of absolute disinterested interrogation. At these moments it was as if one had suddenly fallen under the infinitely neutral scrutiny of a supernatural being. It made my heart stop. But he couldn't have seen. I told myself I was imagining it.

We never went to his house. *My mum doesn't like people coming round.* It was left at that. His father had died when Kelp was only two years old, whereupon his mother had moved from Chester (and, it was intimated, the middle classes) via mishandled money and shit luck to Begshall and the council flat in Mere Street. I had seen her a few times, since only Lordship Park separated my street from his: a wiry woman with his white-blond hair (scraped back and tied), a hard, coltish face and slender eyes – not the green of her son's but plum dark and withdrawn from the world. *My mum doesn't like people coming round.* I had seen her in her winter coat – woollen, an incongruously loud red – speed-walking back from the off-licence with – there was no mistaking it – a clinking carrier bag. *Don't ask, Pen, I think she's an alcoholic.* Thereafter we had left him alone about it.

We were unpopular at St Dymphna's, our self-containment being an affront. The Trinity, to the facetious Grammar; to the High (Pen mortified) the Queers. For a while we managed with a stretched effort to dismiss the girls (Grammar *or* High) as *girls*, that is to say, as beings who had failed to be boys. But as terms passed and hormones twitched the defence showed signs of strain. Adolescence, mongrel-like, went about its business. Pustules rioted. Boys hitherto thought negligible specimens evolved into baritone giants, scalps oozing grease, faces bacterially aflame, penises (showers after games) transformed from the bald shrimps of childhood into pubescence's hairy king prawns. The girls stopped being *girls* and became – treacherously – girls. They had breasts, over which they kept their arms folded. Hips arrived. Skirts climbed. Earrings, nail varnish, lip gloss. By the middle of the second year our system of denial was moribund.

'I'd shag Pamela Merril,' Pen said, one wet afternoon in a bus shelter, where, with cigarettes and a half-bottle of Lamb's Navy Rum, the three of us were truanting.

'So would I.'

'So would I.'

Pamela Merril had stopped wearing knee socks and started wearing thigh-highs. We'd been waiting for one of us to pluck up the courage. (Pen found courage in unlikely places: impatience; weakness; fatalism; desire; boredom.) It was a relief to accede, to let the revolution begin. Now all other objects of consciousness must move aside to make room for the central matter, the desirability or otherwise of girls. (There was the other central matter for me, but I wasn't saying anything about that.)

Saturday afternoons we shoplifted in Manchester. A routine established itself: calorific breakfast in the station's greasy spoon; half an hour's Galaxian in Leisure Zone; train to

Manchester; quick inspection of the import record shops, then down to the business of thievery. Home, without fail, on the 17.32, which got us back in time for hot-panted Catherine Bach in *The Dukes of Hazard*.

Points were scored in inverse proportion to the desirability of the stolen item. Thus between us we accumulated onions, screws, toilet rolls, cushion covers, dentagrip, surgical stockings, anchovies, saucepans, ladies' hats, laxatives, door knockers, a cat basket and three toupees. One day, in a Market Street HMV, Pen sat down on the floor, slid a Kate Bush poster all the way up his trouser leg, then Long John Silvered out of the door. No points – Kate Bush's desirability being luminous – but our admiration for sheer chutzpah. The following week Kelp topped him by walking into a sweet shop (bottom rung on the risk ladder) with his school bag, saying, 'Hello, Mr Shopkeeper,' to the cardied nonogenarian at the till, tipping the counter display's entire stock (about eighty items) into the bag, zipping it up, saying, 'Good-bye Mr Shopkeeper,' then walking out of the shop.

What's the big fascination with Manchester, all of a sudden? My mother wanted to know. I told her import record shops. *Is that illegal?* she asked, with raised index finger. Of course not, I told her, of *course* not.

Sundays were spent in Pen's attic. He had his own sock-scented bedroom, but the attic was the one place he could escape the cling of his younger brother, Gareth. Pen's mother, Mona (whom everyone, including Pen, called Mogs), had had Pen when she was thirty-two, then eight years later fallen foul of Vatican roulette (as my own mother had with me, precipitating final surrender to prophylactics) and had Gareth. Gareth had Down's syndrome. Excruciating for Pen, Kelp and I knew; some deal cut with Mogs: Gareth was allowed to pester us for a while (he didn't do any harm, just wanted to be there with us, and to clamber about our laps and shoulders); then Pen would look at his watch, have a word with Mogs, and Gareth would be lured away with a chocolate biscuit. Whereupon we would retire to the attic (Pen hugely relieved and disgusted with himself) to listen to records, drink pilfered booze, smoke cigarettes with our heads stuck out of the windows, and discuss the desirability or otherwise of girls. None of us had had sex *with another person* – as Feeney would have said – a state of affairs we never tired of lamenting, but for which, secretly, we were thankful, being terrified of not being up to it when the time came. Or, in my case, of being up to something entirely different.

I didn't tell them about Malone. What would I have told them? Listen, I know this sounds unbelievable, but when I was eight I accidentally killed this Irish bastard called Callum Burke. However, a priest I'd met six months earlier came by and resurrected him. He knew I had something wrong with me, you see, and decided to stake a claim for God in my soul.

Pen would have scoffed, desperately; desperately because he was in fact an inveterate and pants-wetting believer in the supernatural. Kelp, too, would have let it in without demur. Not being believed wasn't the problem. The problem was that telling them about Malone would have meant telling them about *It*. Unthinkable. Nights, I lay awake, glairy with seed and crushed by the weight of *It*, deafened by the noise of the stream of self which roared along, as in an underground tunnel. Only I (and God, and the Devil, and Ignatius Malone) knew where the doors to it were hidden. The rest of me was available for limitless inspection, certainly by Penguin and Kelp, but probably by anyone who bothered to look. There simply was no traceable connection between one Dominic Hood and the other. Most of the time, even the me of the upper chambers carried on (playing Galaxian, shoplifting, conceding the merits of Pamela Merril's thighs) as if in ignorance of the me of the lower.

Meanwhile the me of the lower chambers got on with its business. Mrs Walker (of the green eyeshadow and veiny hands) and daughter were older, now, and not alone. These days they hobnobbed with celebrities. Chris Evert, Lindsey Wagner, Debbie Harry, Pan's People, Jenny Hanley, Jaclyn Smith, Caroline Munroe, Brit Ekland – the list went on to include more or less every televisual woman I'd ever noticed, famous or obscure, all furnished with evil streaks and violent appetites they never dreamed they had. They didn't all have to be attractive, since it added piquancy to see beauty abused by ugliness. I remained the accomplice. (Misogyny, the coquette, insisted from behind coyly fluttered fan on a female representative.) The essential relation, however, was the same: sexual pleasure increased proportionally according to the victim's suffering.

I had read – and found out, among many other garish facts, what *they made tapes* of. A book of serial killers shoplifted from Begshall's W.H. Smith showed the famous headshots of Myra Hindley and Ian Brady, his eyes impregnable as those of a fish, hers, under the slight frown, curiously interrogative. It had been agreed, the book said, that the tapes (played for the jury) would never be made public. I studied the photographs for hours. *They know it,* an inner version of my own voice said. *They know, now, what it is . . .*

No they don't, Malone's voice insisted, calmly. I imagined him sitting behind me, crammed into a small chair, bony hands on bony knees. *The Devil is a liar* – mischievous wink – *and a liar never keeps his word.*

I continued to take long, scalding showers and baths. 'We can move your bed in there if you like,' my dad said, alerted by the gas bill. 'Then you'll only have to come out for meals and to see your bloody mates.'

Most of the time I blotted out my fear of Hell. Of *going* to Hell. That I had stopped going to mass was irrelevant: The discovery of my true nature had confirmed and solidified the structure and logic of the spiritual realm. *Masturbari ergo Satana ergo Deus.* I wondered, in a spirit of clinical curiosity, what would happen when I started having sex – to remain within Feeney's idiom – *with another person*.

In tandem with all this an insatiable appetite for fantasy sagas. *The Lord of the Rings*, *Narnia*, *The Weirdstone of Brisingammen*, *The Chronicles of Thomas Covenant*, Arthurian pulp by the pound. There was no imaginary world so morally banal that its triumph of good over evil failed to bring a lump to my throat. Ditto lugubrious hymns and sad carols: *In the bleak mid-winter, long, long ago.* A British Airways commercial: *bringing people* (slow-motion montage of multi-racial and intergenerational embraces) . . . *together*. The rankest sentimentality had me swallowing, blinking, getting up and leaving the room. I didn't understand. Like the fear of Hell, it was blotted out. For a long while, it was blotted out.

Three school years passed, measured publicly in attic Sundays, bus-shelter evenings, cigarettes and empties, simultaneous equations, *Twelfth Night*, French declensions, shoplifting, *how much would you have to be paid to* conversations and the endless speculation about girls. Privately they were measured in torture tableaux and urgent ejaculations, visions of Malone and of my soul: a delicate yolk with, at the centre, the Devil's incrementally expanding bloodspot. You hurt them, you see, you hurt them and look into their eyes.

You look into their eyes. If you can look, and see them, really *see* them . . .

Then, with the strange digits of nineteen-eighty (plump, futuristic, for the first time ever bringing the notion of the year 2000 out of the realm of science fiction) beginning to suggest themselves, things began to happen.

To begin with, I met Kelp's mother.

As if it were the most natural thing in the world – as if all the *My mum doesn't like people coming round* had never been – he asked me back there one evening after school. It was early December. We had walked through Lordship Park with collars up against freezing sleet. Trees bare-knuckled and leathery. Darkness, skirls of wind. I had asked no questions, treated the invitation as if it meant nothing; in spite of which chit-chat dropped away by the time we reached the house in Mere Street. I've wondered, since, why he let me in. I thought for a long while it was because he'd felt the first stirrings of his condition, intimations of what he'd soon have to deal with, sensed that there was no point in keeping her out of our ken any longer, since he'd be following in her footsteps. But the truth is, of course, that he was a fourteen-year-old boy not sure of anything, and that she was a lot to carry, on his own, and that he, after three years of lighting each other's fags and sipping without wiping the bottleneck, trusted me.

Thirteen Mere Street. Just behind the front door a dinner plate with a brown quarter-moon of congealed gravy and a handful of stiffened chips. Next to it an untouched slew of windowed envelopes. In the living room, an exhausted couch and unmatching armchair, nicotine stains on the walls, a television with sound down and picture rolling. Loaded ashtrays, strewn clothes, many more empties than was seemly.

Kelp's face went tight, resolved on soaking up my shock. Randomly, he picked up a half-drunk cup of tea and took it through to the kitchen, where he emptied it down the sink with a look of compressed disgust, as if this cup, specifically, was to blame. 'I might need your help, Dummie,' he said, without turning.

Stella was in the low-ceilinged bedroom, in bed, under what looked like several duvets. Behind the drawn curtains the window was an oblong of softly burning amber. A crack admitted a sliver of untouched sun, which in turn revealed motes moving as in plasma. Stale cigarette smoke, burped booze, farts, neglected linen. I didn't dare cross the threshold, but stood instead on the landing with my wrists gone heavy and my jaws locked.

'What?' she said, when Kelp shook her. 'Piss off, Frank, for Christ's sake, will you?'

'It's me,' Kelp said, standing up straight. 'Is Frank here?'

Stella groaned and rolled over.

'Mum!'

'What?'

'Wake *up*.'

She did, with great reluctance – and noticed me in the bedroom doorway. 'For fuck's *sake*,' she said, grabbing the bedclothes close. (Not quick enough: a glimpse of one bare and solid armpit and the strap of a pink vest.) 'Jesus Christ.'

'Don't overreact,' Kelp said, taking a Silk Cut from the bedside table pack and lighting it, unopposed. 'It's only Dummie.'

She waved me away, violently, and began a fit of coughing. I retreated to the hall, where, a few moments later, Kelp joined me.

'He's in the bathroom,' he said. 'Come on.'

In the bathtub, to be precise. Asleep, in a flimsy grey suit and tartan socks. Late fifties, with a thin, drink-blasted face, lank, dyed black hair and a faintly happy smile.

'Get up, Frank,' Kelp said.

'Hair,' Frank said, petulantly.

'Frank!' Kelp shouted. 'Get up you miserable cocksucking spiv!'

One pink eye opened a sliver. The dried lips ungummed themselves, disclosing a set of shamelessly brilliant dentures. Then eye and mouth closed again.

'Frank,' Kelp said, bending close to the long ear. 'If you don't get up, I'm turning the cold water on.'

'Mmuuur,' Frank said. 'Nun.'

Kelp straightened again, took a drag of the Silk Cut, passed it to me, exhaled, considering. 'Ten minutes, Frank,' he said, loudly. 'Then I'm back up here and I'm turning the cold on.'

'Azza good boy,' Frank said. 'Azza good lad.' He rolled onto his side, foreplayed dentures and lips with a dexterous tongue, then sank back into oblivion.

'Who the fuck is he?' I asked, back in the living room. Kelp stood with his hands in his pockets, surveying the devastation. He looked exhausted.

'Friend of my mum's,' he said. 'Piss-head. Birds of a feather and all that. You don't have to hang around here, Dummie. I wouldn't.'

We did the washing-up, which took an hour and a half. Then we bin-bagged the empties and turfed out the butts. Kelp hoovered, Domestos'd, Hazed, and settled the telly's vertical hold.

Stella emerged at last, in pink jogging pants and a black roll-neck sweater. She found us in the kitchen, with mugs of tea.

'Sit down, Mum,' Kelp said. 'There's tea.' He got up to

pour it from the newly washed pot. Stella took a seat opposite me. Lit a Silk Cut; eyes narrowed, briefly in the
sidestream smoke, then went cold and focused again.

'How much is he charging?' she said to me.

I raised my eyebrows, not understanding.

'To get to see the Mother.'

'Ignore it, Dummie,' Kelp said.

'Only he normally prefers to keep me under wraps, don't
you, love?'

'Yeah,' Kelp said. 'Here's your tea.'

'What with me taking a drop more . . . a drop more than
the recommended daily . . .' She didn't finish. Instead looked
past me, glazed, momentarily.

'Frank!' Stella bawled, suddenly, tipping her head back.
'Frank, get out of my house, will you?'

Small noises followed. Frank, precariously, on the move.

'Does he know about it?' Stella said, quietly, looking not
at Kelp but at me.

'No.'

'Are you going to tell him?'

'I suppose so,' Kelp said. My head tennis-umpiring.

'Well,' Stella said, making her eyes wide, as if to demon-
strate wonder to a two-year-old. 'Well!'

Frank poked his head round the kitchen door. He had
attempted a wash-and-brush-up, without success.

'Cup for me is there, Stell?'

'Strangely, Frank,' Stella said, 'no, there isn't.' A wee flash
at me with her eyes this time, bringing me into collusion.
Suddenly the house's mess not so important.

Frank beamed and scratched his ear. 'Right. Right. You
down the Firkin tonight?'

Stella lowered her head and picked at a stain on the
Formica.

'Time to go, Frank,' Kelp said.

'Right, right,' Frank said, clinging to the doorframe like a crane fly. 'Mebby see you down there later, then, Stell.'

'I'm listening for the sound of you withdrawing, Frank,' Stella said, not looking up.

'Right you are. Ta-ra, then,' Frank said, and shuffled away, coughing. We heard the front door close, softly, behind him.

Stella slumped forward and laid her check on her folded arms. Her eyes remained open, however, looking at her son, me utterly excluded. The unidentifiable peripheral noise – traffic, I supposed – subsided, and the kitchen went quiet. Stella moved her hand over to Kelp's, touched it, just, barely, hooked her index in his for a moment, elicited a tug of recognition, then relaxed and withdrew. She slid back up to her original position, facing me with a sad smile.

'Due to muteness, is it?' she asked.

I made a face of pleasant incomprehension.

'"Dummie",' she said. 'On account of your inability to speak, I presume?'

Oh. A joke. Kelp sipped, gave me a bright look over the rim of his mug.

'Dominic,' I said. 'Dommie. Dummie.'

She looked at me, weighing up, I could tell, her ability to resist behaving badly, making something further deformed from the encounter. Let it go.

'Sorry, love,' she said. 'You must be wishing you were somewhere else.'

'I'm okay,' I said, looking down at the table top (a spot-welded baked bean Kelp's swipes had missed), then up, to be greeted by her face denuded now of all but its tiredness. To my horror, she reached across for my hand, took it in hers. Hers warm from the mug, mine schoolboyishly nibbled. A squeeze, which, not knowing what else to do, I returned.

Her eyes filled, briefly – a slight distress in the chin – then she was over it. She cleared her throat. 'You two've tidied up,' she said.

'Or maybe it was the elves,' Kelp said.

She smiled.

'Take a fiver out of my purse,' she said, exhaling smoke, mashing the Silk Cut in her saucer.

That night Pen and I went with him up to the lodge in the shadow of Hargreaves's mill. (These days Begshall's cotton mills have been knocked down or put at the disposal of disposable income as home-improvement centres, health clubs or lofts, but back then you could still find Blake's satanic edifices, wrecked, giantly redundant, haunted by the ghosts of machine-hum and dogged northern graft.) Hargreaves's mill, grandly ruined, with glass-fanged windows and crenellated walls, was on a hill overlooking the reservoir. The roof had fallen in and the walls had been pillaged for brick; now only a jagged perimeter remained. Less than ten years ago, the mutilated body of a missing seven-year-old boy had been dredged up here; case still open.

It was sleetless now, but windy, and we sat (on a bin liner) on the bank with caps pulled down and collars rattling. Pen had brought a quarter bottle of Lamb's Navy Rum; fiery gulps, shudders, then the warmth, spreading.

'She's got second sight,' Kelp said.

'What?' Pen said.

'Second sight,' Kelp said. 'ESP. Clairvoyance. My mum. Uri Geller. Stella Geller.'

His glasses were in for mending. Without them, his face had the look of a harmless wild animal, a gazelle, perhaps.

'Oh, right,' Pen said, swigging, gasping. 'Yeah.'

'It started when she was about twelve. Periods and seeing

things. They'll tell you it's all connected. Hormones. Fertility. The *moon*.'

'Who'll tell you?' I said.

Kelp snorted. 'All the weirdos. Go to a mind, body and spirit convention. Go to a *white witch*. Even the fucking doctors'll believe it's for real if they can tie it to PMT.'

'What are you talking about?' Pen asked.

'Shut up, Pen,' I said. Then, to Kelp, 'And is it connected? To the hormones, I mean?'

'Dunno,' he said. 'Might be, for all I know. You'd think you'd go and get it checked out, wouldn't you? Egg-heads and science and what not. She says you don't. She says, somehow, you just don't.'

Pen passed the bottle, and Kelp took an excruciating swig.

'Let me get this straight,' Pen said, lighting a Rothman. 'You reckon your mum's a . . . Your mum can see the future?' Trowelled-on credulousness – bogus, I knew. I kept thinking of Stella, the scraped-back hair and scoured face, that glimpse of armpit, jogging pants. Of course: ordinary people, if at all.

'It's because of my dad,' Kelp said, flatly. 'Her. The drink. Because he died.'

A long pause, the lodge reservoir lapping, Pen newly attentive, smoking seriously, now, shoulders hunched. The wind hissed in the grass.

'He was an architect,' Kelp said. 'He was going to a site. It wasn't ten minutes from where we lived. This was in Chester. I don't remember, being only two.'

I swigged rum (Christmas and piracy and Jamaica and Lamb's Navy Rum poster girl Caroline Munroe), contorted for a second, then returned the bottle to Pen. Kelp stretched his legs out and crossed his ankles.

'The site was only ten minutes away, so my dad was going

to walk. She called down to him and told him to take a brolly. It was going to rain. She knew. Seen it. You think it's all assassins and planes blowing up and whatnot. It isn't. Most of the time it's trivial crap. Tickets sold out. Train late. The weather. So my dad laughed and took a brolly. Didn't even look which one, just picked one at random from the stand in the hall. Turned out later he'd picked a really feminine one, with flowers on it.' He smiled at that: a gram of ironic compensation. 'It did rain,' he went on. 'She was right about that. But there was an accident. A car came off the road. It was a young couple, arguing. The bloke went to hit the girl, lost control of the wheel. Split-second stuff. Amazing, isn't it? Anyway, they hit him, my dad. He went back against a wall. Smashed his skull, massive brain haemorrhage. Died before the ambulance got there.'

Pen and I very quiet now, him having not taken a drag or a swig for a long time. Kelp with hands in donkey-jacket pockets and white hair-wings streaming from under his cap.

'She'd seen the rain, you see? But not the accident. Selective premonition. That's the way it is. You get to see what you get to see. That's all. She might have seen the accident. She didn't. She saw the rain.'

Several moments passed, Pen and I looking at each other across Kelp in the middle, Kelp lodge-transfixed, with a gentle smile and bright eyes. Pen (I sensed) abandoning in rapid increments any hope that it might not be true, that he might be entitled to make a joke.

'Fuck my dog,' I said, eventually.

'That was twelve years ago,' Kelp said.

'Fuck my dog,' I repeated.

Kelp eased the bottle from Pen's grip, lifted, took a gulp, forced himself to keep still as it went down.

'Yeah,' he said. 'That's about the size of it.'

We walked the long way home, via Pen's, where, having swallowed a final belt of the Lamb's, he said goodnight, or rather, *Right – baaaaaarp – that's me, homosexuals*. For a moment, after his front door closed, Kelp and I stood in silence. A little ritual we'd evolved: listening to the sound of suburbia. Whispering trees. The audible solidity of detatched houses. The wind had dropped now, and the night was cool and fresh. We breathed deeply through our noses, both, it dawned on us (belatedly, as always), drunk.

'It's because of me,' Kelp said.

'Eh?'

'My mum. The way she is. The drink. It's not because of my dad. It's because of me.'

Cigarettes. Rothmans. The last two. I lighted us both. His bitten fingernails.

'She wanted to kill herself,' he said, as we began walking. 'After my dad died she wanted to kill herself, but she couldn't, because there was me.'

'Come on,' I said.

'I read it in her diary.' He stopped walking to quote: '"Now there's just prison. And a five-year-old jailer who doesn't even know I'm behind the bars."'

Half a dozen mental false starts, then my resignation to having nothing consolatory to say. I wondered how old he had been, reading that.

'She's doing it slowly,' he said, as we began walking again. 'Stretching it out until I'm old enough to take care of myself. Can't be much longer now.'

Later, we stopped in a back street for him to pee. (I wanted to, myself, but knew I wouldn't be able to, in front of or even alongside him.) It was only a few moments, but it left me with one of the half-dozen images of him that will last me, I suppose, to my grave. He stood, legs apart, forearm resting against the wall, head resting on forearm, face concealed.

Masturbation collapsed that night, or shied away from something. Kelly–Burke and me in my room at Logan Street. (I had given up trying to stop this creature's oscillating transsexualism, or sometimes hermaphroditism. Generally I kept it out in favour of less ambiguous staples, but increasingly it forced its goosefleshed, burping and toe-nail-varnished self into the proceedings.) Pen's mother crouched, naked in the corner, myself and Kelly–Burke taking a breather. But that wasn't what I shied away from. There was someone else in the room. Another victim. Tied, prone, behind us, as yet untouched. Kelly–Burke, remembering, having caught its sour breath, was all for it, and turned – *Let's do this fock'n cont* – but I wasn't ready. I wasn't ready. Would never. If I should just turn. Would never. Stop. Hands down. Stop.

I did stop. Sat up in bed, breathing hard. Malone had been watching. Malone was always there, somewhere in the room, larger than his normal dimensions, with the translucence and shiver of a hologram. Malone was always there because Malone was the option to fight, or to walk away, or in any case to *take your stand against the Devil's schemes*.

Bedside light, water, rosary, my flaking copy of *The Lord of the Rings*. Sickness and disgust pleasingly familiar. A base-note of desperation, urgency, excitement. Christ help me. I wasn't . . . I wouldn't. I wasn't.

'You all right, Dum?' Kelp said to me the next night in the attic, when Pen had been verbally abused into going downstairs to make a pot of tea.

'Yeah,' I said. 'Fine.'

'Something's wrong,' he said.

'Nothing's wrong.'

A freighted silence. I stood at the open window, smoking, looking out over Pen's neighbourhood of gardened semis under a faintly starred dusk. Kelp was on his knees, flicking through the vinyls. *Joe's Garage*, *Physical Graffiti*, *Horses*, *Beggars Banquet*. The flicking slowed, then stopped. I knew I wouldn't be able to stand it if he looked up at me, the green eyes through the specs, the raised eyebrows of gentle enquiry.

'We're out of fags,' I said. 'I'll go.'

He didn't say anything. There were these exchanges, which left both of us quiet and raw, as if from gratuitous insult. Passing him that night in the attic, I remembered passing my mother's hip years ago, the curiosity about whether she was going to lash out. Then remembered, too, that I had known she wouldn't, that sadness was her finally arrived at state.

Later that night, after the Bionic Woman (cybernetics conveniently on the blink) had been mutilated by a fishnetted Jane Seymour and a basqued Jaclyn Smith, I thought of what *had* been wrong — specifically and locally wrong, as opposed to generally and pervasively. What had been wrong was that downstairs, moments before, I had crept up on Pen in the kitchen with the intention of giving him a fright. (Penguin was — and I daresay still is — easily and spectacularly startled. At some of his great frights he has executed leaps, spins, shimmies, jerks, once or twice things that looked like Latin dance moves. If the opportunity to startle Pen was there, you startled him. That was the way it was.) Therefore to the open kitchen door on tiptoe.

Pen sat on a stool with his back to me, waiting for the electric kettle to boil. Gareth sat on his lap, facing me over Pen's shoulder, clinging like a monkey. The gesture was a reflex of shared blood, structural care, Pen most likely thinking of something completely different. Though he had seen me, Gareth said nothing, just stared. Eventually, the kettle boiled and switched itself off.

'Right, fat-pants,' Pen said. 'Come on. Get off me.'

I had backed away, swallowing, blinking, with a feeling of fracture down my sternum.

◆

Holly has no sentimentality. No photographs, no box of love letters, no ravaged soft toys, no mementos, period. She opens birthday cards, reads them, throws them away. She chooses *Alien 3* over *Casablanca*, *Last Exit to Brooklyn* over *It's a Wonderful Life*. The apartment is spartan, cursorily or functionally furnished. There were things on the walls when she moved in: a laminated subway map; an aesthetically worthless abstract in oils; a Prince tour poster; a Man Ray calendar from 1998. She left all of them where they were. Another opportunity to affirm her disengagement. That I had nothing – no *things*, no *stuff* – piqued what might have otherwise been her momentary interest. I moved in with a single bag, the same one with which I'd left London.

'Is that it?' she'd said.

'That's it.'

She hadn't made an occasion of my official arrival. She'd been vacuuming, only switched off for this exchange.

'Easier when you move out again, then,' she said with only a shaving of humour. Then she switched the vacuum cleaner back on.

She's softened since then, very slightly. Last night, in bed, after long, abstract fucking in the dark, I felt her becoming aware of this feeling I've started having towards her, a feeling which arrived in the wake of what I've taken to be my last fit of laughter, a tightly curled presence in my chest which must now in excruciating increments over an undetermined time open. (It's not quite a certainty that it will open – or survive the opening. More of a troubling suspicion; and a question about whether Holly will still be there to see it.) She lay on her back, eyes open in the dark. I lay on my side, facing her. Normally she doesn't like to be touched at all afterwards, but I had put my right hand on her midriff and had not been asked to move it. I felt her feeling that I was about to say something.

'Don't say anything,' she said

◆

'I've got a headache,' Kelp announced, Manchester-bound, two weeks before Christmas. The carriage was full and stuffy, the train rollicking. 'I had this dream last night,' he said, 'that my head had been turned into an alarm clock. Excruciating ticking. I tried to pull it off, but blood started trickling out where it was joined to my neck. When I woke up, my actual head was right next to the alarm clock.'

Pen and I had been revising our top five women. Catherine Bach's position at One was safe (for eternity, Pen claimed), but he wanted to make room for Princess Ardala from *Buck Rogers in the 21st Century*. Nastasia Kinski's Number Five was precarious.

'Is there some reason you thought we'd give a fuck about your head?' he asked Kelp.

'No, Pen,' Kelp said, looking out of the window. 'I'm sorry for disturbing you.'

It was a dull, close afternoon, with a parcel of thunderheads over the city. Occasionally, feeble rain fell, without alleviating the atmosphere. The shops were hot and crowded.

We lifted a potted plant, a malt loaf, a tea cosy, and some small rubber monsters for sticking on the ends of pencils, but Kelp's heart wasn't in it. I caught him rubbing his temples, squeezing the back of his neck, pinching the top of his nose, as if not all the excruciating ticking had ceased. I shoplifted him some Nurofen and a bottle of mineral water, but it didn't help.

'There's a fuck of a lot of flies in this carriage,' Kelp said, swatting, on the 17.32 home. 'Doesn't anyone else object to these fucking flies?'

'What flies?' Pen said. 'There aren't any flies.'

I remember it, now. I've had cause to remember it, over the years. At the time, my mind was elsewhere. (There had been a haughty-looking older woman in Debenhams, with puff-pastry hair and a pancake of make-up. I'd inferred loose underarms, a gamy anus, a modicum of seductive varicosis. Her, certainly, and perhaps the glossed and porcelain-headed junior on the Lancôme counter . . .) Kelp, tutting, got up and changed carriages.

'Where's he going?' I said to Pen, who had his nose buried in a shoplifted *New Musical Express*.

'Who knows,' he said, barely looking up. Then, after some visible thought, 'Okay, it's official. Kinski's out.'

'The Princess?'

He shook his head. 'Bird from Transvision Vamp,' he said. 'I'd forgotten her. In at Three. Filthy. Absolutely fucking *filthy*.'

I didn't think much about it at the time, excited as I was at the prospect of having Julia home that evening. We – Pen, Kelp and I – had adopted the requisite cynical stance towards Christmas, but secretly I was excited. Along with crying at British Airways commercials and wobbling tearily over words like *honour* and *courage* and *grace*, I longed for my sister's visits; not just her unpredictable glamour – new hair-dos, clothes, words, ideas, stories, paintings, sketchbooks – but her ability to rescue the season's rituals from bankruptcy. *Ma!* (horrified) There's no *brandy snaps*. Are you *mad*?

But it wasn't to be. She came home that evening miserable.

'What's the matter?'

'I don't want to talk about it.'

'You don't want to talk about it?'

'Your hearing is working.'

Fucked and fucked-over (her words, later) by a visiting sculptor from Madrid. I didn't know that then. Then I just noticed greasy hair and distressed nail varnish. The public line was regret at not having taken a year out before starting her MA. 'I'm sick of painting, sick of fucking *talking* about it', at which my mother's head ducked as if from a blow – Julia! – and me wondering whether my father wouldn't have given her a clip, degree or no degree, for the mouth on her, had he been at home. Thereafter Julia more careful; but still, you knew, poisonous. 'And in any case' (to me, privately), 'it's all fucking installation stuff, now. Paint's a sort of obscenity, unless you squirt it from your fanny onto a mannequin dressed as St Francis of Assisi.' All one to me; but I didn't like the baggy jumpers and saggy-arsed jeans, nor the sound, one night, of her crying behind the locked bathroom door.

Christmas, with its evocations, did me no good. It smelled – sherry, stuffing, pine needles, Advocaat, wrapping paper – of the time before corruption.

'What's the matter with you?' Julia said.

Boxing Day evening. Half a dozen friends of my parents clogging up the living room. Julia had sneaked off – upstairs, I'd assumed – and I'd decided to follow her example by claiming the front room. I was contemplating – *madness* – a quiet fifteen minutes in there, having noticed that not-really-my-Aunty Carol, in her own, heavy-jawed and freckle-chested way, was crying out (how could I have missed this?) for imaginative treatment. She didn't have a daughter of her own (was barren, in fact, which now that I thought of it only raised her erotic stock), but not-really-my-Aunty Phyllis did, a winsome thirteen-year-old with damson-coloured eyes and small shoulders. I'd stayed at home partly to see how she was coming along, young Janet, and had been miffed to discover that migraine was keeping her home with her dad. She would do, I'd decided, *splendidly*.

But there was Jules, fairy-lit in the bay window seat with brandy balloon and Marlboro. Behind her, Logan Street was already under deep snow, and still the big, surprising flakes hurried down out of the darkness.

'What do you mean?' I said, taking a cigarette from her pack and (parents ensconced) lighting up. She observed, briefly contemplated censure, discovered she didn't care.

'You're like a fucking *cloud* in the house,' she said. 'Is something the matter?'

'No.'

'Something is the matter.'

'Nothing's the matter. What's the matter with *you*, for fuck's sake, come to that?'

A moment, then, in which we accepted each other's unspeakables. In the street, a boy in a blue anorak slipped and fell on his backside. His friends laughed.

'Got a girlfriend yet?' she said.

'Oh yeah,' I said. 'Have *you*?'

'Don't be a smart-arse, Dommie.'

'Don't be a pain-in-the-arse, Jules.'

We subsided.

'You'll make yourself sick like that.'

I flinched. Then interpreted: the cigarette. I'd been drag-ging, furiously. I stubbed it out and got up.

At the door, I said, 'Sorry, Jules.'

She leaned her head back against the window frame. 'What for?' she said.

I didn't know. Except that her clouds of glory were gone, replaced now by an aura of London, worries about money, dull allusions to *him*, talk of getting a flat, a job, a life. Her life now, when I thought of it, evoked an image of the capital (where I'd never been): chains of coughing traffic, office lights on in the early dark, a place with the secular and depressing seriousness of *News at Ten*. For the first time – considering this in the doorway – I felt a shudder of doubt about the facts of my past and the conditions of my present. An accelerated damp of the spirit. Would Julia, if I were to tell her – about Malone, about risen Burke, about *It* – believe me? *I believe that* you *believe it, Dommie.* It tilted in, then, for an instant, the other world, her world, the world in which I'd be referred to psychiatrists, or put on drugs, or both.

'Nothing,' I said. 'Forget it.'

That night, depressed, angry and mildly delirious I dragged the rosary's red teardrops through a gobbet of my own shot-out semen. What, after all, had I seen? A boy with a bleeding mouth, motionless on a stone slab. Very still, granted, but not *indubitably* dead. Like all great magicians Malone had shown the before and the after but had cloaked (with bogus rosary-hunt) the in-between. The moment of transformation always hidden. Why else silk-drape the vessels of transubstantiating bread and wine? *We've forgotten the power of prayer*, he'd said. I tried it. Praying often gave me an erection. *Now I lay me down to sleep, We whip dat bitch an' make her weep.* He did voices, the Devil. Black, Hispanic,

German, Oxbridge. But now for the first time, elicited along with scrotal stirrings by the blasphemy a very sane, quiet American psychotherapist who didn't believe in the Devil at all. I waited. A terrible and unidentifiable silence, my hands stilled from the shock of what they had done.

Eventually, uncertain of whether the silence was the universe's sudden emptiness or God's held-in breath, I fell asleep.

Then, in the attic on New Year's Day (for those of you who doubt, God or Malone or the Devil might as well have said) Penguin produced the ouija board.

'Thought I'd been through all the stuff up here,' he said. 'It's all rubbish. But I found this last night.'

The attic's open windows let out the smoke and in the smell of the back garden's snow. Kelp sat half-lotused in the armchair. I nursed a cracked teacup of Lamb's Navy Rum, lolling on the couch. Pen sat at the little table with the ouija. It was an old wooden board, circular, bordered by a flaking gold alphabet, YES and NO in the middle. The pointer was a small flat triangle on three rollers.

'Count me out,' Kelp said.

Pen raised his eyebrows. 'Come off it,' he said. 'This is right up your street, isn't it? Channelling and prognostication and whatnot. It's in your genes.'

'I'm not doing it,' Kelp said. 'You're on your own. And if you want my advice: *don't.*'

Pen grinned scepticism – desperately fake. 'What about you, Dummie?'

'I don't think so.'

'Come on.'

'Nah, it's all bollocks.'

Pen cleared a space on the white table and set the board down. 'Yeah, yeah, yeah,' he said. 'Come on.'

Kelp lit a cigarette, got up and went to the open window. 'Don't do it,' he said, smiling. 'I'm just saying: don't do it.'

I joined Penguin at the table.

'What are we supposed to do?' Pen said, hands very emphatically in his pockets. 'I mean, is there . . . you know . . . is there . . .?'

'Put your finger, just lightly, on the pointer,' I said. 'Then I'll put mine on, like this, and—'

It moved. Before either finger had touched it, in a quick, fluid curve straight off the edge of the table onto the floor, where it clattered, then was still.

'Told you,' Kelp said, looking out into the rain.

'Fuck,' I said. 'Fuck. *Fuck*.'

Pen had frozen, finger poised.

'Pen,' I said. 'Pen . . .'

'Told you,' Kelp repeated.

Pen took a pace backwards, away from the table. 'Did you see that?' he said, in a helium-swallower's squeak. 'Did you fucking *see* that?'

'Yeah. I don't think we should—'

'But did you fucking *see* that?'

'Can't you feel it?' Kelp said, in the voice of a Californian hippy girl. 'It's all a*round*.'

'Shut up,' I said.

'I can put my hand out and—'

'Shut *up*, Kelp, for fuck's sake.'

All three of us shut up. Pen and I stood gawping at each other. Kelp sat on in the window, one knee drawn up. Outside, birds twittered.

'Shall I tell you my story?' he said, at last. 'Or are you going to have another go with the board?'

★

'A few years ago, my mum started doing it. Had a little circle. You'd be surprised. Even in Begshall. I used to sneak down and spy on them from behind the living-room door.'

He extinguished the cigarette, pocketed the butt, got down from the sill and slid to the floor, back against the wall, knees up to his chest, fingers laced round shins. Penguin and I sat side by side on the couch in the calm of deep shock.

'It was what you'd expect,' Kelp said. 'Sometimes nothing, sometimes people pissing about, knocking the table with their knees. Sometimes my mum three sheets to the wind, faking it. Other times, though, it would fly. They used a glass, you know, a tumbler. I've seen that glass move so fast they couldn't keep their fucking fingers on it. Someone would sit by with a pencil and pad, translating. Transcribing, I mean, whatever the word is.

'They used to get all sorts. One spirit who just spelled out swear words, over and over. Someone else who kept talking about a fucking insurance claim. An Indian chief. Someone else who talked gibberish – then when they looked more closely, found out it wasn't gibberish, it was Latin. Sometimes weird smells would come in the room. Chocolate, once, overpowering. Another time shit. I used to watch. My mum charged – quite a lot, I think, though she wasn't bothered about the money.'

No. Of course not. I knew what she was bothered about, that Catholic girl with the Sight, and the imprint of God's injustice.

'Anyway,' Kelp said. 'One night they contacted this spirit, Charlotte Anne. She told them she'd been murdered. She told them where she was buried, what year, where the man who'd done it was in prison. They checked. It was all true. She came night after night. My mum started asking questions about my dad. After a while, she stopped the other people coming round. That's when I started sitting in, transcribing.'

Pen chain-smoked, robotically, where he sat. The last of the day's light aureoled Kelp's hair.

'Charlotte Anne wouldn't answer questions about things like God or Heaven. She just wouldn't answer. My mum wasn't bothered about the details, anyway – she just kept asking about my dad: was he there? Could Charlotte Anne bring him to talk? She begged her. At first, Charlotte Anne seemed vague about it. She'd answer weirdly, like she'd been hearing a different question. Once, she said something about not being able to reach the fifth level.

'Then, one night, she changed. She seemed to come awake. She understood everything exactly. She said she knew my dad, that he was in a different place, that she could bring him. I don't know why, but I knew it wasn't her. I wrote on the pad and held it up for my mum to see: "This isn't Charlotte Anne." But my mum didn't . . . She thought it was her. The spirit sort of kept it going, drawing it out. My mum just kept saying: "Please let me talk to him. Please bring him. Please, please, please" and Charlotte Anne kept feeding her details about my dad's life that were true, that no one else could have known. It was like he was keeping her talking. Like he was trying to trace a call.'

'Who was?' Pen said, quietly.

Kelp ignored him. 'Eventually, after what seemed like hours – you know, I had fucking pages and pages of writing – my mum was at breaking point. She didn't ask any more questions. She didn't *have* any more questions. She had cramp in her arm from keeping her finger on the glass. She looked absolutely drained. Like she'd aged. Years, *years*.' He shook his head. 'Won't forget that,' he said. 'The way she looked. Christ. Anyway, she said: "Will you bring him?" It was silent for ages. The spirit spelled out: "You will pay my price."'

He stopped not for theatrical effect, but because he was back there. The low-ceilinged room, the closed curtains, the table. Very gently, he reached into his jacket's top pocket, took out his No. 6, lighted from the Zippo, dragged, needfully. The first exhaled funnel of smoke drifted up, then was sucked out into the rain.

'My mum said: "What price?" The weird thing was, I wasn't surprised when I spelled out the reply. Like I'd known beforehand what it was. When I wrote, I separated the words in the right places automatically. Didn't even feel like it was me writing them.'

'What did it say?' Pen said, very carefully. 'What was the price?'

Kelp tilted his head back (as Stella had, hollering at Frank to get out) and blew two thick, shivering smoke rings.

'"I want your souls,"' he said.

It had become an awkward intuition between the three of us that the Queers lifespan as an acceptable joke was over. Homophobic pragmatism aside, there remained brute curiosity. Harmless fantasies did nothing for me. Had never done anything for me. I might as well have imagined mathematical formulae or the contents of the Begshall telephone directory. Would the presence of a harmless *other person* be any different? Would I be, banally, impotent?

Linda Kirby was a Protestant from Holcroft High. We met at a party in the first week of the new decade and started going out with each other, which meant staying in with each other. Penguin started going out with Linda's friend Mandy (who didn't let him stay in with her much, forcing him into lies about what they had and hadn't done); Kelp didn't start going out with anyone, and regarded Pen and me with gentle distaste. 'Courting evenings', as he called them, he stayed in (or went to the library) and read Dostoyevsky. Guilty, we promised we'd dump the girls after our mocks, which exams stood between us and summer like a gang of thugs. Until then, we claimed, not unreasonably, girlfriends helped with the Stress.

Penguin maintained a perpetual myth that he and Mandy were on the cusp of consummation. Kelp and I tormented him.

'Have you shagged her yet?'

'This Saturday. Babysitting. Put fucking money on it.'

'Have you licked her out?' Kelp asked.

'Course he hasn't,' I said.

'Has she sucked you off, Pen? Has she swallowed your jiz?'

'For God's *sake*,' Pen said, with a face like *he'd* swallowed his jiz.

'*Course* she hasn't,' I said. 'She hasn't *wanked* the poor bugger off, yet.'

'She fucking *has* wanked me off—'

'He probably hasn't even sucked her tits,' Kelp said, arms folded, shaking his head, sadly. 'Wouldn't be surprised if he hadn't even *skwonked* her tits.'

'I'm fucking warning you . . .'

'Linda told me that Mandy's beginning to wonder if he even *wants*—'

'Of *course* I've sucked her fucking tits! I've had her whole . . .' vague, agonized gesture and unpleasantly curled lip . . . 'I've had her whole fucking knocker in my entire fucking *mouth*!'

Linda wasn't pretty (neither was Mandy, for the record – even Pen would agree), but she wasn't without allure. She was a stone heavier than me, with a broad, oily, hard-boned face, enquiring eyes, and dark hair in a violently artificial spiral perm. Her body demonstrated with near parodic overstatement the formula for female anatomical desirability, namely that it increased in proportion to the nearness to each other of the sex parts: she had, yes, high breasts, a fleshy backside and a flat belly, but more importantly the very short upper body which brought these three features so provocatively close to each other. It was such an accommodatingly short sweep from breasts to belly, belly to bottom, bottom to belly and belly back to breasts, that the mere thought of touching her could leave a fondler pre-emptively jaded.

Her years at Holcroft High (one of the roughest schools in Begshall) had left her academically vacant and filled with a heavy, directionless energy. She didn't expect to pass any of her exams, nor had she any idea of what she wanted or could do in the world. Saturdays, she worked at Chop and Change hair salon, sweeping up, washing hair, making coffee, chatting – but she didn't see herself carrying on with it. (I mention this because Linda for ever eroticized the smells of hair care; even now, five minutes in the right salon can equip me with a melancholy erection.) A relationship going nowhere, we both knew. It piqued her, the question of why she was going out with me, since she didn't like me, and was well aware that I didn't like her, either.

The scene: Linda's bedroom. The time: 8.00pm. The unbelievable facts: her parents, ten-year-old sister and eight-year-old brother are all downstairs watching *Dirty Harry*; her bedroom door doesn't lock; she has made no objection to my rolling up her sweater, nor to my stroking, squeezing, nibbling and sucking her braless breasts, nor to my hoiking up her denim skirt, nor – the temptation to freeze her and dash off to phone Kelp and Pen almost overwhelming – to my cupping, through the white cotton knickers, with the tentativeness of incredulity, the piping hot mound of her cunt. It has drawn reverence from me, the little aura of heat around her mons, heat as distinct and intimate as that around a low wattage lightbulb or newly baked loaf. It has given me a glimpse of sexual tenderness and its close, difficult relationship with sexual hunger. *Oh*, I've almost let out, *oh that's so very . . . so very lovely . . . What an extraordinary, delicate, beautiful . . .* I haven't let it out, naturally. Not out of strategy or cool, but because the flesh (*in the flesh*) has revealed the great and futile distance words will have to travel if they are going to get anywhere near it.

These are the facts, and they are all unbelievable to me. It hasn't occurred to me, that I might arrive here without resistance or negotiation, that she might *like* it. Nonetheless here we are.

I don't know what to do. I have the schematic, of course – put your mouth . . . see if she'll let you . . . grab the . . . now lick there – but not, really, the *desire*. The intimacy is a physical and psychic assault, unbearable. *How do people bear this stuff?* I'm thinking, easing the knickers down from Linda's co-operatively lifted hips. *How do they stand the intimacy?*

But she guides my hand and fingers, gently at first, then with increasing insistence and a peculiar, sustained frown on her broad-boned face – until I've found the required spot and the required rhythm – and I discover there's a whole other league of not saying anything demanded by this whole other league of intimacy. Her frown is urgent, perplexed by pleasure, and its fixity contrasts sharply with the tireless swivel and grind of her hips. I can't bear to look at her – and then I can, and not the connections between us but the gaps – all those *gaps* – combine in a potent aphrodisiac and I find myself intolerably hard, and know that I will remain so until she does to me whatever it is she's going to do.

To my amazement, she comes, or appears to, gripping my forearm with her left hand and scrunching the duvet with her right. Under the frown the hard, yellowy-brown eyes don't leave mine (our mouths, like anemones, making word-shapes but no actual words) until the very last moment, when as if it has been yanked by a rein and bridle her head lashes away and the bizarre, speechless, shuddering contact between us is broken.

At which point, having absorbed from all sources the idea that girls couldn't, by definition, like sex, I'm expecting a mood swing, recriminations, a different kind of silent treatment, at the very least her getting up and uglily pulling her knickers back on.

But no. Proceeding initially as if I'm insensible (a piece of meat, I think) Linda slithers down the bed on her side and gives my erection an investigative squeeze. Redundantly, tumescence being absurdly, *satirically* visible under my jeans. *She's going to put it in her mouth.* A neutrally delivered bulletin. A disinterested conclusion from a curiously disparate set of premises: the boiled-vegetables smell of her house; the no lock on the door; the threadbare carpet and the fake sheep-skin rug; the knickers not put back on. *She's going to put it in her mouth.*

I'm expecting, I suppose, some version of the frowning ecstasies of a moment ago – but this is completely different. She doesn't look at me (*That will come later, when we're more used to each other* – another bulletin), but undoes my fly, gently lifts the elastic of my underpants, and makes *absolutely no gesture of horror or revulsion* as my cock springs out and very gently thwacks her chin.

★

On a rock in the pink evening desert Malone stands, hands in cassock pockets, white hair ruffled by the frailest edge of a breeze. Not smiling, not shaking a fist. Just watching to see what this will be for me.

This one brief image, then Linda's mouth opens and closes round me – and all other images disappear.

'Spose you're going to brag to your mates, now.'

I lay next to her on her pink duvet, blinking, recon-structing my detonated history, breathing through my mouth.

'No,' I said.

'Think I'm a slag, then?' With a dash of contempt (for whom, I wasn't sure). 'Think I do this all the time?'

'No?'

'Well I don't, right?'

'Right.'

'It's only the third time I've done it.'

That I found hard to believe. Nonetheless some ques-tions answered. Chiefly that I was capable – to my astonishment – of normal sexual activity. She had sucked me with diligence (though as if her mind were shut down or occupied by something else entirely) until I had come, whereafter, immediately following the final bulletin – *She's going to swallow it* – she had quietly but audibly swallowed my semen. In her now. No images. No *mental* images. There hadn't been room for any. At first because mere sensation (the shocking heat of the *inside* of someone's mouth) obliterated all other experience. Later because the actual image of Linda – the broad-boned face seen from a new angle – sucking and licking my cock remained a thing of inexhaustible delight. Disbelief. Proof. Disbelief. Proof. Disbelief . . . Proof.

Walking home, then, after that first evening, humbled by initiation, I wondered if I hadn't found the antidote to *It*. The air, after all, was crisp and fresh. Frost on the estate's tarmac winked. My limbs felt honourable, rightly aligned, and God had blessed me with one last Rothmans left in the pack to complete the moment. There hadn't been much looking at each other, afterwards, nor much of an inclination to speak and risk our vocabularies' inequity. But at the door (*ta-ra, love*, called to me by the presumably idiotic or indifferent parents in the living room) there had been an odd little moment of mutual visibility. Nothing more than the acknowledgement that the little flame of intimacy wouldn't last – or if it did would remain dwarfed by everything else mismatched – but still, a glimpse, however slight, of what it might be like to do what we had done with people we *liked*.

The brave new world lasted until I got home, went straight to bed, and, after half an hour's flimsy resistance, masturbated.

As per usual.

I went to parties with Linda, grudgingly for walks and to the pictures, had frequent, gymnastic mutually reciprocal and imaginatively harmless oral sex with her (she was saving her hymen, a mighty relief to me) – but manufactured a completely different fantasy version of our sexual relationship for private use in my head. One that she wouldn't have liked. One that *no* one would have liked.

Not *during*. During, the actual Linda and the actual fellatio were sufficient. Sensually pleasurable, mundanely, acceptably sinful. But later, in the absence of the actual Linda – *by myself*, as Feeney would have said – things were very different. Different in all the familiar ways.

I never *did* anything to her. Never suggested – with the

ambiguous levity required for such proposals – that she let me tie her up, or spank her, or tie her up *and* spank her; with good reason: I didn't want to tie her up and spank her. I wanted to tie her up and (best just to state it plainly) torture her.

I had looked *It* – and myself – up in the *Collins*.

sadism: *n.* **1** a form of sexual perversion characterized by the enjoyment of inflicting pain or suffering on others (cf. MASOCHISM) **2** *colloq.* The enjoyment of cruelty to others. **sadist** *n.* **sadistic** *adj.* **sadistically** *adv.* [F *sadisme* f. Count or Marquis de *Sade*, Fr. writer d. 1814] see *brutality* (BRUTAL) **sadist** brute, beast, savage, monster, devil, sadistic, cruel, monstrous, brutal, brutish, beastly, ruthless, perverse . . . algolagnic

There was, I knew, a permissible pantomime of cruelty ('Sorry, love, was that a bit hard?'), a mummery in which the paraphernalia of cuffs and canes, masks and manacles was half the fun. I knew, not being culturally blind, the costumery, the trappings, the accoutrements. All uninteresting to me. In my imaginary world handcuffs had no glamour; they were practical necessities. I knew what *consent* meant. One wasn't granted a share in the Devil's secret if one's victim gave *consent*. That was a fundamental: a willing victim was no victim at all.

Passing through the living room late one night (my mum and dad, exhausted after an evening's long-postponed painting and decorating, asleep like untidy children on the couch) I glanced at the television screen, where, just audibly, a small-hours Open University boffin said, 'Of course the fantasist's conviction is that nothing exists in his fantasy except that which he would translate into reality *if he could do so with*

impunity. This conviction, analysis shows us, is a delusion . . .'
I crept past and hurried up the stairs.

Duality was addictive. Alone, each half of me caused pain; but in perpetual oscillation between the two, I was filled with a sickening energy. I throbbed with potential and deceit. The future was ravenous for me.

I didn't realize the breadth of the future's appetite. I didn't realize the future was ravenous for *all* of us.

◆

Today, in a bar on 12th Street between First and Second Holly and I sat in a window booth with American Spirits and chilled Brooklyn Lagers. She had an hour between the gym and the start of her shift at McLusky's downtown. The sun was out and it had seemed a harmless enough idea. But ten minutes after we'd sat down the sky had clouded over and her mind had gone wherever it goes. She stared out of the window. At nothing, I thought.

The bar was dim and all but empty. Culture Club's 'Do You Really Want to Hurt Me?' had come on quietly from the jukebox, played out, achieved no discernible atmospheric change. Now the room was silent again, but for the air-conditioners' hum. I had a feeling that if we sat there long enough the song would come on again, with the same absence of effect. The pierced and pony-tailed bartender sat on a high stool on the wrong side of the bar, chain-smoking Chesterfields and reading Norman Mailer's *An American Dream*.

I followed Holly's gaze out of the window. She was staring at a handmade poster beside the door of the dilapidated building across the street.

THE DEAD ARE ALIVE AND SENDING MESSAGES TO THE LIVING IN

100

THIS CHURCH, it said, in lettering of assorted colours. I read it aloud. Holly didn't move.

'What do you think of that?' I asked her.

'Nothing,' she said. 'The dead are the dead.'

◆

'I've got a stinking headache,' Kelp said. 'Right behind my bastard eyes.'

We were in the kitchen at Mark Eccles's post-O-levels party. Mark Eccles was the only child of wealthy parents whose predilection for Andrew Lloyd Webber weekends in London left him in sole charge of the house. 'Serves them right,' he shouted from the top of the stairs, with raised brandy balloon and smouldering cigar. '*Starlight Express*? *Starlight* fucking *Express*?' It was unusual for us to have been invited, but the Queers thing had dropped away in the face of Linda's and Mandy's sexual clout, and in any case, school being over (for the summer for the Grammar, who would go on to A levels in October; for ever for the High, who would go on to minimum wage or the dole), an attitude of tolerance and inclusiveness temporarily prevailed.

Having shed the Queers, Pen and I were single again. Untrue to our word we had not got rid of the girls after mocks, but had been got rid *of*, in Pen's case by Mandy before the mocks had even come round (certainly before penetrative sex had come round), and in my case, having limped on past them (and the summer holidays, and the Michaelmas term, and Christmas) with pointless arguing and breaking up and getting back together and having increasingly elaborate oral and digital sex, by Linda, who had, at the start of our final year, dumped me and started going out with Jason Pilling, who was eighteen, and had a beard and a car and a job in his dad's painting and decorating business.

In Mark Eccles's kitchen Pen sat cross-legged on a worktop with a king-sized jar of pickled onions between his thighs. Against everyone's expectations (including his own), he'd passed six O levels, enough to buy him two years and A levels at Begshall Tech, from where, like the rest of the Grammar, he expected to go on to university. 'First,' he said, 'I'm going to eat a great many of these onions, for which I . . . for which I have passion. Then' – indicating for me to grab and pass them – 'I'm going to eat that box of After Eight mint chocolates. Thank you, Dummie. And please' – crunching the first acid bulb, squirming with the shock of it – 'if Her Mandyship should happen to arrive, tell her I am not disposed to discuss the past.'

Two hours later, drunk, and, having half-heartedly nibbled some magic mushrooms, experiencing occasionally vivid and pixilated versions of various objects, I found Kelp in the dope room, reading an Enid Blyton book about two rabbits called Binkle and Flip. The room was sour with smoke. The smokers themselves were beyond the point when any more smoking was required, but they carried on, regardless. In a corner, a slim boy with greasy black hair and girlishly long fingernails was awkwardly arranged on – or rather *in* – a near-beanless bean bag, playing 'Wish You Were Here', repeatedly, on Mark Eccles's Fender acoustic.

'I think we might be approaching a pickled-onion episode,' I said, squatting down beside Kelp.

(I had encountered Pen in the moist back garden. He'd been on all fours, breathing heavily, staring at the grass.

'You all right?' I asked him.

He looked up at me with glazed eyes and a thread of spittle dangling.

'Pen!' I barked. 'Are you okay?'

He had smiled, weakly, and bobbed his head a couple of times. After a few moments in which his concentration had been absorbed by something in the grass, he had said, inexplicably, 'Guernica.')

'Fuck Penguin,' Kelp said now, massaging his head. 'I feel terrible.'

He looked it. The rims of his eyes were raw. A bad odour on his breath – more than the reek of alcohol – something sweet and sick-roomish. His voice was tight.

'Did you take anything?' I asked him.

He shook his head, irritated. 'Headache,' he said. 'Behind my eyes. Feels like a fucking boomerang stuck in there.'

Suddenly, he jerked his arm and waved it in front of his face. 'Did you see that?' he said.

'What?'

'That fly.'

'I didn't see it. Are you sure you didn't—'

'Fucking hundreds of flies in here.'

I looked hard at him again. The downside of those eyes was that their death killed his whole face.

'D'you want to go out and get some air?' I asked – but he stood up, abruptly, and glared at the room's stupefied crowd.

'Somebody in here has shat his pants,' he announced. 'And it's not me.'

After which (the smokers' predictable array of faint frowns, peacefully raised brows, gentle smiles, 'Wish You Were Here' having faltered, then resumed) he stormed out of the room and locked himself in the toilet. When I followed him and knocked, he shouted back: 'I'm all right, Dummie. Leave me alone.'

Penguin was no longer visible in the back garden. I stood on the patio with pilfered bottle of San Miguel and just-lit

Silk Cut. An unBegshall-like night: balmy and honeysuckle-scented air, the garden's perimeter of intriguing darkness, snail-tracks and daisies visible in the kitchen's thrown oblong of light. I felt (with the sinking-in realization that *school* – at least of the uniformed and repressive St Dymphna's variety – was over) light-headed and uneasy. Reminded, too (much *more* uneasy), of why this sort of consciousness, in my own company, without an object of distraction, was never a good idea.

Suddenly, the raw sound of retching from the shadows. Then, in piteous soliloquy: 'Jesus . . . *Christ*.'

At the bottom of the garden a stunted oak grew from a corner. Beneath it, the rank Eccles compost. On a low branch, clinging, Penguin, unmanned by copious spewing.

'Dummie,' he said, then reached for something to which to attach the address, 'Dummie . . . fuck.'

'What are you doing up there?'

'They put me up here.'

'Who?'

Pen groaned, dry-heaved, mewled. 'Do you think you could . . . you know . . .?'

'*What*, for fuck's sake?'

'Get me down? Get me . . . I'm not happy up here.'

'What are you? Mad?'

'That fucking compost . . .'

'Can I get you a pickled onion or anything?'

The foliage rustled from his shudder. He made a straining noise, as if to deliver himself of a formidable turd.

'I won't forget this, you know,' he said. 'When I get down from here, you're going to die. That's all. I'm going to kick your fucking buttocks to slush. I'm going to—'

A synchronicity, then. The final, thumped note of Led Zeppelin's 'Rock and Roll', and, in the silence succeeding it, a female scream from upstairs. Then silence again. The house suddenly grave and attentive.

For a moment Pen and I froze. Then, turning, I set off across the lawn.

'What is it?' Penguin called after me. 'Oi! Fucking *hell*, Dummie.'

Upstairs, a handful of revellers outside the kicked-in bathroom door. All the Eccles' inset halogens on, the room filled with their mauve-tinted light.

'What's ee ad?'

'Fuck knows. Ee dinray any of that acid, did ee?'

'Luke at state of im.'

'Kelp!' I said. 'Kelp, can you hear me?'

He lay with oddly disposed limbs on the bathroom tiles looking as if he'd fallen from a great height. Pockets of frothed spittle in the corners of his mouth. Eyes closed, the white-blond hair in sweat-stiffened fronds, a slug of snot poking from one nostril.

'Fuck, Dominic, what's up with im?'

'Azee been like this before or what?'

'We should . . . We should . . .'

'Leave im alone, I reck.'

'Mebby someone . . . D'you think it's . . .?'

I touched Kelp's face: oven-warm. Around me, in the crowd, the idea crystallizing that this was, in fact, not a joke.

'Dial nine nine nine,' I said.

The ambulance was medicine-flavoured, cluttered with instruments of what looked like Oceanian shoddiness. One expected LCD displays, winking lights, fibreglass, stainless steel, economy of design. Instead rattling and archaically valved oxygen tanks, a sad blanket, rubber tubes, things not battened down properly.

'Has he taken any drugs?'

Me in the back with strapped-in and plastic-masked Kelp; also a sandy-haired and suntanned medic in peppermint green.

'No.'

'Sure?'

'Yes.'

'Have you?'

'No. Just drink. Handful of magics.'

'How much has he had to drink?'

No judgement, merely the need to establish facts.

'I don't know,' I said.

'What about you?'

'Eh?'

'Was it a good party?'

'Not really.'

He smiled, the tan flattering to teeth and periwinkle eyes. 'You two mates?' he asked.

Constriction in the throat. 'Yeah.'

'Well don't look so worried, sunshine' (giving my shoulder a slap), 'I'm not sure what's wrong with him, but he's not going to *die*.'

I discovered Casualty. Orange plastic chairs and taupe walls. Nothing to read except the signs: NO SMOKING. PATIENTS AND STAFF ONLY BEYOND THIS POINT. ASSAULTS ON MEMBERS OF STAFF WILL RESULT IN CRIMINAL PROSECUTION. The room's festive spot was the neoned and occasionally gurgling soft-drinks machine. Other than that, the aesthetics of nullity. Stella wasn't answering the phone.

At about 1.00am, Penguin turned up. His face was pouchy and his hair stiff with grease. He was soiled, from flowerbed, vomit, tree and compost.

'What's wrong with him?' he asked me, the two of us having stepped outside to share the last of the night's cigarettes.

'I don't know. Nobody's told me anything. Admissions nurse obviously thinks we're smack addicts.'

'Did you phone his mum?'

I gave him the explanatory look.

'Oh,' he said. 'How long's he going to be in?'

'God knows. Pen, he looked fucking *dead* in the ambulance.' A lumpy silence. 'Medic said he'd be okay, though.'

'Yeah? Well he'd know, wouldn't he?'

'I spose. Give us a last drag on that.'

No one told us anything for another hour. In defiance of his chair Pen fell extravagantly asleep.

Then a thin young bald doctor with a brown beard and emerald-green eyes emerged and went over to the nurse at the admissions desk. Pointed my way, he approached. I nudged Penguin, to no effect.

'Are you the person who came in with Gregory Kelp?'

'Yes. Is he okay?'

The doctor smiled, clicking his ballpoint furiously. The young, bearded, earnest face had a clean, rubbery look, as of unnatural wakefulness – the impostor's mien of over-efficiency, I thought – knowing the thought was madness. 'Yes,' he said, clicking. 'Given us some interesting questions, though. We're keeping him in tonight. Do you want to see him?'

'Yes, please.'

'What about your friend?'

Pen was asleep with his neck crooked and his palms open. He looked like St Theresa in ecstasy.

'I'll deal with him later,' I said.

★

Ward 4F, in another part of the building. Half a dozen instructions on how to get there, and after following the first three I was lost. I stood in a blindingly lit and heavily disinfected corridor feebly looking around for someone to ask.

Suddenly, at the far end of the corridor, a door on the left opened and Ignatius Malone hurried out. He didn't look my way, but turned in the opposite direction and headed in giant strides towards the swing doors. Before I could get a word out, he had bashed through them and disappeared. They flapped in his wake.

Seven years.

The drunkenness had worn off, as had the mushrooms' occasional pixillation and slight dimensional warp. Not for one moment did I think I might be even partly hallucinating.

It's never too late to seek God, Dominic. Seven years. Is it every seven years? Is that the pattern? *A futile rage with his own imperfection.* He's no fear of dogs, then? The universe either does or doesn't have a . . . Either there's a plan, or we're . . .

I ran after him.

The swing doors gave onto (of course) a T-junction, of which I was standing in the middle of the horizontal. One long hallway stretched ahead, empty but for an orderly awkwardly wheeling a posse of drips. If Malone had gone that way he'd still be in sight. Left and right corridors, on the other hand, both cornered within ten or twenty paces. At his speed he could have rounded either one . . .

I went left. Round the corner, two nurses, one with an empty wheelchair, the other with her little cape on, presumably clocking off.

'Did you see him?'

'Sorry?'

'Did a priest just come this way?'

They looked at me. Naturally they did. My state. The hour. Presumably, given the racing blood, my *face*.

I turned and ran back the other way. Alarmed the drip-wheeling orderly, somewhat.

'Oi!'

'Sorry.'

'Stop pelting around like that.'

I made the corner. Turned. Nothing. Empty corridor with more swing doors at the end. I jogged down it, peeking quickly into the rooms on either side. *The Last Rites*. Check the register for miraculous recoveries. Very funny. Not here. He's not fucking *here*.

I had known. Felt the logic of the moment beginning to slip from when I'd taken left instead of right. Left hand the Devil's. Should've gone right. Should've gone *right*, idiot.

I ended up in the hospital's main entrance. No sign. *We don't keep a record of visitors*. Of course not. Of course not.

For a moment I sat down in one of the chairs. *Be calm*. Think. First, find 4F. Kelp. Doctor said all right, so that means all right, but go now and find. Tomorrow check with Father Feeney. Miss Warburton, maybe. Still alive? God knows. People know him. If he's here, you'll see him. Be calm. Find 4F.

Underneath all of which: *One look at you and he'll know. He'll know.*

I went with as much appearance of sanity as I could muster back to the desk.

In 4F Kelp was sitting up in bed drinking a glass of water. Very bony, the face; the hair still sweat-damp, dark where nurse fingers had scraped it back – but his eyes had returned to peppery life. No discernible trembling. Relief went through me, uncramping muscles. With it – daring, wildly precocious – an inner analyst which wasn't the Devil: *The woman punished is the woman you are. She's in love with him.* Correlatively, one of my ankles gave. A clownish wobble, with sudden pain – then balance, and the inner analyst gagged. Kelp, looking under the blankets, didn't see.

Then he did look up, grinned. I sat on the bed.

'This dress they've got me in is wide open at the back,' he said. 'I think I might have tied it up wrong. Either that or it's to stop you running away.'

'What the fuck *happened*?' I said. 'What did the doctor say?'

'Where are my grapes?'

'Don't fuck about. What did they say is wrong with you?'

He made a dismissive face. 'Low blood pressure.'

'Bollocks. My mum's got low blood pressure. You were *foaming at the mouth.*'

'Did you phone my mum?' he asked, not looking at me.

'Yeah.'

A half-look, then, which I confirmed.

'Fair enough,' he said.

'But I mean maybe she's—'

'Shut up, Dummie. Never mind. Got any fags?'

'No. You can't smoke in here, anyway, arse-finger.'

A rubber-shoed nurse with the look of a transsexual walked past the ward door pushing a drip. For no reason except that the event seemed to happen in surreal slow motion, the two of us watched her.

'It's about you and Pen,' he said, suddenly, when her squeaks had died away.

'What?'

'What I saw. Tonight. Maybe it's hormones after all.'

110

One understands immediately, but goes through the motions of not understanding, quite. 'What you . . .? What you saw?'

'You know what I mean.'

A very long pause, then, neither of us looking at each other.

'Something's going to happen here,' he said.

◆

CHAPTER THREE

And Death Shall Have No Dominion

'Eight across,' Holly said, this morning. '"Form of discipline." Four letters.' She goes through phases in which any moment of unemployed consciousness is unbearable. At such times she does crosswords, one after another.

'Cane,' I said.

She thought for a few seconds, tapping the pen against her teeth.

'Self,' she said.

I looked out of the window. These flecks of ironic design persist. I don't know what to do with them. I've never known what to do with them. Design has come into and gone out of my life like a ringed and dexterous hand – outstretched for handshake, then whipped away for the nose-thumb just when I've thought it safe to grasp. I've never been able to complete it, this most basic gesture of agreement. Or never been allowed to. By the designer. Or the absence of one.

Nothing to do but go on.

★

'I want to ask you something,' Holly said later.

'Okay.'

'Why are you with me?'

We sat in the sun at an outside table at Bandito's on Second Avenue, drinking frozen margaritas. The sex that had followed the crossword had moved up another gear. It had revealed a heightened sensitivity to each other's touch. Also much looking at each other between caresses, a mutual recognition of the welter of things unsaid, a joint owning-up to our histories. (The thing in my chest uncramps by degrees, with agonizing slowness.) Kissing her ankles, her elbows, her eyelids, I was gnawed by my own insatiable appetite for treating her with tenderness. Something with the tone or echo of infinity drove me to her finiteness – the ends of her fingers and toes, lips, eyelashes, nipples, ear-lobes – nothing more or less than the old impossible demand, that the soul express itself through the body; but still, it was new to us, and she felt it, too. Lovemaking stretched, expanded surreally, bent time with its abstruse and stumbled-upon equations, escorted us to the boundaries of ourselves and showed us the space of being beyond, from which, terrified and with appetites whetted, we just about managed to draw back.

The price being, afterwards, the persisting presences of our unshared pasts. And given those pasts, questions about our presents, our futures.

'I don't know anything about you.'

I hadn't answered. Had felt instead a crippling inertia.

She left a long pause. Very raw, this business of talking about what might be taking shape between us.

'I'm no good,' I said, eventually. 'I've done some things.'

'So have I.'

'Not like these things.'

She looked down into her drink. 'You have no idea who I am,' she said. 'What I've done.'

'No,' I said. 'That's true.'

'It's bad to start feeling things for someone who has only bad feelings about herself.'

I didn't reply. A cab pulled up nearby and a young couple got out and hurried into the bar. When the cab drove away it left in its wake one of those rare urban lulls in which human and automotive traffic as if by consensus disappear. For a few seconds Manhattan might have been a city after an apocalypse. Holly looked away down Second Avenue, into the road shimmer. I knew she'd noticed the stillness. I knew she was thinking that it wouldn't last, that at any moment it would be shattered by a police siren on Eleventh or the jukebox in the bar.

She looked at me. It wouldn't quite evaporate for either of us, the memory of the morning, of our angelic translation, the shock of tenderness, and of the terrifying suggestion that we might take the risk of speaking to each other about who we were.

'What do you want in life?' she asked me.

'Not to do any harm,' I said.

◆

Kelp didn't know what was going to happen. Or when, beyond soon. But Pen and I, he maintained, were in danger as long as we stayed in Begshall. We had to get out, if only for a short while.

'Oh come *on*, Dummie.'

'Oh come on Dummie *what*?'

'It's a *wind*-up.'

'You weren't there. You didn't see. He might be wrong, Pen, but he's definitely not kidding.'

Pen and I were in the Coopers' Arms, where everyone bar the landlord was under age. We had arranged a Kelpless meeting, to (in Pen's words) *consider what to do about it.*

'And you believe him?'

I thought back to Kelp in the hospital. Him looking down the bed to where his feet made peaks under the blankets; his thin arms at rest; his voice absolutely normal. *I don't know what, exactly, but something's going to happen here, something awful.* What? I'd wanted to know. Like an earthquake? In *Begshall*? He'd blinked, slowly. *It's you and Pen. I don't know what, Dummie, but it's real. I swear on my mother's life. You've got to get away from here for a while. It'll be all right, but you've got to get away. Trust me.*

'Yes,' I said to Penguin. 'I believe him.'

'Oh, for fuck's sake—'

'You've seen his mum.'

Pen looked at me as if I was stupid. 'His *mum*?'

'I mean his mum's clairvoyance.'

'Oh, you believe that, do you?'

'What and you don't?'

Pen's own arguments did this to him, got him to admit the thing he'd set out to deny, or vice versa.

'I'm not saying I don't believe it, as such, but—'

'What about the fucking ouija board then?'

'What about it?'

I made a face of exasperation. Pen responded with wincing and palming the air. 'Okay okay,' he said. 'I'll grant you the ouija board thing was a bit fucking . . . I'll grant you I don't have an explanation for that . . .'

'But?' I said.

He sighed and his shoulders slumped. I knew what it was. It wasn't that he didn't believe. It was that he didn't want to *go*. The motions of scepticism must be gone through if only as a means of postponing *getting out of town*, and all the parent-wheedling, deceit, and expense that would entail.

'Come on, Dum, for fuck's sake,' Pen said.

'What?'

'What? *This*. Kreskin and the fucking prophecy of doom. The world's not . . . I mean the world isn't . . .'

'What?'

'The world isn't *like* that.'

I remembered something else. A five-year gestation, now here it was. 'He knew my name,' I said.

'What?'

'Kelp. That first day in the bogs. Just before you came in, he said, "I'll tell you something, Dominic," then you burst in with "CUNT" written on your head.'

Pen made a face of minor constipation, looked at the floor as if for explanatory assistance, then back at me. 'So?' he said.

'So how did he know my name? *I* didn't tell him. How could he possibly have known my name if he didn't have some sort of . . . capability?'

Pen leaned back in his chair again. Went slowly through the business of lighting a Rothman and swallowing the last mouthful of his half. All with fake tight-lipped complacency.

'Unconvincing,' he said. 'First of all, I wasn't there, so I've only got your word for it. And second of all—'

'You don't say "second of all".'

'What?'

'There's no such idiom.'

'What?'

'Never mind.'

'What the fuck are you talking about?'

'Never *mind*. Second of all *what*?'

'*Second* of all,' Pen said, then paused for a self-congratulatory smoke ring, 'the world's just not fucking *like* that.'

We left the Coopers' with him still going through the motions of scepticism, but by the time we parted company silence had taken its shape between us.

'Think about it, Pen,' I said.

'Yeah, yeah, bollocks, whatever.'

'I mean it.'

'Yeah, yeah. Kiss my ring.'

But at his front door, he turned.

'You really think something's going to happen?' he said. 'I mean really, seriously?'

'I don't know.' I thought about it for a moment. 'D'you want to wait around to find out?'

For as long as I could I avoided being alone with him. But in our world that wasn't very long.

'Your mum's thing,' I said.

Pen was late for our rendezvous at the cenotaph in Lordship Park. Now that the weather was warming up we did our drinking there. Kelp and I sat in the sunlight with our backs to the iron list of dead. We'd picked up a bottle of Merrydown Extra Dry on the way. Sat down, taken two or three sips apiece; then been clamped by awkwardness.

'That's a non sequitur, I think,' he said.

'Your mum's thing. Is it just seeing *events*? Or does she . . .?'

We didn't look at each other. It hadn't occurred to me that *he* wouldn't know what to say, either. *How do people bear this stuff?* I'd wanted to know, watching Linda's fierce frown and precisely rotating hips. Now, how did people bear *this*? This was worse: intensity without pleasure. Intensity with awkwardness. The world *was* like 'that', we would all deep down admit. The worse horror was that the world was like *this*, too.

Silence drifted over us and settled. I got up and lit a cigarette. Tossed him the pack. I stood in profile to him, smoking, feeling the warmth of the sun on my back. Pen appeared at the edge of the lawn, raised a hand (or more likely gave us the vee) in greeting.

'This guy came to one of her séances, once,' Kelp said. 'Claimed he'd died and come back on the operating table.'

I had thought, poking the manicured turf with the toe of my trainer, that we would wait it out. Let Pen arrive and relieve us. Apparently not. I looked up, but Kelp was staring at the grass. The sunlit Merrydown glowed, its fizz all but gone. I picked it up and took a long swig. Passed it to him. All without meeting each other's eyes.

'I've heard this one,' I said, for something to say. 'He floated up out of his body towards a bright light. Got called back by his wife and kids or whatever.'

He nodded. 'I'd heard it, too,' he said. 'But do you know what that light *felt* like?'

I looked to see how close Pen was. I had an overpowering conviction that, whatever it was, we had to get it out of the way before he joined us. Kelp continued staring at the grass.

'He said it was like confronting your mother and father with everything you'd ever done or thought of doing,' he said. 'Total nakedness.'

I wanted to reach for the bottle. Couldn't, in case we looked at each other.

'Oi, nangleberries!' Pen called. Neither of us acknowledged him.

'He said he felt the exact dimensions of his own shame,' Kelp said. 'And he felt this space around it, going on for ever.'

The day was very still around us. Pen's approach audible now in the grass.

'What happened to him, this guy?' I asked.

'He's Meths Eddie,' he said.

Meths Eddie was a bearded, barrel-chested alcoholic who wore a fur coat all year round and staggered about Begshall's town centre babbling incoherently.

'Meths Eddie?'

'Meths Eddie,' Kelp said, as if the name had made the two of us stupid.

'Tell that homosexual there he owes me three fags from yesterday,' Pen said, coming up.

Pen held out as long as he could, but with diminishing conviction. By the end of the week he had retreated from alleged disbelief in Kelp's 'sight' to anxieties about the cost and practicalities of the trip. (The trip. We started calling it 'the trip' out of the need, I now believe, to recast it as a *project*, something we could own and plan, something over which we could exercise control, an achieved leaving rather than one thrust upon us.)

'And where is it we're going, pray?' he asked Kelp, in the Coopers' Arms. 'Where is it, exactly, Kreskin, that we'll be *safe*?'

Kelp, very perky since his night in hospital, very saucy and indifferent, uncharacteristically ravenous for food and drink, answered with his mouth full of salt-and-vinegar crisps, spraying slightly. 'South,' he said; then a sip of Guinness, and his fingers fishing the Levis top pocket for Golden Virginia and papers. 'I'm thinking Cornwall. I was conceived there, you know.' On my mum and dad's honeymoon.'

Penguin looked at me, blinked, slowly, with elaborate tolerance.

'We might wander about a bit on the way.' Kelp said. 'See the country. Hitchhike, maybe. You know.'

'Oh yeah,' Pen said. 'Hitchhiking. Good idea. Let's get hats, too, with "Please bugger me and leave me in a ditch" on them.'

'Some are born to leave,' Kelp said, this having become his (to Pen deeply irritating) misquote of choice, 'some achieve leaving, and some have leaving thrust upon them.'

'Yeah,' Pen said, stubbing out his cigarette, 'and some have *bollocks* thrust upon them.'

I showed my mother and father a brochure for campsites in the South West. I showed them my Youth Hostel Association membership card. I showed them (when the time came) an open return coach ticket to Torquay. I left out, naturally, all mention of hitchhiking.

'I hope you realize we're trusting you and your pals to do this *responsibly*?' my father said, while my mother sat on the edge of the couch with her knees tight together and her fingers laced. 'I hope you understand that this is all, Mister, on the basis of you not getting up to anything stupid?'

'I know, Dad.'

'And you'll call us every day?'

'Every *few* days, Mum.'

'Oh *God*,' she said, as if I'd just stabbed her.

'All right all right,' my father said. 'He's not stupid. He knows. You know, don't you?'

'I know, Dad.'

So we left. Scrabbled together laughable savings and cleared out. Kelp relaxed as Begshall receded. I saw it in him at the end of our first day out from home. We had settled for the night (illicitly) in a field in Cheshire, just south of Alderley

Edge. In the dusk we sat around the camping stove listening to the little kettle's whispers and tonks. I saw his face, different.

'You all right?' I asked him.

Pen looked up from cigarette rolling, sensing the question's weight. (It was in keeping with the spirit of the Road, we'd felt, rolling one's own. We kept the tobacco moist with bits of fruit. Banana-flavoured Golden Virginia. Apple. Pear.)

'I'm all right,' Kelp said. 'I feel good.'

'Well, that's the main thing,' Pen said.

A few moments of quiet. A bat whirring about, then disappearing.

'This is the right thing to do,' Kelp said. He smiled, broadly, as from sudden inner pleasure. 'I know you think it's bollocks, but it's true. It doesn't matter if you don't believe me.'

'That's just as well,' Pen said, then rolled, licked the Rizla, lit up.

Later, I walked away to the hedgerow to pee. Dark and clear night, brilliantly starred. The enormous globe, hairy with grass, puckered with mountains, a-slosh with seas, the great weight and age of the planet – then me, minute, tethered by flimsy gravity, pissing into one of its zillion rustling crevices. A condensed vertigo; sudden adrenalin at knees, ankles, scalp. I finished, zipped up, then stood still, looking out over the hedge to where the neighbouring field dropped into darkness and the stars came down. The same mini-vertigo or nausea when I'd seen Malone at the hospital that night. Now, standing in the dark, I imagined a thin, wriggling and crackling electrical charge between us, from my navel to the small of his back. Which image *made* my navel tingle, so that I put my palm over it. *Father Malone travels a great deal.* Nonetheless. There – my navel *hurt* – was the twitching electric capillary or umbilical, to which the world's size was a matter of indifference.

I turned and walked back to the light of the stove.

It's too dangerous to hitchhike in England now, and I suppose it was too dangerous then, but I don't remember us being worried much. We got into cars with complete strangers and were shot through motorway-sliced England, added to by the shadowy histories and fettered desires of those behind the wheels. We didn't have to ask. The miles unravelled overlaid by our drivers' confidences, the slipstream filled with tales of constipated lust and freeze-dried regret, stories of stunted dreams – 'I fucking knew the bastard wouldn't leave me a penny' – and petrified shame – 'It sickens you, doesn't it, that I could do that while she was upstairs, *dying*.'

Our road MO was simple. We picked a spot on the map, split up, spent the day listening to the world's multiple personalities while cows and pylons rolled by, then regrouped at our destination, changed, older, ready for each other's company at the camping stove or (very occasionally) fire, where we would create vast suppers, eclectic (tinned tuna, wine gums, Boursin, pilchards, digestives, a roasted onion, a French stick, bacon grill, a Flake), but rounded off always with roll–ups, sugary tea, then nightgowns (*much* longer than nightcaps) of Lamb's Navy Rum, Caroline Munroe devoutly toasted.

We had a two-man tent of satirical cheapness in which, when we could be bothered to erect it, all three of us slept, in a sockish fug. For the most part we relied on the provocatively named survival bags, which allowed for quick getaways in the middle of the night.

122

'Getaways from what?' I'd asked Pen.

'Butchers,' he'd said.

It came as a shock to us, the sensuousness of sleeping out-doors. To fall asleep in a warm sleeping bag with the night air trailing over one's face and throat and fingers and wrists. Things reintroduced themselves to us in the pantheistic flesh: trees, blocks of blue sky, stones, horizons, the wind; the earth was urgently and at all points on its scale alive, when one rubbed up close against or wandered about in it. We thought of all the Begshall hours – bus stops and drains, traffic lights, garages and felt, absurdly, some pin-pricks of species-memory, of the elemental time before all that non-sense. This inner sadness and longing was concealed from but intuitively apparent to each other, and dealt with instead by incessant carping about the heat, or the drizzle, or the uncomfortable night, or the difficulty of preparing a satisfy-ing meal.

We stank, of course. In hindsight, I'm amazed drivers ever picked us up – or allowed us to remain in their cars longer than thirty seconds after they had picked us up. We smelled of life outdoors, Golden Virginia, citronella, sar-dines, diesel, tarmac, grass, dung, feet, pits. We smelled – incredibly – good to each other, but surely bad to everyone else.

'Funny thing about Arthur,' Kelp said, in South Cadbury, on the seventh day out of Begshall.

'Arthur who?' Pen said.

'*King* Arthur, bladder-head,' I said.

Kelp sighed through his nostrils. 'It's understandable that the fact has passed you by, Pen,' he said. 'Engrossed as you so often are in things like Mars bars and the scratching of your arse, but South Cadbury, that is to say, this locale, here, where we *are*, is commonly regarded as the site of the court of Camelot. I don't want to burden you with information that will get in your way, but every now and then it occurs to me that you might like to . . . well, you know . . . *look about you.*'

We sat on a hill not far from the site, looking out over the downs. Sandwiched between dun horizon and a low bruise of cloud the sun was setting in strands of copper, plum and gold. Our embattled tent, erected in defiance of the bylaws, rattled and flapped in the wind. Pen, who was indeed eating a Mars bar (in his distinctive manner, by nibbling off all the outer chocolate before what Kelp described as a pornographic engagement with caramel and nougat), didn't look up, but said: 'Pubic turds.'

'What about King Arthur?' I asked Kelp.

He was on his haunches, ministering to camping stove and pinging kettle. 'I was thinking,' he said, 'that towards the end he becomes nebulous. It's the other ones you remember. Merlin, Guinevere, Lancelot, Morgana. By the time Arthur gets it in the neck he's just a sort of invisible centre.'

Pen rolled over onto his back, contemplating his work on the Mars bar. 'In *Excalibur*,' he said, 'would you rather shag Helen Mirren or Cherie Lunghi?'

Kelp licked the Rizla and rolled. I tossed him the lighter. 'On the other hand,' he said, 'it's his legend, not theirs. Because he dies. Dying *inflates* him.'

'He doesn't die, though, does he?' I said. 'He goes into a kind of sleep.'

'I'd *say* Cherie Lunghi,' Pen said. 'But I'm put off by her name. Too much like fungi. In your groin. Because you haven't dried yourself properly. On the other hand, there's that bird at the beginning. What's her name? Migraine. Gets shagged by the bloke in the armour. That's not to be sniffed at, a woman who'd put up with that. How's that tea coming, cock-face?'

Funds were low (greenhorn overspending), so we made a meagre evening meal of vegetable stock, red Leicester, rice pudding, and a loaf of slightly tough Hovis slathered in raspberry jam. After which we sat round the small fire Pen had got going (also illegal, but a week on the road had made us contemptuous of the law) with regulation Golden Virginia and rum tea. Peace descended upon us, humbly, courtesy of salt-flavoured air and madly constellated sky; a deep pleasure in the feeling of full bellies and the fire's warmth.

'It's a shame it's all got to end,' Kelp said. He sat opposite me, cross-legged, orange-tinted by the fire between us. Pen lay in his sleeping bag, up on one elbow, awake, with a tired and dirty face. Kelp's face, too, was grimy, swiped on one cheek with fire smut, but still a thing of androgynous beauty. The high bones and angel hair, the cat eyes. In all the years since the toilet cubicle, none of us had seen the others naked.

'The trip?' I asked him. Pen's eyes, which had closed, opened, surprised.

Kelp took a sip of rum, shook his head. 'Not giving a fuck,' he said. 'In a few years, we'll all care about all that stuff we don't care about now.'

'I don't think I'll ever care about *power steering*,' I said.

'Or inflation,' Pen said.

Kelp smiled, looking into the core of the flames. 'It'll matter,' he said. 'There'll be a mortgage. And we'll want *better stuff*. There'll be *employers*.'

'I mean, what *is* inflation?' Pen asked. 'Everybody's always going on about inflation. Why can't some cunt just *de*flate the bastard?'

A moment. The fire's busy soliloquy, peppered with

sudden hisses and Zulu clicks. Pen, I knew, was worried that Kelp wanted to say something serious. I thought how beautiful it would be if we could acknowledge . . . if we could just . . .

'It'll never come again,' Kelp said, as a breeze lifted his hair.

'Yeah, yeah,' Pen said. '*Carpe diem* and all the rest of it. So what?'

'Jesus Christ, Pen,' I said. 'That was . . . that was *correct*.'

'And once again,' Pen with mellifluous tolerance, 'they underestimate this superb genius.'

'Now you've fucked it up. You don't say "superb genius".'

'Why not?'

'You just don't. It's . . . I don't know why, but you don't.'

The mood crumbled. I watched Kelp let it go, chuckle, begin rolling a cigarette. Tiny internal deaths, these moments that reached out for some ritual or enactment – but didn't find it.

'Yeah, well,' Kelp said, topping himself up and taking a gulp. 'Anyway.' Then a pause. Then 'Anyway, anyway, anyway.'

We went to Stonehenge, having deliberately missed the festival. Salisbury's disgruntlement was still evident, along with galaxies of litter and the after-shape of the crowd, who had come asserting a connection between prehistoric calculus and twentieth-century rock and roll. Finished with, the city (and the monument) laid bare the fraudulence of the idea. A Rastafarian had been stabbed to death. A girl from Scotland had been gang-raped.

In a hot lull the three of us shared a bench near the cathedral. Sunlight whitened the square. Old ladies' soufflé hairdos blinding. A resinous cedar round which the benches

126

were arranged blotched us with shadow, in and out of which pigeons – balding, club-footed, with the look of having been petrol-dipped and blow-dried – tottered, pecking at and occasionally tussling epileptically with rubbishy bits of food.

Two men approached us, loose-boned and weather-beaten, one, forties, dark, with grey flecks in his shaggy hair and beard, dressed in baggy and indeterminate trousers (over which a little paunch) and a cheesecloth shirt which had once been white, the other thirtyish, smaller, dirty-golden, with a greasy vulpine face and pale-green eyes, sporting bike-oiled jeans and threadbare combat jacket.

'Praise the Lord!' the older one said.

'Praise His knees!' his companion said.

They squatted down in front of us.

'The three strangers,' the younger one said.

'The three *gun*slingers,' the dark one said. 'Boys, what's your business?'

Pen began rolling a cigarette – registered immediately by the younger, manifestly a scavenger.

'No business,' Kelp said. 'Just hanging out.'

'Just hanging out,' the dark one said, then gave a bass, meaty laugh, slapping his friend on the shoulder. 'Now what do you think of that, Jim?'

'I think it's cool,' Jim said, tucking a greasy strand behind his ear – the same strand, rapid-fire, three times – a tick. 'I think it's fucking *cool*, you know?' Still observing every movement of Pen's rolling, very seriously.

'Just hanging out . . . heh heh heh—' again the bass laugh. The beard full and fat, like a pelt. 'Well I'm Jake, friends, and this is my friend Jim. Shall I tell you what *our* business is?'

Pen didn't lift his head.

'By all means,' Kelp said, smiling.

'The fucking *Lord* is our business,' Jake said. 'And He's a Lord with a fucking *sword*, right?'

'Aha,' Kelp said.

'People think "Jesus",' Jim said, eyes lecherously following Pen's first inhalation, 'and they think' – with terrible scorn – '*mmnaah*, some hippy pussy in sandals, right?'

'Right,' Kelp said.

'*Right*,' Jake picked up. 'But those cunts are wrong. *Dead* wrong, right?' The laugh again, adjusting his position from squat to half-lotus, Jim following suit, both of them mottled with cedar shadow. Pigeons veered on quick-stepping legs, then returned. The two old ladies who had been sharing the neighbouring bench (both sunburned, both liver-spotted, both with mild Parkinsonian head-wobble) got up, by arthritic degrees, and left.

'The *meek*?' Jake said, suddenly, as if he'd overheard us whispering about them. 'Don't talk to me about the meek.'

'Yeah, the meek,' Jim said, watching Pen's roll-up. 'They kill me.'

'Don't even *talk* to me about the meek,' Jake said.

'Could I offer you gentlemen a cigarette?' Kelp said, handing over his tobacco and papers, unable to bear Jim's nakedness any longer.

'When the Lord comes,' Jake said, with a grin of delight and no acknowledgement of the gift, but deftly and greedily rolling nonetheless, 'He's coming to vanquish His enemies, to divide nations, to raise armies on either shore, setting man against his brother, till man exists no more.'

'And the meek shall inherit the earth,' Pen said, quietly.

Jim and Jake looked at each other, then, and shook their heads with converts' gleeful resignation.

'You know what, Jim?' Jake said.

'What, Jake?'

Jake's arms wide, inclusive, and a bright, beard-splitting grin of good teeth, one of them gold. 'I love doing the Lord's work,' he said. 'I fucking *love* it.'

Harmless, we decided, and in any case they had a Volkswagen van in which they offered to drive us up to the monument just before sundown.

'No point going during the day,' Jake told us. 'It's all fucking kagouls and foreign brats. You'll end up killing someone. Remember that American bloke you nearly killed, Jim?'

The van ride was something. There was a carton of fresh whipping cream on one of the seats. Pen, blindly, sat on it. It exploded between his legs. It wasn't mentioned for a few minutes, then Jim, riding shotgun, said, quietly, 'You know, Jake, I'm feeling a lot of anger about that cream.'

To which Jake, after a substantial silence (Pen with screwed-up face, wiping, ineffectually, Kelp and I in quashed hysterics looking out of the window), replied: 'That's understandable, Jim. That is, when all's said and done, understandable.'

There was an edge to the driving after that. Jake tutted and chuckled in what appeared to be mild disapproval – *fond* disapproval, even – at the injudicious meandering of an old lady cyclist in front, whose weaving made passing her perilous. 'Dear Lord,' he sighed, as we approached her. 'Ninety if she's a day and still out on her old two-wheeler.' Then he leaned across Jim and screamed: 'Get off the road you fucking old *wreck*.'

We reached Salisbury Plain when the sun was going down in gashed reds and molten golds – all very unEnglish. The baked land was cooling; not a breath of wind stirred the dry grass. We got out and sat on a bank fifty yards from the stones. A handful of tourists milled, snapped and cam-cordered, but within half an hour – our camping kettle on the boil, Jim and Jake helping themselves to further roll-ups – they were gone.

Kelp got up and walked to the perimeter fence.

'Mystical moment, I expect,' Pen said, cracking open a pack of jammy dodgers.

'Pagan rubbish,' Jake said. 'Do you know how *sad* this makes him?'

'Makes who?' Pen said.

Jake rolled his eyes. 'The *Lord*, for Christ's sake,' he said. 'Those who are not with Him are against Him. He that is not my brother I shall crush . . . and vomit forth in the wilderness.'

Kelp reached out and took hold of the wire.

'Can't do that,' Jim called. 'Oi, friend. Can't go in there. Pressure pads.'

Kelp turned. 'What?' he said.

'Pressure pads,' Jim said, plucking a strand of Golden Virginia from his bottom lip. 'Under the grass. Ultra-sensitive. Step on the fuckers, sets the whole alarm system off.' Three quick behind-the-ear hair tucks.

'*Pressure pads*?' Pen said.

'Ever since that twat sprayed the CND symbol on,' Jake explained. 'The entire area inside the fence is pressure-sensitive. Put a foot in there and the dogs are on you.'

Pen looked at me, trying to squint out the truth.

'German Shepherds,' Jake continued. 'There's kennels underground. A pretend hippy got savaged two years ago. Tried to sue the National Trust.'

Pen chewed his biscuit, cogitating, weighing up. 'Kelp?' he called, after a while. 'Come away from there.'

That night Jim and Jake stayed in the Volkswagen van, us with the tent up close by. A supper of porridge and biscuits, then the mugs of tea laced with rum. The land very gentle now.

'I like our little stove,' Kelp said.

'Fuck the stove,' Pen said, cross-legged in the doorway of the tent. 'I could be lying on Mandy's bed with my head up her skirt. I could be lying there with her actual skirt over my head. I just want you to know that.'

'Only if you'd killed her,' Kelp said, stretched out, fingers laced behind his head.

For a while we fell silent. I had no idea that I was going to say what I said next.

'I want to ask you something,' I said.

'Is it going to be boring?' Pen said.

'Why not kill people?' I said. A pause. A sickening and exhilarating feeling of the earth suddenly dropping away from beneath me.

'What?' Pen said.

'Why not, if you don't believe in God, or Heaven or Hell – or any kind of punishment after death – why not torture and kill people?'

Pen rolled his eyes.

'Listen,' I said. 'It's a fair question. Suppose you *like* to torture people to death, right? It gives you *pleasure*. And suppose you were guaranteed immunity from any kind of punishment, in this life or the next. Why not do it?'

'Prison,' Pen said.

'No no no no you're not *listening*, bollock-brain. *Guaranteed immunity*. Right? No *punishment*.'

Pen puckered his lips and closed his eyes, cogitating. 'Because no one would like you,' he said.

I opened my mouth for exasperated dismissal – then faltered, wondering if he didn't have a point.

'Dummie means,' Kelp said, lighting up, inhaling,

exhaling with tilted-back head, 'is there some reason for not murdering people that isn't related to *consequences*. He means is there some *abstract* reason for not murdering people.'

'For pleasure,' I added. Kelp wasn't looking at me.

Pen took out his own tobacco and papers. 'Yeah,' he said, 'but what about . . .' He hesitated; the flimsy and unpredictable relationship he had with his thoughts . . . 'What about those women who lift trucks because their kid's trapped underneath?'

'What about them?' I asked him.

'No, no, that's not what I mean. I mean, what about if it's a mother who shoots someone who's going to butcher her kid?'

I watched Kelp's eyes close. He'd been through a phase of keeping his hair very short, which Pen and I hadn't liked, but it had passed. Now the brilliant straw nest was back. 'The only thing your contribution to any discussion reveals, Pen,' he said, 'is just what a sorry fucking state your mind is in.'

Penguin lit, inhaled, squinted, tried to look shrewd. 'Can't answer my question, though, can you?' he said, then closed his lips with man-in-the-street satisfaction.

'Your question's *irrelevant*,' I told him. 'You're not following anything.'

'And so they evade the issue,' Pen said, breezily, chin raised. 'Can't answer? Tell him he's not following.'

'Jesus Christ,' I said. 'Forget it. Give me one of those, will you?'

'There's no abstract reason,' Kelp said, lying down on his back. 'It's just that you'd lose your sense of humour.'

I caught Penguin's tossed Golden Virginia in both hands, glared at him for the rotten throw. 'Can we stop talking about this crap?' he said.

★

In my dream that night I was walking up Logan Street towards home. Evening, possibly, or the weirdly lit hour before dawn. Halfway to number 17, a derelict old man appeared at the top of the street, on the opposite side. We stopped and looked at each other. I felt immediately uneasy. He smiled – horribly vital – and began walking towards me. At which point two things happened: I noticed that he had a large wooden peg driven through his left foot; and, somewhere far away, getting nearer, a police siren began to wail. I woke to local chaos.

The siren had transferred itself to the waking world. Lights were on, somewhere nearby. There was movement, very close.

Just time to note these three conditions before a flapping body crashed into the side of the tent and brought the whole thing down on top of me.

'Jesus Christ, Dummie, get out of there!' Pen hissed. 'Get *out!*'

For a second, Penguin was tangled on top of me, then he was up again, yanking at the tent, randomly, pegs flying, guy ropes pinging. 'For fuck's *sake,* Dominic, get *out*, will you? Fuck fuck fuck *fuck.*'

I scrambled out. Wide-eyed, mouth open, Pen was running about in short bursts with his hands out and his knees bent. A light had come on in the Volkswagen. Lights had come on around the stones, too, and somewhere, a dog was barking.

Jake's head poked out of the van's passenger window. 'What's going on, boys?' he asked, looking wide awake, as if the two of them had been not sleeping but sitting and communing silently in the dark.

'I fucking knew it,' Pen said. 'I fucking *knew* it.'

'Oh,' I said, understanding. 'Oh.'

'Open the door, open the door!' Pen was hissing, having collapsed the tent – sleeping bags and rucksacks still inside it – and dragged it like swag over to the van. Jim opened the door and stepped out, fully dressed.

'Be not afraid,' Jake said, turning the engine over, 'for though the Devil walks among you like a ravishing . . . for though the Devil roars, like a howling . . .'

'Get in, Dummie,' Pen ordered. Dogs, plural now, were definitely barking. The siren stopped. From the other side of the road a powerful searchlight came on and swept towards us.

'For God's sake get in the van!' Pen barked.

Volkswagen ignition. 'Praise Him,' Jim said, businesslike.

'And also with you,' Jake said.

I ran to the perimeter fence. No sign of Kelp. The search-light groped and splashed the stones.

'Fuck him, Dummie, get in the van!'

'If we're getting out of here,' Jim said, indifferently, 'we need to go now. Response time's around four minutes. Police get here shortly thereafter. Me and Jake don't have dealings with the police, do we, Jake?'

'That's right,' Jake said. 'Render unto Caesar that which belongs to Caesar.'

'Dominic!' Pen shouted. 'Into the van! Now!'

We drove.

Pen was in the back, lying on the floor with limbs spread protectively over the traumatized tent. 'We left the stove,' he said, dismally. 'We left the fucking *stove*.'

A mile away and half an hour later we stopped in a small clearing in the middle of a forest. Jake had driven through three fences and a hedgerow, crossed a lane, and somehow found a narrow track which ran deep in under the trees. Pen had gone very quiet and thick-faced.

We got out, inadequately illuminated by the van's interior light. I sat down with my back against the front wheel and rolled a cigarette. The trees were tall and gently susurrating benevolences around us, opening, when one looked up, on a circle of milkily starred sky. Jim and Jake, with a feeble torch each, poked around the clearing, gathering kindling. In ten minutes they had a fire going, atop of which their own little camping kettle.

'Dunno how we're going to find your mate,' Jake said. 'You two might have to bite the bullet and go to the police tomorrow.'

'Good,' Pen said, sinking down next to me. 'Then we can go home. I hope they arrest the bastard.'

Silence closed, the fire's soft tufts of flame shimmying up into the dark. I knew Penguin was depressed. His eyes had gone small. I thought of Down's syndrome Gareth, the mongoloid eyes, looking at me. The back of my throat, without warning, threatened tears.

Then Jim said, tucking his hair, 'Something funny about your mate, I thought. Got a bit of a weird aura, you know? Bit of a twilight zoner.'

'You noticed that, did you?' Pen said, dryly.

'We know,' I said.

'You know what *I* think, don't you, Jim?' Jake said, returning from an audible and pungent piss, still zipping up. Jim nodded, meaningfully, patently without a clue. '*I* think,' Jake continued, lifting the kettle, pouring, 'that the Lord might be putting His touch on that boy.'

A night of dread. Words glowed and faded like breathed-on embers: 'missing', 'police', 'abducted', 'arrested', 'lost', 'found dead'. Pen sat all night wrapped in his sleeping bag with his back against a tree, horribly alert, unable to speak, beyond the odd truncated pronouncement: 'If he's dead, I'm not the one telling his mum.' 'If we go to the police, Dummie, you'll have to talk.' 'We've got his stuff.' 'He won't have a fucking clue where we are.' *How can people do these things*? In my sleeping bag I curled onto my side, stomach a knot, face daubed with heat from the fire. Sickness rose and subsided, rose . . . and subsided. Alternated, rather, with clenches of excitement. *How can people do these things*? Perhaps, stripped and strung up in a soundproofed cell of perspiring brick, Kelp was about to find out. I saw him in a blacker version of the predicament he'd been in that first day in the toilet cubicle, no trace of comedy this time; his torturer emerging from the shadows, string-vested and obese, tight slacks revealing the genital punnet, face sheened as if from a steamy kitchen, eyes remote with desire. Which of them was truly my brother? I imagined myself (why bother with the string-vested vicar?) looking into Kelp's face. Perhaps with Mrs Walker (why not?) putting the finishing touches to her lips in the shadows. His look would say to me, in the last analysis, *We love each other, Dummie*. My look would say to him, *Yes, I know*. How would we proceed from there? Kelly–Burke had known. I had known. That's why I couldn't turn round. *Let's do this fock'n cunt*. It hadn't been bearable. When you loved somebody, it offered you two things. One was the love itself. The other was . . . the other was . . .

The wood shifted, partly consumed, and fell in on the fire's heart.

'We're out of fucking rum,' Pen said.

In the morning – no sight or sound of Kelp back at the stones – we resolved, miserably, on reporting to the police. Jim and Jake, much crumpled after their night in the van, drove us down to the city just after first light and dropped us off at the cedar-shaded bench in the shadow of the cathedral where we'd met the day before. It had been my and Pen's slim hope that Kelp, were he able, would make for this spot. But he wasn't there. Nothing was open yet. Zealous, deadening sunlight, and the streets deserted, the stone intricacies of the cathedral, its chilly lake of shadow.

'Best not to mention us,' Jake said, over the VW's idle. Jim, in the passenger seat, nodded, and did the hair-tuck. 'Have to say you walked it back.'

Kelp's disappearance had scotched the proselytizing somewhat. Long-eyelashed Jake did, however, sketch a ministerial blessing above our heads, while Jim rootled mysteriously in the glove box. 'May His love and power keep you, the many . . . for the solitary lamb that wanders shall not remain lost, nor prey to demons of the wild . . . nor—'

'Amen,' Pen concluded – prematurely, from Jake's clipped nod and gunned engine.

'I've just got to sit down a minute,' Pen said, after they'd gone, and sat down, still with his rucksack on. Kelp's pack, now an awful symbol, stood forlornly at my feet. Last night's soul-wrestling had been an unaffordable luxury; daylight made that plain, at least. Kelp was missing. Anything (didn't *I* know), *anything* could have happened to him. The thought of Stella receiving the news sent a contained charge through my skin. I opened my mouth to say as much to Pen, but was delayed by the sudden approach of a small, L-plated and disproportionately noisy motorbike (like the maddening half-broken larynx of a teenage boy), which drew up alongside us, brayed, bletted, roared, then went silent as its driver and passenger dismounted. The pilot was a pretty, malnourished girl with big-lashed eyes the colour of blueberries and a wide, lippy mouth. The doffed helmet released a cascade of very dark, very corkscrewy hair. Impossible not to note, too, the apple-sized and braless breasts, made much of by a cropped and clinging pink T-shirt. The passenger – Kelp – took his helmet off and smiled at us.

A moment of silence. Relief from fingernails to folicles.

'Oh my giddy pants,' Pen said.

'It's a *tape recording* of dogs,' Kelp told us. 'Security's two old duffers with a torch. Not even *two* torches. I could've painted the *Mona Lisa* on there. I could've *dismantled* the thing.'

I buried it. All the night's contents. *When you loved somebody, it offered you two*—no. Gone. Buried. This was the road's grace: its sudden switchbacks and hairpins forced you to forget what you had been looking at only moments before. Not that I needed forcing, having woken that morning exhausted and filled with self-loathing. I had dreamed that I was part of a small group, men and women, all very fat and uglily cosmeti-cized, in a futuristic society. We patronized a secret club, where it was possible to take showers in human blood. Soap, shampoo, loofahs – all very prosaic – except that through the cubicles' frosted glass we could see our enforced donors, held in place by science-fictionish contraptions, growing weaker as their blood went to the washing of our armpits, toes, genitals. The great thing was to shower until they died.

Kelp had observed us making our getaway ('Cheers, by the way') and had set off in pursuit, but had lost us after the first field. When the geriatric hoo-ha at the monument had died down he'd gone back and waited. Eventually, bored, he'd decided to walk the nine miles back into town, where, tagging on to a young and largely hallucinating group of rev-ellers disgorged from a nightclub, he ended up at an all-night party (a labyrinthine squat) in the bingeful company of com-plete but affable strangers, among them, seventeen-year-old

Nancy. A night of hitting-it-off-straight-away. They'd just finished breakfast at an early-morning café, and shared the vaguely beatified look of complete exhaustion. (Pen and I asked him, ocularly, when she wasn't looking: *Have you?* Ocularly he replied: *No. But . . .*)

She ought to have been sassy, but she wasn't. She was shy. The sort of shy girl who nonetheless has her own L-plated motorbike and takes quantities of drugs. (*The best kind of shy girl*, I knew Pen was thinking.) She blinked like a puppet, slowly. Her top lip was chapped, and made an appealing smear of her mouth. Take off the mascara and eyeshadow and she'd look unwell; with it, she looked shyly mysterious.

'I've got to buzz off,' she said, a few minutes after Kelp had finished his narrative. She gave his hand a squeeze, then, the two of them giggling, a peck on the cheek. 'You know where you're going, do you?' she asked him.

'Yup,' he said.

Small air-patting movements from Pen, representing his just managing not to manhandle her onto the bike seat. Then the froth of hair was pinned under the helmet and the spare looped onto the cow horns. Another embarrassed laugh exchanged between her and suddenly majestic Kelp, then the machine brayed into life.

Very muffled: 'Nice meeting you.' Pen and I nodding like lobotomized dogs. Then, treble-farting exhaust leaving bluish fumes, the bike pulled away.

'And where *are* you going, bastard?' I asked Kelp, as the sound of the engine faded.

'Not me,' he said, with a grin which expanded into an enviable yawn. '*Us.*'

'What are you writing?'

'Just a journal. Things I remember.'

This evening Holly and I lay on our backs side by side after aborted sex. We had kissed, with increasing appetite — then she became agitated. Wouldn't look at me. Kept jerking her head to look elsewhere, as if the apartment contained darting spirits; eyes angry when she did look at me. Her body kept moving, but her eyes closed as if consciousness was unbearable. She felt my hesitancy and said, *Go on, do it, go on, do what you want. What do you want?* Then when I tried to kiss her mouth yanked her head away and hit out at me. She caught me in the eye and I had to sit up, wait for it to clear. She had lain still, breathing through her nose, face turned away.

Silence, some new nakedness between us.

'There was a woman on television the other day,' she said.

Then after a long pause, 'She'd been raped by a gang of men.'

I waited, saying nothing.

Slowly, she rolled onto her side away from me. I heard her take a cigarette, light it from a matchbook, inhale, breathe out. The thing in my chest moved, slightly, fine fronds of pain spreading from its core. Outside, the city's conversation, its insistence on carrying on. In an hour she'd have to be at work. Her, the same woman as the woman lying here on her side, smoking, uninterested in her own beauty, perhaps beauty in general. All matters of indifference to the city, which would still demand that she get up and go to work.

'She said that all her memories, all the good memories of her life up until it happened, were still there, but she couldn't touch them. She said she didn't feel entitled to them any more.'

Without turning, and knowing it wasn't wanted, I reached behind me and put my palm on her shin. I listened to her smoke the cigarette out. The room darkened.

'I've got to get ready,' she said, then sat up and swung her legs out from under my touch.

◆

Nancy lived in Burcombe, a tiny village a few miles out of the city.

With her friend Jill.

'Now listen to me, Dummie,' Pen began, as we walked up there (Jim and Jake forgotten) that evening.

'Mine,' I said. 'She's mine. Foregone conclusion.'

'All I'm saying is—'

'Not interested. Don't even dream.'

He walked in silence for a while, then said, in a higher than usual voice, 'All right. We'll see. I'm just saying. We'll see.'

'Me and Nance in her room,' Kelp said to me, bloke-to-bloke, for Pen's benefit. 'You and Jill in Jill's. Pen'll be all right down on the couch.'

Dung-scented Burcombe was a handful of dwarfish cottages, a farm or two, an all-purpose shop, a pub, a post office and a bus stop, all clustered round the intersection of three very minor roads. Friesians in a deep-green field stood on their solid legs looking at us as if we might be the bearers of news they'd been awaiting for millennia.

'Hiya,' Nancy said, opening the door with a grin and a whiff of patchouli. 'Come in.'

The cottage was small and thick-walled, coal-fired, smelling of marijuana and incense-cloaked damp. Furniture cast-offs: an auntie's couch, a mum's coffee table, a granny's paunchy and shuddering fridge. If Nancy and Jill hadn't lived there it would have been a hovel. Courtesy of the DHSS, however, they did live there, and had transformed the place into a junky paradise: bits of farm machinery; pine cones; feathers; blue glass; mandalas; bleached or anthropomorphic branches; a sheep's skull; stones; a bird's nest; a ram's flaking horn; Buddhas in fake jade and brass; Fonda and Hopper; a Sacred Heart tambourine.

'We found all this stuff,' Nancy said, skinny shoulders hunched, fingertips in pockets. 'Didn't cost us a penny. People throw incredible stuff away.'

Nancy – soft Wiltshire voice and slow-blinking puppet eyes – moved around slowly, with very slightly raised eyebrows, handling objects carefully. Jill was smaller, stockier, feistier, with leonine hair and little chimpanzee nostrils. There was a supple and fiery self in there, I believed. The eyes (hers were small and sly-spirited, two fierce works of gold and brown, peppered with black) never lied. Her cheeks glowed after the first glass of our abysmal plonk. 'Nance, I've told you,' she said. 'You've got to stop bringing strange blokes home. There's no room left in the garden.' She performed, somewhat, but never unironically; you'd be able to get through that, once she trusted you.

Pen, meanwhile, was in a state.

'I want to have sex with Jill,' he said to me when we crossed paths at the outside loo. 'I just want you to know that, now, so there's no confusion later. I really, *really* want to have sex with Jill.'

The girls cooked a fibrous but thrillingly spiced vegetarian hot-pot for supper, which we ate – accompanied by Joni Mitchell's *Blue*, candles, and more of our thin red wine – sitting on the creepy-crawly grass in the cramped back garden. 'Pisses me off having a conscience,' Jill said. 'I still miss it:

142

roast lamb, cold chicken, sausages' – closed eyes, orgasmic inhalation and groan – '*bacon*.' (Pen's upper body tilted towards her, as if reeled in.) 'I just really miss *meat*,' Jill ended, opening and flashing her naughty eyes.

'So do I,' Pen said.

After dinner the three of us washed up while Nancy and Jill 'revived the living room' – blatant euphemism for a strategy meeting. I say the three of us washed up; not strictly true. Kelp washed, I dried, Penguin flapped like a demented bird.

'Take it easy there, Pen,' I said.

'Don't overdo it, man,' Kelp said.

Pen rubbed his eyes, scratched his head, shoved his hands into his pockets, pulled them out, rubbed his eyes, scratched his head.

'Why don't you just ask her?' I suggested.

'What?'

'Why don't you, instead of fannying around in here, just go in there and ask her if she'd like to have sex with you?'

'Very funny.'

'Go on.'

'Don't push me, Dummie.'

'Go on, you jessie. She'll eat you for breakfast.'

'I'm warning you.'

'Well put some of these dishes away then, flannel-face.'

Dope was brought out. Nancy, knees together, ringlets tucked behind each pink, lobeless and silver-hooped ear, sat in one of the ectoplasmic armchairs and rolled joint after joint with dreamy precision. A joy to watch.

'Didn't do any work today,' Jill said.

'Didn't do any yesterday,' Nancy said.

'Don't think I'll do any tomorrow,' Jill concluded.

Pen, fatuously stoned, with humble eyes said, 'Would it be all right if we stayed here for the rest of our lives?'

'No,' Jill said. 'But it's obvious you're expecting to stay for the rest of the night.'

A brief and sacred silence followed, in which every detail of ourselves and the cottage was perfected. Then the girls giggled. Nancy, blinking slowly over a broad, lips-together smile, presented us with a newly minted spliff then stood up and took Kelp by the hand. He looked over his shoulder at me, en route to the stairs. I'd expected a grin, but saw instead a tiny, fleeting acknowledgement of virginity; this in the look, yes, and something else, equally slight: the recognition that such sweetness of timing, such luck, such purely gifted *life* comes so rarely – for some, never. Then he was gone.

I had a contorted episode of swallowing and blinking and not quite knowing whether I was getting up from the couch or not.

'You all right there?' Jill asked. She was roseate and low-lying in her armchair, eyes and hair full of firelight, feet (in grey hiking socks) up on the coffee table, chubby hands latticed over her belly.

'Yeah. Yeah. Sorry. Faded out a bit.'

Penguin had gone (unsteadily, narrating himself) out for a pee.

'Look, don't take this the wrong way or anything,' I said, 'but my friend really likes you.'

'I know.'

'Eh?'

'I know.'

'Oh.'

A pause. 'What about you?'

Another pause. The fire's forked tongues tearing themselves apart.

'What about me?'

'Don't you like me?'

Again constriction in the throat. Blinding intellectual recognition of her desirability. Very faintly, a flicker of actual desire, too. But primarily the suspicion of some giant and proximal sadness; chiefly the threatened ambush by tears. Absurd. Ab*surd*.

'Oh yes,' I said, voice fracturing on delivery. 'I really like you, too.'

The ensuing silence (but for the fire's snap and chuckle) of formidable charge and mass, what with the two of us looking directly at each other, seeing with that raw, freakish kind of seeing, the exact and closable distance between us.

'That's the biggest fucking spider I've ever seen,' Penguin announced, returning, chastened, somewhat, by night air and arachnid. Somewhere within me a voice said: 'Practise virtue. It's as simple as that. *Practise.*'

Not prompted by this, exactly, but alarmed by the vague threat of a crying jag, I stood (with imprudent, blood-rushing and head-spinning haste), swayed, flailed, slightly, and excused myself.

'Wasted,' I said. 'Bit of fresh air. Behave yourself, Pen.'

Three candle stubs flickered in the back garden. I lay down on the grass, exhausted. Watched the Milky Way for a while. Fell asleep.

I woke – sour-eyed, thick-tongued, dew-damp and possessed of an importunate erection – just after the sun had come up. The garden was an abrasive assault in stereo and Technicolor. Not quite in time with my member, my head throbbed. I lay still for a moment, very conscious of the thinness of my eyelids and the thermonuclear nature of the sun. But I was dehydrated. (Of course, the thought of . . . There was, after all . . . and hadn't I earned it, in any case, practising virtue like that?) Thirst first. I crawled to the kitchen, knelt, clawed myself up with the aid of a chair, stood upright (thinking, *The ascent of Man*), and drank in ecstatic swallows a pint of cool but not cold tap water.

I knew, with both inward grin and inward shudder, what the material would be. Those puppet eyes of Nancy's disbelieving, disbelieving, disbelieving – *But she's my best friend* – yet what's to disbelieve, when, Igor-assisted and egged on by me, with the little chimp nostrils flared . . .

Where? Surely not standing up in the spidery outside toilet? Certainly not in the moist garden, overlooked by the back bedroom (Christ Almighty, look at *that*). Which left only the living room or the kitchen, and these two divided by the short flight of stairs – short enough, I wagered, that a masturbator might not have time to get himself in order should one of the upstairs inhabitants, woken by raging thirst or bursting bladder, come thumping down without warning.

The practical obstacles at first irked, then, by degrees, deflated me. Conscience a poor second to detumescence.

Not with ire, but gently, very saintly, with pity for his rage, I asked Satan to get behind me. (A slip, that: 'Get behind me,' Jill hisses, giving Nancy a bloodying belt. 'And open your fucking mouth' – but no. No. A flicker – but no. I'll tidy up. Indeed. By God I'll tidy up, with reverence for every roach and cork, for this, too, can be God's work. There is nothing, nothing so small and ignoble that it cannot, in the right conditions . . .)

I tidied, quietly, very pure, the humble logic of emptying mugs and scraping into bins a great help. This, I knew, this *overcoming* of oneself, in humility, this was grace. And there, look, ah, one of Jill's hiking socks, tugged off sleepily, no doubt, one plump fist rubbing her eye.

At the top of the stairs was a very small landing with a cramped bathroom facing and a door on either side. I knocked, softly, on the one to my left. No answer, nor resistance to my gentle push. Half-open curtains and one stripe of sunlight crossing the rumpled bed, where Penguin and Jill lay in each other's arms. Well, actually, not in each other's arms; Jill lay on her back with a shut face and both arms thrown behind her head, as if she'd lifted, then been relieved of, a dumbbell. The lion's-mane hair would have its own heat; I wondered if Pen had made the most of it. Not to mention the nude armpits, the furious nostrils, the pulses of wrist, throat and groin, the sacrum's golden down or the spaces between the toes. Had he (as I did, before meting out diabolical injustice) lingered? I doubted it. Pen himself lay on his side with his face resting on Jill's thigh, frowning, as if under mild interrogation. If he woke and moved very gently, thigh and cheek would separate with a soft tearing sound.

I retreated and stepped across (after a brief and cretinous struggle with tears on the landing) to the other room. This door wasn't locked, either. I poked my head in. The curtains were wide open, though the window, west facing, admitted a gentler light. Another rumpled bed, Nancy lying on her back with the sheet chastely up over her breasts and her white arms down by her sides. She was only asleep, but she had the look of a composed and lovely corpse. Kelp, standing in just jeans by the window, turned and saw me. A moment, then. Me with eyebrows raised in reflex preparation for the nudge-nudge remark, him filled with a new, humbly initiated version of himself, wondering if the bliss through which he'd passed was visible, seeing (all this in less time than it takes to tell) that it was, and that I knew, and wouldn't ruin it. I wondered if he was thinking about his mother.

'I'll put the kettle on, then,' I said.

A thing of beauty being a joy for ever, I still have it precise and clear, that morning image of him by the window and her in the bed. I imagine it, these days, as a tiny, enamelled bit of my brain. I've made use of it, from time to time, like a talisman. As I have, when required, of what came next.

Kelp, skinnily wearing the window's soft light, straw hair standing where their last tussle had left it, hands in pockets, still humming from the baptism, turned, saw that I was wondering about loyalties, grinned, and said, 'Then it'll be time to be thinking of leaving.'

'She was like an angel,' Pen said, one evening, through the fire's smoke. 'She was like a sort of demonic sex angel. Of *course* there's a God. Because she was a blessing, you know? A reward. Do you know what she said to me?'

I knew.

'She said: "I do everything." Just that. "I do . . . *everything*."' A pause. 'It's been bothering me, you know?' he said. 'I think I've thought of a couple of things I might not have done.' He sat cross-legged, hair stiff with grease. We were in Devon, by the River Dart, just south of Buckfastleigh. The sign had said: 'KEEP OU PRIVATE FISHING', the missing T of which had, in our liberal judgement, invalidated the proscription. Besides, it was an irresistible spot. The river icy cold and bottle green, no more than twenty feet across and each bank floored with large, flat, comfortable stones, overhung with conspiratorial trees through which the breeze passed in tranquillizing susurrations. Kelp, claiming blackberries in the field above, had gone off alone, and now Pen and I sat with the fire between us, waiting for the kettle to boil.

'You're not listening to me, are you?'

'I am.'

'Might as well talk to the fucking trees.'

'I am listening. What didn't you do?'

He held up one hand, palm outwards, the Zen guru quelling the acolyte's impatience. Began rolling a cigarette with great care and a pacific smile, as if he had discovered the universal meaning of such small actions. 'It's very hard for me, Dominic,' he said. 'It's very hard for me to explain the experience with Jill. Words, you see? Words—'

'Did you have anal sex with her?'

Coincidentally, he coughed just then, spluttered, rolled onto his side, nearly lost the tobacco, then sat up and pointed at me with the pinched Rizla. 'That's just what I've come to expect from you. My God, man' – *cark* – 'You see? That's the way you think' – *cark* – 'still in the old ways, still shackled to' – *cark, cark* – 'still with such limits of understanding . . . The flesh. I mean the body, the *actual* body. Whereas with Jill . . .' Leaning back on his elbows he meditatively inhaled, then grinningly exhaled a self-congratulatory cone of smoke, disturbing the cloud of midges that had gathered above us. 'Whereas, of course, with Jill . . .'

'I'm beginning to wonder if you did anything at all with the poor cow,' I said. 'You're never specific. I don't think, in fact, that you even—'

'I *spunked* on her *feet*, bastard-head,' Pen snapped. 'How dare you? How *dare* you impinge . . . How dare *you* impinge my—'

'Im*pugn*. Im*pugn*, you idiot.'

'It was spiritual. *Spiritual*. That's what I'm saying. That's what I'm getting at. I don't expect you to understand, really, my son. I pity you. I mean, I do, actually, pity you.'

'There's nothing spiritual about spunking on someone's feet,' I said. But he was lying on his back now, looking up at the gently rustling leaves.

'You see, Dominic, when it's her – I mean when it's *her*, the one you've been waiting for – you just know. You *recognize* each other. Kelp's explained it all to me. We were separated at birth.'

'What?'

'The thing with your partner – your *soul*-partner – is that before this incarnation – this one, I mean, now, your life here on earth since being born – *before* your birth you and your soul-mate were actually one being. One united *entity*. The two of you. Together. As one.'

'Dear God.'

'Then birth happens, and you're separated. It's a terrible thing. Traumatic. The other half of you could be *anywhere*. The whole world, you see? You might even have been born in different countries or whatever. *Your* other half, Dummie, might be a girl in Russia or Venezuela or somewhere. But you've got no choice: you're doomed to spend your life searching for her.'

The camping kettle began to whistle. I removed it and poured into our two teabagged cups. 'You've got the powdered milk,' I said.

'Whereas in my case,' he continued, 'she happened to be in that little cottage in Burcombe. Right there. I've lain awake these nights thinking how incredible it is that she wasn't born in Mongolia or Siberia or Polynesia or something. I mean, it's extraordinary, when you come to think of it. In fact, it disturbs me, slightly, to think of it. To think of how we might never have met, to think of the years, the long, *hard* years, Dummie, that I could have spent scouring the planet in search of her. And yet there she was. And there *I* was. And the circle was complete, and the search was at an end.'

★

Until that night I'd confined my self-abuse to public toilet cubicles, surrounded by shitswipes, pricked by thoughts of hidden vice officers or state-of-the-art surveillance, frequently deflated by the walls' dyslexic advertisements: 'Tall 10″ cock luv to spunk in yor moth', 'Want arse licked out? Ring Bernie – he's good!' But I managed. Stood with shut eyes and plugged nostrils, calves and quads quivering, lips tight together or drawn in gargoylish glee, until the deed was done. After which, masochistically, for guilt, many deep inhalations. *Yes, boy, suck it in, for this is the smell of yourself, these authors your brothers, this filth your own.* Then a decoy toilet flush and a quick wash-and-brush-up before re-entry into public life. Let shit be the ruse, then, if it was my element: I told Pen I was going for one, when I woke him getting out of my sleeping bag late that night.

'At night?' he said, groggily. 'That's disgusting. That's *wrong.*'

It required some effort, picking in the dark through grabbing undergrowth and snapping twigs, not to surrender to fear. *Presences* thronged the unmoonlit hollows. Nonetheless I crept on, until thirty paces or so saw me established, supine, between the half-exposed knuckles of a giant and gossiping oak.

The surrender was exquisite. Every penny of virtue carefully collected in the cottage at dawn – cleaning, tidying, step by step discovering the secret wealth of *abstinence* – squandered now.

That morning at Nancy and Jill's a handful of ordinary things – the slight hangover, the sunlit rooms, the post-coital sleepers upstairs, the soul-imprint left by my little act of selflessness in letting Pen have Jill – had constellated to form a thing of holiness and great beauty. I had been scoured and elevated by it. Virtue worked by revealing these sacred artefacts.

Now, something else worked. The thing that demanded their defilement. It worked with urgency and insistence. Had *been* working ever since that morning. Ever since I could remember.

Therefore I put Nancy on her knees and myself in cahoots with Jill. The predictable machinations: beatings, burnings, lacerations, floggings, degradation, violation upon violation, each cruelty sounding new depths of pleasure, each act confirming the Devil's hint that this way Divine wisdom lay, each new assault suggesting it would finally be enough to reveal his truth once and for all. But falling just short, always just short. There was some essence or extremity the details couldn't quite discover. The closest I came to it was in letting the camera vacillate between Nancy's look and Jill's, Nancy's (between gagged screams) tear-streaked, pleading for the recognition of *all the love and friendship* the two of them had shared, Jill's, flushed, meeting it, steadily, granting the recognition – *Yes, that's right, we have* – then raising her eyebrows as with curiosity before the next cigarette burn, or lash, or punch, or kick. The elusive essence was here, in the victim's appeal to love, in hatred's recognition and transcendence of it. I love you. I know. I *love* you. I know. *I love you . . .*

I washed my hands in the river, now with disgust as the aegis against fear. Dawdled back, in fact, in contempt of whatever the ether might hold. The forces of darkness could surely have no quarrel with one of their own.

Kelp was awake when I got back to camp, sitting on a moonlit stone by the river, smoking, drinking Lamb's from his tin mug.

His response to my greeting sounded choked.

'Kelp?'

'That was some dump, Dummie. I hope you buried it, like a dog.'

The longer utterance gave it away. He was – or had been, until seconds ago – crying.

For a moment I sat in silence, numbed. I'd never seen him upset, never imagined it possible. It was wrong; an aesthetic crime. I froze, awkward. Then the thought that he had, at last, seen me for what I was. A thrill that I meant enough to him for the knowledge to do this. Then fear of losing him. Then uncertainty – and, in the seconds that passed with him dragging his sleeve across his nose and sniffing and laughing, and struggling to swallow rum and keep the roll-up alight, the conviction that it was none of it anything to do with me. Relief and deflation. A glimpse of it, the liberation of being exposed; now gone. I remained alone with myself.

'It's okay to laugh, Dum,' he said.

'What's the matter?'

He shook his head. Took another swig. Needed a moment. I took out my own tobacco and papers and began rolling a cigarette for myself. In the river-freshened night, the innocent smell of tobacco and apple gave me a specific dose of misery. Giggling Jill polluting me, directing my come onto Nancy's open wounds. Now Kelp with tear-silvered face, shared rum and the moon like a petal of honesty.

'Bad dream,' Kelp said, not looking at me, but over towards the river. 'My mum. Dead.'

'Christ.'

'Textbook stuff,' he said. 'Too late to say all the things. Woke myself up blubbing.'

'Give us a light,' I said.

The Zippo's clack and rasp sustained us, gave him the last moments required for recovery. We smoked for a short while in silence, passing the rum back and forth. There had been a moment when I could have put my arm round him. Should have put my arm round him. Only a handful of such moments are available; I had squandered this one too. I felt it go, a precise subtraction.

'She's funny, you know,' Kelp said.

'Your ma?'

'Funny ha-ha, I mean. She can make me piss myself, sometimes. And brainy. You think I'm brainy. It's nothing to the brain on her.'

'I think she's cool,' I said. 'Very cool. You know that.'

He nodded, as if I'd asked for his agreement. Fidgeted, picked up a stone and tossed it into the river, which received it with a *choink*.

'I always . . .'

'What?'

'I never thought there would be anything I could do,' he said.

'Anything you could do?'

'I never thought anything I could do would help, would be any use to her.'

Horror again: new tears suddenly welled and fell. Me rigid with shock a second time. His laughing half crying or crying half laughing. 'Oh Christ. Fuck. Sorry. Sorry Dummie. Disgusting, I know.'

At the centre of my paralysis the thing I knew I should say: *She knows you love her. That helps her, doesn't it?* Too pinned to spit it out. Nancy's face pleading for the recognition of love. Jill and I recognizing it; our warm arms lifting their weapons.

He wiped his nose on his sleeve, got himself under control again. Relighted his roll-up. 'Sorry, Dum,' he said again. 'That fucking dream.'

'It's okay,' I said. 'Don't . . . It's fine. It's fine.'

A pause. Pen's snoring, the water moving past softly, the odd ruffle and frill.

He looked up at me. Smiled. Looked away again. 'It's all right,' he said. 'I know you think I'm fucked in the head.'

'Don't be a *hole*.'

'You don't know how these things work.'

'What things?'

'Curses.'

'What do you mean?'

'It'll . . . They're liftable, curses.' He laughed, hearing himself.

'You think it'll lift the curse?' I said. 'If we . . . If this turns out to be . . .'

He shook his head, not in denial, just in despair of being able to explain. 'I know you think it's bollocks,' he said.

'Of course I don't.'

'I don't blame you. Half the time I think it's bollocks myself. Except I know it isn't. Or it is, and I'm fucked in the head.'

I inhaled smoke, deeply, without a scrap of respiratory resistance. A cricket nearby chirruped. Kelp stubbed out his cigarette and flicked it towards the water. His question, when it came, startled me.

'What's wrong with you, Dummie?'

A long pause, me unable to look at him. I picked and *choinked* a succession of small stones of my own, felt or imagined I felt the force of him pressing on me, wanting to know. Him not sure what it was he wanted to know. I dragged, heavily, threw a much larger stone: *Chooonk* – too loud and vulgar, a breach of the moment's etiquette. I was close to telling him. I could feel the shape of liberation into which, telling him, I would move. If we had looked at each other then, I'm convinced I would have been visible, immediately, clairvoyantly, the maggoty core no less than the starlit surface.

We did look at each other, eventually, after the speechless moments had piled up; whereupon I wondered – his expression of barely veiled intensity – if he was going to make a pass at me. I ask myself, these days (these days of Holly and Manhattan and having decided not to do the Devil's dirty work), whether that wasn't a moment from which – the stunned embrace, the appalled and reinventing kiss – from which a wholly different future might have flowed. I ask myself whether that wasn't the last time when a choice of mine could have changed everything. I ask myself what might have happened had the possibilities swarming between us just then been left uninterrupted.

But they were interrupted.

Penguin sat up in his sleep, his head, in its bobless bob-hat, silhouetted. 'The goat of the committee,' he said; which woke him from whatever dream to the discovery that he was alone in the dark. All alone. In the dark. 'Dum?' he said, quietly. 'Kelp?' Then he sat very still in silence.

Kelp kicked my foot, gently.

'Ready?' he whispered.

'Ready,' I said.

'You're not listening to me again,' Pen said, a week later. (A week? I don't know. Days. Something. The road's relationship to time was febrile.)

'What?'

'I *said*,' he said, 'how come it's always Fauntleroy who gets a lift first and me and you who are hanging around in the fucking rain?'

'I don't know, do I?'

'Well, I'll tell you: It's fat old spuds who think he's gay.'

One of Pen's pet theories.

'They pick him up because he looks like a fairy. They think he's going to toss them off in the slow lane – which he probably does.'

'Probably.'

'Yeah. Well, it's getting on my nerves. You look a total twat in that, by the way.'

My yellow kagoul. Rich, from him in his orange one, his dad's, two sizes too big, which, with hood toggles pulled tight, made his head look abnormally small.

'I said it's getting on my nerves, Dummie.'

'I heard you.'

'I mean, how long are we supposed to keep at it?'

'Who knows? Ask him.'

'Load of bollocks anyway.'

We didn't like talking about it.

'If we go back via Nancy and Jill's,' I said, 'I'm going to seduce Jill away from you.'

He had been bent over his rucksack, rootling for tobacco (or chocolate, or Lamb's Navy) but when the words got through to him he stopped, straightened, and turned to me with closed eyes, raised eyebrows, open mouth and denunciatory finger. Something ornately obscene, I'm sure, had we not been interrupted.

A white Audi travelling at about eighty miles an hour roared towards us, slammed its brakes on, locked its wheels, skidded twenty or thirty yards past us, spun a complete volte-face, accelerated back towards us on the wrong side of the road, slammed its brakes on a second time, locked and volte-faced again, stopped for a moment, then snarled into our layby.

Pen and I stood with our mouths open and the rain falling into our faces, each looking (I now imagine) as if surprised by a lubricated penetration. In the moment before the passenger door swung open I saw that the car had been knocked about. One broad, dark scrape ran the entire length of the wing nearest us; a wheel missed its hub cap; the rear side-window glass was fractured; dozens of dents flecked the body. A new car, but abused. When the passenger door flew open, a skeletally thin fortyish woman with dyed blond hair fell out onto the gravel, laughing hysterically. She got up. The unseen driver gunned the engine. A fresh wheeze of laughter. Staggering, she opened the back door. The unseen driver said: 'Get 'em in quick if they're comin', Ange, for fuck's sake.'

'Come on come on come on come on come on come on,' Ange said, wildly beckoning with ringed fingers, grin and stiletto wobble. 'Come on come on come on come on.'

So Pen and I got in, without a word. We slid into the back with the obedience of package tourists. Packs on laps, faces delicately smiling with dread, both in full knowledge of what a terrible idea getting in had been. Door-slam, engine-growl, then the spun gravel and unassimilable lurch, and Pen's small sounds of psychic haemorrhage.

'Don't worry about the car,' Ange said, lighting a joint with a malachite and gold desk lighter, her roomy smile revealing equine teeth the colour of Scrabble tiles. 'The car's a friend's of ourziz.'

'Are *fink* you'll find,' the driver said, reasonably, 'that the car's *nicked*, as a matter of fact.'

Pen and I looked at each other. 'This was a mistake,' he said.

'Might wanna think about slowin' down a bit, babes,' Ange suggested, as we merged with three lanes. 'Guests an' all.'

Sandalwood-aftershaved Tony eased off the gas, dragging

us down to what was for him a laborious crawl of a hundred and five. I wondered, looking out, whether our hosts weren't known on the road, since many of its other users seemed to *get out of the way* the moment we hove into view. It was as if an invisible (and presumably ironic) police escort preceded us.

'Beg pardon,' Tony said, exhaling jointsmoke. Then with a glance at us in the rear-view: 'Ange does the etiquette, I do the driving.' He was small and compact, round-faced, with a close-fitting 1974 footballer haircut and nicotined finger-tips. The open white shirt revealed girlish bubs and a drum-tight paunch.

The joint came back to us via Ange, whose hands were veiny and deeply tanned, with nails painted milk-of-magnesia white. Her eyes – sparkling lilac in a pile-up of mascara and lash – were inconstant, sometimes seeing you, sometimes dimensionally elsewhere.

'Sixteen years,' Tony said, of their partnership, two joints and a whisk of miles later. 'Bin like this from the word go. I seen 'er in this place in Camden an I juss knew. You juss fuckin *know*, you see?'

'Yes,' Pen said. 'Yes, *exactly*.'

'We went for an Italian in this right snotty place,' Ange said, Tony squeezing her narrow thigh in affirmation. 'Shit-faced by this point, mind you.'

'Plastered,' Tony agreed.

'An I says to Tone, "You up for a runner?" Coz I knew 'e was. I juss knew. An you grinned at me, didn't you, babes?'

'Yeah.'

'An we fuckin *legged it*. Laughing? Christ.'

'You recognized it in each other,' Pen said, leaning forward, gripping their seat backs. 'It was like you were joined together in a previous existence and you'd spent your lives searching for each other.'

'Right,' Tony said. '*Right*. That's exactly right. Bonnie and Clyde, et cetera.'

'Romeo and Juliet,' Pen said, with dilated pupils and a veneer of perspiration. 'Tristram and whatsername. Insult.'

'Iseult,' I said.

'Whatever,' Pen said. 'The point is, when you know it's each other . . . When you, each of you . . . There's each *other*, isn't there?'

'You've said something, there,' Tony said, nodding, as we barely missed the giant wheel of an articulated lorry in the middle lane. 'You've fuckin *said* something, there.'

They were only going as far as Tintagel (allegedly King Arthur's birthplace, Kelp would have informed Pen), which by the time they dropped us there – stoned, traumatized – we regarded as a blessing in not much of a disguise. Pen got another lift within ten minutes from a bohemian family in a Citroën. They would have taken me, too, had I not minded sitting on someone's lap. Queasy, disorientated, I was happy to let them go.

Profligacy, I thought, three hours later, when a handful of scrappy local lifts had taken me a measly twenty miles. Complacency. *Hubris*. I'd been deposited in a hitchhikers' black hole, a minor road T-junction of such undriven-by proportions that I wouldn't have been surprised to come across the remains of previous travellers, the bones of their still outstretched thumbs long since picked clean. Worse, the dope had given me sporadic gut-rot, crippling when it had me in its grip. I swallowed the last mouthful of water from my bottle, then picked the lane that headed approximately south.

Half an hour and three explosive bowel movements later (having thanked God for seclusion – and dock leaves, in the absence of toilet paper) I sat down in the shadows cast by a

160

row of silver birches which overhung the lane. Opposite me a chalky path led through rough grass and brilliant gorse twenty yards to a small church of dark stone. A complete anomaly in the landscape. Four worn steps up to a gothically arched doorway, double doors, open. Thirty or so mossed headstones toothed the land to the left of the building. No flowers. No new graves. These dead were long dead.

My head throbbed and my guts squirmed, though I knew I had nothing left to void. The sun ringed my cranium like a hot crown. I stood up, head thumping, and took a few steps towards the church. Sunlight blazed on the white path. When I looked back to the trees, I saw the magpies.

The first not five feet away, waddling up and down the lane. Two more under the nearest of the gorse bushes. A fourth, fifth and sixth with sable and ermine very distinct against the path's chalk. All six brilliant in the sunshine.

One for sorrow, two for joy, three for a girl and four for a boy, five for silver, six for gold . . .

No. That was wrong. That was a modern version of something older. That was, in fact, the lyrical half of the theme to the children's television programme *Magpie*, featuring presenter Jenny Hanley, of husky voice, high cheekbones, long eyelashes, and straight fall of centre-parted blond hair. She'd been one of young Dominic Hood's regulars, usually torturing some of the pigtailed Girl Guides or rubbery gymnasts who not infrequently appeared on the show. *Five for silver, six for gold, seven for a secret never to be told . . .*

With creaking wings a seventh magpie alighted on the corner of the tower. I took two steps forward and collapsed onto my knees.

Blood twittered in my ears. I thought: If this was my father, he'd ditch the rucksack and try to get to his feet. So

I ditched the rucksack and got wobblingly to my feet. Bronchioles sizzled. Curious now, I lifted my right hand, palm down, level with my face. Not just a tremble, but occasional wild jerks as if to ward off flies. Extraordinary. I took three more paces towards the stone steps. Each one partly diffused the dot-swarm. But then an eighth magpie joined its fellow on the tower, from whence the two flap-flapped in ungainly unison down to the headstones' beds of shadow. Down on one knee I went again.

'Fucking hell,' I said, standing, more as a test of my ability to speak than as an expression of discomfort. But, having said it, found that I'd crossed the remaining distance to the steps. Now when I looked up I could see past the open door to the cool-promising stone of the vestibule and the wet lip of the font. *That* would be nice to dip into – my whole head, preferably. If I could just force myself up . . . these . . .

On the top step I turned and looked back. There, in the middle of the crooked white path was my abandoned rucksack, its orange and blue nylon bestirred to brilliance in the sun. A ninth magpie, larger than all the rest, came in a low swoop from the lane's birches, settled on it for a moment, then sprang down to the grass and commenced walking around erratically, like a despot delivering a tirade.

A caress of nausea as I closed and opened my eyes, held off by flickering images of my father's face, laughing, Pen and Kelp sitting with their backs to a tree, Julia white-bathrobed and towel-turbaned, sitting with ankles crossed, painting her fingernails – then receding, allowing me to stand upright, turn and walk into the salving shadow of the church.

Deserted. Pale walls and dark floor of icy granite. One stained-glass window behind the altar, half a dozen others unstained and latticed flanking the nave. An iron-grilled centre aisle with eight pews on each side. Butter-coloured candles of mighty girth burned in transept and apse. The tabernacle stood to the right of the altar, loosely hooded in gold velvet, a spartan Christ in painted wood gorily crucified above it.

I sat down in the nearest pew, head still a thing of shifting neural bergs and sluggish blood but relieved, at least, of its dot-swarm. Nothing of the recent minutes (hours, millennia, whatever they had been) was clear. Why had I left my rucksack behind? Hard to imagine returning to it, walking out, descending the steps, crossing the daisied and buttercupped grass, the magpies. Hard to imagine getting a lift, making conversation, drinking tea, reuniting with Penguin and Kelp . . .

One Hundred Hymns and Carols. Each pew had a slew of dog-eared copies, plus a scatter of CAFOD donation envelopes and the parish newsletter, called, sensibly enough, *St Benedict's Newsletter*, one of which I took in palsied hands and began to read. Predictably, obituaries and births, progress on the tower's renovation, CAFOD bring-and-buy at Mrs Derrick's on Tuesday afternoon, Father Gorman still in the chemo unit at Bodmin, your prayers requested etc. . . . Confession times . . .

The church very still now. Belatedly, I realized that God was here. Had been from the moment I crossed the threshold and fingertipped the font. Now here I was, distinct and visible, alive to the burning and particular mass of my sins under His eye. A shudder and a feeling of fracture in my chest.

The design – God's Plan – had chosen this moment to reassert itself.

I looked down at the last, poorly photocopied page of

the newsletter. Wherein (God sitting back to light a cigarette for the indulgent re-read, the slow knuckle-crack, the smile) all the details of the day cohered at last, just as they had six years ago when I sat in meditation on Burke's manslaughtered body speaking its blood bubble onto the stone.

A VISITOR FROM ABROAD, the headline read. The picture showed two priests shaking hands. One was thirtyish, fair-haired and partridge plump, the other was so tall that I could see the photographer's struggle to get the head in the frame without losing the handshake. Tall and old surely beyond his years, his smile was lips-together and sensually curled; above the animal cheekbones the light eyes faced down the flash. The Beckett thatch was brilliant white, the tanned face almost black. Even in monochrome Malone carried the salt whiff and sand dazzle of his journeys.

I stopped snivelling. My head cleared. Somewhere behind the altar a door opened and closed. No one appeared.

It was hello and *bon voyage* to Father Ignatius Malone last month, when he visited us here at St Benedict's. Recently in Rome, Father Malone was calling on old friends in the Parish before flying to India to renew his work among the poor and the sick. He will be visiting Mother Theresa in Calcutta with, we are told, a communication from His Holiness Pope John Paul II, then travel south to Madras for a stay of indefinite duration. Tea and cakes were provided by Mrs Cole.

Navel tingling, I looked up. A liver-spotted woman in her late sixties with a croissant of lacquered white hair and slack jowls stood in front of the altar with a yellow duster in one hand and a can of Mr Sheen furniture polish in the other.

She looked terrified, but determined on politeness. When I stood up, she took a step backwards.

'Can I help you?' she said. Not Cornish. Home counties.

I held up the newsletter. 'Father Ignatius Malone,' I said.

'Who?'

'The priest, the exorcist who was here.'

Duster and Mr Sheen gripped martially now. They might be her only weapons, but by God she was willing to use them. 'What d'you want?' she said.

It was very difficult to be orderly. I stepped out from the pew and took a couple of paces towards her, brandishing the newsletter. She backed up against the altar, cleaning accoutrements at the ready. I stopped.

'Sorry,' I said. 'I don't mean to alarm you.'

'What is it you *want*, dear?' she said, straightening, slightly ashamed of herself.

'I was wondering,' I said. 'In the newsletter here it says that Father Malone came to see you last month. Do you remember at all?'

'Of course I remember,' she said, haughtily, strabismus quivering at the implied Alzheimer's. 'Of course I remember. I made the *cakes*.'

From which emphasis, evidently, her belief that the entire visit would have been impossible or pointless without them.

'Yes, the cakes,' I said. 'You'd be Mrs Cole, then?'

'Yes.'

'I see.'

I saw what? What was it I wanted? she had quite properly asked. What was there to want? He had been here. He had gone. That was all.

'He's gone to India, then,' I said.

'That's right, dear, yes. Do you know him?'

We looked at each other, me with an emptily beatified

face, her with a suspicious one. Cautiously, with the lightest application of digital pressure, she gave the altar rail a *psssst* of Mr Sheen and began to rub it with the duster. If I was dangerous, perhaps the motion of slow polishing would calm me down.

'What?' I asked.

'Did you know Father Malone?'

Yes, Mrs Cole, I did. Six years ago I manslaughtered one of my peers and the good father saw fit to raise him from the dead. You wouldn't think, to look at me, would you, that . . .

'Was anyone here troubled with . . .?'

Pssst. 'With what?'

'With . . .' I couldn't say it. Instead stood mesmerized by the loose skin of her forearm as she worked rhythmically at the fingerprints.

'With what, dear?'

'Nothing. Nothing. It doesn't matter.'

'You all right, are you?'

'Yes, I'm all right.'

For a moment we stood thus, me with outstretched newsletter, her languidly polishing. He had been here. He had gone.

'Do you have trouble with magpies?' I asked. Imbecilic. I followed quickly with 'What I mean is: are there unusually large numbers of magpies around here at this time of year?'

Fortunately, she was sufficiently mad not to regard this as a non sequitur. 'Oh no,' she said. 'No more than anywhere else, I expect. Trouble we've got is with ants.'

'Ants?'

'Blighters are everywhere. I can't think where they're coming from. They ruined Father Gorman's seed cake.'

'Father Gorman on chemotherapy,' I said. 'Bodmin Hospital.'

'Yes, poor chap. I made one to send up with Mrs Derrick, you see. Only left it in the vestry kitchen one night. In the morning they were all over it.'

'That's a shame,' I said.

'Course, I'll make him another one,' Mrs Cole said, then *psssst, psst*, 'but you know, I mean, he's not getting any better.'

'Yes,' I said. 'I see.'

'You could leave me a message for Father *Duffy*, if you like. *He's* still here.'

But I had turned away. My head had been relieved of its burning diadem, my gut disencumbered of its wind bolus. I wasn't coming down with anything. It was just God, working, as per repute, in mysterious ways.

'I hope Father Gorman gets better,' I said, from the door.

'We can always pray for him,' Mrs Cole said, then stopped rubbing for a moment and straightened, a candle's lozenge of flame held in one of her lenses. 'It's so easy to forget the power of prayer,' she said.

Outside, the sun was still shining and the magpies were still there, in a semi-circle round my rucksack. Not a cloud, now, in the high blue sky. I looked at the birds. They looked at me. Something still here, certainly, a quietly blazing presence to which my skin alerted me the moment I crossed the threshold.

Then, as if in response to a subsonic signal, all nine magpies took flight. In a moment, they were gone. Only my dazzling rucksack remained, alone on the path. The air cleared. The last vestiges of nausea faded.

I collected my pack and walked back towards the lane. When, five minutes later, the VW van pulled up, precisely at the level of my outstretched thumb, I took it with nonchalance, the last cheeky curlicue of an already baroque design. The door slid open with a soft roar.

'Praise be to Jesus,' Jake said, grinning.

'And Blessed is the Holy Beard,' Jim said. 'The wandering lamb that was lost is reunited with the shepherd, because verily is the spirit . . . because the flock is mightier than the . . .'

'You look like shit,' Jake said. 'Where's the other two?'

'Fuck knows,' I said, climbing in. 'You got anything to drink?'

St Ives was hot, sunny, and infested with summer tourists. The streets smelled of beer, sun-tan lotion, fish and chips, ice-cream, traffic and the sea. Braless mums from Birmingham with wrecked hair and varicose veins held hands with pink-shouldered dads in paunch-hugging vests. Normally unseen bodily bits were bare to the generous weather: toes, backs, midriffs, knees – the pathos of the Great British Body's reckless heliolatry. Children rode the peeling shoulders like midget mahouts with plastic spades for goads, their mouths ice-lolly-dyed betel or woad. Groups, *gangs* in fact, of blokeish men, pendulous with downed pints, swaggered in too-tight shorts and criminally obvious perms, each with clutched lighter and fags, each with sun-surprised face and pickled eyes.

Kelp and Penguin were on the beach, Pen, Buddha-like, facing the sea's late-afternoon glare, Kelp curled up next to him with Pen's denim jacket draped over his shoulders, shivering.

'Oh, it's you bummers, is it?' Pen said, seeing who I had in tow. 'By the holy chimp of Manchester.'

I collapsed to the sand. It had been a garrulous journey

with Jim and Jake. (Jake had driven and stayed sober. Jim and I had drunk the best part of a bottle of Scotch between us. 'People think we're *queer*,' Jim confided in a bellowed drawl, meaning him and Jake. 'People think we're *homosexual*.'

'Easy there, brother,' Jake said, loudly, to the windscreen.

'Not that there's anything wrong with that,' Jim said. 'Apart from the sin of sodomy, unfortunately—'

'Let he who is without sin,' Jake interrupted. 'Let he who is without sin.'

'But we're just . . .' Jim's face had taken on a curious expression of pain and happiness. 'We're just *friends*, for Christ's sake.'

'Friends in Christ,' Jake said, swerving for something.

'I mean, Jake's always . . . Jake's always *been* there for me, haven't you, Jake?'

'I have, Jim.'

'Fucking everyone thinks . . . Fucking no one really appreciates the importance of fucking *friendship*, these days.'

'Friendship,' Jake said, chin up, hands at a quarter-to-three on the wheel, 'is bigger than love.' Then, after a pause, 'Which is why Jesus most definitely did *not*, probably, fuck Mary Magdalene. Or any of the apostles, for that matter.'

After which, all three of us had observed a few minutes of respectful silence.)

'What happened to Jenny Hanley from *Magpie*?' I asked the golden granules under my nose. 'She was gorgeous.'

'He has tasted of the fruits of the vine,' Jake said. 'Whereas I myself am in full command of my faculties, having let the cup pass from my lips.'

Kelp struggled into a sitting position. 'Christ, I feel fucked,' he said.

'Fauntleroy's got the shivers,' Pen said.

'I need a drink,' Kelp said.

He didn't look too bad. Admittedly his hair had darkened with dirt and grease, and the side of his face had sand stuck to it, but the green eyes were still alight.

'I've got to ask you about magpies,' I said.

'Yeah, yeah,' Pen said. 'Jenny Hanley. She's probably a cleaning lady somewhere. With big dewlappy arms.'

'No, no, *birds*. There's a rhyme—*oof*.' Lying down had been a mistake, the manoeuvre tipping whatever Scotch was in me directly into my cranium for a gloves-off assault on my brain. 'Oh dear,' I said.

Jake, sober and akimbo with the light behind him, said, 'Since we are all here gathered present . . . That is to say, since the Lord has seen fit to reunite the brethren . . .'

'Amen, Jacob,' Jim said.

'Let the brethren drink in celebration. Jim has recently been blessed with a giro, and I know, from long fellowship, that he'd be honoured to—'

'Actually, Jake—'

'To celebrate this renewed fellowship *in* Christ.'

'I don't think I can drink any more,' I said. A large and bellicose seagull with a red spot on its beak was walking back and forth across my line of vision. I recalled an animal behaviour titbit: the red spot was a target for seagull young to peck at when hungry. It stimulated regurgitation in the adult. Parent bird spewed, offspring ate the vomitus. I wished, with tearful sincerity, that I hadn't been able to remember that. Kelp's teeth chattered – a burst of machine-gun fire – then stopped.

Pen reached down and placed his hand on my head in benediction. 'You can and you must, my son,' he said.

We ended up, after much weaving and staggering through St Ives's labyrinthine streets and cobbled alleys, in an old, low-ceilinged pub called the Brig (nautical accoutrements, jukebox, fruit machine), where, since it was still early, we managed to find a booth to ourselves.

Under duress, Jim got a round in, visibly pained. When he returned to our booth with the tray (Scotch for me, brandy for Kelp, lager tops for the rest) he had acquired a second tic to go with the behind-the-ear hair-tuck, an eye-twitch and slight head-jerk. 'Now don't start with that,' Jake said, as Jim squeezed in alongside me. 'It is easier for a camel to pass through, et cetera, eh? Et cetera, eh?'

'Fuck off,' Jim said, quietly, then began rolling a cigarette

The pub filled up. A young couple with nothing to say to each other sat nearby, drinking round after speechless round, her biting her nails, him smoking, alert and businesslike, both yielding, incrementally, to their lives having taken this shape. A few fisherman types enjoyed a vociferous ecstasy of *oooo-aaarr*ing at the bar, encouraged by the landlord and his permed wife, two old codgers played dominoes at a corner table; and, much to my unease, a group of white-skulled skinheads stood around the jukebox, looking bored. One with tartan jeans, one with a wee swastika on the back of his left hand, one with lively blue eyes and one (ah, more rococo flourishes in the shameless design) thick-limbed with a low-browed look of distant familiarity.

Pen had noticed them, too.

'I think perhaps *staring* at them isn't the prudent choice, Pen,' Kelp said. He had just returned from the gents. On his way back to our booth one of the skins (the familiar one; me suffering the awkward internal manoeuvres that would take me to recognition) had made an exaggerated pretence of being startled by him, and the group had laughed, wealthily. 'I think maybe *not* staring at them might be the golden move, if you see what I mean.'

'There's only four of them,' Pen said, looking down at the table top. 'There's *five* of us.'

The three of us looked at Jim and Jake. The two of them looked at us, then at each other, then back at us. At the end of which mute exchange all relevant information was in.

The skins were very obviously keeping an eye on us now.

'Let's leave,' Pen said.

'Leaving will provoke them,' Kelp said — then another rattle from the machine-gun teeth. 'So will staying.'

'Brothers, brothers, chill, *chill*,' Jake said, as if with inbuilt echo. 'The Lord watches over His flock e'en as the shepherd of the fields.'

'I can't have any violence, Jake, you know that,' Jim said. 'My kidneys . . .'

'Come on, Dummie,' Kelp said. 'Let's get a round in.'

'Isn't that going to draw attention to us?'

'We just carry on as normal,' Kelp said, getting shakily to his feet. His face was booze-bright and (brandy's curative powers notwithstanding) fever-flushed. Certainly he was drunk. As was I, as well as being superconscious of those bits of my body that would start clocking up pain if the skins decided on assault: head; elbows; stomach; knees. The booth had at least been a kind of shelter. Now we were out in the open with our backs to them.

'You eighteen?' the landlady demanded in her budgie voice.

'Yes, we are,' Kelp said. 'Actually, I'm twenty tomorrow, as it turns out.'

She tightened the corners of her mouth. 'Sure you're not *forty* tomorrow?' she said. 'We get raided, you two are going to be in ott bleddy wodder. Juss so's you know. Ott *bleddy* wodder, got it?'

Suddenly a loud burst of laughter from the skins, just as

the song on the jukebox (Carly Simon's 'Nobody Does It Better') ended.

'Say something,' Kelp said. 'Make conversation with me.'

Which request exposed a howling conversational cavity. In desperation: 'Did your mum and dad really stay here on their honeymoon?'

The next song started. Bachman-Turner Overdrive, 'You Ain't Seen Nothin Yet.'

'Not here,' Kelp said. 'Place called Zennor about five miles away. We're booked in for tomorrow night.'

Both of us were staring at the landlady's pulling action as if hard enough staring would reveal what was going on behind us. It took me a moment to take in what he'd just said.

'Booked in?' I said, finally managing to look at him (he remained in wide-eyed profile, one smoke-coloured vein up in his temple). 'What are you talking about?'

He was flushed now. His hair – that luciferous mop – was full of static. Single strands stood out, moving gently in the pub's fug.

'Actually,' he said, 'I think I'd better sit down. I don't feel too grand. Can you manage?' He pushed himself away from the bar and wove unsteadily back to our booth. Wolf-whistles and exaggerated limp wrists from the skins. You ain't seen nothin yet. B-b-b-*baby* you ain't seen nothin yet . . .

A very heavy hand on my shoulder.

'Dominic.'

I turned, powerfully encouraged by the hand, which had transferred its grip from my shoulder to the back of my neck, and took a look at Callum Burke, now, at sixteen, a fully grown man.

The mind's a curse, the senses a stupid conspiracy. What one wants is to not take it in. What one gets is saturation with detail. He was, for a start, a good head taller than me. Hormones had delivered to chest, shanks, shoulders, wrists; the puppy-fat had turned to dumb (but effective) bulk; the jaw had lengthened and the left brow now showed a silver cedilla-shaped scar. New smell, too, cigarette smoke and an abrasive aftershave, boot polish, denim – an overall effect of blue collar masculinity.

'Dominic fucking Hood,' he said, with a generous grin and a neck-squeeze. 'Fucking amazing. Fucking *amazing*.'

One of his fellows approached, Burke's height, but leaner, with a musket-ball skull on which the hair, should it ever be allowed back, would be as blond as Kelp's. The information zones – eyes blue and alert with long eyelashes, mouth dexterous and sensual – informed without ambiguity.

Burke continued to squeeze and chortle and not quite look at me, but his companion met my eye glacially in order that I might see in his own the absence of any willingness to be reasoned with. Naturally he wanted me to try reasoning with him.

'Now, the thing is,' Burke said, leaning close, one speck of spittle entering my middle ear with a tickle, 'we've got a situation here, haven't we?' He let go of my neck and put his arm round my shoulders, giving me a for-he's-a-jolly-good-fellow shake, while I remained ocularly locked with his friend. 'A situation is what this is, roight?'

He moved aside and with a gentle master of ceremonies extension of the arm, introduced me to the other two skins across the room, one much older (perhaps in his late twenties), the other (with swastika tattoo) our own age, who smiled and lifted their pints in a cheers. My drinks and change stood waiting for me on the bar. Burke's hand returned to the back of my neck.

'Give my mates a smoile, now, Dominic,' he said. 'Go on,

give 'em a noice big one. That's it, go on. A noice . . .
big . . . There you go. That's it.'

My smile laboured, the grin of a sick man.

'Chroist, I bet you wish you'd chose another pub,' Burke
said, at first struggling with, then mastering his mirth. The
Irish and Cornish had bled and intermingled around those
rhotic rs. 'Still, do us both the whorled o good, spect.'

I didn't spill a drop on my way back to the booth.

'We can't unprovoke them,' Kelp said. 'They've got to be
met.'

'It's just me they want,' I said, heavily 'I know the one
with the fat head. I twatted him when we were kids, believe
it or not.'

A long silence of astonishment Then Kelp released a
sudden giddy bit of abruptly terminated laughter.

'You mean me and Jake could just get up and walk out of
here?' Jim said, unable to stop himself. All of us – even
Penguin – looked at him.

'Jim,' Jake said. 'That was an unworthy thought, brother.'

'No, no, I mean . . . What I meant was—'

'Don't be a fucking *coward*,' Jake said, with very precise
enunciation. 'Cowardice is like lying. You know that.
Ephesians, for fuck's sake: "Be strong in the Lord and in His
mighty power. Put on the full armour of God so that you
can . . ." something something . . . "for our struggle is not
against flesh and blood, but . . . but . . ."'

'"But against the rulers, the authorities, against the powers
of this dark world and against the spiritual forces of evil in
the heavenly realm,"' I completed. Thanks to Malone, the
only bit of scripture I knew by heart. Something else for
which Malone was to be given credit, along with the survival of Callum Burke.

'It's a certainty that we're going to get twatted,' Kelp said.

'Agreed? I mean that's *going* to happen. The only thing we've got to decide—'

'Is whether we *all* have to get twatted,' Jim said.

'Is what we can do, *given* that we're going to get twatted,' Kelp concluded.

'Oh, God,' Pen said. 'Please don't anyone listen to him.'

'It is a far, far better thing that I do now,' Kelp began, getting to his feet, but replaced the end of the quote with a bass and protracted belch. With dropped jaws and inert limbs we watched as he crossed to the fruit machine, bent and pulled out its plug. The oldest skin nudged Burke. Kelp went over to the jukebox. B–b–b–baby baby you ain't seen—

A *thunk* of amputated electricity. Heads turned in the sudden silence. The landlord leaned over the bar, owlish brows furrowed. The landlady, pulling a Guinness for one of the cable-knitted seadogs, craned to see what was going on. The rumble of conversation reduced to a murmur, a simmer, then whispering, then silence. Kelp strode into the centre of the room and raised his arms. His face was red and (I knew) piping hot. 'Ladies and gentlemen,' he said, with theatrical projection. 'Ladies and gentlemen of the Brig, honourable proprietors, mariners, friends. My companions and I find ourselves in a sticky situation. These gentlemen here' (indicating Burke & co) 'want to beat us up.'

'Shut–it, faggot,' the blue-eyed and fine-mouthed skinhead said, flatly.

'He's going to get us killed,' Pen whispered, not to me but to the indifferent universe. He was on his feet. So was I. So were Jim and Jake.

'The situation,' Kelp said, ignoring the command and panning his now silent audience, 'as I was just explaining to my friends here – two of whom are ministers of the Church, by the way – is very simple. Nothing will satisfy these rogues except that they give us a damned good hiding.'

'Shard-arp for God's sake,' an irritated voice called from a smoky corner. Two of the heavily made-up women snickered.

'Now look yur,' the landlord began.

'Landlord, *please*,' Kelp said, as if *particularly* disappointed in the landlord, of whom he'd had such high expectations. 'Please. This is a serious business.'

'Anythin in ere gets bleddy broke, you lot'll be sent the bill,' the landlord said.

'I'm callin the pleece,' the landlady said, but a beard and eyebrows scowl from her husband (hot micro, dodgy Scotch, iffy pasties) stopped her. At my side I'd felt Pen's euphoria at the mention of 'the pleece' surge and die. In tiny incre-ments I edged out from the booth. Pen followed, not out of loyalty or courage, but because he was holding on to the tail of my jacket and lacked the will to release it.

'We can't escape the violence because it's not about us,' Kelp said, face sweat-speckled, arms spread in a gesture of audience inclusion. 'It's about them. The rage – and make no mistake, it will *be* rage – is because they cannot escape themselves.' He turned his back on Burke and took a couple of paces away, as if with complete confidence that he wouldn't be touched. 'What they want is our fear. They want us to be *afraid*. They want to look into our eyes and see us hoping for *mercy*.'

The blue-eyed skinhead of the sensual mouth put his pint down and picked up by its neck a bottle of Pilsner from the table next to him. I knew what that meant: among other things, that they were ready. We, naturally, weren't ready, were by definition never ready.

'Out,' the landlord said. 'Come on. The lot of you. Outside. *Now*.'

'Bout that time, I'd say,' the oldest skin said. His head, hairless like his compadres', was a phrenologist's dream. Eyes the brown of old blood set in deep orbits, a lilac shaving shadow. I couldn't believe – the pub's air gridlocked with undischarged energy – that they hadn't touched us yet. Pen and I, like blind man and guide, had edged out into the centre of the room, well within range of the Pilsner's swing.

'But, sadly, my *dear* boys,' Kelp said, turning, showing empty palms (the '*dear* boys' might have been Wilde's, entering a homosexual brothel), 'it isn't going to be like that. Our fear is ours and ours alone to give.'

The Pilsner skin stepped closer. Kelp turned and pointed at him. 'So fuck you,' Kelp said; then to the two hanging back, 'and fuck you two,' then finally, bringing his perspiring face within inches of Burke's, 'and most especially, very *very* much fuck you, bubble head. You can all suck the cock of Satan and drink his black jiz.'

Someone at a nearby table said, 'Jesus *Chroiss.*'

One of the women hiccupped, once. Then Burke headbutted Kelp in the face.

On impact, Kelp's smile imploded. His head snapped back. A moment of stillness as he righted it (having not, to my astonishment, collapsed) in which his features struggled to rediscover their logic. Then blood hurried out of his nostrils, over his lips, down his chin and onto the carpet. He put his hand up to his mouth, frowning like a miffed toddler. Burke, having made his opening gambit, observed.

'I'll tell you what,' Kelp said to him. 'That really hurt.'

The bottle-wielder took a step towards me, drew back his arm, made the last adjustment to his weight and stance, then swung the bottle at my head.

For no reason that I could think of then (and none that I can think of now) the bottle didn't break. I crashed to my knees and fell forward under a weight. The weight was Penguin, who, having been either unwilling or unable to release his hold on my jacket, had staggered down feebly onto my back. A boot thudded into my ribs and I screamed. Pen rolled off me with a whimper. I wondered what was happening to Kelp, what sort of changes he was going through. Chairs scraped; the pub's punters were reacting, backing away from the unpleasant dramatic nucleus as from someone's sudden splatter of vomit. Then everything went strangely quiet, the thick silence of a room filled with silent people. I put my palms flush to the carpet, pushed, got my knees under me, then sat up.

Kelp was sitting on the floor with his back to the bar, his mouth and nose a mess of blood. He was scrutinizing something in his cupped hand. Ange, in wrinkled black cocktail dress and jet necklace, squatted next to him, also examining. Burke was laid out on the floor. Tony stood facing the Pilsner-wielding skin in what looked like a satirical Marquess of Queensberry boxing stance. The two of them regarded each other for a moment, then Tony knocked him out.

A straight right of unbelievable speed, accuracy and force. The skin's knees buckled and down he went, Minnelli eyelashes fluttering, then out cold. Tony turned to the two remaining. 'Anyone else?' he enquired politely.

The two remaining shook their heads.

'It's one of my incisors,' Kelp said.

'Nah,' Ange said. 'Thass wunna yer teef, love.'

God knows what put it into the heads of Richard and Stella (née Mitchell) Kelp to spend their honeymoon in Cornwall in winter. Perhaps Stella had seen something – typhoid on the Costa del Sol, terrorists in Morocco, earthquakes in Greece. Whatever the reason, it was to the Seaview Hotel,

Zennor, Cornwall, that they came in January 1965 ('Exactly nine months before I was born,' Kelp said, with raised index finger), astonished that Richard's Anglia had made it and with the simple agenda (no doubt) of keeping each other warm for a week of early nights and Church-sanctioned coupling.

A mile out of the village we stood in the road looking up at the hotel through a gap in the hedge where a gate used to be. The Seaview was a large, white-painted Edwardian house set in an acre of rough grass and wildflowers. (Beyond the house, fifty yards of bluebells, buttercups, daisies and dande-lions before the rickety fence and sheer drop into the sea.) Crows loped around the garden and idly spiralled the chim-neys. Seagull shadows flickered on and off the whitewash. Not a dilapidated place, but certainly weatherworn, wind-shaken, salt-scoured.

This was Pen's final concession. In snatches out of Kelp's earshot the two of us had carried on an argument about what should follow from the fight in the Brig. For Pen the conclusion was simple: he'd had enough of all this shit and was going home, prophecy or no.

'Just one more night,' I had said.

'I'm going home, Dummie. We're going to get ourselves killed. *He's* going to get us killed.'

'Come on, Pen, it wasn't his fault. It was *my* fucking fault, if it was anyone's fault. It's me Burke had it in for.' (How much thinking had I done about this since the pub? How keen was I to contemplate the distant effects of miraculous causes?) 'One more night,' I said.

'Bollocks to that.'

'Come on. What difference is one more night going to make?'

'Forget it.'

180

'You're being a cunt, Pen.'

'I'm not being a cunt, Dummie. You're being a cunt. A *stupid* cunt, in fact.'

'Look just do this one thing for him.'

'What one thing?'

'Just stay tomorrow night in this fucking hotel.'

'No way.'

'I can't believe you'd be so . . . such a fucking *tight*-arse. When you know . . . When you know . . .'

'Promise we'll go home immediately after.'

'I promise.'

'Swear to God?'

'I swear to Almighty God.'

'Okay. One more night, then that's it. I don't give a fuck.'

We had checked in (eyed suspiciously at reception) and been shown up to our room, which was west-facing on the third floor with a view of near-parodic drama: biblical cloud and shafts of light shot straight down into the sea, calling up greens, blues, purples, silvers; in the distance, an approaching mass of gun-coloured thunderheads. Pen, having found in a bedside table along with a Gideon Bible a *Dictionary of Birds in Britain*, was at the room's one sash window, trying his hand at ornithology.

'Where'd the money come from?' I asked Kelp.

'It was foreseen from the outset, Dummie,' Kelp said.

'Yes, but—'

'They're all Black-headed,' Pen said. '*Larus ridibundus*. Cracking name, though.'

Kelp lay on his back (on one of the room's two proper beds, the third being a camping cot which, though he didn't know it yet, we'd allotted to Penguin), with arms folded and ankles crossed. He was shivering again.

'It's a bit gross, if you ask me,' Pen said. 'I mean, the

actual room where your mum and dad actually—Ooo! *Larus fuscus*. Big fucker.'

Kelp, with chattering teeth, sat up and searched in his pack for rum. Calm – then furious rootling. 'Fuck it,' he said, coming up empty-handed. 'No medicaments. You two?'

'How do you know it was their room?' I asked him, having discovered, via Pen's rucksack and my own, that we had not a drop between the three of us.

Kelp, groaning, got under the covers. 'I just know,' he said.

'Or it could have been *Larus marinus*,' Pen said. 'Have we got any binoculars?'

Kelp rolled himself into a shivering ball. 'I feel like a fucking germ,' he said.

It wasn't a bad place, the Seaview Hotel, and might have been a positively good place in winter, when the guests were dirty-weekenders and ruminative geriatrics. As it was, couples with children occupied all the other rooms. Staff tripped over pushchairs, barked their shins on trikes, closed their eyes and concentrated on *not committing infanticide* when the brats screamed fit to splinter the skull.

A topless four-year-old with a large ribcage and dirt and ice-cream round his mouth confronted me and Pen at the bottom of the stairs.

'You don't live here,' he said, sticking his face out.

'Fuck off, you deformed little cunt,' Pen said.

Kelp was worse by mid-afternoon, but refused fuss beyond being allowed to remain in bed with all available blankets, one of which he wrapped round his head, Bedouin style. 'Got to sweat this fucker out,' he said. 'Show it who's boss.'

So we left him and went out along the cliffs. The thunderheads had come up. The sea, marbled with whitecaps was the colour of bad meat. Pen's *Larus ridibundus* sailed out, banked with dangling feet, then returned, screeching. A marker buoy *tang-tanged* all alone on the swell – a terrible existence for an object, we agreed.

'We should get an early start tomorrow,' Pen said.

It hadn't been discussed further, the business of whether Kelp and I were heading home with him the following day.

'He might not be well enough,' I said.

We walked the rest of the way to the headland in silence. *It's about you and Pen. Something's going to happen here.* Did Pen still believe it? Did I? Did even Kelp? And yet there had been Burke, the weight of design, the shameless architect's fingerprints. There was no denying the unease I'd felt since St Benedict's. The queasiness that came with seeing the pattern. I'd thought of the welter of ordinary things with which the three of us were rich: smiles and cigarettes and sips and the sound of each other's laughter – and still there came (via the reappearance of Burke) the insistence from the ether that the invisible ruled the visible, that there was, verily, magic in the air.

Eventually, with the rain now a mealy-mouthed drizzle, we stood looking down at the sea smashing itself on the cliffs' shins. Mesmerizing, the tilt and thud, the suck, crash and hiss, repeated endlessly. Either a giant, impenetrable purpose or a giant, meaningless habit.

For a while Pen stood staring down past his feet into the roiling water. Eventually, without saying anything, he turned and started back towards the bay.

Kelp's condition had worsened by the time we got back to the hotel.

'You don't look too fucking chipper there, Kelp,' Pen said, squatting down by the bed.

'Well, that might be because I don't feel t–t–t–too fucking chipper, Pen,' Kelp said.

Pen felt Kelp's forehead. 'Fucking hell,' he said. 'I could fry an egg on that.'

'Please don't,' Kelp said.

'I'll go and ask the landlady if she's got anything,' I said.

'A yeast infection,' Kelp said. 'I don't want any of that.'

'I mean Lemsip or something.'

'*Lemsip*? That's not going to help. I need *rum*. Or, in the absence of rum, Caroline Munroe.'

The landlady wasn't available, but a chambermaid gave me a thermometer.

'You don't know whose mouth that's been in,' Pen said. 'Better put it in his anus.'

'I'll put *you* in my anus,' Kelp said. 'What do you think of that?'

'It's probably what he wants,' I said. 'Open.'

Kelp's temperature was a hundred and one.

'How bad is that?' Pen asked.

'I don't know,' I said. 'Is that serious, Kelp?'

'Oh, yeah,' Kelp said. 'Good idea. Ask the patient.'

Pen, affecting weariness, turned back to his bird-watching. 'Look,' he said. 'You've got a *slight* temperature, I'd say. Nothing to be alarmed about. If you're going to be a granny about it me and Dummie'll rustle you up a Beecham's powder or whatever. It's your own fault, anyway, for getting pissed and butted last night.'

'Well,' Kelp said. 'I'm glad we've got that cleared up.'

Jim and Jake drove out to see us at around four o'clock. By then the rain had set in. It blew about in swathes over the sea. Clotted-cream teas were on offer at the Seaview; downstairs china was tinkling and chairs were being drawn up. The hotel's springer spaniel was thumping the carpet with its tail. Jim and Jake entered, wide-eyed, recking of marijuana.

'He's sick,' Pen explained, pointing to the room's invalid. We had taken Kelp's temperature again. It had risen to a hundred and two.

'We've got to give him *something*, for fuck's sake,' Pen said, when Kelp, still with blankets wrapped round his head, had begun to babble somewhat. 'Even if it *is* only rum.'

It was decided that Jim, Jake and I should drive into St Ives for medication.

'How come you get to go with them?' Pen wanted to know.

'Fine,' I said. 'You go. Give my regards to those skins if you run into them.'

'I'm not saying I *want* to go, Dummie. God, you're so *hasty.*'

I squatted down to examine Kelp's fiery face. He looked rotten. He was glazed with sweat. His eyes were bright, the orbits the same bad-beef colour as the sea.

'Listen,' I said. 'I'm going to get you some stuff, okay?'

He stared at me, smiling and shivering.

'Fucking hell,' Jim said, over my shoulder. 'He looks terrible.'

'Look, Kelp, I think we should get you a doctor,' I said.

Kelp's hot hand shot out from under the blankets and grabbed my wrist.

'What?' I said.

But he just shivered, and said, 'Vavavavavava.'

Pen, it was agreed, would track down the landlady and get the number of a local doctor. 'All doctors' secretaries are evil bitches,' I said. 'Don't let her tell you the doctor can't come out on call or any such shite. You tell her it's a sixteen-year-old boy and he's got a temperature of a hundred and four.'

'I thought you said it was a hundred and two?'

'Yeah, well, they don't know that, do they?' We were standing in the hotel's lobby. I could hear Jim and Jake struggling to get the Volkswagen started. On the fourth or fifth attempt, the engine caught. Heavy rain fell.

'Don't do anything stupid,' Pen said. 'And get some food, will you? I'm starving.'

I'm trying to remember why, exactly, I had that *Dictionary of Birds in Britain* with me in the van. I can only assume that Pen had put it down and that I had picked it up. Its cracked spine opened it where I was meant to look.

Originally a rural bird, the magpie (Lat. *Pica pica*) was wont to prefer mature or neglected pasture land, especially areas of thick hedges. A member of the crow family, this much-maligned bird, wrongly regarded as a pest, suffered serious population decline in the first half of the twentieth century, until a shift into urban areas (approx. 1940 onwards) took it out of the range of the farmer's gun. Adult sexes are marked alike, with pied plumage (head dark, flanks and belly white); a clutch of 5 to 8 bluish green eggs is laid any time from April onwards. Juveniles have short tails and remain under parental care until September. The superstitious tradition which sees the magpie as a bird of ill omen persists today, most commonly expressed in the saying, '*One for sorrow, two for joy*', though folklore specialists tell us that this is a truncation of a longer rhyme of Scottish origin.★ Defences against the solitary magpie's bad luck include making the sign of the cross, 'doffing' (lifting) one's cap or hat to the bird, or even spitting three times over the right shoulder.

> *One's for sorrow, two's for mirth,
> Three's a wedding, four's a birth,
> Five's a Christening, six a dearth,
> Seven's for Heaven, eight's for Hell
> And nine's the Devil his ane sel'.

In St Ives's Spar we pooled resources and bought tangerines, a French stick, a packet of jammy dodgers, a half of Lamb's Navy, and a pot of raspberry jam. Jim bought a newspaper.

Things would have turned out differently (or perhaps not; probably not) if Jake hadn't rolled down the window, through which, sly and tentacular, came the odours of fish and chips from a take-away across the street. As it was, we counted up what we had left. Enough for one fish and three bags of chips, a few of which I vowed to save for Pen, rubbery though they'd be by the time we made it back to the Seaview. I scrambled from the van and joined the queue in the irresistibly named *In Cod We Trust*.

I had placed my order and was staring out of the fogged window when I saw Kelp's mother rush past, frowning, collar up, hands clutching her coat together where buttons or zip should have been.

I did what one does at such moments. I thought: That was Stella Kelp I just saw. And with more or less simultaneity thought: No, that wasn't her, because she's three hundred miles away in Begshall, hung over.

'Thur you go, moi luvver,' Mrs Chips said, loud enough to suggest that I hadn't heard her the first time. I turned from the window, paid, then hurried to the doorway. But she was gone, whoever she was.

'And lo,' Jake said, grinning, 'it was found that the fish could be divided among them. They all ate and were satisfied.'

'This is my fish,' Jim said, sniffing from behind his *Sun*. 'And with it I am well pleased.'

I opened my mouth to remind him that this was in fact *our* fish, then stopped.

'Oh my God,' I said. 'Oh. My. God.'

'56 DEAD IN MANCHESTER TRAIN CRASH,' the headline said.

'Jim?' I said, very calmly. 'Just pass me that newspaper a sec, will you?'

The *Sun* had devoted all but eight of its pages to the disaster. (The Page Three Girl had been demoted to page twenty-eight, but she was there, holding her breasts and beaming over her bare shoulder, blond hair ablaze in the studio lights. 'Good to know you can rely on *some*thing,' Jim said, later.) The 15.03 from Newcastle to Manchester met the 17.32 from Manchester to Blackpool North – via Begshall. One train, the Manchester-to-Begshall local, had had a green signal. That had been established. The other, the Newcastle-to-Manchester Intercity, might have failed to stop on a red. Fifty-six dead and the wreck only twenty-two hours old. There were fears that 'the death toll' could be as high as a hundred and fifty. It was, the *Sun* said, 'a matter at this early stage for grim conjecture'. Photographers had been busy. Shot after grainy shot of survivors and relatives. Calls for a public enquiry. Questions to be asked. Lessons to be learned. Heads to roll. The 17.32. From Manchester to Begshall. That got all shoplifters home in time for hot-panted Catherine Bach in *The Dukes of Hazard*. Fifty-six dead. And us, alive, three hundred miles away.

Jim, lifting his eyes from the as yet undivided fish, saw my face.

'What's up?' he asked.

I showed him the front page. 'It's our train,' I said. 'We would've been on it.' Neither him nor Jake quite assimilating. 'Fucking hell,' I said. 'Fucking *hell*.'

'Christ,' Jake said. 'Yesterday, was it?'

Suddenly I saw what he was thinking. What anyone else would have been thinking.

'Oh, my God,' I said, and leaped from the van.

I ran around two blocks twice before I found a phone box.

'Hello?'

'Dad?'

'Who's that? Ronnie?'

'No, Dad, it's me, Dominic.'

'Oh, hello, son. Are you all right? Where are you?'

'I'm in Cornwall. Listen, I just heard about the crash at Manchester—'

'Oh, that's a terrible bloody thing. They're showing it to us on the news. Bloody—'

'Dominic?' My mother said, having summarily confiscated the receiver from my dad; I could hear him in the background, complaining.

'Hi, Mum.'

'When are you coming *home*?'

The single word crammed: pain, longing, fear, need, love. Come *home*. It felt good not to have to lie. 'I'm coming home very soon, Mum. Maybe even tomorrow.'

'Come home *now*.'

'Soon, Mum, I promise. I just wanted to know you were okay. The train crash—'

'Oh, sweetheart, it's awful. *Awful*. One of the boys from your school, somebody Eccles. Mark Eccles. They think he was on the train.'

'Mark Eccles is *dead*?'

'They don't know. They haven't . . . I just kept thinking how lucky I am that you were away. If you were here, Saturday, you'd have been with your mates in—'

'I know, Mum. I know. We're lucky.'

'Julia phoned last night. People cut in half. When are you coming home?'

'Mum, my money's running out. I'll call you—'

'Don't come by train!'

'Okay, okay.'

'Come by coach!'

'Mum, I'll see you soon.'

'We love you, sweetheart.'

'I love you, too, Ma. Look, don't worry. I'll be—' but that was my one coin gone.

'They're okay,' I reported, back in the van. Jim and Jake had saved me a third of the fish, but I was beyond eating it. *Something's going to happen here, something awful.* I sat in silence for a moment, trying to imagine Pen's face when I told him. My body had discovered a new stratum of relaxation.

'Let's go,' I said. 'They'll want to phone home.'

Jim had pounced on and wolfed down my bit of fish and was in the process of licking his lips when something across the road caught his eye.

'Oh, shit,' he said.

A seen-better-days white transit van stood opposite, its slide-back centre door open. Figures inside, obscured by shadow. We didn't need to see them. We didn't need to see them because the one standing akimbo with his back to us — tartan jeans, black braces, shaved, phrenologist's wet dream of a head — was sufficient for us to infer their identities.

'Oh,' Jake said.

'They couldn't have found out where . . .'

'Yeah. I don't . . .'

The grown-up skinhead opened the driver's door and jumped in. A hand from the shadows slid the side door shut with a clunk.

'I don't like this,' I said. 'I think we should get going.'

The transit's driver door slammed shut. No mirror, no signal, just the manoeuvre – a quick swerve out into the road, then acceleration away up the hill.

'I really think we should go,' I said. 'Now.' Jim had already turned the van over twice without ignition.

'Come on, man,' Jake said.

'Shut the fuck up,' Jim said.

'Come *on*, man,' Jake repeated.

'Shut the fuck up,' Jim said.

'You're flooding it, for fuck's sake.'

'I am not flooding it.'

'You're fucking *flooding* it.'

'I am NOT FUCKING FLOODING IT.'

I had a clear mental image of the transit weaving the lanes on its way to the hotel. Very white the van, very green and lush the fields, very thick and dark the hedgerows. It looked like a toytown model.

'Keep at it, for Christ's sake,' Jake said.

Jim's fringe quivered. I opened the door and jumped from the van.

There was someone in the phone box, naturally, an enormous, hairy and soft-shouldered man in a white string vest. I opened the door just as he said: 'f'the syme proyce as the turkaye'.

'I'm sorry,' I said. 'You've got every right to stay on this phone as long as you like, but I've got an emergency, a real emergency, and I was wondering if you could just—'

He yanked the door out of my grasp with such force that it brought pain to the tips of my fingers. 'Owl on a minnit, Rodge,' he said into the mouthpiece. Then, to me: 'Git the fook a why from ere, yow.'

I scanned the street. A chemist. The Spar. A tobacconist. Public toilets. A pub.

A pub. The Three Pigeons. I was aware, peripherally, of Jim and Jake at war in the turning and turning VW. Time compressed and expanded. I raced in slow motion, watched the pub's door ache open at my hand's shove, saw day-drinker faces and amber pints swim up from the smoke and gloom, saw the phone on its cradle.

'Directory assistance, which name please?'

'The Seaview Hotel, St Ives – no, Zennor, Cornwall.'

Then the plummy recorded woman: 'The number you require is . . .'

I burned each one into my brain and dialled.

Engaged.

I jammed my jaws together and raised the receiver above my head. I would have smashed it, too, had I not caught the landlord's eye. He was leaning on the heels of two mighty hands and scowling at me from the darkness of a Zapata moustache and two ferocious eyebrows. I lowered the hand-set and lifted a conciliatory palm. Smiling, feebly, I hung up and dialled again.

The cruel click of connection that deludes for a split second, then *pooooop-poop, pooooop-poop, pooooop-poop* . . .

I really might have done some damage then, landlord or no landlord, had the door not opened and Jake appeared.

'She's running,' he said. 'By the grace and glory of the Lord.'

How much time had we lost? Hard to say. Surely no more than five or ten minutes. The three of us sat hunched forward. The rain was soft and steady. Jim drove and chewed his fringe.

'And I saw an angel coming down out of heaven,' Jake murmured, 'having the key to the Abyss and holding in his hand a great chain.'

'Can't see a fucking thing,' Jim said, then *whumped* the steering wheel with the flat of his hand. 'There's smears of crap all over the windscreen, Jake, for Christ's sake.'

'Peace, brother,' Jake said. 'A bad workman, et cetera. Eh?'

It was slow going. Pedestrians milled and shuffled and overflowed from the pavement into the road. Traffic lights, zebras, pelicans. All the town's colours and forms distinct: the Woolworth's logo; a keep-left sign; a girl's denim skirt and red espadrilles. On a traffic island a seagull – *Larus fuscus* – did mute, earnest battle with the plastic hoops from a six-pack. The rain burst on the tarmac in rings.

'Stop!'

Jim jumped on the brakes. By some minor miracle nothing hit us from behind.

'Jesus Christ,' Jake said. 'Easy there, James, *easy*.'

Jim rested his head on the steering wheel. 'I can't take this,' he said. 'I know that's a sign of weakness, but I can't take all the . . . all the . . .'

'What's going on?' Jake asked; but I was already halfway out of the van.

I shouldn't have been surprised that she turned a moment before I opened my mouth to call to her. (Wondering, in fact, how to address her. Stella? Mrs Kelp?) We stared at each other. A short period of silence, then the necessary conclusion that there would be no politeness or convention.

'Where is he?' she said.

'Close by. We're on our way there.'

She was making a superhuman effort not to become hysterical. The blood went around my skull in audible spasms. I felt sick.

'I can't see where he is, exactly,' she said. 'Take me to him.'

In the van she sat wrapped in the black coat with her face closed and small, eyes cold with resistance to exhaustion. Jim and Jake went quiet and careful with their movements, as if the entire physical world now deserved their reverence.

'This is Kelp's mum,' I said. 'We need to drive her to the hotel as fast as possible. Right now.'

Three sets of lights favoured us and we roared out of town. The rain thickened. Jim peered ahead, his nose almost touching the glass.

'He's at the Seaview Hotel in Zennor,' I said. Her eyes didn't react – since her own history wasn't important now. 'He hasn't been well, but it's just a fever. I think he's got good old-fashioned flu, actually. Pen's calling a doctor from the—'

'Please don't speak to me,' she said. 'It's not your fault.'

She leaned forward and placed her pale hand on Jim's shoulder. 'Drive faster,' she said. Speaking a painful effort for her, obviously. 'Faster,' she whispered. Rain shadows freckled her face.

Jim drove faster.

Penguin returned from the Quest for the Landlady and the Phone Call to the Doctor (both successfully completed) to find Kelp fully dressed – in a great many clothes, not all of them his own – sitting on the edge of the bed, frowning.

'What are you playing at?' Pen asked him.

Kelp shook his head, teeth still a-chatter. 'I need some air,' he said. 'I'm fucking suffocating in here. And there are flies.'

Pen didn't like the look of him. 'I think you'd better get back into bed,' he said. 'You're raving.'

'I'm not raving, buttock. I'm asphyxiating.'

'Kelp, do not be a clinker. You look like a corpse. Anyway, the doctor's coming. You'll have to stay in bed.'

But the patient was adamant. 'I'm inhaling my own germs,' he said. 'I feel like a genie in his bottle in here, with the cork . . . It's no good opening the window. I just need to step outside for a minute. Just for a minute.'

There was nothing Pen could do, short of pinning Kelp to the bed, so he let him go, with the warning that dire consequences would follow should the doctor materialize and there be no patient to see. Kelp promised to go no further than the hotel's front porch. 'Just a sniff of fresh air,' he said. 'Just a c–c–couple of inhalations.'

'Yeah, yeah,' Pen said. 'Don't interfere with anyone. Especially that chambermaid, because I think there might be a little understanding growing up between her and me.'

The four of us sat in silence as the van ploughed through the rain. Knobs and knolls of old Cornish land, the seals on its legion chipped and shattered dead. Dark trees gestured against the sky. Friesians like black and white standing stones in the grass. A lay-by with a mustard-coloured Escort parked at a tilt, missing a back wheel. I was thinking (I think) that I knew nothing about anyone. Kelp's mother, Jim and Jake, Penguin, Julia, Kelp. It followed, didn't it, from their not knowing what there was to know about me. It followed, didn't it, the possibility of their own occult centres, from the actuality of my own.

Something made Pen change his mind, though he knew not (and knows not) what. He was lying on the camping cot with his fingers laced behind his head when a strange feeling stole over him.

'Like someone was drawing a cold blanket over me,' he said, afterwards. A long time afterwards. 'It started at my feet and moved all the way up to my chest.'

He didn't like it, but sitting up and swinging his legs over the side of the bed did nothing to dispel it. The hotel had gone quiet. He got up, crossed to the open window and looked out. He was going to hold his hands out in the rain then wipe them over his hot face. For his face had become hot. The left brain was telling him that he had absorbed Kelp's virus, that the hot and cold shenanigans were nothing more sinister than the first symptoms of flu. The right brain, on the other hand, was darkly and persuasively busy. He reached out into the rain.

'That's when I heard them,' he told me later. 'It was just a couple of doors clunking shut, but it scared the shit out of me.'

He didn't know, obviously, that the doors were the doors of a white transit van, and that the hands that had slammed them shut belonged to Callum Burke & co. He didn't know that they had tracked us and come fixed on revenge, that same four in their same clothes, one with split lip, another with tooth loosened by Tony's hard, straight right. He didn't know what he was doing when he drew his hands in, wiped them quickly across his face, then crossed the room to the door and stepped out onto the landing.

'Drive faster,' Stella said, but Jake was struggling to hold the road as it was. It was a shared knowledge between the four of us, that we couldn't go any faster, that there were set limits, now, to what we could do, that the division between ourselves and our experience was dissolving and that we were moving ineluctably into an event.

A farmhouse of blond stone sailed past on our right, a bright-red tractor trundling towards the gate. Jim switched the headlights on.

'It's not far from here,' I said. 'You should be able to see it on the left after the bend.'

'I know where it is,' Stella said, fingers at temples, shut eyes buried in a frown. For the first time, stupidly, I found myself wondering how she had got here. I imagined her waking (pink-vested, under unwashed duvet) in the Begshall night, revisited after the long, barren stretch as if by an incubus. She had thought herself finished with all that. I pictured her staggering, head in hands, through the room's strewn clothes and kicked-off shoes; dressing, the cold fabric abrasive to the heightened skin; laryngitically calling a taxi; boarding (no luggage, just the battered handbag) a train. A different train, that is. One that hadn't bloodily disgorged its passengers. Fifty-six dead and us not among them. Three hundred miles away. Safe.

'Oh Christ,' I said. 'Hurry *up*.'

On the landing between first and ground floors Pen paused to lick and seal a roll-up. Patting his pockets for matches, he rounded the banister, took two steps down, and saw them.

The skins stood in the hotel's reception with their arms loose at their sides, large-lipped and fish-eyed Callum at the head. To his left, the driver with the rucked cranium, the other two grinning just behind. They were considering Kelp, who stood (now in purloined balaclava) hands in pockets directly below Pen. There was no one else around.

'He looked up at me,' Pen said, afterwards. 'He looked up at me with that fucking stupid grin. You know what I mean?' (I knew. I know. I see that grin these nights, at Holly's window, six floors up.)

Burke, alerted by Kelp's glance, looked up and saw Pen.

'Never mind him,' Kelp said. 'I'll take the lot of you on single-handed, enfeebled as I am by a deadly virus. I'll kick your buttocks to slush and ram your heads in it. What's the matter? Come on. I'll blow my fucking pants off at you if you stand there gawping any longer.'

The sort of daredevil manoeuvre Penguin was calculating as he stood observing from above was one he had only ever seen in Marvel comics and action adventure films. He knew what was going to happen. The skins had very little time to get in, do their damage, and get out again. At any moment they would rush forward and Kelp would go down.

'You know what you look like?' Kelp said, but he wasn't allowed to tell them. They leaped towards him in unison. As Kelp spun and ran for the kitchens they sped after him in eerie silence; only the last (and smallest) of the four suffering the full weight of Pen's airborne attack.

Courage or madness – Penguin had jumped. Over the banister and all but head first into the upturned face of the fourth skin, upon whom he fell with such mass and hysteria that it was several moments before his target recovered his wits and proceeded to turn the tables. 'He looked so surprised,' Pen chuckled, later. 'He looked so *amazed*. I wish Kelp could have seen that fucker's amazed bald face!'

Kelp saw nothing of the kind. He was busy slaloming through the steam and rattlecrash of the Seaview's kitchen with Burke's reduced posse on his tail, flinging everything he could grab into his wake. An aproned cook screamed and held up her floury hands as if at gunpoint. A cat got under his feet and sent him sprawling over the lino. He got up in an instant and was off again. He glimpsed an old man in a lumberjack shirt (the owner in Stella's day) sitting in an alcove spooning soup into a brilliantly dentured mouth.

With the high-octane fuel of fever he ran, tipping chairs, tables, plates, pans, dishes and cups into his slipstream. He ran and fumbled until his palms found themselves flush to a white-painted wooden door which opened onto a stone step, cold rain and a bright stretch of green grass.

What calculations did he make? What details did he notice? Did he consider and reject running for the cliffs, or was it blind instinct that turned him inland? Did he see the speedwell and buttercups? The dozen molehills? The daisies? In an alternative vision I see him go straight for the cliffs and leap off into the rainy sky, taking flight. I see the sea swinging under him. I see him climbing higher, growing smaller, vanishing, Burke and chums skidding to a cartoon halt at the land's edge – or, better still, unable to stop in time, pitching forward, scrabbling (a gulp into camera), then plummeting . . .

At random or instinctively or by split-second design he ran to his right at full tilt. He could hear them behind him. The door had swung and banged three times after him; he could hear their breathing and the *putch-putch* of their boots. He was thinking that as long as he ran they would be drawn away from Pen. He didn't know (of course he didn't) that by the time he spotted the gap in the hedge that led into the road Pen already had a broken wrist, two fractured ribs and a Hitler tash of blood. He didn't know that there were fifty-six dead and ourselves not among them. He didn't know that he'd been right all along. He didn't know (did he?) how close we were, bringing the black-and-white news with his mother through the driving rain.

The fever strength was giving out. His chest was empty and scorched, each bronchiole starved crisp. Blood waltzed in his legs. Wind and rain flung themselves against him, splashed the girlish bones and darkened the fiery hair. He would have been grinning, I'm sure of that. He would have been filled with fever and his own history, regretting nothing, surely, as, without slackening his pace, he leaped through the gap in the hedge, into our headlights, into our myth.

CHAPTER FOUR

◆

Black Magic

'You heard of Denis Merchant?' Holly said.

'No. Who is he?'

'A medium. A *performing* medium. I went to one of his things a few years back.'

'What was it like?'

'You've seen them, haven't you?'

'Only on television once.'

'Him saying: "I'm getting a gentleman in his sixties . . . Is there a Philip in the audience, from Queens?" and someone's hand goes up. "I'm getting coronary death, right? And you had something of his . . .?"'

We were on the fire escape, me having been woken by Kelp, her having been woken by me. She'd been speaking with her cheek resting on her pulled-up knees, voice slurred slightly as a result. Now she lifted her head and stared out at the opposite brownstone.

'Not once in the whole thing did any of the dead say

anything of importance to any of the living,' she said. 'I was waiting for it. *Stop seeing her, Dave or you'll die. I know about the poison. The money's buried in the schoolyard. I'm going to get you, you murdering bastard.* Nothing.'

We were silent for a minute. She returned her head to where it had rested on her knees.

'How long do you think this'll go on?' she said.

◆

We buried his body on a lawn-scented day of misty rain in St Joseph's graveyard. There weren't many of us: half a dozen of Stella's relatives who kept to themselves; Penguin and myself, our parents, a handful of teachers from St Dymphna's. The mist flirted with becoming rain. A few umbrellas went up, reflexively, then came down again, having felt disrespectful. *Gregory Alexander Bernard Kelp, 1965–1982. At rest*, it claimed.

I had stopped myself wondering what was going on in Mrs Kelp's heart. From the first moments of comprehension – in the silence after the thud, when the engine had died and the rain had with suspect synchronicity stopped – to nasal Feeney's soporific rite over the grave, Stella had said little, and what little she had said was ominously composed. Offers of help with the funeral arrangements politely but firmly declined. She stood to one side, watching the lowered coffin, face stripped of its habits, ungloved hands hanging at her sides, feet slightly too far apart – this last giving her a profane look.

The wake was a tense affair at the council flat in Mere Street, everyone afraid of speaking, not knowing what horror might come out. Instead we moved our feet around and bit off the corners of our sandwiches, tasting nothing.

Pen and I went into the empty back garden to smoke;

both on Rothmans now, having abandoned roll-ups in silent agreement, one of a bundle of things (Lamb's Navy Rum, Caroline Munroe, summer, Volkswagen vans) we would never be able to enjoy in quite the same way again. The rain had stopped. The air smelled of Begshall: wet litter, exhaust, drains, damp brick. Pen was in a suit, his first, and one which would never be worn again. I was in one of my dad's, visibly altered by my mum. There was one anorexic apple tree at the bottom of the narrow garden, so we stood under it, more because it symbolized concealment from our parents than because it in fact concealed us. Not that they would have dared censure us for anything, being terrified of our silences, of what might be happening inside our heads, of what it all might *mean*.

'We should have told Nancy,' I said. 'She should've been here.'

'D'you think she would've wanted to?' Pen asked.

I thought back to the morning in the girls' cottage (a lifetime ago), my paltry victory, the few cruel moments of grace. I remembered Nancy lying asleep, pretty as a tulip, Kelp at the window, stunned by the night's bliss. I saw him turning to me, hair like spun glass. *Time to be thinking of leaving.*

Pen was precariously balanced. I knew anything might set him off.

'I think you should write to them,' I said. 'Tell them what's happened.'

'You reckon?'

'I know it was only a night . . .'

'I know.'

Grief wasn't inside us. It was a substance filling all the space around us from which we were separated by a thin membrane of disbelief. Actually, that's not true. There *was* no grief, not for me. Merely a numbing throb of guilt and bottled hilarity at its absence. Death's first lesson: you don't feel what you're supposed to feel. Its second: you lie, and say that you do. It was only shock, I know now; but at the time it was a vertiginous liberation. Your best friend is dead. You feel nothing! What next?

I had been staring at my shiny black shoes in the grass; when I looked up I saw that Pen was crying, one of the worst sights I'd ever seen. The suit was a cynical master-stroke, ridiculing him on top of his pain. Not that that was the source of my horror. The source of my horror was the gap between Pen's tears and my own indifference. I put my hand on his shoulder. He sniffed and wiped the tears away, briskly, as if they'd been a silly aberration.

'Best go back in, then,' he said, ducking out from under my hand.

I waited a while after he'd gone, feeling as dry and frail as a tumbleweed. Bits of all the things Kelp had ever said fluttered in my head, but I couldn't grasp any of them. Surges of bloody concupiscence, too, despite the cigarette, the dismal tree, the lightness of being, the death. Good to know you can rely on *some*thing, as Jim had said, long ago.

From the kitchen, where I'd stopped to pour myself the first of the afternoon's many drinks, I saw through into the toilet, the door of which, ajar, revealed Stella, sans black hat and gloves, standing very still, weight on one leg, staring into the strip-lit mirror. She stood for a long time, blinking at her reflection, not moving. There had been no tears all day. Nor were there now.

The cistern refilled, then went silent. Stella remained in stillness. Eventually, since she showed no sign of moving, I took my drink and went back into the living room.

★

It wasn't my plan to break into St Edmund's that night. Or rather, it wasn't *my* plan; I can't answer for my subconscious, or whichever insatiable power was pulling the cosmic strings.

'Where are you going, sweetheart?' my mother asked.

'Pen's.'

'Are you all right?'

'Yeah.'

'Oh, Dominic I'm so—'

'It's okay, Ma, I'm fine. I'll stay over, probably.'

She didn't say anything. Just put her arms around me – while I remained rigid – then smiled with useless sadness. I turned and went out into the wet dark, empty of intention.

Intention and everything else. Dominic Hood potent with numbness. There was something beyond or beneath it and in defence against which it had reared up. I didn't know (or didn't let myself know) what it was. (Now I do. It was shame.) Therefore I walked the small-hours streets in mediocre rain, drunk, laughing, until I found myself – a vague or gentle gravitational drift – in the empty yard at St Edmund's. Staring at it for a while, face hot and tender in the drizzle. Then walking groggily around it and peering into its classrooms. Then finding the window on the Infants' toilets ajar. Then hoisting myself up and slithering head and shoulders first (ribs gouged by the latch's prong) into the lavatorial block, assailed on entry by the ammoniacal past and the shrinkage of heights and widths: the tiny urinals and stalls; the miniature desks and chairs; a line of blue in the corridor's tiles I'd always had to look up to see, now lower than my own shoulder.

The medical room wasn't locked. (In the school hall I had stood in the dark and felt not just the floor's tilt and swing but a summons as if from the seven-year-old version of myself still lying on the starchy cot. Nothing gentle about this pull. I had run there – tripped, barked my shins on the stairs, got up fast, felt nothing.) Nurse Maggie long gone, I supposed. Certainly no whiff of Charlie or Juicy Fruit. Otherwise the room much the same. Light enough from the street to show me the outline of the archaic weighing scales and the sheen of the laminated circulatory man. *Ah, there's a boy here.* There was a boy here. A boy died. A boy came back. A different boy died. Doesn't prove anything. Should have been me. Disgusting and now disgusted filthy me. Cut them open and shit in their wounds. *Truth*, that's what. Alive, alive-o. *It was hello and bon voyage.* The damned are the saved and the saved are the damned. Miracle mix-up. Or the malice of miracles (*stop this, hold on to that indifference*) . . . singing cock-ups, and mix-ups alive, alive-o . . .

I lay down on the cot and lit a Silk Cut. (I had inherited Kelp's Zippo. Mrs Kelp had pressed it without a word into my hand at the funeral. Had to force myself to use it, flinching at its clack, rasp and flame, the distinctive reek of its fuel.) The school's presences hushed, knowing I was beyond them. *Hail Mary*, I had said, *full of grace, the Lord is with thee* . . . Some part of me (I realized, tears rolling with a curious absence of emotion down the sides of my head from the corners of my eyes to my ears) had been waiting, since Kelp's death, for certainty that God (or Malone – God . . . or Malone) was either dead or malicious. On the cot, now, in the rain-shadowed room with the medicine smells, I knew it was worse than that. They were a challenge, a dare: you must look at the horrors of the world and find a way back to faith in spite of what you saw. I had a glimpse of what the purer version of myself might be capable of: enduring the loss, keeping the rage and disgust down, finding meaning through suffering. But it was only a glimpse. There was so much shame, and the shame made me angry at the thought of getting better.

Sore throat now. Nicotine and whisky headache. Limbs fiery and bloated. Bladder full. Sluggishly, I rolled onto my side, unzipped, and pissed on the floor.

Through the rank end of summer, Pen and I were horribly awkward. Autumn – the first A-level term at Begshall Tech, scraped through, hatefully. *Fundamentals of Sociology. The Nellie, a cruising yawl, swung to her anchor.* Winter. Christmas a jolly obscenity, Easter not even a ripple. *Understanding Society. It is a truth universally acknowledged.* Academic life began to make itself available as a pleasant distraction. *The Marxist model of society sees capital as. Hardy uses the landscape as a—*

Then, at the beginning of the summer holidays, I met Deborah Black.

◆

Names and places have been changed for the protection of the persons involved.

But they haven't. Come what may. My challenge to fate, to the Stylist's heavy hand. Dominic Hood, Deborah Black. The design argument in two surnames. Holly, my darling, you must take this document and do with it what you will. And I, in good and weathered faith, will listen for the phone, the footsteps on the stairs, the pounding on the door.

◆

Deborah lived with a woman who was not her mother and a girl who was not her sister in Eastfield, a private old people's home in Begshall's one salubrious quarter to the south-east of town. I was there, in spattered overalls, to paint and decorate.

A friend of my father's had had his apprentice go lame after a five-a-side spill and was looking for a cheap and willing pair of hands. My indifference having been noted, and my parents subscribing to some meaningful connection between Art A level and home decor, I was put forward and hired. My first job was with hot gun and scraper in an unoccupied third-floor room. Very satisfying, the suddenly burgeoning bubo of blistered paint, the scrape, the naked wood. I took my lunch with a copy of the *Star* (the *Sun* too wordy now; my appetite for tabloid cynicism and pictures of celebrities insatiable since 56 DEAD) alone on the landing, Dougie's salt-of-the-earth aphorisms and *I-always-says* having several times that morning had me on the edge of mute violence. Halfway through my first ham sandwich and thermos coffee, a door on the floor below slammed on what was surely an argument and sullen footsteps came eight stairs up, perceived the new odours of my handiwork, slowed, then stopped. I sat with my back against the corridor wall, ankles crossed, half-eaten sandwich poised. She came up the last six stairs slowly, then pivoted at the banister head.

Lovers don't finally meet somewhere, Rumi says. *They're in each other all along.*

'Hi.'

She didn't answer, but regarded me from the stairhead. I did have the satisfaction of seeing that my presence had shoved aside whatever disgruntlement the row downstairs had left her with. Replaced it with curiosity. Opportunity. Something. The dark eyes very still and intelligent. A jolt in the body of my inert self.

I took a sip from my flask top, having managed not to scrabble to my feet like a puppy.

'Haven't got any matches, have you?' I said. 'Can't find mine.'

A pause. The sound of hot and urinous Eastfield, which was sometimes (as now) a faint hiss.

'I'll get some,' she said, then turned and went back down the stairs.

As a child I had had visions of the infinite, usually when running a fever. One was of a small car travelling as if on a conveyor belt through an endless matrix of tunnels and pipes, the pipes all in cross-section. Potentially endless, like hell. Emptiness and repetition and inescapable concrete details. That was the infinite. Eastfield had it, too. The institutional radiators and polished floors attested: for ever was here. I felt it, waiting for her to come back.

The woman who wasn't her mother was the deputy matron, Mrs Lingard, Deborah's guardian. I refrained from questions.

'How long are you coming here?' she asked. The room – of a recently cancer-devoured blind lady, Deborah said – was small and dim, with hospital bed, industrial lino, charity-shop dresser and wardrobe, both of dark wood. Funereal, but with one shaft of spring sunlight coming in through the sash window, which, to dispel the odour of torched paint, I had opened wide. Deborah lay elbow-propped on the stripped bed, one knee bent, shoes kicked off to reveal alluringly undainty feet, one painted toenail visible through a hole in the nylons. I was awake now, bristling consciousness around a core of silence.

'I'm not sure. Couple of weeks, I reckon.'

'Longer than that, rate you're going.'

'Could be. Maybe I should slow down.'

A pause. One slow blink. 'Har har.'

Har har. That was as good as it got.

'Used to the stink of piss and shit yet?' she asked.

'No. But I've sorted out the ethics of euthanasia.'

'The matron broke one of the grannies' hands last week.'

'What?'

'You're looking up my skirt.'

'Sorry.'

She came and stood in front of me. An inch shorter. Black eyes and hair cut Cleopatra style. We had spent our time not quite looking at each other. It was an instinct in both of us, to keep a part of consciousness averted from each other.

'You look a fucking idiot in those overalls.'

'Would you like to come out for a drink with me?'

'Why?'

'Why do you think?'

'When?'

'Tonight?'

'Can't. I'm babysitting the bitch's vegetable.'

She had very gently taken hold of my overalls' marsupial front pocket and was pulling it, gently, this way and that, a gesture not completely lost on me, busy as I was trying to settle her last phonemes into words. Bitchizvejtuble. Bitch's. Vegetable. Mrs Lingard the bitch. And the vegetable?

'Why don't you come round?'

'Tonight?'

'Yes, tonight. Maybe I'll let you look up my skirt.'

Instant scrotal swarm. The skirt was old. Its little packet of cunt heat. Smell of warm cotton. Nylon static.

'What time?'

She considered. 'How long from where you live?'

'Twenty minutes.' A burping second-hand 50cc Honda for my seventeenth. Me an ungrateful wretch at the time, then by degrees slipping into the liberty bestowed by L-plates and a provisional licence.

'Give me your number,' she said. 'I'll phone you when she's gone.'

I kept my mouth shut.

'Bring some booze,' she said. 'You got any blow?'

Penguin had just purchased a bag of Californian grass, but that would mean going round there and coming up with a good reason for not sitting down and smoking it with him. In dealings with Deborah, the will to secrecy superseded all other forces from the outset.

'I can get some next time,' I said.

'Next time?'

'My apologies. Appalling presumption.'

'Shut up. Come here.'

With the exception of her hands in my absurd front pocket no other parts of our bodies touched; only our mouths met, without bumped teeth or misangled heads, rested upon each other, tasted breath, tongues, lips. Tasted or touched or sipped recognition. You juss fuckin *know*, you see?

The blood in my cock an idling truck's throb. A moment longer and my body's screamed imperative to grab her waist and pull her hard against me would have had its way. I got a sense of her: the hours and days of her flesh, weariness, hand–me–down clothes, perpetual agitation. But she put her hands on my chest and pushed herself gently away from me.

She went to the door, stopped, turned, and looked at me. 'I'll phone you,' she said.

At home I went methodically through prosaic preparation – shower, shave, nail-trim, earwax removal, bowel movement (necessitating second mini or loin shower), pilfered tot of Teacher's, clothes pulled on with ritual precision. Perceptions crackled, fizzed and purred. Humble objects recognized me, spelled out the great deadness and certainty of having met her.

Her.

In Julia's old room, now mine, I sat on the bed and watched the street's little bits of glamourless life, thinking of Where They Were Now: Kelly weighed fourteen stone and had added two braying, scarlet-faced bastard toddlers to the Saunders household. Elaine and family had emigrated to Australia. Stew Fletcher was an apprentice mechanic, engaged to a thin and incessantly complaining girl who ruled him with a rod of iron. These were the facts, and they meant nothing to me. Kelly and I said hello when we passed in the street. It was a long time since I had even wondered if she remembered. Time had told. Unwanted motherhood, bills, the treacherous body – *life* had come and taken up all the available room. The past, memory – all undesirable, all exiled.

The bed made a small *boing* under me. This bed, the same bed. There had been sunlight, Jules's white haunch, sudden knowledge, the blaze and dismay of my mother in the door-way, the discovery of myself. Now, this evening, there was sunlight again, Logan Street's long shadows, and myself, alert for the first time since Kelp's death.

Images of that day returned, momentarily – Stella sitting with coat clutched on the wet roadside; bloody-nosed Pen limping up; Jim vomiting into the hedge; the VW's pleas-antly surprised and blood-spattered face; the *Sun* on the tarmac, flapping its pages of 56 DEAD for attention – then receded as if sucked into a black hole of my own inner space. This had been the way of it, bits of memory flashing, then

212

disappearing, whisked down into the void the dead part of myself had made ready. I had invented or given birth to this new, speechless version of Dominic Hood, who banned questions, thoughts, attempts to connect present to past.

But now there was something.

Deborah. The name already a psychic tattoo. I thought back. Plump face and dark eyes, smallish breasts and very slight pear shape. One misangled canine that gave her mouth its latent sneer. Nothing overtly seductive, but a suggestion of heaviness around the hips and a current of impatience that ran beneath her surface. Stripped of superfluity Desire was in those spaces between the ideals. Ever since the funeral there had been in me an agitated demand for something. I didn't know what.

I sat on the bed, looking out into Logan Street as if trying to absorb all its details, to make them precious and say good-bye before death.

The phone rang.

A two-bedroomed basement flat went with Mrs Lingard's position, and I found it, as per Deborah's instructions, at the back of the building, down a flight of mossy stone steps.

'Who's that?'

'None of your business. Stay in there and don't fucking move.'

Alice Lingard, the not-all-there girl who was not Deborah's sister, lay belly down on the living-room carpet, chin in hands, face flickered over by the television's light. Fifteen? Sixteen? Hard to tell. Ginger bunches and an eight-year-old's dress of ox-eye daisies, but avocado-sized breasts and frankly pubescent hips. I noticed large knees and a dusting of freckles, a small face of pigletish prettiness.

'Izzy yer boyfriend?'

But Deborah closed the door and led me into her room. 'What did you get?' she wanted to know.

Vodka, a whole bottle, courtesy of an advance negotiated from my dad on expected wages from Dougie. Deborah went to the kitchen and returned with glasses. I sat on the bed while she poured in silence. An indifferently lived-in room. No posters, no paintings, no attempt to lift it beyond function. Only White Musk and the dresser's Manhattan of bottles and jars testified to her sex, the rest loveless and strewn with clothes. We clinked glasses, me convinced she could hear my inner calculations of the hows and whys of her situation.

'Where's she gone, anyway?' I asked, meaning Mrs Lingard.

'She's got a bloke,' Deborah said. 'Believe it or not, someone actually wants to fuck her. How much would you have to be paid for that?'

I smiled, took a sip. 'I love what you've done with this room.'

A silence in response that made me think for a moment I'd hurt her feelings. Then I realized she couldn't think of anything with which to counter, was impatient with me, or the world of words. I imagined sudden violence (she had the packed-away power in her shoulders and thighs), mirror smashing, crockery throwing – a fury at the lack of fit between herself and everyone else.

The silence brought forward Eastfield's smell, its hiss of empty time. She sat against the headboard with her stockinged feet in my lap. She hadn't changed or bathed, I could tell. The afternoon's white blouse and bottle-green skirt. Very adult or worldly, the not bothering. She had, however, made-up. Lavish mascara making spiders of her eyes and a lipstick of pale pink, additionally liquid-glossed,

214

an act nearly satirical on a mouth as naturally wealthy as hers.

'You must be wondering,' she said. Her foot had discerned my erection and was squeezing it in a gentle rhythm.

'Yes,' I said.

'Have to wonder, then, won't you?'

'That's okay with me,' I said. 'Although I should warn you that if you carry on doing that I'm likely to show signs of gratification.'

Again she said nothing, nor acknowledged the litotes. Talking wasn't going to help.

We clambered towards each other.

'Take this off. Go on.' Her voice with its blade of impatience. 'Lick them.'

The experience divided into two strands. One, *see every detail of her nipples and feel the lacy hummock of her clever little cunt and see her lips those pink fucking lipsticked lips so close to my* and so on, through the stream-of-pornographic-consciousness that resided (unmoved by Kelp's death or anything else the world might try) in a state of ever-readiness in my mind. The other, panic. Sudden tilts that tipped me flailing towards the lip of the void. Either that or I left my body, and had to swim uglily back into it.

'Christ, you're beautiful.'

'Shut up.'

There was something else there – when we could bear to look at each other. I thought at the time it came from her. Now I know it might just as well have come from me. It was an acknowledgement that there was something more, something towards which, together, we tended. I wondered if it was, against all reason, love.

Love. The word flared, all the colours of a Sacred Heart, and with it adrenalin and another sickening pitch towards the gulf, all my history collapsing in on itself like a star, an impossible density; the whole past now horribly internal, compressed into something the size of a musket ball buried in my skull. All the while Deborah's body and breath a kind of insistence, the pull of a birth; bodyweight and flesh and occasionally meeting eyes. Her skin had the smell of a slightly stale towel. Dominic Hood knowing and not knowing what to do, how to be, who he is. Was. Is becoming.

A pause. I lay on my back with my shirt off and my trousers undone. Deborah, topless, with hoiked-up skirt, sat astride my thighs, left hand loosely clasping my liberated erection. Her lipstick was a mess round her mouth and her cheeks were red. A few strands of her hair had lifted with static. My heart thumped; ears, lips, hands and cock throbbed. The central heating had come on with a commentary of shudders and clanks and now her bedroom was stuffed with wads of heat. I thought of all the people who had died in this place, had mewled and screamed and leaked and dribbled and coughed and vomited and hallucinated and shat and ground their teeth into death. Deborah's face was hot. Somebody had smashed her, somewhere. Structural damage. It came off her pure and passed into the space I had ready for it. There was a phrase, *deep structure*, from somewhere, cosmology, mathematics. Something wrong in the deep structure. It had allowed her – among many other things – not to bother washing between the afternoon and now. Her face knew a place below language. She had been forced there. She went there, spent time there, came back.

We stared at each other. I looked away. Whatever it was I recoiled, momentarily, retreated into reaching up and squeezing her breasts and encouraging with upthrust hips her hand around me, all of which she understood, held back for a few seconds – *I've seen you, now; you can't pretend; all right a bit more of this* – then tightened her grip on me and leaned forward until our mouths met and kissed.

'What do you want?' she said. We lay on our sides, facing each other, her wanking me with calculated intermittence, me with my left hand holding her away from me the better to see her face, my right hand, under bunched-up skirt and eased-down knickers, roaming. *What do you want?* She had asked it looking directly at me, without urgency. I didn't know. Did know. We had owned up to it, in the two or three moments of looking at and seeing each other, her misery, and mine. The sudden closeness shocked, was flecked with dread.

She lifted her vodka mouth off mine, and said, quietly, looking with absolute conviction into my eyes: 'You like it, don't you?'

At which I came, copiously and in violent thrusts, into her spittled hand. She raised her eyebrows very slightly on receipt of this – soft pornography's deliberate fake surprise at the confirmed intuition – then let her features settle back into cold observation. I had been what she had expected. She was satisfied.

Satisfied of her acuity, that is. I, meanwhile, had been reintroduced via ejaculation to the boundaries of my own skin, hair, blood and bone. I was an undivine thing with feet that clumsily stepped, hands that touched, great lump of a head with its cargo of wobbling tripe. I hadn't come with a girl since Linda. I'd forgotten the deadness that followed, the desire to be anywhere – *anywhere* – else. This was different. There was nowhere else. These moments had a tight, detailed quality, in which I felt curiosity about her (*Deborah*; the hard and soft of the name curled and uncurled in my head), all the unseen territory, the anger and stinking history (*She's not my fucking mother*, she'd said of Mrs Lingard), all the rich invisibles.

Therefore, still trembling, *shivering*, as if the inevitability of these movements induced physical cold, I descended. *What did you do today?* Thick-skinned rib cage and the sharp slope down into belly and mons. *You all right, Dum?* I kissed. Licked and dipped into her navel. *You look different.* Proceeded. *What's up, fig-brain?*

Her body alternated between registering pleasure – voluntarily spread legs, upthrust and gently swivelled hips – and expressing irritation – sudden yanks on my scalp, spells of tantrum-prelude breathing through her nose, a certain twist of the spine which seemed intent on throwing me from the bed; even, at one stage, throat clearing.

'Stop.'

'What's wrong?'

'Stop.'

Finally. After perhaps half an hour. We disengaged. She sat up and began righting her clothing, I did the same. What would, not all that long ago, have been felt as panic at having failed would now (if I had failed) be felt as just an absence of surprise. Dressed again, she lit a Marlboro and crossed the room to the window. She pulled the curtain aside and looked out into the dark. I felt exhausted.

She turned from the window, moved to the desk, pressed PLAY on the ghetto-blaster. Some music I didn't recognize – bland, processed pop in tinny voices – then she switched it off. Three more hurried drags on the Marlboro. I couldn't think of a single thing to say. My mouth felt bruised and dry. There was something in the room with us.

'I'm going to make some coffee,' she said.

There was a Sacred Heart in the mildew-scented hall. I stood and looked while Deborah made the drinks. I was aware of Alice on the living-room floor, unsuccessfully trying to conceal her scrutiny of me with felt-tips and an inaccurately coloured colouring book open on the carpet in front of her. I examined the holy portrait. Blond Jesus with eyes of pellucid blue. The tiredly parted robe and pornographic heart. BLESS THIS HOUSE. Manifestly He had not. I wondered if the picture belonged to Mrs Lingard, and if so whether, post-coitally, she got down on her knees to ask forgiveness.

You like it, don't you?

In the lounge with vodka and coffees we sat on the couch, Deborah again with her feet in my lap. Alice, movements deprived of even the rudimentary art sixteen normal years would have bestowed, coloured wildly on, book, head and tongue much moved around.

A penis-squeeze from Deborah's toes. I looked at her. She looked at me. Hard to bear; we looked away. But Deborah continued squeezing. Tumescence again in half a dozen surges of blood. Something in the room with us. She climbed onto my lap in silence. I sensed rather than saw Alice look up, briefly, then return to her colouring with vigour, felt-tips squeaking. Deborah kissed me. Lewd and dead the shove and flick of her tongue, coffee- and cigarette-flavoured, worldly, too, with the flash of alcohol. I couldn't see Alice, but felt the gentle heat of her shame as from a little fire in the room. Deborah lifted herself slightly, braless breasts beneath the white blouse brushing my face with their hardened tips. I slid my hands under the hem of her skirt and pushed it up over her buttocks, as if presenting the spectacle to Alice. Deborah's breathing quickened and a slight frown appeared on her face. She kissed me as if distracted by something, some perplexing sensation inside herself. The thing in the room with us pressed upon me, me the delicious bruise. Alice's presence and the shame it sent out ravished the exposed parts of me: wrists, face, throat, hands, scalp, insinuated the logical extension: to be completely naked, to fuck Deborah in front of her. Alice's shame then would wash milkily over us. *What do you want?* Cramped magic that had waited years for full liberation. I glanced over Deborah's shoulder and caught Alice looking: eyes with their history of being stumped and bullied by the world's rules and powers. *Our* eyes met, mine and Alice's, then she forced herself back to fierce colouring. Deborah paused, sat back on my thighs, looked at me. For the first time (fingers finding her wet and open) I returned the look without guard. Silence like an invisible spirit or will plaited us. On the silver screen we would have smiled evilly, I suppose (*they made tapes*) or winked, or at any rate said something to confirm our allegiance. As it was we remained still, her with her palms on my chest and her hair hanging in two dark sickles towards me, me with my fingers close to the heat of her cunt.

Then she dismounted, and the two of us sat side by side, holding hands. The thing in the room which had pressed the bruise of me drew back a little, half placated, seeing where we would go.

'Alice.'

'Umm?' Not looking up.

Deborah remote-controlled, and *Brookside*'s scouse babble softened to a trickle.

'Alice.'

'What?' Still not looking up.

'Look what I'm doing.'

'I don't want.'

'*Look*, I said.'

Alice looked, and so did I. Deborah had her tongue stuck out between her lips, as in childish insult.

'I don't want,' Alice said.

'Come on.'

Alice very deliberately colouring now, with diminishing accuracy. 'No. I don't want.'

Deborah's voice shifted down a gear. 'Alice.'

Alice's red felt-tip stilled, bleeding an expanding spot into the fibrous page. Her face went through a short sequence of expressions – disappointment, confusion, misery – all in a moment, then returned to its frown of concentration. The pen moved: she *would* colour. She *would*. My face glowed as if brash sunlight were resting on it. Mechanically, not looking at me, Deborah had removed her hand from mine and placed it round the ludicrously visible bulge made by my erection.

'It's because he's here, isn't it?' Deborah said, squeezing.

Unable to check her curiosity, Alice looked up. The exquisite feeling of visibility. A great, wordless distance now, a featureless plain exponentially expanding between myself and my life. Penguin whizzing past and away, shrinking over a remote horizon. Alice's shame and fear reached out to me and fuelled the metamorphosis, the new version of myself coming into being with every burgeoning moment, all that Deborah and I hadn't said forming an umbilical between us.

'His name's Dominic,' Deborah said. 'He's playing, too.'

At which Alice jammed her jaws together, with such pressure that her head shuddered. She might have been trying to pass a cripplingly large turd.

'Stop that.'

Alice continued shuddering.

'*Stop* it, I said,' Deborah repeated, still in the lower register. Alice stopped, but looked away, out of the window. Deborah left a pause, time for Alice to understand that no amount of displacement activity – shuddering, looking out of the window – would be sufficient.

'Watch,' Deborah said. 'Alice. Watch.'

Deborah leaned towards me. 'Touch tongues,' she said.

'What?'

'Touch tongues with me.'

Which, when I did, evoked childhood, Julia, the taste between anode and cathode on a battery. The memory added its portion of shame to the transformation. *Shshsh, Dommie, it's all right, it's a dream.* Even curiosity about Deborah was pushed to one side as my self went through its soundless mutations. Alice, having watched in spite of herself, mouth open, fringe aloft with static, suddenly came to, remembered her predicament. Under Deborah's stare her face readied itself for tears.

'See?' Deborah said, gently. Then very firm: 'Don't you dare fucking cry. Don't you *fucking* dare.'

On the muted television the tail end of a brightly coloured commercial for Persil. *Brookside* returned. Via remote control Deborah removed the last vestiges of sound from the set, but refrained from switching it off. Eastfield's quiet exhalation, now louder.

'Pull your knickers down,' Deborah said.

'No.'

'Go on.'

'I don't want.'

'Do you want me to tell your mum what you've been doing?'

Caricature scowl from Alice. To be borne, all this must be construed cartoonishly, much larger than life. She lived her life with Deborah like this, I saw, futilely attempting to rephrase misery in the idiom of children's television. *There's that nasty girl again! Whatever will she do next?*

'Do you want me to get the photos and—'

'No!'

A little pause here. Alice's face crumpling, righting itself.

Just that daft game. The thing in the room with us gesturing with sly generosity towards its promise. *All this I offer you if.*

'What are you?' Deborah, rhetorical again.

No reply from Alice.

'What *are* you, I said.'

The reply in exaggerated boredom. 'A dirty girl.'

'Say it!'

'Amma dirty girl.'

Silence. The capitulation a gift for the two of us to unwrap.

'That's right,' Deborah said, having unzipped and released me. 'You are. A very dirty girl.'

Something happened to time and something happened to space. Moments didn't pass, but came into being and remained, perfected, like exquisite baubles. The room's absences – the empty air between its objects – gently stiff-ened into pliable presences, so that every position we adopted felt cushioned and supported. My body in sensual increments transfiguring, as if a pith was being painlessly burned away. Around us an intoxicating paradox of silence and sound: no space in the room for the slightest reverbera-tion; nonetheless every object speaking the sly promise like deafening blood. Alice crouched on the carpet in front of us, knickers round her ankles, dress lifted up to her waist, fore-head flush to the carpet. She was humming, a pretence of having taken her soul elsewhere for safekeeping. For a while Deborah and I had merely sat and observed, my hand between her legs, hers between mine, fingers moving mechanically. Then she had got up and stood over Alice. Impossible to say how long she stood there, looking some-times down at Alice, sometimes up and directly at me – which look sometimes brought us close to sheer fusion and sometimes measured a terrible distance between us. Then one stockinged foot raised, and placed carefully on Alice's buttock. A slight shake, as if testing the cheek's consistency.

'Deborah?'

My own voice, dry and thick in the jammed room, surprised me. A terrible moment of self-consciousness, the world rearing up like a snake. Nor had I any idea what I was going to say. Deborah looked up at me; her head came up slowly, as if she was drugged or weak with sleep. A surge of panic, upwards from the tips of my toes. Panic – but an immediate counterforce from the presence that was with us: the offer to turn the sound of my voice and the flash of self-consciousness into something else, to make of it a new symbol of permissiveness. *Look: I can do this and talk.* I opened my mouth. Deborah was breathing heavily.

Then the doorbell rang, startling all three of us.

The interruption – the matron, Mrs Vickers, with a message for Mrs Lingard – unsettled me. Deborah, too. Alice, snivelling, ran and locked herself in the bathroom. Deborah stood outside for a few minutes, threatening in the reasonable low register, then inhaled and exhaled, deeply, once, through her nose (disgust, boredom, momentarily exhausted rage), and returned to the bedroom, where she lit a cigarette and pressed PLAY again. The unidentifiable pop of earlier.

Eschewing the bed, she sat knees up to chin in the desk chair, the shin of one black stocking laddered. I sat on the bed. We had returned to our earlier selves, with a part of consciousness averted. I had the feeling that if I were to refer to what had just happened in the living room, she would have no idea what I was talking about. She got up, crossed to the window, opened the curtain, moved very slightly to the music, let the curtain drop, sat down again in the chair.

'Don't know what time she'll be back,' she said.

'Does she ever stay out all night?'

'Sometimes.'

The same tumbleweed lightness that was mine at Kelp's grave.

Deborah got up and crossed to the bed. Lay down. I felt tired at the thought of her having a history.

'Why don't you fuck me?' she said.

I crashed the moped on the way home. Going too fast down Blackstock Lane I slammed the brakes on to avoid a hedgehog. Hit a welt or gravelled divot, skidded, went down (with unexpected gentleness) on my left side and let the machine slide away from me. Friction burns through left jacket sleeve and leg of jeans; corresponding grazes, a gauze of blood welling up. The alcohol had worn off, so the pain was a welcome wrap. Unable to face getting back on the thing, I began wheeling it, slowly. There had been rain, earlier, and the air was damp and fresh. I was still in the environs of Eastfield: suburban gardens, a park, the crematorium. The unfamiliarity of all this something to shove between this evening and all my life before it.

We had done it all but fully clothed. Deborah had seemed to get virtually nothing out of it, except the pleasure of watching someone – me – in extremis. Something for her in the first coupling, perhaps, sufficient Alice residue to carry her part way to pleasure, but it had petered out by the second; and by the third she was spectating, her body scornfully co-operative. Afterwards it was just a question of buttoning and zipping in silence. Deborah had got up and gone back to sit knees up to chin at the desk. It hadn't surprised me that the music was put back on, nor that when it was turned off a few minutes later silence solidified between us.

Hard to tell how long passed before she said: 'She's going out again a week on Saturday.'

At home – vaguely conscious of having lost my virginity – I had a long, scrupulous shower, brushed my teeth, and slipped naked into bed.

In the desert at evening, Malone stood still, cassock skirt ruffled by a breeze. The face, rumpled and scoured, looked out at me. No expression of censure or scorn. Just the patient grey-green eyes, looking past the dirt of the day into the future I carried in myself like an empty amphitheatre.

'A week on Saturday' wasn't referred to the following day, when I was back on the Eastfield job with hot gun and scraper. Nothing was referred to. Not as if the night before hadn't happened, but rather as if not referring to it came naturally to both of us. Instead, during my lunch hour, we masturbated each other in the funereal room on the third floor. In total silence until, feeling me close to coming and wanting perhaps to flex the muscle of her control, Deborah said again: 'You like it, don't you?'

With the expected result.

'Can I see you tonight?'

'No.'

'Why not?'

'The bitch is in.'

'Let's go out, then.'

She shook her head.

'Or you could come to mine.'

'I don't want to.'

'Why not?'

'I don't want to.'

'Why not?'

'Look, shut up will you, for fuck's sake. You're giving me a fucking headache.'

This was to be the way, her calling the shots. Nothing to lose as far as she was concerned. I – with everything to lose – shut up.

I didn't see her for the rest of the day. The following day not at all. Thereafter the weekend, and since I didn't have her number I was at a loss. I rode out to Eastfield Saturday and Sunday evenings, thinking what I don't know, that I would be able to sneak in or crawl through the back garden and tap at her window. But her room remained unlit. The only voices I heard were Alice's and Mrs Lingard's.

'What is it with you?' Pen said, late Sunday night, after my aborted secret mission.

'What?'

'I mean what is it?'

A pause. Rain on a bus-shelter roof. There had been no telling him. If I thought of telling him I got angry. The past's wailing to be connected to the present filled me with anger.

'It isn't anything,' I said. 'Fuck off.'

'Fuck off yourself. You're going weird.'

'I'm going weird. Yeah.'

'Why don't we go away somewhere?'

'No.'

'Why not?'

'No.'

'Jesus fucking Christ.'

A few moments of slackening rain; then, as if it had been caught napping, the downpour's redoubled ferocity. Cars crawled past, wipers frantic, drivers hunched forward, peering. I got up and walked to the doorway. Pen, with match hand–cupped against the wind, lit a Rothmans. His face yellowy orange in the little flare of light.

'I'll see you later,' I said.

He looked up at me. I saw the whole reflexive mechanism of him stall. *Oh yeah, good idea*, he should have said, or *Don't be a fucking nangle*, or *Are you out of your pubic mind*? But he didn't. For the first time our history impotent. His face emptied of expression, achieved the innocence of shock.

I turned, with the feeling of a limb being slowly torn from its socket, and walked out into the hammering rain.

Monday morning dragged. Lunchtime came and went. No sign of her. With a sort of calm insanity I decided to walk down to the basement flat and knock on Mrs Lingard's door. Some question, a workman's question — it would come to me — and if it didn't I would simply enquire after the whereabouts of the matron. I downed tools.

In the reception hall I came across two care assistants lifting a white–haired old woman who had had a fall.

'Can you stand, Elsie?' one of them bellowed.

'Yiss, I can.'

'Come on. Let's get you sat down.'

The old woman had her head down, as if ashamed. I recognized her as soon as she lifted it. Less than ten years ago I had lived for her encouragements in red. *Very imaginative. Neat work. 4 Good Marks.* Miss Warburton.

'Can I help you?' one of the care assistants asked me.

'Nigel?' Miss Warburton said.

'It's not Nigel, love, it's the painter's lad.'

'That's Nigel.'

'No, love, it's not. Come on now. Let's get you sat.'

'I was . . .' I said.

They weren't listening. They were absorbed in guiding

Miss Warburton (not gently) to one of the hall's wing-backed chairs. I retreated, slowly, watching. Terrible, incremental articulation to get her seated.

'Do you need the toilet, Elsie?' Again bellowed.

'No, I'm all right, thank you.'

'Are you sure?'

She didn't answer a second time. I saw how it was: flashes of dignity. *I will be* right outside *this door*, she had said, with index finger raised. Now her hands shook, holding the cigarette they'd lit for her. *Astronomical, but good try!*

Deborah was in the empty third-floor room (now painted and dry) when I got back.

'Where've you been?' she said. 'I've been waiting here fucking ages.'

When the unreferred-to Saturday arrived, I went to Eastfield from a chemically deadened afternoon with Pen. His parents and Gareth were on holiday in Greece; but despite having the whole house to get stoned and drunk in he'd moved his portable television up into the attic (where he all but lived), which so desecrated the place's memory as to make it bearable. He got drunk and stoned without glamour, alone, with express anaesthetic purpose. He had taken to watching *horse racing*, stoned, low-slung and with feet up in the attic's gutless armchair. Horse racing, football, snooker, indoor bowls. Cricket.

'D'you want some of this, Dum?'

Another joint. I didn't. I hadn't wanted any of the last one, either, or the better half of a bottle of vodka. I felt vague, with, underneath, great anger ready to leap up. Hours had passed with us not saying much. In a monotone Pen had explained odds, stewards' enquiries, the going. We could manage, just, on this diet. Nothing had been said about the night in the bus shelter. It was as if we had agreed to make a parodic spectacle of ourselves.

At the door – dull afternoon of low cloud, Pen's garden sullen – I tried to give him Kelp's Zippo.

'I don't want it,' he said.

'I think you should have it.'

'I don't want it. It wasn't given to me.'

'That doesn't matter. That's just his mum. *She* wouldn't know.'

'No, Dum. Ta.'

'Go on.'

'I don't fucking *want* it, okay?'

The ugly emphasis to which we were prone now. Followed, as always, by silence, a little lump of confusion.

'I'll see you, Dum. Give us a call.'

'Yeah. Okay. See you.'

Used to be Kelp and I would look back from the end of the drive. Pen mooning or giving us the vee. Now I heard the door close before I was three paces away.

'What are these?' I ask Deborah. (All the way over from Pen's I've existed in a state of suspension, preventing either belief or non-belief in what Deborah and I might do to Alice when I get there. It's tiring, this averting one's consciousness from both certain past and possible future, like forcing one's eyes not to focus. But I'm getting it. Let other things occupy the space: the pent weather; the pavement rolling under me; all the present's disinterested details.

Alice is in the kitchen, sullenly finishing the remains of her burned dinner. The two of us are lying on Deborah's bed, her on her belly, me, lower down, on my side. I've taken her stockings off. Two white and satiny scars the width of a finger, horizontally, one across each calf. Me with the nerve to ask after long wondering and her very loudly not saying anything about them.

'None of your business.'

'Okay. Sorry.'

'Turn you on, do they?'

'No. I just . . . Sorry.'

I can feel the deadness of her. The labour it is for her to speak.

'I think you should let me paint this room,' I say.

'My mum used to leave me with my granddad. One day I wandered off. When I came home, my granddad burned my legs with the poker. Stop me wandering off.'

A pause.

'Will that do?'

'Jesus Christ.'

'She was a whore,' she says. Then in mock little-mite nursery rhyme: 'A whore, a whore a tewwible whore, wan off when I was ownee four.' Then in her normal voice: 'With a nigger.'

'What about your dad?'

'Stop talking.'

'Okay, sorry.'

'Stop *talking*.'

I lie very still. I'm not thinking of anything in particular, just trying to exist, to live with the ever-expanding core of numbness and the frantic periphery of excitement. In the world I inhabit now – the world I've been inhabiting for more than a week – I feel, powerfully, the certainty of my parents' death. They will die, be dead, be finished, the stream of their love cut off. And I will still be here. The world and all its rubbish of television and chemicals will still be here. This certainty of my parents' death has done something to my skin, taken off a dull layer, left me in sensual nudity. *Nothing will happen nothing will happen nothing will happen.*

'Finished!' Alice calls, as instructed.

For what seems a long while Deborah and I remain still.

'I've finished!' Alice calls again.

Another minute. My skin now like a living organism. *There's no. But there's. She's. We'll.*

Half an hour of amicable Snakes and Ladders before this moment. Beginning with friendliness serves a more refined aesthetic than would simply pouncing on her. Her uncertainty is our aphrodisiac; we've watched her moving from radical doubt (she remembers last time) to guarded comfort (oh, they're *not* going to) to flat dismay (they are) with steadily waxing delight. We force ourselves not to hurry.

In the bathroom, I stand behind Deborah (both of us undressed) holding her breasts, my cock pressed tight between her thighs, its blood-packed glans just visible, protruding below her vulva like a strawberry deformity. Alice lies naked and prostrate in the bathroom's doorway, whispering nonsense to the carpet, her red hair spread around her like the fronds of an undersea plant. The freckles go all over her, we've discovered. Discovered, too, the flesh's stupid obedience: her nipples, for example, are dials which, when twisted, increase the wealth of her pain and our pleasure simultaneously. I've knelt on her arms with my hands pressed over her mouth while Deborah sits astride her 'tuning her in'. The screams vibrate through my palms. It's almost hilarious to us, Alice's incarceration in her own body, the discomfort that guarantees in our care. At each point – right up to the moment of action – I've heard my own calm voice: I won't do this. I'll do this, but no more. I won't do this. I'll do *this*, but no more. At the edge of each

232

transgression I've felt sure that now, *now* will reality rip and God's wrath come through. God's or Malone's. I've approached the tip of each violation with steadily escalating excitement and disgust, sure, *sure*, of the intervention to come. Nothing has come. I've got bigger and more sensitive, felt my will expanding into spaces it's never occupied before. It's not the absence of God (or Malone) that I feel but the presence of something else, a rich and pregnant observation, this and the terrible dare to choose not to go on with it.

'Keep your eyes open.'

But I cross over. The moments surrender one by one. Alice's face, crumpled with pain (words flash, *distress, misery, suffering*) is a clue; if we keep it in front of us long enough we will see our way through into truth that will turn us once and for all into giants or gods ourselves.

'Keep your eyes *open*, I said.'

Deborah's voice is cold and angry, with barely restrained fury underneath. My own importance astounds me. My reverence for every detail of perception is the angel's for every infinite detail of the Divine. I wonder how much more is possible before my transfiguration is complete. Alice's face measures the precise quantity of her misery. The thing in the room with us wants us to be brave, to press on.

Deborah's jugular is petal-soft and blood-warm where my lips touch. She wants to badly hurt Alice, I know. I know she wants to badly hurt her because I want to badly hurt her myself. Holding Deborah in my arms I can feel the need to surrender (after dozens of deliberate slowings-down and withdrawals) to that thing which is either a luminous truth or a luminous lie but which in any case is a luminous promise, there, in front of her, waiting. I can feel her driving towards what must surely be a perfection or apotheosis, the building conviction that the last steps into divinity or revelatory nothingness are finally before her. *We are so huge, so huge.*

Why, why, why, why, why, is an irritant tacked onto the end of each beat of my pulse. I don't know *why*, only *that*. That I myself am the carrier of a great golden calf of rage before which, if I am willing, bowing down will liberate me along with her. I'm not quite sure of my balance, bearing this idol. Deborah has taken Alice by the hair, not violently, but with a gentle insistence.

'I don't *want*.'

Of course she doesn't, and there are Deborah's ribs flaring under my hands. Our body heat yields not quite unity, but exquisite collusion. The world shrinks to a negligible rind.

Deborah tilts Alice's face up, lightly slaps and accurately spits into it. It's not enough. How can it ever be enough? How is it possible that it's all so unsatisfactory and so nearly perfect?

'Look at it,' Deborah says, meaning her cunt and my cock, the little hermaphrodite gargoyle they make together. Not that Alice has a choice, unless she closes her eyes, which she's learned not to do. Snakes and Ladders. Now this. She can't remember how.

'Kiss it,' Deborah hisses, very close, I know, to an angry denouement. 'Kiss it, *kiss* it you useless little fu – huh – huh – huh—' because the articulation can't quite survive under the sudden weight of pleasure as she comes (as do I, with near simultaneity, a gobbet of sperm striking Alice on the chin as Deborah yanks the hair to get a clean look at the dirt of it), her own eyes unable to resist closing, opening slowly, her mouth a curl of disgust.

◆

A lovebite, on Holly's breast. Not given by me. No attempt to conceal it.

She lay with one arm bent up behind her head, the other by her side, not looking at me. A silent, eloquent presentation.

I looked for the version of myself that would have ignited with jealousy. It was still there, visible, like a thing preserved in formaldehyde. I felt a fondness for it. I could go back, admire it, walk round it, smile. But not, apparently, release or reanimate it.

Simplest to lie down next to her, not touching. The bite will change colours over the next few days, reminding us both of being teenagers. I had an image of a man's dark head against her breast, her face with eyes open looking elsewhere.

Very gently, I leaned up and over, then bent my head, kissed the place where she had been marked.

We lay still for a moment, without speaking. Then she rolled onto her side, away from me.

◆

We live in a mitigating world. Not much room for freely chosen evil between the devil of nurture and nature's deep blue sea. Deborah's character witnesses? Psychoanalysis. Neurophysiology. The human genome project. Put enough of them on the stand and Deborah disappears completely. Put determinism on the stand and we *all* disappear.

She shuffled her stories, held their details in contempt.

Actually, I had a twin sister. But my mother killed her. That's when they took me off her.

Really?

My mother's in a psychiatric hospital in Manchester.

Jesus Christ.

Or rather, she was, until Mrs Thatcher decided it was time to reintegrate the nutters. Now she wanders around the Arndale in her nightie, stinking of shit.

I know you don't like to talk about it.

Neither would you if Kirk fucked you in the arse every night then made you lick his cock clean.

After which particular confession she got up and swept with one swipe the entire metropolis of bottles and jars off the dresser, most of which, however, didn't break.

Difficult to sift. She could have just refused to talk about it at all. But some desire for a narrative, however unreliable, would have its way. 'Kirk', I gathered, was Mrs Lingard's estranged husband and the father of Alice from a previous marriage. He and Mrs Lingard had adopted Deborah, but had then (alcoholism having done for Kirk's ex) ended up with Alice as well. 'That was just about it for Kirk,' Deborah said. 'He fucked off.' (She laughed, flatly, when she told me this. Forced.)

All this information came in the early days, flippantly – though once or twice with passionless tears. As time went on, she talked less and less about herself, and eventually less and less about anything.

I said nothing to my parents about Deborah. Mrs Lingard did know, however, greeting my introduction with weariness and irritation. She was waiting for Deborah to be gone. I was allowed in Deborah's room, but not to keep her company babysitting, the theory being that Alice needed more watching than the two of us alone together in the flat were fit for. Needless to say Deborah and I treated this and all other proscriptions with contempt.

Alice irritated us. The parameters of what we could do with her (*to* her) pricked us almost beyond bearing. Deborah's eyes would well up with fury because she wanted so much and was allowed so little. The route to the heart of it – it . . . yes, *It* – was there before us and yet we could take only the first few steps. The Devil (who was it in the room with us if not him?) garlanded us with suggestions – or rather the same suggestion, repeated: that it was only a matter of courage. We need only reach out without fear . . .

Deborah had long since established the formula for managing Alice: an early coercion into sex games (I'd seen the grim Polaroids), the revelation that such practices were filth, followed by the demand for more as the only guarantee against exposure. We couldn't mark her, obviously, beyond the odd scratch or bruise which would pass as play wear-and-tear or be explained by Alice as her own clumsiness – and that was what pained us most. At times, seeing Deborah's frustration at having to hold back from real damage, my heart ached for her.

Naturally I had very bad dreams. Other people's dreams being boring, I'll limit myself to one, since there is one, a particular one, which more or less stands for all.

In the dream I wake up in the middle of the night lying in my bed. The bedroom door is locked and there's a huge creature moving around the room in the dark, breathing. A wolf. A very big wolf, intelligent and vicious.

Nowhere for me to go. I'm just lying there in the dark waiting for it to attack. I realize that had I not woken up the wolf wouldn't have known I was there. But I have woken up, it *does* know. The sound of its husky breathing and heavily padding paws is unbearable. I see glimmers of eyes and teeth. I hear wet chops open and close. All of which seems to last a long time – then suddenly it rushes me. I feel the dreadful weight as it leaps onto my chest. Its slaver falls onto my face.

But it doesn't attack. The jaws lunge and snap – inches

from my face – but never touch me. Stranger still (and this is what wakes me at last on a giant inhalation) is that the wolf speaks to me. Between gnashes and snarls it demands: 'Don't you know who I am? Don't you know who I am? *Don't you know who I am?*'

I don't remember much of the other parts of my life from those weeks. My parents were wraiths, my mum, when she could, taking my face in her hands and looking with a faint frown, as if she might see, somehow, whatever sickness was turning her son into a stranger. My secrecy and self-disgust were translated into – among other things – extreme politeness and a permanently tidy room. I ate all the meals my mother put in front of me. She looked at me as if suspecting the work of a giant intestinal worm: consumption without nutrition. Most of the time I didn't really believe I'd done the things I'd done. Looking at myself would have made no more sense than sticking my hand in a fire.

Alice went away to a summer school for a month.

One afternoon, alone in Deborah's room, I went through her handbag. Mrs Lingard was out. Deborah, with the period cramps that crippled her, was doubled up in a hot bath.

I didn't expect to find anything. I wasn't *looking* for anything. Rather I was in that state of listless empty-mindedness – a kind of blankness or moronism – in which any action might rise up, motivelessly, and claim my agency. Therefore, suddenly, the handbag. Cigarettes, contraceptive pills, a scatter of biros and broken biro bits, an address book with no addresses in it, a Flake wrapper, lipstick, hairbrush, compact, purse. In a little inside pocket, receipts, unused stamps, and a thin sheet of letter paper, folded small, clearly having been once crumpled.

Dear Deborah

This is a hard letter to write, as painful for me as I imagine it will be for you. Maybe the best thing is just to come straight to the point.

It's not going to work, is it? You know what I mean. Your coming here. It's making it so hard for Sylvia and me to work on *our* difficulties, you see, which, despite appearances, are formidable, I assure you. And it's confusing Jenny very much, poor thing.

I had thought, initially, that the best thing would be for us to meet alone – maybe go away for a weekend or something – but as Sylvia pointed out: what's the point of a relationship that won't do either of us justice? I know this may sound hard. I know. But in the end, I know you'll have the strength to understand. You've my blood, after all, which is good for nothing if not being tough as old boots! You've got your life, and I don't want to intrude. That's my other fear, you see: seeing you has been an overwhelming experience for me after all these years. Really overwhelming. What worries me (and Sylvia – who by the way really *isn't* the monster you must think she is) is the thought of how much the love I feel for you will take me away from the life and responsibilities *I* now have. You underestimate yourself, talking the way you do: you could very easily turn an old man like me into a lovesick fool, hanging on your every word without a thought for anyone else!

You've turned out such a mature and bright person. That's how I know you'll understand. It goes without saying that

Whatever it was, it would have to go without saying, because that was the end of the sheet, and no amount of further rootling turned up its successors. I wondered why she'd kept only this one. And whether this was the last. And whether her mother had been any better. And why, since nothing of the kind had happened to me, I, like Deborah, had turned out to be a bearer of the old disease.

'I'm getting out,' she said in the dark the next night, knowing I was still awake. She had started letting me in through her window after hours. Therefore the two of us (me allegedly at Penguin's) squeezed into her single bed.

She meant of Begshall. Of this.

'I could come with you,' I said.

There followed a very long pause. Despite the bed's narrowness we were lying on our backs, side by side. I turned my head to look at her profile. The unblinking stare wasn't theatrical; she wasn't aware that I was even looking at her.

After several minutes in silence, she turned onto her side, away from me, without a word.

A week before the first of my three good-byes to Deborah, Julia came home, ashamed of the money she'd recently made. A lucrative (for her) painting backlash after the first wave of installation fever.

'It's being engineered,' she told me. 'The whole fucking thing's about gallery owners, not painters. The painters think it's great. The painters think the world's *seeing the light* again, after all this . . . this . . .' She made a face, one which knew that her intolerance of installation work rested chiefly on her unwillingness to acquire the requisite language. 'Another two years,' she said, 'and we'll all be doing portraits on the prom in Blackpool. Ah well, grab it while you can, I suppose.'

My palms were hot, my face thick. I was inflated by

everything I concealed. Pinpricks everywhere, waiting for the conspicuous balloon of me to land.

'Julia Thatcher,' I said.

'Fuck off. Anyway, Tories are actually personally generous. It's the socialists who are tight-arses. Personal generosity inversely proportional to . . . whatsit, the generosity of their ideologies.'

She was twenty-three now, sharp-featured, with a look of quick and cynical truck with the world. Tawny hair in a straight fall to the middle of her spine. My father's long legs. A deep mistrust of *joining* anything, and an irritable relationship to her own beauty. There had been lovers since the sculptor from Madrid, but none had lasted. I found myself mildly surprised that the thought of having sex with her didn't do much for me – knowing nonetheless that such things were just a question of working oneself up in the right way.

'Besides,' she said, 'I'm buying a flat.'

'That's nice. Where?'

She stopped unpacking and looked at me. Looked at me properly. 'What the fuck is the matter with you?' she said.

'What? Nothing.'

'Are you on something?'

'Course not.'

'You look weird.'

'Oh yeah, well, cheers.'

'Mum and Dad say you're never here.'

'So?'

'They say you don't see Penguin much, either.'

'What a lot they say.'

'So who is she?'

'She?'

'Come on.'

'There is no "she".'

'We've had this conversation before,' she said.

'So?'

'One day we'll have it without you lying through your teeth.'

'You're amazing, Jules,' I said. 'Absolutely amazingly full of bollocks.' Desperate. 'Have you brought me anything from London or what?' I said.

Julia made a wry face and lifted the last layer of clothes out of her suitcase to reveal what was obviously a framed canvas, heavily wrapped.

'Don't say I never do anything for you,' she said.

It was me, sitting face-front in an armchair in a room with no other furniture. A small fair-haired and white-dressed female figure with her back to the viewer stood looking out of the room's one window, which gave onto an urban landscape. The picture was executed in large, painterly blocks of colour, reverentially sub-Hopper, but with Baconian disturbance in places: the side of my head, the woman's feet, the windowsill, one patch of wall. The whole thing, including frame, was no bigger than a tabloid news-paper. It was signed, but untitled.

'Don't sell it yet,' she said. 'Wait a few years. Preferably until I'm dead, in fact.'

She had taken to recording her dreams. She kept a Dictaphone by the bed, so the narratives would be spared the warp of writing. 'It's all rubbish,' she said. 'But it's funny. You do start to see recurring things. Numbers, colours, animals. I dreamed this one *twice*, believe it or not. Your fault for pre-tending you haven't got a girl stashed away.'

A girl stashed away. Two girls, Jules.

★

'Well, I do remember him, you know,' Miss Warburton said. 'Millicent says her memory's better than mine, but it's not.'

'I'm sure it isn't,'

'She tells lies, you know.'

'Does she?'

'Oh yes. They're like that, some people. Wicked. Is my wardrobe coming today?'

I sat by the window in her room drinking a cup of thin tea. The curtains were half closed. She had had a slight stroke since her fall, and was allowed to stay in bed a good deal. Her skin had shrivelled, giving her a skullish look. A thin, reptilian dewlap from jaw to clavicle. Short silver hair damp and wild from a tropical sleep. I had spent half an hour trying to bring Deborah to orgasm with my mouth, for the last fifteen minutes of which she had lain barely moving. I had stopped. She had remained lying on her back, staring up at the ceiling. She had felt far away, sealed inside some shell, and for once it made me afraid. The great sculptures of silence we had made, the terrible collection of them, their dark value. I hadn't been able to think of a single thing to say. With every second that passed I had become more convinced that at any moment I was going to open my mouth and start screaming. I was convinced of this. If I started, I would never be able to stop. Then, without a word, Deborah got up and went to the bathroom. She had locked the door and begun running a bath.

A care assistant had directed me to Miss Warburton's room.

'You were saying, Miss Warburton, about young Ignatius?'

'Elsie, love, Elsie. Oh yes. That lad – well, I say lad as shouldn't, him being a priest and all and met the Pope but he did cure my tooth whatever the wherefores of it.'

'You were telling me about his mother.'

She snapped her dentures and looked out of the window. For a moment locked up as tight as a clam. 'Yiss, I was. Don't be so impatient.'

'I'm sorry.'

'They lived on Brewer Street that's come down since. It were coming down while they lived there. They were the last ones. All the others had been given council houses. They were to move the week of the fire.'

'An accident, was it?'

Again the clamped teeth, this time with a strange clench that stretched the neck tendons. I waited.

'That's what they said. There was always t'other story, as far as I know.'

A trip to the library could confirm it, I supposed. As in detective films. Part of me imagined myself doing all this. The numb core rested in certainty that I wouldn't bother.

'They say a couple of men broke in. Been watching her. Everyone else in the street gone.'

'He saw what happened? Ignatius saw it?'

'I don't know, love, I don't know.' A very weary sigh, then. A little self-righteous head-shaking at the wickedness of the world. 'She died, poor lass. Sommat went wrong wi' im, after that. He were out of school and in hospital a long while. But when he came out he were right as rain. Like sunshine coming out of him.'

I thought of him watching what happened to her. What they must have done. What he must have seen. I had a glimpse of something, remembering the wolfish grin he'd given me, escorting Burke back through the woods: it wasn't virtue beat the Devil, it was cunning. The pure, the simply good, the meek, they weren't part of the war. It was the ones who found their way back to the light through *cunning*, they were the victories that counted. I glimpsed this, half-understanding, but as if from a distance. It made me feel exhausted. The same dog-tiredness I'd felt confronted by Deborah's invisible history.

'And did he really cure your tooth?' I asked her.

She looked out of the window, took her glasses off, as if tears were coming. They weren't, but she had acquired the elderly's appetite for emotional performance.

'Some children . . .' she said, then tailed off. 'I don't know, love. But he put his hand there, you know, bold as brass. Standing next to me while I went through his times-tables book. I felt it go. Just felt it go.' Now she did shed a few tears. I sat and held her hand, dry-eyed, no lump in the throat, nothing. The ration of even sentimentality gone. Now just that thing to which sentimentality used to be partner.

The afternoon I said the first of the three good-byes to Deborah Black, I had my last fight with Penguin.

'You haven't paid me back for the last lot, Pen,' I said.

'I have.'

'No, you haven't.'

He had been awkward — more awkward than usual — through the horse racing, and very visibly not smoking any weed, though the last of the attic's stash of spirits had seen us into bad-tempered drunkenness. He owed me money (borrowed for marijuana) and now he wanted to borrow more.

'I can't fucking believe you can sit there and say I haven't paid you, when I distinctly—'

'You haven't paid me back.'

'Yes, I *have.*'

'No, you *haven't.*'

He knew he hadn't. Knew, too, that if he just admitted he

hadn't I'd lend him whatever I could spare. But we had allowed disgust between us. A store of disgust had been available to us ever since the funeral and now discharged itself erratically. It was a relief to us, in fact, to be able to let some of the disgust out.

'Never thought I'd see it, Dum,' he said, feet up in the armchair, face pinched with anger.

'See what?'

'You. The day you turned into a fucking . . . The day you started bothering about fucking *money*.'

'I'm not bothered about money. I'm bothered about you *lying*.'

He turned, at that, and looked at me with a version of his face I'd never seen before: adult.

'Don't,' he said. 'Don't fucking use that word with me.'

'What word?'

'You fucking know what word. Don't you talk to me about lying.'

Don't get up and go. Stay here. You don't have to tell him any-thing, but just stay here.

I got up. The smell of Mogs's spaghetti bolognaise drifted up from downstairs. I put a five-pound note on the table.

'Keep it,' he said.

'Don't be stupid,' I said.

He wouldn't look at me, either, now, ashamed of how much he needed the money. 'You pick that fucking fiver up and put it back in your pocket, Dummie. I'm not fucking kidding.'

'Pen—'

'Pick it *up*.'

I picked it up and put it back in my pocket. Went to the trapdoor.

'Tell your ma thanks, but—'

'Just fuck off, will you?' he said, staring at the television screen.

Deborah went into Alice's pocket and pulled out Kelp's Zippo.
'I never,' Alice said. 'I *never*.'

I felt tired. A measure of exhaustion equal, almost, to the measure of desire. The core of me, that numb bulk of deadened certainty I had carried all the way to this summer's end, seemed diminished, whittled down to a thin but stubborn lode. I hadn't noticed it happening, except for the fatigue like a weight given to me to carry every day. I ached, moved forward through the circles of desire abrasively, every pleasure carrying a correlative contribution to the weight of tiredness.

'This is daft,' Alice said, in her voice of fractured jollity, her face wet with tears. Returning from summer school, she had let in the mad hope that this wouldn't happen any more. Now that it had, there was both misery and, at a deeper level, the comfort of familiarity. She crouched on the floor with her face against the carpet, backside raised. Deborah had shoved the handle of a plastic hairbrush into her anus and now sat back, on her haunches, like an intelligent but perplexed animal, occasionally giving the brush a shove or wiggle, as if not sure of how to proceed.

Nonetheless we got onto the bed and hurriedly adjusted our clothes, gracelessly exposed the parts of ourselves needed. With the first flash of Deborah's cunt a great surge of energy or weariness went through me. I had to force myself not to think about her, her history, the prints the human world had left on her. *Dear Deborah, this is a hard letter to write*. If I thought about any of that I would be useless to both of us; any of that would rear up between us, blocking the magic of collusion. Therefore I shut it out.

She was urgent and impatient with me. When I kissed her she turned it into a wrestle, as if I was the space around her closing in, pulled away from me, then clamped her big mouth on mine. She made noises as if someone had cut out her tongue, as if she would speak if she could.

For a while she had me fuck her, hard, simply, in front of Alice (who between tears grinned as to an invisible angel, grown-uppishly waiting for all this nonsense to be over) on her knees by the bed, unable to look at us. Deborah stared at Alice, occasionally spat or swiped at her, all the while muttering to herself – curses, to judge from the sibilants and fricatives; these accompanied by facial contortions of disgust bordering on pain, as if no outward signs, neither obscenities nor gurns, could begin to show how revolting this was, all of it.

Then, suddenly, she stopped moving altogether.

Still inside her, I raised myself up on my elbows. For a moment our eyes met, not with the usual bright deadness of agreement, but with uncertainty (mine) and panic (hers). I opened my mouth to ask what was wrong, but at that moment her face contorted as if in terrible pain. Her fingers, wrapped in my hair, clenched. She shuddered, turned her head to one side. I thought she was going to vomit.

She didn't. Just shivered for a moment, then seemed to get herself – whatever was going on inside her – under control. She didn't look at me, but loosened her fingers in my hair, pulled my face towards her, moved her hips, kissed me.

I didn't understand, or know what to do, so I moved with her, slowly, until the rhythm came back, and we began another slow descent to the state in which every humble detail of the room would blaze and deafen with the Devil's promise.

In waves, a feeling similar to listening to music or looking at an empty sky: the division between me and my experience, between subject and object, burned away. I wasn't there. Or rather, *I* wasn't there. No me and no it. Just a curiously burgeoning event into which I had been assimilated or by which I had been destroyed. Passing into and out of these phases was a process of falling asleep and coming to. There was no knowing of my own absence until my own presence had been thrust back upon me.

Coming out of one of these – the fourth or fifth in the timeless hour – I knew something was wrong.

At some point Alice had been gagged and stripped and put on her back on the bed. Deborah was on all fours over her, with me coupled to her from behind.

The elsewhereness, the giant and fillable emptiness into which Deborah and I had begun to expand seemed to shrivel or crinkle, to shrink and tear around me like a desiccant skin, then to vanish, leaving me cold and exposed.

Deborah was delivering between gasps and sighs her mumbled litany. I couldn't pick out more than the odd word – fuck, pig, yes, cunt, shit, piece, eh? – but whatever the rest they enhanced her transformation. A tremendous energy surrounded her body in a hot aura, making me acutely conscious of the absence of one from my own. I felt with disgust the unexceptional nature of my knees and knuckles, belly and scalp, my dreadful and particular corporeality. I felt the exact, dull dimensions of who I was.

The room's molecules dropped out of cahoots, left me with a terrible intimation of matter's deadness. I pulled out of Deborah, suddenly. She made a strange noise, something like 'haih', but didn't stop what she was doing. Her face was set in contempt or nausea, the dark eyes half closed, the wet lips martially curled, the skin flushed and glazed with sweat.

I knelt beside the bed and regarded her for a moment, filled – almost filled, I should say – with reverence. But seeing her warmth only exacerbated my own feeling of cold, and I stood up and took hold of her wrists.

I wasn't thinking when I said, 'Stop it, Deborah.' I wasn't thinking that if I didn't remove her hands from Alice's windpipe Alice would run out of air and lose consciousness, and that if the pressure was maintained she would stop breathing and die. I didn't think I was doing the right thing. I vacillated, during the silly-looking struggle that followed. I wasn't by any means resolved. The beauty of Deborah's face – her incomplete transfiguration – distracted me, repeatedly.

But eventually the fingers came free and Alice drew a mighty inhalation, succeeded by a long fit of choking and coughing. She rolled off the bed and crashed onto her hands and knees on the floor. I saw her from the corner of my eye, but could only pay partial attention to her, occupied as I was with Deborah, who was writhing in my grip. She had been pulled back from the brink of beatification. Now she looked furious and bereaved. There were tears in her eyes.

She got a hand free and used it to administer a blow to my face, part slap, part scratch. Two of her fingernails drew blood. A lovely warmth rose in my cheek.

'Get dressed,' I said to Alice, not taking my eyes from Deborah. She would have left me behind. Without compunction she would have gone on ahead of me into the Devil's promise. I didn't know why I hadn't been able to go with her. It felt a paltry failure. My body was goosefleshed. I looked at one of my shoes on the floor. Then a sock, my underpants, my jeans. The thought of dressing depressed me.

Deborah said not a word. We looked at each other. Her face was clayish with anger, but I knew she would consider a sound or word from herself a defeat.

I began to dress. Deborah got up from the bed and picked her yellow dressing gown up from the floor.

It took a long time to coax Alice from the bathroom. I was worried that Mrs Lingard would return before I'd finished. But eventually, after much soft talking and a raft of promises, she emerged, with face pouchy from crying and arms wrapped round herself for comfort. She shrank against the wall when Deborah appeared – but my beloved ignored her, passing both of us on carefully placed feet and with averted face. She went into the bathroom and locked the door.

'You know what these are, don't you?'

The wretched Polaroids. Alice on a kitchen chair with chin on knees, struggling to chew and swallow a placatory bourbon.

'No more, all right?'

She didn't understand. Neither did I.

Kelp's Zippo lit first time.

A week passed. Two. Nothing happened. I didn't phone Deborah and she didn't phone me. I existed in a state of near idiocy, one in which something as simple as an orange might detain my consciousness for an hour. I took long, empty minded baths. I returned to my A-level texts with plodding diligence. *Marlow ceased, and sat apart, indistinct and silent, in the pose of a meditating—*

Then, one night, I woke myself up crying. I stopped as soon as I was awake, but the feeling of loss was like a hardened cavity in my chest. I dressed, went downstairs, made and drank a cup of tea, and, at first light, walked out, circuitously, to Eastfield.

'What do you want?'

Mrs Lingard looked haggard. Her breath smelled, stalely,

of instant coffee. Alice, wide-eyed, with brown lips and liquorice bootlace dangling, peered out from the hallway behind her.

'Is Deborah in, please?'

She looked at me. Compressed mouth and narrowed eyes, bagged with tiredness. The last few days the weather had turned brisk. Now heavy wind moved a flocculent sky. A few drops of rain whisked about. At the bottom of the home's back lawn, the gardener was burning rubbish. I thought of the Polaroids, Alice's image, blistering, bursting, stinking the kitchen up. No more, all right?

'No, she's not here.'

Her voice rasped. Alice in the background wound the other end of the bootlace round her finger.

'Oh,' I said. 'Okay. Sorry to bother you. D'you know when she might be back?'

Something in the fire snapped like a broken bone and coughed bright sparks. I knew before the words were out.

'She's not coming back,' Mrs Lingard said. 'She's gone.'

CHAPTER FIVE

◆

And Love Shall Have
No Dominion

'Sometimes something happens to you,' I said to Holly last night. 'And it becomes the thing against which everything else has to make sense.'

It was after two in the morning. We were sitting at an outside table at a little bar called Asmodeus on the corner of First Avenue and 6th Street. The heat's unreasoning phase had passed. The city's afterglow, now, and some occasional movement of air. Five other outside tables, three of which were occupied: two couples, desultorily winding their night out down, and one deeply suntanned man in his forties wearing only khaki shorts and loafers, reading the *New York Times*. (The novelty of being up, out, and lazily drinking tall drinks in the small hours has never worn off for me – as I believe it never wears off for any of the city's expats. Even Holly, I think, still derives some grim satisfaction: the mad hour, the mad weather, no one thinking of going home to bed.) She had met me here straight from her shift at

McLusky's, smelling of the restaurant, fried food, cigarette smoke, perfume. It doesn't help my case that I find her irresistible in this state.

She sipped her Tom Collins, not looking at me.

'Or against which everything else fails to make sense,' she said.

Later, the bedroom's thickened air woke me. Holly lay on her back with her arms away from her sides and her legs slightly parted, as if for suntanning. Not much light from the street, but enough to show the treasure of her, the fortune of flesh and blood that refuses to diminish, no matter her own indifference to it. Briefly, before getting up, I tried to imagine how I'll feel when I've lost her. Small. Shrivelled down to a leathery essence, to be blown about by wind and weather. A few months ago this image (I saw myself, something like a dried chilli with legs, head and arms, being buffeted and drenched by wind and rain) might have brought on a laughing fit. Now it brought just a thin feeling of sadness, and a little signal of unexceptional tiredness from my bones. I got up and went into the living room.

'I got rid of the gun,' I said, quietly. A ghost is no reason not to keep your voice down when someone's sleeping in the next room. He looked tired. I wondered what this was costing him, in his scheme of things. Whatever it was costing him, he raised a slighter version of the smile.

'You look faint,' I said. 'Fainter.'

The smile wavered, slightly. He looked over his shoulder for a moment, then back at me. The air buckled.

'Kelp?'

I moved towards the window. 'Look,' I said, 'I'm leaving here, soon. I'm going. I won't have a choice. Okay? Mission accomplished. You don't need to—'

254

The air swelled again, a balloon of heat pressed up against me, then he flickered, raised his hand, and dissolved.

It occurred to me for the first time, a few minutes later, on the fire escape, breathing the ghostless air deeply through my nose, that I'm not the only one for whom the clock is ticking.

◆

It took me until 1992 to move to London, in the footsteps (or so I had always imagined) of Deborah Black, by which time I was twenty-seven, and not hopeful of my life amounting to anything. With the exception of two growing fears (they grew on the very edge of consciousness, the psychic equivalent of a peripheral visual disturbance) the content of those nine years between Deborah and London beggars my belief now, though it seemed inevitable at the time. On the surface, three years' English at Bristol, two years of a doomed PhD (*The Window and the Bomb: Revelation and Terror in the Novels of D. H. Lawrence*); academic fatigue, the deferral we all knew was terminal, eighteen suicidal months back in Begshall shuttling between tawdry jobs and the dole, finally the inescapable TEFL training and two years' joyless teaching in Manchester.

On the surface.

Beneath, a minute-by-minute assimilation of my own deviance. *Of what I had done*, as the prayer said, *of what I had failed to do*. The discovery, post-Deborah, that the two Dominic Hoods of youth were alive, kicking, and ready to recommence their pas de deux, albeit now confined within the hall of his own skull. 'Of course, the fantasist's conviction is that nothing exists in his fantasy except that which he would translate into reality *if he could do so with impunity*. This conviction, analysis shows us, is a delusion.' A delusion. The phrase visited me like a succubus in the small hours. Picked its moments and repeated itself. Became a question: *a delusion?*

It had patience, this question, I knew.

For almost a decade I was haunted by the memory of Deborah Black, I was about to claim. But the memory didn't haunt me; I haunted the memory. Went to it, at night or in the deadened hours of empty afternoons, woke it up, reminded it of all the fun we'd had, made it do things with me. There had been, in nine years, a dozen or so Linda-ish liaisons, honouring their prototype in that they afforded 'normal' sexual pleasure, subsistence suckings and fuckings and lickings, while the essential or Deborah'd Dominic Hood stood to one side, aloof, as if watching his dog chase a ball. I chose girls I didn't like or who didn't like me (sufficiently). In the fantasies that followed, Deborah and I got to know this dozen, searched and found out their distinctive talents for suffering or collusive cruelty. Each of them had something different to offer.

Love was out of the question. My fear was that there would come a time when love could no longer be *kept* out of the question. The same essential or Deborah'd self that spectated on my functional couplings not only knew that love might come, but demanded its arrival. The Devil had a question for love. The question was what love would do when it met him.

'I like it here with you,' one girl, Caroline, had said to me, post-coitally, in my Manchester bedsit. Light from the street on her bare shoulder and hip. A suggestion of intimacy waiting to be unwrapped. I had felt it, too. We had made each other laugh. I never called her, after that night.

I didn't imagine Deborah thinking of me. Imagining Deborah as a living, growing being at all, in fact, was impossible. *Where a little boy and his bear will always be playing*, wrote A. A. Milne at the end of the Pooh books, freezing Christopher Robin in the cryogenics of the collective imagination. Or a not so little boy and his girl. None of the dozen Lindas evinced the least surprise when the figure on the administrative end of poker or cigarette burn or hammer or whip turned out to be a seventeen-year-old girl in a white blouse and bottle green skirt, with a hole in the toe of her stocking.

Since Mrs Lingard's bald dismissal on the doorstep, mention of London had always ruffled the ether. Visiting Jules there over the years I had scanned the crowds, strained my peripheral vision, repeating, inwardly: *She won't be here, she won't be here, she* won't *be here . . .*

My other fear was of the unmagical world's speed and skill. *I don't think I'll ever care about power steering.* I didn't. But life without Kelp, Malone or Deborah had gobbled the best part of a decade quick; and left me with what? A national insurance number. A vocabulary. A driving licence. A degree. The intellectual ability (unwanted and generally ignored) to see instead of any ultimate reality a wardrobe of its deconstructible costumes. Nothing I wanted.

'Okay,' I said to Julia on the phone. 'You win. I'm coming. Can you put me up for a bit?'

'Well, thank fuck for that,' she said. 'What's brought that on?'

'I can't stand it any more,' I said.

'Can't stand what any more?'

I was in the Logan Street living room for this call. My mother was in the kitchen, making me cheese on toast.

Love might be—

'This feeling that I'm running out of time,' I said.

★

The day before I left Begshall (never, I swore, to return), I went (after a long time of not going) to visit Kelp's grave.

It was a cold morning in February with a high blue sky and a fierce wind. I didn't know why I was going. *The flesh has gone. The organs briefly slithering in the lined casket. Now bones, and the white hair. Not him. Yes, him.*

I did know why I was going.

'Are you going up to the cemetery before you go, love?'

My mother, very casually, the day before. Instant prickle of shame, threatening a blaze. It had become a quiet, wretched obsession of hers since 56 DEAD, that we had survived. That two of the three of us had survived. (She shopped artfully if I was with her, with a list and route that pulled us close to the church. 'D'you want to pop into the cemetery, Dominic?' *Almost* completely disguised disapproval if I said no. I could hate her for it, the intrusion, the appropriation. But every month she went up with flowers; and I never did.)

At the gates, I stopped to smoke a cigarette, for the first time in a long time wishing – uncomplicatedly – that Pen was here. We had reunited, somewhat, after Deborah's departure, but lost touch again during the university years. Letters, regularly enough, for the first couple of terms (he was at Lancaster, architecture), drinks at Christmas and Easter, but by the summer he had a steady, ballbreaking South African girlfriend (business studies) called Tanya, pronounced 'tenure' by her, whom I loathed, and who loathed me. Pen loathed her, too, I suspected, but she was attractive, in a Pekinesish way, and Pen was viral with lust for her. He seemed attentive to the air around her, and moved his hands as if patting her aura or checking for invisible irritants. I didn't hold it against him (what had I to hold against anyone?); she had, after all, a provocative irritability (not to mention the sauce of unmentionable apartheid), and I knew how desire could work with that. But the letters petered out. Vacations, increasingly, had seen us avoiding Begshall. By the end of the third year, I didn't even have an address for him.

I missed him now, with the cold making my eyes water and the green grave I couldn't bear to approach.

'Good heavens, would that be Dominic Hood there almost settin' foot in a chorch?'

Violet-jowled Feeney had emerged from the vestry in trilby and it seemed to me very inadequate overcoat. A brief window for escape while he focused — two or three seconds — then recognition, and me pinned.

'Morning, Father,' I said. 'How are you keeping?'

'Oh, I'm grand, grand. Yourself?'

Five minutes. Ten. Utterly absurd chit-chat. My cynic wondered if the priest could smell it through my coat. Unable to bear it any longer, I pulled the hip-flask out and unscrewed the top. 'Can I tempt you to a drop, Father?'

'Well, for the cold, you know, for the cold.'

He sipped and passed to me. I thought of the three of us, never bothering to wipe. Couldn't wipe now, obviously. Sipped, thinking, *From the lips which speak Transubstantiation.*

'Grand send-off for the old girl last week,' he said, with a backwards nod and an air of confidentiality.

I must have politely looked blank.

'Did you not know?'

'No. Who?'

'Old Miss Warburton, poor thing, gone on now, God bless her. Did she not teach you at St Edmund's?'

Eyes closed for a moment. Real sadness and a flash of pity. Not for Miss Warburton (although there *was* something, some dismal extension of hope for her afterlife), but for the child I had been. *Astronomical, but good try!*

'Yes,' I said, opening my eyes, resigned to finishing the whole flask with him now. 'She was my favourite teacher, when I was little.'

'You and a good many others,' he said. 'We'd Father Malone here for the service was a pupil of hers. Did y'ever meet Father Malone, Dominic?'

The wind dropped for a moment, but the heavens gave nothing away; just the endless blue smile.

A stubborn flicker of excitement, like a firework struggling to start up.

'He's not still here, by any chance, is he?' I said.

Feeney, having measured his swig for penultimacy and handed me back the flask, wiped his lips with the sleeve of his coat. 'Eh, no,' he said. 'No. He left after the funeral.'

Crackle. Hiss. A dud. No – another shot spark. A speck of light.

'You wouldn't happen to know where he was going, would you, Father?'

'Back east,' he said. 'A couple of days in London, I think, then back to the missions. There's no keeping up with a fellah like that.'

London received me with gigantic and benign indifference. On arriving, I discovered Julia had lined me up for a job interview at a publishing house called Cornerstone.

'Christ, Jules, *why*?' I said. 'I don't know anything about publishing.'

'Shut up,' she said. 'You can *read*, can't you?'

'Jules—'

'Look, it's just an entry-level position, Dominic. You'll probably be photocopying and making the tea. But it's more money than the dole and it's something you could do for a while at least. Unless you'd rather work in McDonald's?'

I went to the interview. Cornerstone had large offices in Covent Garden overlooking the street performers' cobbled square. They also had a very simple publishing agenda abbreviated by its employees to CC: conservative and commercial. The house had been established (the result of a cocaine-fuelled *bet*, it was alleged) by an English art dealer and entrepreneur, Clifford Gill, who had made a million fifty times over in the Sixties and now lived in and reigned from New York, with fingers in everything from real estate to pharmaceuticals, and for whom Cornerstone was nothing more than an eccentric's lucrative hobby.

My boss, David Drake, was a receding and benevolent queen in his late fifties with a high forehead, sharp blue eyes, long jowls and over two hundred bow-ties who had flailed over to Cornerstone during Mrs Thatcher's second term when the literary house to which he used to belong went bankrupt. Since then he had discovered in himself what he called (in a deliberate metaphorical pile-up) 'a nose for the reek of the middle-brow.'

I didn't care. Cornerstone met my three criteria: I could afford to get out from under Julia's feet, I could smoke at my desk, and I wasn't required to wear a suit.

After a dismal six months in a bedsit I moved into a shared house in Shepherd's Bush. Three other precariously maintained lives to which I (lonely, I think now, just plain lonely) added my own: Sorrel, Helen and Joe.

Sorrel, with glitzy green eyes, snuff-coloured bob, pop-kittenish body and just-barely maintained delusion that fucking her way to wealth wasn't her last available route out of poverty, took up residence in the gallery of Deborah Accomplices the minute I set eyes on her. We made the relevant evaluations immediately – namely, that I would have sex with her and that she wouldn't have sex with me – arriving at a mutual visibility that formed the basis of all transactions thereafter. She knew what I thought of her – too lazy to engage in anything more demanding than strategic sex – and was, during very occasional silent looks, willing to let her eyes own up to it. There were these piquant moments, me staring with Christly intelligence, her with chin up, defiant at the edge of self-loathing. We both enjoyed the nakedness of it. It was real, if nothing else. *And you're still getting nowhere near my pants*, the starlet eyes added, this being the curlicue, the flourish at the end of the glance, just to keep me in my place. She temped, read magazines, plotted, simmered, and did whatever she could to avoid herself.

Joe, six-three, big-knuckled, with festive blue eyes and a look of John the Baptist, was a carpenter by trade, guitarist by calling, and still, at the age of thirty-five, broken-hearted from the demise of his relationship with Tina, who, four years before my arrival at 47A, had achieved mythic status by leaving him for a Fucking Marketing Executive. He got up at the crack of dawn and went off to work in a state of near disbelief at his own tiredness, worked all day filled with hate for his site manager, then got home around seven with the evening's medicaments: six-pack of Holsten Pils; pie and chips; marijuana; videos. I don't know how many times I watched *Blade Runner* with Joe (nor how many times I watched *Angel Heart*, *Terminator*, *Terminator II*, *Excalibur* [Cherie Lunghi, Pen, for the record, Cherie Lunghi], *Brazil*, *Highlander*, *The Abyss* and *Aliens*), but I know it was a lot. The two of us would retire to Joe's room (a room crammed with all the accoutrements of the adolescence he'd been unable to leave behind), him cross-legged on the bed, me hunched in the spineless armchair, smoke, drink, watch the films, and talk – when I could get him off Tina and the

FME – about how much we would like to have sex with Sorrel, which was also a lot.

Finally there was Helen, who was an English PhD (*Aw a Muddle! Morality and Class in the Novels of Charles Dickens*), compassionate, bright, humorous and honest. Also, however, depressive, and in the grip of an occasionally audible eating disorder. When I moved in she was copy-editing for a legal firm, crippled not just by the meaninglessness of the work but by her willing acceptance of it as her lot. 'I've got this quiet voice inside me,' she told me one night, the two of us drunk. 'I used to hear it all the while I was writing my thesis. It used to go: *You're going to finish this and end up on the checkout in Sainsbury's*. And I'd lie there thinking: *I know, I know, I know*. Funny how they're right about things, those little voices.'

Once, having succumbed to the effects of a hangover, I came home from work early and heard her crying, quietly, in the bathroom. Not sentimentality but, to my astonishment, a tiny, pure desire to comfort her came over me, and I moved towards the bathroom on impulse. I was taken by surprise, however; the bathroom door was open, and there was Helen in hoiked-up nightie, sitting on the toilet, weeping. Noble desire, but also the impact of the scene's prosaic details: the smell of her shit (fruity, cattle-sheddish); the grotesque comedy of her attempt and near-catastrophic failure to reach the bathroom door and swing it shut; the bathroom's characters – mat, loofah, Andrex, plunger, sponge – each with its little personality and each observing this wreck of Agape and awkwardness from its unique inanimation. For a moment Helen and I saw each other.

Then it was gone. She lunged for the door, looked ridiculous, made me despise myself for wanting to laugh. In the end she hid her face in her hands, unable even to tell me to go. I turned and retreated to my room, where I lay down with throbbing skull and cried for a while, then masturbated, gloomily (Deborah, Sorrel, Helen, all the predictable alignments), then cried again, then fell asleep.

The two fears drove me out into the city. I told myself I didn't know what I wanted. Only what I was afraid of. Presumably there was a word for the condition. In any case going out was all I could do to stave off the other fear, that I was running out of time. A dream of being in a plummeting lift, watching the wall of the shaft rush upwards, inches from my face. The dream became a mental fixture, permanently available for consultation: *This is your life*.

'The George,' Joe said, when I asked him for a recommendation. He was sitting in front of the television fast-forwarding through the drowning scene in *The Abyss*, drinking a can of Holsten Pils. 'Off Charing Cross Road,' he added, not taking his eyes from the screen. 'On the left, after Foyles. Goslett Yard. In there till closing, then the Astoria a block further up.'

'Why them?'

He smiled, sipped his beer, burped with modulation. He was remembering something, some zest for life in the days before Tina and the FME. 'Because that's where you go if you've got fucking shocking taste in music,' he said.

I took his advice.

'Aren't you afraid?' I asked the girl who later that night (both of us drunk and bad-tempered) took me home. I had followed her up the stairs to her studio flat in Mile End. She had opened the door, entered without a backward glance. I had lingered in the doorway.

'Afraid of what?' she said, bored.

'I could be a psychotic cannibal serial killer,' I offered.

264

She stood with her hand on her hip and the hip itself cocked. She had a full-cheeked face, tuftily cut and heavily waxed bleach-blond hair and very large and blackly made-up eyes. 'You?' she said, with the air of someone who had had first hand and disappointing experience of such characters. 'Er . . . no.'

I followed her in.

'Look, if you're going to go inside me you've got to use a condom. There's some in the medicine cabinet in the bathroom. Although,' she added, slinging her denim jacket and plucking at her earrings, 'to tell you the truth, I've gone right off the idea, myself.'

Since, down on all fours, she seemed not to object to an investigative prod I pushed my cock into her anus. 'Hmm,' she said, not in pleasure, but with the suggestion of an earlier suspicion confirmed. (Thanks to Aids, the Eighties had been anal sex's decade. Millions of people who had never thought of having anal sex began thinking about nothing else. Campus health officers' T-shirts said: ANAL SEX? MAKE IT SAFE! The women I slept with at Bristol had had their relationships to their anuses transformed. Moderate sophistication required at the very least an acknowledgement of the orifice as an object of desire. But who aspired to moderate sophistication? Real sophistication was taking it – admittedly with tight-shut eyes and squeaking molars – *up the arse*.) So the little 'Hmm' in Mile End not much of a surprise. Nor much of a surprise that she – Shana – seemed unmoved by either this or any of the fiddling about with her I did after I had come. Afterwards we lay side by side, smoking and feeling nauseated, her no doubt wishing it was still early enough for me not to stay the night, me reaching out mentally towards how beautiful she would look, helping me hold down Cornerstone's new receptionist while Deborah heated the implements.

'How old are you?' she asked.

'Twenty-eight.'

A pause, indicating, I supposed, that she was older. All the room's objects well aware that we wouldn't be seeing each other again.

'This is what it's like, by the way,' she said.

'What what's like?'

'Going out in this city,' she said, stubbing out her Marlboro. 'Going home with people you don't know and trying to fuck them.'

I didn't go anywhere near 'the S & M scene'. I was not interested in scenes. Scenes were pretences. Pretend victims, pretend crimes. The theatre and props were of no more relevance to me now than they had been years ago. 'Real pain' was administered at such places, allegedly. Very well, but pain wasn't the object. Suffering was the object – and which willing sufferer truly suffered?

Cornerstone, *work*, was a comfort. Any work would have been. Unemployed consciousness brought one or the other of the two fears, sometimes both. If I stopped I heard ticking: time's clock or love's bomb. *Love is the question for the Devil. The Devil is the question for love.* I worked. Within two years I had a handful of authors of my own. My typing improved. I got to know the proofreader's hieroglyphs and the publicist's bright armour, the copy-editor's withering superiority (perfunctorily veiled with a question mark), the receptionist's omniscience and the sales rep's binary system of anxiety and ennui. About half the staff had taste and self-consciousness (in other words knew they were churning out mediocrity) and therefore drank disgustedly, with a kind of grim determination; the other half didn't think, and drank happily. In any case there was a good deal of drinking. Coupled with my social consumption, it took its toll. A string of

266

viruses, ringworm, chest pains, a bout of scabies, two doses of NSU, and, most mornings, a bloody toothbrush. All concealed from those immediately around me, though Julia eyed me askance.

My sister had a good deal of money and a share in a lucrative gallery. She was *known*, as much for her on–off relationship with paint (there had been diversions into mixed media and installation projects) as for her original oath of loyalty to it at the Royal Academy's 'A New Spirit in Painting' exhibition back in 1981. (She barely remembered swearing it, having been drunk at the time, chiefly, she remembered 'vomiting and vomiting' in one of the bathrooms, and being slung into a taxi by no less a man than Nicholas Serota himself.) Corporate commissions came from the United States, Germany, France, Italy, Japan; the Saatchi Gallery had bought the first three of her *Beatitudes* a year after opening in 1984, and the following year she had found herself one of the half-dozen darlings of Mary Boone in New York. Her address book revealed to snooping me numbers with exotic names attached to them: Francesco Clemente, Miquel Barcelo, Robert Combas, Eric Fischl, Christopher LeBrun, Sandro Chia, Mimmo Paladino, Julian Schnabel, Nacisse Tordoir. She had kept the tiny flat in West Kensington, but worked from a studio in the East End, a big, ugly building somewhere between Stratford and Leyton bought cheap from a liquidated trucking company and converted. Globetrotting Clifford Gill was one of her collectors.

'I hope you didn't sleep with him to get me the job,' I said to her, one night at her flat. It was late. Rain rustled outside. We sat each in an armchair, the fire muttering between us, Al Stewart's *Year of the Cat* down low on the hi-fi, Julia with white knees showing through Levis holes. (She dressed like a tramp, these days: boots, old gardening jackets, a moth-eaten cardie. When she glammed up for an event, the transformation was startling.)

'Don't be insane,' she said. 'I'd rather spend the night in a septic tank.'

'Speaking of which,' I said, 'how is your love life?'

As expected, the slowly closed eyes and curled lip. On the surface, the comedy version of disgust or wits' endedness; beneath (I knew, she knew I knew) something approaching violence or despair. She had recently come home to find her (now-ejected) boyfriend having himself robotically fellated by a prostitute on her, Julia's, bed.

'It wasn't the infidelity,' she said, now, after my pressing. 'Although God knows that was fucking shite. It was the look on his face. It was amazing, really, seeing someone you thought you knew. Seeing a completely new expression on his face.'

We let the last track of record play out.

'Do you remember Malone?' I asked, when it had finished. I had dreamed of him the night before. He was standing on a dune in the desert at dusk. I was circling him, in the air, very slowly, proportions more or less those of a helicopter and the Statue of Liberty. A tiny particle of something blew off the edge of his ear and went sailing away on the air. Then two more particles. Then a dozen, hundreds, a swarm. A sand sculpture. The breeze swirled around him. Half his head was gone, and most of his right side. He was saying something, but I couldn't understand. I woke myself up, shouting.

'Who?'

'Father Ignatius Malone. Weird-looking priest used to drop in at St Edmund's once in a blue moon. Dark face, white hair. You told me he was an exorcist.'

I watched her thinking back.

'God,' she said. 'I'd forgotten all about him. What, have you seen him or something?'

'No.' A pause. 'No. It's just . . .'

She waited.

'Just that I remember always thinking that if I had to make a last confession — I mean *really* a last confession, if I was *dying* . . . I mean if I'd committed some fucking awful sin . . .'

'You haven't done something, have you?'

Quick quick quick 'No. But I've always thought that in the end I'd want him as my confessor. I don't think he'd dick around with the penances. They'd be real.'

'What are you on about?'

I grabbed my jaw and slowly twisted — *crick* — my neck, as he had done in the medical room all those years ago. I wished I could do the same for every joint in my body.

'Dunno,' I said. 'You saying about the different look on his face.'

'You don't still go to confession, do you?' Julia asked.

'Of course not. Bloody hell.'

'I do.'

'*What?*'

She laughed, one humourless bark. 'Shocking, isn't it? Not often. Hardly ever, really. Sometimes, though.'

'I can't believe it.'

'Bless me, Father, for I have sinned.'

'Christ, Jules, I'm amazed.'

She nibbled a fingernail, spat a bit out, nibbled again. 'I'm amazed myself,' she said. 'I read the Sermon on the Mount the other day. Sat here crying like an idiot.'

'But confession,' I said. 'I mean, *confession*?'

'It's not the priest. It's the act of telling the truth about yourself.'

'But a priest?' I said. 'I mean why couldn't we— Why not go to a therapist or an analyst or a counsellor or something?'

'I don't know. Because there's no poetry in it. No beauty and ugliness.'

'No magic, you mean.'

'Yes. No magic. Magic is the missing thing.'

'God help us, Jules.'

'God help us all, Dommie.'

Woken one Tuesday in the small hours by the return of the wolf and his *don't you know who I am*? routine, I found Helen sitting on one of the kitchen's high stools, staring out into 47A's rubbishy back garden. She was bundled up in her pink towelling bathrobe, hands clasped round a huge mug of tea. The Fosters ashtray contained eight B&H butts. Within seconds of my arrival she had another on the go.

'What about that bloke from HMV?'

'What about him?'

'I thought you were going out with him?'

'Oh yeah,' Helen said. 'We were practically engaged.'

Sarcasm. Therefore not suicidal. Suicidal, Helen lost all humour, including sarcasm, and instead became tenderly solicitous of everyone, of Sorrel in particular. Suicidal, Helen devoted herself to making Sorrel feel good; she must preempt the universe's nasty habit of pointing out Sorrel's gifts (or rather gift, physical beauty), by pointing it out herself, by juxtaposition of her own plainness.

'You working tomorrow?' I asked, then almost flinched at the abstractedness to which the question testified.

'Yeah,' she said.

'You should get some sleep.'

'I should get fucking cosmetic surgery.'

I moved to turn the light on, but she said: 'Don't. Please.'

So I set about preparing a bowl of Frosties, illuminated by the fridge's open door.

'I'm one of those women people think should do herself a favour and become a lesbian,' she said. 'They don't realize *women* wouldn't fancy me, either.'

'For fuck's sake, Helen,' I said. More eloquent compassion.

'Oh, *sorry*,' she said. 'Christ, I didn't mean to spoil your cereal or anything.'

She got off the stool and stood with her back to me, looking through her translucent reflection out into the night. When she bowed her head I knew it would only be a matter of moments before . . . There. Crying. Silent, but discernible through the shuddering shoulders.

Again the horror of mixed feelings. Finding myself moving towards her with the intention of giving her a hug – unstrategic, spontaneous, propelled by what I can only describe as simple compassion – I cringed internally, remembering what I (and Deborah and giggling, heavy-handed Sorrel) had put her through in my head less than eight hours ago. How was it, how was it *permissible*, that the one didn't prohibit the other?

I put my arms around her. The dressing gown smelled of baby powder, her hair of Flex shampoo.

Not quite relaxing into the embrace, holding on to the minimal dignity of pain, she continued crying and blinking, both of us aware of her tears falling *tip, tip* onto the lino.

'It's hilarious, isn't it?' she said. 'That I should still want . . . that someone like me should want . . .' A sudden alarming shudder in her, then rigidity, the determination to drink this cup to the dregs. 'My whole fucking life,' she said. 'It's like a brilliant set of premises, with no conclusion to make them worth anything. I want . . . I . . .' But she couldn't say it; even without the unswallowable egg of misery that had come up in her throat, she wouldn't have been able to utter it, that dirty four-letter word whose absence from her lips and life was, by degrees, killing her.

I put my head on her shoulder, toying with the desire to give in myself, to take the opportunity for a purgative sob. But I couldn't, quite. Not, at any rate, with the image of Sorrel (raised eyebrows, slight smile) cigarette burning and observing . . . cigarette burning and observing . . . cigarette burning . . .

'Why don't you give it up for a bit?' Julia said.

'What?'

'The life, for God's sake. The bloody West End. *Drinking*.'

'I'm looking for love,' I said.

'Well, you're not going to find it dressed in its underwear at the Astoria, are you?'

In the summer of 1994 47A went into a depression. Joe lost his job and went on the dole. Helen indulged in long periods of venerating Sorrel, so much so that even *Sorrel* began to feel uncomfortable.

'What's wrong with everyone?' she kept asking. 'This place is beginning to feel like a . . . like a . . .' Similes weren't her strong point.

'Her *arse* is her strong point,' Joe said, staring into his beer can. He had recently bumped into Tina, now pregnant by the FME (FME no longer) and living in Notting Hill. It had depressed him. He had already been depressed by the loss of his job (and the lies and shenanigans involved in keeping his room in the house resulting therefrom); seeing his erstwhile beloved big-bellied with another man's child had only made matters worse.

I suggested he have sex with Helen.

'Tried,' he said. 'She wasn't interested.'

In the general malaise, I made a pass at Sorrel.

'Oi,' she said, quietly. Then, when I didn't stop, 'Oi!'

We were in the living room, both having come home, separately, drunk. A joint later I was having my face slapped.

'Dominic, for fuck's sake.'

'I might be in love with you.'

'You've lost your mind.'

'Do you deny there's something between us?'

'Yes.'

'You've felt it, though. Come on, I know you've felt it.'

'I'd like to go to bed now.'

'Exactly.'

'Alone, you prick.'

'You've been giving me the come-on all night.'

At the living-room door she turned, hands on hips. Some triumph, apparently, me having shown myself not such a hot ethical shot.

'You make me fucking sick,' she said, then turned on her heel (a gesture spoiled by a momentary wobble) and stomped upstairs.

New Year's Eve that same year hauled me out into the West End's shuffling traffic and congested streets. Drizzle, and a cold wind, the pubs tropics of aftershave and perfume with bar queues five deep. Hope, lies, resolutions, memories, the 31st's distinctive desperation. Infinitely preferable, nonetheless, to my own. I pinballed into Soho. Let the city flip me where it would.

Grandiose. Less than an hour found me at the bar of the George.

Insulated by deafening Pearl Jam and furnished with four double gins I tried a silent toast to the memory of Kelp. Got instead Deborah, the dark eyes' naked recognition. Of me. *You like it, don't you?*

The fourth double went down in an inflagration. Feeling not better but warmer, readier for whatever crippling mundanity the year's remaining hours had in store, I turned from the bar to take stock of the pub's leathered and jabbering crowd.

In the face of all reason, a young woman I'd never seen before was sitting alone at a table opposite, looking at me.

'What were you *doing* in there?'

'I don't know. I was walking past. I went in.'

Natalie West. (Chronology has kept her out of it until now, but even without it I wouldn't have hurried.) A shared house in Holloway. A large room, one wall books, much untidiness. Faint frangipani, old cosmetics. An unmade double bed, with us in it. This was the holy time, immediately after sex that had surprised both of us with its intensity. She'd left two candles burning, but soon even their minimal light had showed us more of each other than we perhaps were ready for, given the wordless escalation of whatever it was that had wordlessly escalated alongside our carnal pleasure, expressed less in the intuitively changed positions than in our compulsion to look at each other from time to time, barely believing the ease with which we were managing all this. Now, with only one of the candles wobblingly alight, we lay side by side looking up at the ceiling, listening to the rain.

'Happy New Year,' she said.

'Happy New Year,' I replied.

We weren't going to say anything about it yet. No hallelujahs. No tempting Fate. We had a welter of talk in us about what had just happened, about the fluke and glory of

it; but Natalie, perhaps, had been here before: all those celebratory words she had had to eat. I had not been in love
before. But there had been Deborah. Now, lying next to
Natalie West and feeling our silent contract of not saying
anything about what this might be, I felt the memory of
Deborah like a fragment of logic. If p then q. If *Deborah*,
then – then what?

'This is going to sound bizarre,' Natalie said. It was a big
bed. Only our side-by-side forearms touched.

'I'm ready for the bizarre,' I said.

'There's somewhere we could go.'

'Where?'

'By the sea. A cottage. My brother's. I've got keys.'

'Now?'

'I told you it would sound bizarre.'

'How do we get there?'

'In my car.'

'You've got a car?'

'Just about.'

'Can you drive?' Stupid. 'The booze, I mean.'

Her foot touched mine, very lightly.

'I'm sober as a judge,' she said.

Autobiography, it seems to me, is the process of discovering
how much you don't want to remember. And how much,
whether you like it or not, you do.

The night drive, for example. Her at the rattling Escort's
wheel, big-eyed, periodically illuminated by the lights of
passing cars, me angled in the passenger seat to observe her,
weathering surges of adrenalin each time the assessment
yielded its truth: something is happening. Something is
happening.

Miles and the graceful procession of pylons. Sometimes

the black shapes of cattle. Farm lights, evoking in the tremulous world of Something Happening ludicrous images of
ruddy rustics with jolly whiskers and tankards raised to the
New Year; a separate part of myself (oh those endlessly
dividing parts) standing back with wry grin and gently
shaken head *dear oh dear oh dear* while another part quivers
near hysteria, having received the intimation that here is a
whiff of salvation. Meanwhile the lights crawl over her,
catching on the wet convexities of eyes and mouth. We
don't talk much, beyond *Look at that*s and *Shall we stop here*s.
Just as the recognition of déjà vu precipitates its demise, so it
will be, we know, with this: if we speak to each other about
what we're doing, the moment will start haemorrhaging
spontaneity. In a matter of minutes, seconds perhaps, we'll be
left with something inert, a shape made of all the things we
haven't bothered yet to find out about each other.

We arrived at the cottage two hours before dawn. North
Cornwall. I hadn't paid much attention to the road signs. A
terrible confusion when I opened the passenger door – the
sea smell, instantaneous, rough, salty, upsetting crates of the
past.

First the sex's emotional ambush then the drive had
sobered me. Under my scrutiny (Natalie with a jiggle of
keys at the front door) lumps of darkness resolved into a
surrounding privet hedge, two trees – one close enough to
knuckle and rasp at the gable end – three other pale cottages
of similar size, one to the right, two to the left. The sky was
low and thick, the air freezing, with the steel taste of snow.

If *Deborah*, then *not Natalie*.

'My brother's just bought this place.'

Evidently. On the way up to the bedroom (Natalie's rootle
in the kitchen turned up rudimentary utensils: corkscrew
and bottle of Tesco's Valpolicella) I had taken in a small living

room and a slightly larger parlour, both scrappily half-furnished, both with ugly calor gas heaters presiding. A smell of wet dog and mould. The bathroom with exposed plumbing and a baizy fungus under the sink. One of the two bedrooms mainly junk, the other spartan but orderly, with heater, curtains, rug, wardrobe and dresser. And bed. Smaller than Natalie's in the Holloway room, but big enough. The calor lit with a comforting *bhup*, heated the air sourly and quickly. Natalie warmed the bottle and poured us a tumbler each.

'I'll put the hot water on,' she said. 'Then in the morning we can have baths.'

She was gone longer than just that would have taken, but came back still wearing the look of perplexed certainty. I, meanwhile, in calm shock, had taken my clothes off and got into bed.

For a moment she stood and I lay and the room seemed impatient. She said, 'I know,' followed by a decisive gulp of wine, then, 'Fucking hell,' and another wild gulp and the glass put down on the floorboards, and her clambering over me still fully dressed into bed.

An unmanly sensual pleasure for me, in being completely naked against her completely clothed, the first rasp of her denimed knee between my thighs providing me with both redoubtable erection and glimpse of my own large store of femaleness. I bore it, while she crawled on top of me and hunted my mouth out with hers.

Some clumsiness, this second time, forced on us by urgency. Certainly I was urgent, discovering the scents on us from the first time, tasting her mouth's vinous realism, finding the soft and hard of her hips, less strange now by the precise advance of one previous fuck. But she was triumphantly graceless too, happy to hurry and bump teeth and thrust uglily, using it, I wagered – us, fucking – as purgative or celebratory psychic shout. I did wonder, on and off, if she wasn't genuinely mad. Difficult to care very much, however, given the pleasure and seemingly inexhaustible lust. There were third and fourth and fifth rounds, each distinctive but sharing a seductive familial resemblance. She was very thin, the only full areas her little breasts and bottom. At moments, courtesy of the curtains' glowing slab of light, I saw her small face above me, large-eyed, alternately present and abstracted, wondering, I supposed, where her old self had gone and when this vortex might release her.

Think of . . . Think of . . . But I put my mouth and hands and hips on her in the dark and there was nothing to think of. She kissed me and the void where thinking of should have been offered itself to me; I changed positions and drew back from it. I heard her breathing and felt all her history open, intricately.

'Let me come on top,' she said. 'Please, please.'

Her voice given like a shocking gift. I opened my mouth to speak (there was nothing to say except like a gout of blood *love* flashing and gone) but couldn't.

'Kiss me. You kiss me.'

Her words got beautifully in the way of apotheosis. I didn't know what to do, when I was there, when *I* was there, momentarily back from the void. What was there to do but kiss her and move inside her then slip back into dissolution?

Love again – did someone say it? It flashed like a rich red vein or precious lode, astonishing me, panicking me, for a moment, into digging up Deborah, her quiet curses, Alice's face gargoylish with misery. *That* truth, I would preserve *that* truth – the other was too monstrous. From the collapsed star of that summer a great repulsion came against this.

If *Deborah*, then . . .

The first encounter, in the London room a lifetime ago, had hinted at this — hence the sculpted silence in its wake — but with no real sense of scale. I hadn't known (had she? I wondered, as she eased herself down onto me again, my hands incredulous at the endlessly renewable satisfaction of touching her) that there would be these deeps, this threat, this suggestion of antidote to the ravages of the Old Disease.

In the last ejaculatory spasm of the last copulation (soreness, like a representative of reality, beginning to make itself felt), I wondered whether, in Natalie West, God, finally, was ready to apologize for saving my enemy and murdering my friend.

Then it was over, and we lay on our backs side by side, blinking, razed.

'A cigarette,' she said. 'I'll give you all the money I have for a cigarette.'

'Your wish is my command,' I croaked, not knowing *what* to say. Or do, or think, or be. I reached down, found my jacket and the crumpled Marlboros. Kelp's Zippo. Enough light (gulls screeching, too, from time to time, *Larus ridibundus*, no doubt) to release the old brass's bit of glowing colour.

'Are you married?' she said, after the first sighed-out smoke.

No putting it off any longer, re-entering the world, finding out about each other. The opposite force, now, to the one which had compelled laconicism.

'No,' I said.

'Girlfriend?'

'No. Nothing. You?'

'No.' A pause. 'Until a month ago I lived with someone. Four years.'

Rebound, then. Cliché. A slight dulling. Surge of panic at not having prepared for already having served my purpose. But there, whether I liked it or not, was her face, its nocturnal eyes and slight pointiness connoting extra-terrestrialism, the burgundy hair in uncombed waves spread coronally on the pillow. Our night had rubbed most of her make-up off; uncosmetic shadows now visible under her eyes. Not just tonight's sleeplessness. I wondered how old she was.

We lay a while without speaking.

'I keep wanting to say things like, "I can't believe I've done this",' she said. 'But I can believe it. I thought it straight away when I saw you in the pub.'

'I'm glad you did.'

'Are you?'

'Yes.' A feeling of emotional nudity. 'Even if this is all it is.'

She thought about that for a moment, then turned onto her side to look at me. I rolled, too, to face her. There had been her perfume, initially (vanilla-ish, but with a trace of something bitter and eastern), and the cling of the evening's pub smoke and drizzle. Now we smelled of her cunt, for which odour there is no description – one gets near only by gesturing elsewhere: poached pears and musk and ironish blood, salt and honey, the sensational flash of brine, something as involved and generous as the whiff of a luxury delicatessen. I could smell it on my upper lip; that, our sweet-sour wine breath, and the bed's scent of iron and old linen. *Even if this is all it is.* Even if a glimpse is all I get, one cruel peep over the lip of the cesspit. *I'm glad you did.* Was I? Was I glad if, after that night, she was going to drive us back to London, drop me off at 47A with a peck and a wave, then disappear as suddenly as she had arrived?

'Is this all it is?' she said.

'Well, that depends,' I said.

'On?'

'On whether I'm prepared to kid myself that that wasn't possibly the best night of my life.'

280

A reflexive grin – compressed by learned caution into a smile. Moments of the two of us slowly blinking, seeing each other, learning faces. She was more than capable, I decided, of whisking us back to London and leaving me with a thanks ta-ra.

'Where is your brother?' I asked.

'In America. He travels a lot. Business.'

'And he's about ready for a Cornish retreat?'

'He'll end up renting it out. He doesn't sit still long enough for a place like this.'

'Maybe he'll give it to you, if you're nice to him.'

'I wouldn't have to be nice. I'd just have to ask.'

'Handy.'

'It might be, one day, when I'm desperate.'

'Tired of London, tired of life.'

'I've been tired of London for years.'

'But not life.'

'No. You surprise yourself.'

'Did he leave you or did you leave him?'

'We left each other. It had been wrong for ages. Two years, probably. Anyway.' The 'anyway' signalling enough of that matter.

'This is a conversation,' I said.

'I know.'

'I knew it would be.'

'Well, I'd hoped, too. But you don't like to.'

'No.'

Which momentarily killed it, naturally, without alarming us overmuch. She got out of bed, stepped over to the curtains and opened them.

'Oh my God.'

Snow. Still falling in large, dirty-looking flakes, the land already under a blue-shadowed quilt. Childhood rushed up, breathless, unable to do anything but gesture and grin. My aesthete prayed, shamefully, that she wouldn't impishly clap hands or beam at me.

She didn't. She looked at me once. As old as me, I now thought, at least. No one younger would have that look at her disposal: weariness, a fleck of rapture, the recognition of the giantness and absurdity of this offering, as if the world had no sense of proportion, no restraint. All that plus the unlikeliness of us living up to it and the mad human belief that we could.

Julia was jealous – of nothing more than the presence of a real woman in my life, which had hitherto only thrown up one-night-stands (her sovereignty unchallenged, she had assumed, in ignorance of Deborah) – but knew she was, and fought past it quickly enough. I had so terrified Natalie with tales of my sister's beauty and fame that the first time the two of them met (for a dinner at the Ivy to which Jules had insisted on treating us) Natalie's nerves drove her to stub a cigarette out in the butter. This impressed Julia, as did the speed and conviction with which Natalie then proceeded to get drunk. Drunk, Natalie was confident and garrulous, so much so that if not for slurred consonants and comedy hiccups one might never guess that she was anything other than sober and bright.

'I like her,' Julia said, when I went round to see her the following day. 'She's alive. And far too pretty for you, you vile toad. I hope she doesn't let you interfere with her down there.'

'I'm afraid she does,' I said.

Jules made a face. 'Disgusting,' she said. Then, leaving pretend-talk behind: 'What does she mean to you?'

If she'd been looking for longer-than-were-wholesome pauses she might have identified this one. But half her attention seemed elsewhere – back in failed affairs of her own, I supposed.

'Nothing I've ever experienced before,' I said.

And if the arrival of Natalie West wasn't enough to suggest Divine recompense, there was also, that summer, my Cornerstone coup. I bought a first novel titled *The Herb Girl*, an atrociously sentimental story set in India about an Anglo-Indian orphan girl adopted by abusive parents, who sneaks out by night to learn the secrets of a solitary herbalist woman (everyone thinks she's either nuts or a witch) in the nearby hills, who teaches her not only how to heal with herbs but also how to take revenge on the wicked adults. Pseudo-exotic landscape, screaming stereotypes, recipes, youth and age, the triumph of love and come-uppances galore. Her name was Kate Durrell, no relation to Lawrence.

A hunch, I'd said to David. We should sign her up for the next one just in case.

'I bought it,' I said to Natalie at her place (a new place, a beyond-her-means studio flat in Finsbury Park, the Holloway room having been an anything-to-get-out stop-gap), perusing her bookcase for the dozenth time. (My secret project: to identify which books she had read and I hadn't, then read them. Love's no-stone-unturned idiocy.)

'Good. Is she pretty?'

'I haven't met her.'

'She's Anglo-Indian.'

'So?'

'They've got the teeth and the hair and the nails.'

'That's Indian girls.'

'Nonetheless. I've seen you on the escalators. Those women with spider eyes and hair down to their arses. I know your type.'

'These are uncertain times,' I said, picking up a battered copy of *Jaws*. 'It doesn't pay to have a type.' The paperback was buckled and smelled, faintly, of sun cream. 'Multiculturalism, innit. That's my feeling. *Inclusivity*.'

'*Vness*,' she said, bringing two glasses of rioja from the rickety kitchenette. 'Inclusive*ness*. Why don't they get rid of you and hire someone who speaks proper English? You look handsome, by the way.'

I turned, took my drink from her and kissed her. She drew back to look at me. A habit. Sudden evaluative scrutiny. Me unable quite to escape the feeling that she wanted to catch me off guard, visibly thinking of something (or someone) else. It wasn't that, she insisted, it was that sometimes – often after an unexpected kiss – she couldn't believe her luck; the equivalent of pinching herself to make sure she wasn't dreaming.

'Majorca, 1987,' she said, seeing *Jaws*. 'Somebody left it behind on a lounger. You'll love this: I was reading *Ulysses*. I stopped and read that instead. There's all that stuff that's not in the film. Richard Dreyfus has it off with Roy Scheider's wife.'

'I know. They meet for lunch and swap fantasies, and she feels herself getting wet, and worries about leaving a stain on the seat. I was only eleven. "Hooper, stiff as a flagpole . . ." I knew what that meant.'

'I'm sure you did.' She took the paperback from me and sniffed it. 'The ending's different, though.'

'Better. The shark dies of exhaustion just as it's about to eat Chief Brody. That was weird. I remember thinking that was a great ending – this fucking unbelievable monster just running out of steam. I mean, I loved the ending in the film, too, but somehow, you know the book's is . . . *truer*.'

'This is *Jaws*, we're discussing, is it?'

'Were you with Mark?'

'In Majorca?'

'Yes, in Majorca.'

She shoved the book back into its slot. 'Yes,' she said.

'Sun-oiled siesta shags?'

Not malicious; just a need now and then to force myself to imagine her, sexually, with someone else. Someone Before Me.

She didn't like it.

'Sorry,' I said. 'Sorry, sorry, that was crap.'

'Here's to *The Herb Girl*,' she said. 'And all who edit in her.'

Natalie was a freelance graphic designer. Which was another way of saying that she was a part-time temp. I asked her if she wanted to come and work at Cornerstone. No. Obviously no, for half a dozen different reasons. She'd got used to scavenging, she said. I let it be, knowing I'd come back to it.

There had been an up-and-down relationship between her and her beauty. There had been the guiltlessly spent wealth of childhood's Being a Pretty Girl and the self-disgusted baggy-pants and shaved head of the politicized first year. There had been (the photographs testified) a reactionary vampish and Mark-endorsed phase just after graduation which I was sorry to have missed, but it hadn't lasted. Irritated, unresolved, but sick of the endless self-interrogation, she had at the time I knew her settled with gritted teeth on a version of herself which refused to apologize for its good looks but had the dignity to avoid making a meal of them. Her hair stayed more or less shoulder-length. She wore light make-up if she was going out and none if she wasn't. *Very* occasionally, extreme glamour, high heels, the lot. Most of the time, however, androgynous casuals and nice underwear. Her blessing – she knew, with horrified relief – was a body that hadn't bothered to change its weight (eight stone) since she'd turned seventeen.

She was, unapologetically, a burper and farter, my girl, the latter delivered often with Roger Moorishly raised eyebrow, the former with open mouth and glassy look of suspended consciousness. The luxury of grossness unfairly affordable because she was pretty and feminine, we both knew, in which respect she reminded me much of Julia. The burps were things of intricacy, *works*. We competed, and had to check ourselves in public. Drunk and gassy, we were once ejected from a Pizza Express in Notting Hill; shamed, hysterical, we staggered out, exactly the sort of spectacle of romantic self-sufficiency that would have had us grinding our teeth in irritation had we not ourselves been its stars. A deal of infantilism in the early stages – risky, we knew, but hard to resist – and in any case countered, we felt, by straight talk and occasional admissions of boredom with each other. She had the advantage over me, having been in love before. Having, now, an *attitude* to being in love, she could to some degree stand back. Whereas I swallowed pretty much everything in earnest: sunlight on the Thames; blue and white skies; park dusks. Any version of the world's message that here, at long last, was rescue.

Almost swallowed it, I mean.

It was a weight to carry, for both of us, the romantic extravagance of how surreally we'd met, and with how much recognition. It existed in our care like a firstborn and beloved child. We might betray it, if we insisted on knowing each other further.

She was afraid of us moving in together. With Mark, domestic intimacy had become domestic claustrophobia; and had riddled romance (though she never *quite* said this) like woodworm. It wasn't that she was resistant to the glamour-lessness of stray toenails and washing up and underpants and mug-rings and hoovering and boredom; on the contrary: it was that she was horrified by her own willingness to sink so deeply into the comfort of such details. A no nonsense streak in her identified the ordinary with truth, the exotic with delusion. She and Mark had delighted in dehumbugging their own romance, had (she confessed) Larkinized them-selves into mundanity addicts. In Mark's case (she suspected) because he knew deep down he had no magic in him; in her own because she knew deep down that she had too much (no nonsense streak or not), and that to release it would be to lose him – and perhaps herself. Therefore they had wal-lowed together in cosiness, both suffering, Mark for fear of her leaving him, her for fear (certainty, actually) that the romantic inside her would rise up and smash their deadening familiarity to pieces. Which of course it did, eventually.

'His belt buckle tinkling,' she had told me, when I'd asked which straw had broken the camel's back. We were in my room at 47A at the time, lying in on a hot Sunday morning, both guiltily considering a cooked breakfast at the Greek greasy across the road. Natalie had kicked the duvet off. I lay propped on one elbow, she on her back, hands by her sides.

'He'd put on a few pounds,' she continued. 'Nothing, really. The beginnings of a pot belly. Which of course both of us had noticed, and laughed about, and for which I said I'd developed a sort of affection, which I had. That's what you do, when something objectionable emerges, you pounce on it with affection, turn it into something lovable, because you know immediately that if you don't you'll have to hate it.'

'Yes.'

'At home, he took to moving about with the top button of his jeans and his belt undone. When he walked, the buckle made a little tinkling sound, like the bell of a cat's collar.'

Delightful, naturally, to listen to tales of Mark's shortcomings while observing the sunlight on her eyelashes, nipples, mons, ankles. All these treasures the poor tinkling bastard would never enjoy again.

'Not loving someone any more,' Natalie said to the ceiling. 'Not wanting to be with someone any more. It's a weird thing. Huge, shapeless.' She frowned, still, manifestly, figuring it out. 'It's there, this huge discomfort, moving around inside you, waiting for some absurd little hook to hang itself on. And then there *is* the hook. The way he clears his throat. A haircut. His laugh.'

'Or his unbuttoned trousers.'

She turned towards me, put her fingertips against my chest. She was enjoying it somewhat, too, the little betrayal of Mark's memory. She still loved him, differently; now and again there must be these retrospective cruelties, to consolidate her newness, to let her not love him in the old way.

'One day I forgot my key and had to ring the doorbell,' she said. 'It was a beautiful summer evening, absolutely still. I heard him coming to answer the door. Tinkling. That fucking belt buckle. I'd been telling him to just buy a bigger pair of trousers. Or go on a diet. Anything. But he wouldn't. It didn't matter. He knew it didn't matter. He knew it didn't matter to me. And it didn't, of course. It was just that hearing it, him coming to answer the door with his top button undone and that fucking belt tinkling . . .'

She rolled away from me again, onto her back. I had a formidable erection, which she knew all about. Not looking at me, she reached for and wrapped her fingers round it. Very slightly sickened at herself, at her understanding of this little juxtaposition and its emotional utility, she turned her back to me and pulled me in behind her. Small deeds to put lost love in its place. Wholesome blasphemies her wiser self knew she was not just entitled but commanded by the gods of transformation to commit.

Anglo-Indian Kate Durrell, twenty-eight-year-old author of *The Herb Girl*, had not the hair (if by that is meant the bottom-length, thick, black hair), nor the teeth (the straight and brilliant white teeth), nor the nails (the unbreakable almond-shaped nails) of Indian girls. Nor was she Anglo-Indian. She was Goan, or Anglo-Goan, since her (estranged) father was completely English. She was plump and histrionic, with straight, henna-streaked hair and a moist, convex face. A lot of nervous, earth-motherish energy, and a loud, urgent delusion that she was an artist. 'My mother's maiden name was Devaz,' she said. 'Which is Portuguese. She was born in Marmagao, which is in Goa, but moved to Maharashtra, which is in India, when she was ten. I've never even *been* to Igatpuri, where *Girl's* set. Just absorbed the place from my mother and a few photographs.'

Uttered with the expectation of a small round of applause. I smiled, in-the-know: ah yes, that capacity for *absorbing* you artists have. Heavens, how do you *do* it?

'The next book's going to be much more ambitious,' she said. '*Girl's* just to get me into print.'

'I see,' I said. 'Good. Good.' *Bad.*

'I want to do something about' – wistful, slight, cautiously confident head movement, eyes looking away – 'European appropriation.'

I told her it sounded fabulous (catastrophic; so much for

the Columbo hunch), and that we'd line Salman Rushdie (Barbara Taylor Bradford) up for a quote.

'Do you think we're ready?' Nat said, one night after sex.

'For what?'

'You telling me what you fantasize about.'

The familiar bloodrush. Familiar because several times over the year I'd come close to a full confession. She had almost convinced me – with breadth of vision, subtlety of understanding, insight, an ability to look the world's horrors in the eye, with *love* – that she would be able to take it. It. But all of It? Not just my imagination's infection with the Old Disease; not just the episodes with poor Alice (some repugnance, admittedly – but I would be judged by my attitude to it *now*, which I might genuinely express as profound regret); no, *It* would have to be everything, *all of it*, with at its heart the loathed ratio: the greater the object of veneration, the greater the pleasure of inversion. With at its heart, the Devil's question for love.

'Why me telling you? What about you telling me?'

'That's out of the question.'

'Why?'

'Because you're a man and I'm a woman.'

'I see.'

'You knowing my fantasies undermines my power.'

'But not vice versa?'

'Yours *needs* to be undermined. You're a man. You've already *got* too much power.'

'Is this a serious conversation?'

'It's as serious as these conversations always are.'

'Okay, Humpty.'

'In that I both want to know and don't want to know.'

'Let's go with you not wanting to know.'

290

'In that the sexual sophisticate in me believes she can handle anything and ought to be tested, while the political realist in me suspects unhandleable horrors.'

'Oh, those political realists.'

'A suspicion your reticence only confirms.'

'It's true,' I said. 'I'm a monster. What else do you need to know?'

There was a book on her shelf she'd found particularly distressing. *The Vietnam Reader.* I, in my programme of mapping her reading, had read it, too. William Broyles Jr, an American soldier in Vietnam, described the effects on his colonel and himself, of watching the removal by truck of dozens of naked and mud-spattered corpses.

> There was a look of beatific contentment on the colonel's face that I had not seen except in charismatic churches. It was the look of a person transported into ecstasy. And I – what did I do, confronted with this beastly scene? I smiled back, as filled with bliss as he was. That was another of the times I stood on the edge of my humanity, looked into the pit, and loved what I saw there.

Distressing, yes, and, safely contextualized as anecdote from an extraordinary place and an extraordinary time, *understandable.* But bring it closer. Bring the bliss nearer to her, Natalie Jane West, edgily in love with Dominic Francis Hood, tender lover, movable to tears and damaged (she was sure, despite his brusque, factual and non-miraculous narrative) by the premature death of his best friend – bring it *here*, to *us.* Was it understandable *then*?

'Details,' she said.

'Just imagine the worst. That should cover it.'

'More evasion. Do you think about me doing it with a woman?'

'That's the worst you can come up with?'

'Of course not, idiot. I'm starting small. Do you?'

'Naturally.'

'Who?'

'Sheena Easton.'

'Very funny. Come on. Someone we know?'

'How do you know I think about you at all?'

'Oh, *charming.*'

'And what, in the name of tartan, is wrong with Sheena Easton?'

'It's because you know I don't want to do it with another woman. If I did want to, you'd stop fantasizing about it.'

'Try me. I dare you.'

'It's because if I did it, it would be an imposition of your control. *Actual* lesbians don't turn men on at all.'

'They do if they're nice.'

'If they're cosmeticized. If they're *feminine.*'

'I told you I was a monster.'

'What turns men on about women doing it with each other is the underlying belief that they don't *want* to do it with each other.'

'Men's underlying belief is that women don't want to do it with *men.*'

'Which is probably why they like having sex with them.'

'You're losing me.'

'Men with women. Because they, men, secretly, *underlyingly* believe that they're getting women to do something they don't want to do.'

'No, it's just that men are amazed that women do want to have sex with them.'

'Which they probably don't, most of the time.'

'Present company excepted, one hopes.'

A pause. It's all right. I can see what's coming. It's all right. This is what she's wanted to tell me.

'Sometimes I have sex with you when I don't want to.'

Thank God. Love can put its arms round this.

'Ah. Probably best if you stop doing that.'

'And I know you know I don't want to.'

Ah.

'And you know that I know you know that I don't want to. And you do it anyway.'

Whereof one cannot speak, thereof one must be silent.

'Because,' she continued, with a hand placed lightly on my belly, 'it's sometimes an act of contempt from you, having sex with me. Not just you. Men. An act of disgust. Of hatred.'

Silence.

'Sometimes I end up wanting to have sex with you when I've started off not wanting to. But then I wonder whether that isn't just because sometimes sex is an act of hatred for me, too.'

Some pressure on the window spoke of barely withheld rain.

'Of myself,' she added. 'Depressing, isn't it?'

'Yes.'

'Do you want to have sex?'

'Yes. Do you?'

'I think so.'

'I'd never do anything to hurt you, Nat.'

'I know. Well, I don't know. But I've decided to carry on as if I do.'

'Please don't have sex with me any more when you don't want to.'

'Even though you like it?'

'One likes wrong things.'

'I know. I like wrong things, too.'

Not wrong enough.

'I want to know you, Dominic.'

'I know. I want to know you, too.'

'I want to know everything. Otherwise what's the point?'

At 47A Joe got another job, and, to the house's and history's relief, a new girlfriend, Laura, who was tiny and Irish (ex-Catholic) with dark wispy hair and lively blue eyes, and who had a cheeky gleam of life about her that seemed within twenty-four hours to have expunged Tina and the FME from Joe's memory. Fiendish consumption of narcotics and alcohol counterpointed charmingly with a soft voice and the gentlest of southern Irish lilts. Laura had taught English, in the war zones of state comprehensives, for four years which had, in her words, worn the feckin skin off her soul; now she worked (with two other women who had set up their own landscape-gardening business) doing a mixture of donkey- and paperwork, learning as much as she could of green and growing things on the job. Joe was besotted. The two of them would roll in in the small hours giggling and whispering and knocking things over. Not infrequently one emerged for breakfast to find them curled up asleep together on the couch, hands up each other's shirts, mouths open, the joint that had finished them off half smoked on the loaded ashtray's lip. The Degenerates, Sorrel called them.

Sorrel, as if in an act of self-satire, had started seeing an older man with wet-gelled hair, designer spectacles and a Prussian-blue Porsche. Concomitant tightness round the corners of her mouth, mornings; long baths; retroussé nose permanently elevated as in avoidance of an unpleasant smell. She'd not long for this world, Joe and I reasoned, this world of 47A, of tights drying on the radiator, baked beans ageing on the lid of the swing-top bin, brown envelopes piling up.

Helen, meanwhile, continued in more or less misery. There were brave periods – gyms and salads, half-hearted applications for academic posts, a boyfriend or two (none of them *half* Helen's worth), Spanish lessons, London walks – but longer periods of virtual hermitage in her room, where a portable television was switched on as soon as she got home from work and not switched off until she went to bed. Often not even then, so that she fell asleep lulled by its babble. She never read, now, in either mode, though her room remained walled in books. Joe and I admitted to each other that something ought to be done for Helen. We admitted it with manly reason, from the summits of our respective happiness mountains, in the way one reasonably admits the need for a domestic repair one has no intention of ever carrying out.

And so to the moment of transition. There must be one if the beloved is to pass from beloved ideal into beloved reality. We were at the shambolic old Hood house in Logan Street one weekend in the summer of 1996. My mother had fallen off a ladder – *wallpapering* – and broken her ankle; Natalie and I (at Natalie's insistence) had driven up for the weekend to make sure my father didn't set fire to the kitchen or wash the household's whites pink. Huge selflessness from Natalie, who had long since seen through my mother's cunning friendship to the truth, which was that she, my mother, regarded my choice of Natalie – educated, uninterested in cooking, and a drinker of Scotch on the rocks – as a rejection not just of her, my mother, but of the Platonic Form of Woman. Not that she, Natalie, stood for any nonsense. My mother's artful inclusiveness – 'No formalities here, love, just kick your shoes off and make yourself at home' – was received with civility but without delusion, and countered (to the delight of yours truly) by Nat's habit of disagreeing with my mother *about me*.

'Course he shoots his mouth off without thinking, that one. Fireworks one minute, apologies the next. You'll have had a taste of the quick temper yourself by now.'

'Actually, no,' Natalie said, very carefully swallowing a mouthful of tea. 'I've never seen anything like that. Dominic strikes me as one of the calmest people I've ever met. It's me who's more likely to start chucking crockery around.'

Raised maternal eyebrows and sideways downward glance, as if to an invisible ally crouched on the carpet. Another careful sip and swallow from Natalie. 'Great cuppa, by the way. Is Julia hot-tempered, too?'

My father, on the other hand, couldn't think badly of anyone who drank her Scotch straight and matched him peg for peg in the boozy run-up to lunch – which meal, being back in Begshall, we called dinner. Nor was he blind to her more obvious merits; I caught him looking with the priapic gleam or the melancholy pain of the tethered goat.

But the moment of transition.

With Deborah it had been a look and an utterance. *You like it, don't you?* A certain cast of the eyes and five words adding up to a long-awaited rhetorical question. *You like it, don't you?* Yes, I did. And if *Deborah*, then—

A tectonic shift no one but me knew to have taken place. I was lolling on the Logan Street couch after much whisky and a cobbled-together tea of mushroom soup, cold cuts, brown bread and butter, pickles, fresh tomatoes, potato salad, Mr Kipling's French Fancies, Lancashire cheese and Jacob's cream crackers (a 'nick-nack' tea, in childhood parlance). My father was with twitching jaws and audible breathing down on all fours trying to programme the video. Natalie was in the kitchen, following called-out instructions from my mother, who sat – foot in cast on pouffe – in the armchair opposite me. My mother couldn't see Natalie, and Natalie couldn't see her. I could see them both. Natalie could have seen me if she'd looked back into the living room. My mother could have observed me had she not closed her eyes the better to visualize her kitchen.

'In the cupboard to the left of the sink, underneath. Where the other pink plastic colander is. Got it?'

'Got it. And the big Pyrex bowl?'

'In the cupboard above the kettle. Left-hand side.'

'Perfect.'

'Cling-film's in that little cubby between the cooker and the fridge.'

'Between the cooker and the . . . Correct again. We should go on telly.'

No response from my mother. Bearing without apoplexy the image of the woman in her kitchen was taking all her concentration. The living room smelled, comfortingly, of the meal and the street's evening, admitted along with the scents of stodgier teas through the open window. My father coaxed a chirrup from the VCR – unsatisfactory, judging by the muted buggers and bloodys. And I, with flesh, blood and bones creeping awake to a curious, tingling seduction, watched Natalie Jane West (all three names required at epiphanic junctures) moving with alternating faces of concentration and abstraction through the humble spaces of my childhood. It wasn't by any means the first time she had been with me to the Logan Street house. There was nothing (excepting, Herr Doktor, my mother's broken ankle) special about this occasion. But as Deborah's *You like it, don't you?* had hey presto'd my climax face to face all those years ago, so Natalie's patience in the teeth of my mother's enmity . . .

No, not precisely that; rather, the mixture of patience, irritation, good humour and pragmatism . . .

No, not exhaustively *that*, either; these components, yes, but also the brute presence of her body in my house, the smells and colours of my childhood, the throb of familial blood, the friendly stink of the street – *whatever* the causes, there was no mistaking what happened: the arrival – in the heart, in the soul, in the head (all the vague locations), certainly in the reliable guts – of the conviction that I must bind myself to this woman for ever. It took up residence, this conviction, at what felt like the molecular level; some weird outreaching song of the genes – and with it, the thought of having a child with her. It appeared, this thought of having a child, like the face of a maniacal horror clown, then disappeared, leaving me completely convinced.

Meanwhile I lay on the couch with no outward sign of transformation.

'Don't bother wi' that soup pan, Natalie, love. Just leave it to soak.'

'I was hoping you'd say that.'

'*Bloody* bastard thing. Dominic, come here, will you. I can't read this without my glasses.'

The attendance, perhaps, of all the kitchen's little domestic spirits around her. *A politically suspect explanation*, she would have said. *Only when she is returned to her place as unpaid domestic labourer is the modern woman truly acceptable to the allegedly reconstructed man.* Politically bankrupt or not, sprites of kettle, hob, bread bin, tea towel and fridge threw their voices into the mix, all in Old Testament idiom: *take her unto yourself as wife; let her be big with the child of your loins; let your love grow even unto the grave and God willing beyond; for she is of your*—difficult not to give in to hysteria. Indeed I did, actually, release a snort of laughter, onto which, on my mother's opening her eyes, I tacked an unconvincing cough.

One wants to say one was filled with tenderness, love. But it wasn't like that. It was nothing more or less than a feeling of comprehensive physical relief, as if my troubled skeleton and musculature had come at last into correct alignment. The greatest temptation by far was to dissolve into fits of laughter, such the giantness and simplicity of the revelation. Natalie, trying to work out the logical place for the sieve, paused and scratched the side of her nose. She had the sleeves of her burgundy blouse rolled up, revealing slim white forearms and pink elbows. A much-sat-on five-pound note half protruded from the back pocket of her Levis. And there it was: all the dead data transfigured into living truth. I saw our future together compressed into a moment: our faces changing, desire having to cope and reinvent itself at each new stratum of familiarity; I saw the gradual dissolution of mutual mystery and romance, its succession by friendship and a sort of tranquil and supernatural loyalty; I felt – with great lightness of being – the bearability of the idea of death, if the life preceding it was bloodily commingled (in children) with hers. A humble little truth: build a truly good life and it will reward you with mastery of the fear of death. It was simple. Having committed to the building of a marriage and family, all sorts of truths came forward and offered themselves.

Cleave unto her, my son, for the days of thy life are as the burning of the leaves.

She did, finally, look out from the kitchen to see me watching her, and we exchanged a look. Not a wink, not a comedy gurn – as we might have – but merely a look of sexual allegiance (*I'll be seeing you in bed, later, won't I*), and very humbly and gently (humility and gentleness akin to that with which I'd cleaned Nancy and Jill's cottage that morning a lifetime ago), very *quietly*, in fact, I relaxed into the knowledge that I had found the woman who would be my wife.

Three weekends later, I went to see Penguin.

Mogs had said, when I rang for his address: 'I know how glad he'll be to see you, Dominic, really he will.' I had pictured her standing in the hall of the big Begshall semi, phone cradled at her jaw, hair (grey, now) wrongly pinned up, hands busy unpicking a hem. Gareth squatting nearby, mesmerized by the carpet. Mr Holt leaning on a spade in the back garden, staring with disappeared top lip into space.

Pen was in Exeter now, still, according to Mogs, rockily with Tanya. I would be turning up out of the blue, which seemed appropriate – and, besides, I didn't want Tanya forewarned.

I needn't have worried.

The house was a three-storey Victorian terrace on a steep street not far from the university. A pub at the top of the hill and a corner shop (archaic, with jars of sweets, brown paper, imperial scales) at the bottom. The student quarter, though one could be forgiven for thinking otherwise given the cars – the Spitfires and Spiders, the Morgans and Midgets, the Alfas, the Jags, the restored Opels and mint Beetles – Exeter's crop being Hugos and Hermiones without brain enough for Oxford, Cambridge, Durham or Bristol. Outside Pen's house, however, a brown Escort missing three hubcaps. Not hard to imagine his feelings about his neighbours. (Nor, I added to myself, ungenerously, Tanya's about the brown Escort.)

Number 32's front door was open, its hall door closed. No

one answered bell or knocker, both of which I belaboured. Tentatively, I pushed the hall door open and took a few steps inside.

The immediate interior's message was plain: a normally well-kept house being allowed to get into a state. A white shirt lay halfway up the facing staircase. A front-wheelless racing bike against the hall radiator knelt on its forks bleeding oil into the carpet. The Yellow Pages lay open next to the phone on the floor. A potted azalea had been knocked over and not set upright. A fug of uncleared-away fast food; unwashed socks; stale fag ends.

'Pen?'

Nothing.

'Penguin? Anyone home?'

The door on my left opened into an uninhabited front room. The door next to it was ajar, and gave onto what had once been two rooms, living room and kitchen, now knocked into one. The television was on, volume down, *Grandstand*, the execrable horse-racing section in the programme's middle. On the couch, someone's wristwatch lay face down on a greasy dinner plate. Mugs, glasses, empties and half-empties everywhere. Open French windows at the rear showed a long, narrow back garden. Just visible, the edge of a red-and-white deckchair, two protruding legs with jeans rolled shin high and feet bare. A newspaper lay buckled on the grass.

I crossed the room and walked out into the garden.

In the deckchair an unshaven Penguin was asleep with his mouth open. Beneath his current state of looking terrible he hadn't changed much, apart from shorter hair (stiffened by sleep and neglect) and a slight thickening at waist and chops. Very wrong attire in this heat, the jeans and the grey cable-knit. A half-empty bottle of Smirnoff nestled between his thighs. His hands, loosely clasped round the bottle's girth, were the hands I remembered, nails chewed to the quick.

I don't know how long I stood there watching him frown and twitch his way through whatever dreams she'd left him. Not long, perhaps a couple of minutes – long enough (aided by the pigeon shadow that rippled over him) for his sleeper's radar to pick me up.

When he opened his eyes (no other part of his body moving, not even a fingertip), slowly, to reveal the aching whites gone pink, I was leaning against the doorframe with my hands in my pockets.

'Ah, Christ, Dummie,' he said, focusing with evident difficulty. 'Can that really be you?'

We went to the pub, the Queen Mary, at the top of the road.

'How long's she been gone?'

'A month.'

He swallowed the Scotch in one, then followed with a slow sip of his John Smith's.

'Your mum didn't say anything about it,' I said.

'Yeah, well, she wouldn't, since she doesn't know.'

'Jesus Christ, Pen.'

'You never liked her, did you?'

I looked him in the eye, wondering for a moment if we still had enough history for the truth. 'No, I never liked her,' I said. 'But then I don't think she liked me, either, did she?'

He shook his head, then sank it into his hands.

'Pen. Pen, come on. Come on, for fuck's sake.'

He shook his head again, slowly. 'D'you know what he does?' he said.

'Who?'

'This' – his mouth small and tight – 'this *cock*sucker she's been . . . Do you know what he does? That's a rhetorical question. I'll tell you. He's a *sociology* lecturer.'

I must have looked like I was struggling to see why this was so terrible.

'Tanya'd have trouble fucking *spelling* sociology,' he said. 'And *more* trouble spelling fucking lecturer.'

'Christ, Pen, I'm sorry.'

He sat back in his chair and swallowed more of his pint. Then, indicating the tobacco and papers: 'Can I scrounge one of those? When did you go back on rollies?'

'A while back,' I lied. Truth was I'd bought the tobacco – my first after years of straights – that very day, in (fatuous, sentimental) memoriam of the glory days.

'Haven't had a roll-up for years,' he said.

'I know.'

'Which reminds me,' he said – then changed his mind. 'Nah. Never mind.'

'What?'

'Nothing, nothing.'

'Pen, for fuck's sake.'

'Yeah, well, if I tell you you've got to promise you're not going to laugh or have me committed or something.'

'I'm not promising anything of the kind.'

For a moment he concentrated – a little out of practice – on rolling. When he'd lit up, inhaled, then exhaled a long funnel of smoke, he scratched his forehead, raised his eyebrows, lowered them, then looked me straight in the face.

'I think I'm seeing ghosts,' he said.

Back at the house we stayed up into the small hours. Pen didn't want to go to bed. He wasn't afraid of ghosts; he was afraid of Tanya's cold half of the mattress. So we sat in the front room with the curtains closed and the lights low, me stretched out on the couch, him huddled up in the armchair. Music was a cassette tape with Dylan's *Desire* on one side and Joni Mitchell's *Blue* on the other. Pen just kept turning it over, hour after hour.

'He didn't say anything,' he said. 'Not a fucking word. Just stood there – well, *hovered* there – grinning. You know? The grin?'

'And you're sure it wasn't a dream? Sometimes, you know, you're—'

'I was awake, Dummie. Utterly awake. I knocked the fucking alarm clock over fumbling for the light. I was awake.'

'Did you say anything to him?' I asked.

Pen shook his head. 'I wasn't scared,' he said. 'Just completely gobsmacked. You know what I thought? I thought: Oh, it's true, then, after all, that ghosts exist. Well, at least that's settled.' He took a gulp of his screwdriver. 'He just sort of hung there for a few moments,' he said. 'Then, when Tanya woke up, he vanished.'

'Tanya was still here?'

'It was two weeks before she left,' Pen said, then paused.

'What?'

'It was a warning,' he said.

'What?'

'He knew she was going to leave.'

'Pen, that's—'

'Don't argue with me, Dummie. I know. *Some have leaving shoved upon them.*'

'Thrust.'

'Thrust upon them. I knew, anyway. Seeing him, somehow I realized I'd known for ages she was going to go. He was trying to get me to see it. I know this is all bollocks, by the way, so don't look at me like that.'

I got up to stretch my legs. It was almost dawn. Parting

the curtains and looking out I saw a silent street, the steeply descending terrace surreally distinct in Magritte-ish twilight. The wind lifted two paper bags for a moment in a languid spiral, then abandoned them. They drifted back down to the concrete and stillness returned. I felt threadbare and hoarse – and sorry for Pen, who was, I knew, slightly ashamed at having kept me awake all night.

Blue, for the sixth time, ended, and the remaining blank tape hissed, softly, one of the deck's spindles with a squeak.

'Why now, by the way?' Pen said to my shoulder-blades.

'Eh?'

'Why now? You. Here to see me. I mean, don't get me wrong, it's fucking great to see you – but what's happened?'

I didn't turn. The paper bags moved again, slightly. An empty Coke can rolled out from the gutter in a gentle arc, then returned. Five years and we picked up conversation as if we'd left it five minutes ago. Another certainty, along with proposing to Natalie – *engendered* by proposing to Natalie – the certainty of the need to see him.

'I'm getting married,' I said at last. 'I want you to be my best man.'

I kept my back to him as long as I could, having no desire to see the effect on him of what I'd just said. I could feel it, anyway, the unconducted anger and sadness in the room behind me. What effect could it possibly have, except to remind him of what he had lost?

Perhaps a minute, in silence but for the deck's hiss and squeak. Then I heard him lighting up again.

'D'you know how you realize you're old?' he said.

I turned. He was cross-legged in the armchair, cigarette in one hand, empty glass in the other. One more day of not shaving, I thought, and people would stop seeing him as needing a shave and start seeing him as bearded.

'You realize you're old,' he said, 'when you realize that inside you still feel young.'

Kelp's ghost didn't come that night (or the next) either to me or to Penguin, though we both expected it. We barely slept. Drank and talked instead, shameless revisitations of the last great English Road Movie. It made tidying up bearable. Doing the dishes. Binning empties. I watched Pen going through these motions like someone remembering how to use limbs until recently paralysed.

'I wasn't ever really happy with her,' he said, sitting on the kitchen floor amid laundry. 'I wasn't ever happy because I knew from the start she'd never be as bothered about me as I was about her. I was constantly afraid she'd go off with someone else. I mean, she could have pretty much anyone, right? I mean, you saw her, didn't you?'

'She was very attractive, Pen,' I said.

'But it was a kind of curse, you see, because actually she hates men. It's a curse because men are incredibly attracted to her. She can get them to do anything for her – and that just makes her hate them more, the weakness of them. The weakness of *me*, Dummie, I'll tell you. Fucking disgusting.'

'Don't dwell on it,' I said. 'There's no point in dwelling on it.'

'Course, women hated her. She had no friends. I don't think, actually, she's ever had a real friend in her whole life. Needless to say I used to irritate the fuck out of her, going on about you and Fauntleroy. You know, I'd start chuckling to myself, remembering something from . . . You know, just remembering something and she'd go, "What?" and I'd say nothing because it wouldn't be funny to her and it would irritate her that it wasn't. But then the more I tried not to think about it the funnier it'd seem and the more I'd laugh, and the more irritated she'd get. She hated it if I didn't tell her — but she hated it more when I did. She never *got* any of it.'

'Why did you stay with her?'

He looked about him at the strewn laundry, then began tossing items into the machine. 'I don't know, really,' he said. 'Apart from . . . well.'

He stopped loading and looked at me. I handed him one of two bottles of Stella I'd just opened. He took a long drink, gasped, wiped his mouth and stood up. Evening sunlight lit one side of his face. He laughed through his nose, once. 'We hardly ever had sex,' he said, turning his face to the window. 'I know what it was,' he went on, unblinking. 'It was that I never felt entitled to her in the first place. Because she was really pretty and I was . . . well. It was like, I couldn't *not* stay, because she was so good on paper. The mystery, of course, is why the fuck she stayed with me.'

'Maybe because you're a good person.'

Another snort, followed by another swig. 'And there's nothing less sexy than a good person,' he said. 'Nah. It's not a mystery, actually. She stayed because she could bully me. She stayed because she was in total control. The more I let her get away with the more she despised me, and the more she despised me, the more . . . the—'

'Shut up now, Pen, for fuck's sake,' I said, seeing sunlit tears welling. 'Put those clothes in the machine and let's get out of this house. Come on, you can show me Exeter's sights.'

In the small hours, long after a murderous pub-crawl and a ghee-heavy bhuna at Pen's local Indian restaurant (where the waiters seemed to find Pen's mere existence cause for hilarity), after the arrival home and inebriated assault on the stairs, the graceless undressing and crooked pee, the slurred *gnights* and the red-edged swoon into sleep, I woke in the spare room pressed down upon by a weight of sadness. I had been crying in my sleep; my face was still wet with tears.

No memory of what I'd been dreaming, if I'd been dreaming at all. In the bathroom I splashed water on my face then towel blotted it dry, gently, pressing the heels of my hands into my eyes.

Pen hadn't gone to bed. He was curled up asleep on the couch in the front room with his hands between his knees. I went upstairs and dragged the duvet off the bed he'd shared with Tanya, brought it down and threw it over him. He didn't stir. I thought bits of things, *Love might be . . . poor bastard . . . it's never to late to seek . . . but if . . .* then on a thermal of sentimentality *all the years* – then suddenly the phrase *all this misery* – then again – dear God – the tears welling, me standing there swallowing, mouth wobbling. Horrified, I went through rooms emptying ashtrays and turning off lights.

An hour into the train journey back to London, a single-line ad in the *Guardian*'s personals changed everything.

'Saint-Ange seeks Dolamance,' it said. 'VM # 2323-751.'
I knew it was Deborah.

◆

Holly is a beautiful woman.

I was in a cab this afternoon, crawling down sun-blasted Third Avenue in slow traffic with every light against. Shop signs and awnings were brilliant in the sun, deli fruit and flowers glowed, oranges, tomatoes, irises, daisies, all urgent and vivid, nakedly alive. I was thinking of how far away from Logan Street time and freedom had carried me when I saw a woman in ravaged Levis and a white halter-top emerge from a corner florist with several bunches of flowers in her arms. Lilies, tulips, snapdragons, chrysanthemums, sprays of baby's breath and fronds of fern; the blossoms obscured her face. All I could see was the short blaze of blond in the sun. She moved slowly, as if killing time, clutching the flowers, then stopping to look in the window of a shop that sold reconditioned wooden furniture. She stood with her weight on one leg, abdomen moving as she breathed, all the flowers cradled in one arm, the other arm hanging at her side, one heavy, bonelike silver bangle on its wrist. She wasn't seeing anything in the store window, but was staring at some place between her own reflection and the display, a visual limbo that allowed her to remain suspended.

My driver was a Sikh with his own silver bangle, and he, too, was observing her. I thought of Holly and the care I want to take with her, of the hours I've spent listening to her troubled sleep (for she dreams a great deal, kicks about, groans, whimpers, sometimes wakes up in tears, after which follows a period of quiet and inconsolable distress, then ten minutes in the bathroom, then the return, pouchy-faced and exhausted, to bed, where my comfort is still treated with suspicion); I thought of the precise weight of her, lying on top of me, spent and consequently (mysteriously as yet) afraid or ashamed, and of her bashed and scarred willingness to go on, disgustedly, with life – I thought of all this and said to myself (and almost aloud to the Sikh) of the flower-carrying woman: Whoever she is, whatever she is, I still want Holly. Only Holly.

At which point she changed the way she held the flowers, uncradling them and taking a grip of the stems so that the heads almost brushed the sidewalk – and I realized it *was* Holly.

As the cab pulled level with her she turned away from the store window and stepped up to the kerb to cross. She didn't see me.

Later that night I woke from a deep sleep, suddenly, caught a glimmer of Kelp's hair and teeth at the window – dispersed within seconds – and realized that Holly was missing.

I found her sitting on the fire escape in her dressing gown, smoking, drinking a Corona, staring down into the empty street.

'I saw you today,' I said to her.

'Did you?'

'On Third. You'd bought the flowers. I thought you were someone else.'

'But unfortunately I wasn't.'

Let that go.

'I don't know how much longer this can go on,' she said.

'How much longer what can go on?'

'This. Us. It.'

Let that go, too.

'I was thinking,' I said, 'that we might not worry about it too much. That we might just leave it alone. No one ever seems to leave these things alone. I think that's when the trouble starts.'

She smoked the last of her Marlboro. Stubbed it out, *ground* it out, in fact, annihilating all but the cork.

'The trouble always starts,' she said.

◆

Love has a question for the Devil, and the Devil has a question for love.

★

She didn't know it was me. I called myself Robin (all aliases come with clues attached) on the phone. Her voice had deepened, but there was no mistaking its flat testimony to the lifelong struggle with boredom. We arranged to meet in the bar of the National Film Theatre. 'Then if you're short, fat and bald,' she said, 'I'll go and see *Bicycle Thieves* instead.' Anyone else would have said this as a joke. Deborah stated a fact. When I asked how I would recognize her she sighed and said: 'If we can't find a way of recognizing each other in the same room it's not going to work anyway.' Then she hung up.

The morning of the Saturday I was to meet Deborah I lay with Natalie in her sunlit bed at the Finsbury Park studio flat. The radio alarm, set permanently to Radio Three, had woken us as for a work day at seven. We'd turned the volume down, half listening, half sleeping: Prokofiev, Debussy, Fauré, Delius. Natalie dozily luxuriating and me clinging to the last shreds of sleep, knowing what leaving them would mean.

Fully awake, however, both of us had become transfixed by a weird piece of music which came up close and threatening one minute then dreamily receded the next. We remained in silence – Natalie, as usual, on her right side with her left leg thrown over my loins – until it finished, whereupon we were told that it was *Tabula Rasa*, by Arvo Pärt.

'Never heard of it,' Natalie said. I could tell from the slight increase in her leg's grip that the music had disturbed her.

'Me neither,' I said. 'But then I'm an ignoramus. How about I go out and get us some fixings for a whopping fry-up?'

'How about you make love to me, slowly?'

Not easy. Under the duvet heat and the (*this* morning) sickening smell of our bodies. I lifted her arms above her head and kissed her armpits, and likewise kissed the pulses in her wrists and throat; her hairline, ears, eyelids, nipples, navel. Anything to avoid going inside her, face to face.

'No, not like that. Wait.'

But I wouldn't. I held her thighs open and descended between them, working my mouth slowly, repeatedly, with gently increasing insistence until her own rhythm took over. She pulled at me three or four times to raise me up, but I resisted, and eventually she didn't care. I thought (lips numb, *fraenum linguae* at tearing point) of all the times I had done this for her in love. I thought of how (once I had graduated from Natalie as sexual object to Natalie as person) it had filled me with gratitude – for the appalling generosity of her opening herself in this way. I thought of how love had revealed the new meanings of such acts. Revealed, honoured, sanctified, rescued from the mind's cynicism and the body's pathos.

Now it was just the easiest way of avoiding her.

'Your turn,' she said, when her breathing had quietened.

'I know you'll find this hard to believe,' I said. 'But I don't think I feel like it.'

'You don't?'

'No.'

'Oh. Crikey.'

A pause. Her considering the possible meanings. There was nothing I knew of to stop her asking the next, the *How come?* question. Nothing except fear.

For the first time since I'd met her I sensed her deciding to avoid something. 'Okay, then,' she said, grabbing a handful of my hair and giving it a tug. 'What about the whopping fry-up instead?'

Natalie was going shopping with Julia. I was to meet them at Julia's for dinner. Beyond knowing I would be late I hadn't

312

planned anything. A sop to conscience: not to lie before it was certain that lying would be necessary. My afternoon was to be spent at the Tate's Cindy Sherman exhibition. The photographs an appropriate prelude to Deborah. Their titillating unreality and disturbed eroticism. The wigs, the noir make-up; telephones, odd angles. In any case Natalie got off the tube at Oxford Circus and I stayed on for Pimlico. Only as the train slowed into her station did she look at me with any acknowledgement of the morning's unasked questions: Something's wrong. I'm afraid. Trust me. Tell me. Soon. Please.

The doors hissed open, and with a last, confused glance at me, she was gone, swallowed by the Saturday crowds.

We were to meet at eight. I arrived at the film theatre at seven and called Julia's.

Natalie answered.

'Why?'

'It's Joe,' I said. 'I ran into him in town. He's in a state.'

'What's the matter?'

'Him and Laura,' I said. 'I think – I think she's going to dump him.'

'You're joking?'

'No, I'm not. I don't know. *Joe* seems sure of it. I think he thinks . . . Well, never mind. The point is—'

'Are you all right?'

'What?'

'You sound funny.'

'No, no, I'm fine. I just think I should—'

'You sure nothing's the matter? With you, I mean?'

'Honestly, love, I'm fine. I think Joe just needs someone to get hammered with. I'm sorry.'

'Don't be silly. It's all right.'

'Tell Jules sorry.'

'I will.'

'Okay. I'm sorry.'

'Dominic?'

'Yes?'

A pause. A shouting silence.

'Nothing. Just . . . I love you.'

'I love you, too.'

She might have said something as I put the receiver down. I couldn't tell. I wonder often whether it would have made any difference.

These days the bar in the National Film Theatre is a joyless place of tubular steel, interrogative lighting and overpriced baked potatoes. Back then it was dark and smoky, peopled by film buffs and fake bohemians who sat in earnest pre-screening conversation or displayed studied eccentricity in the hope that they would be taken for brilliant madmen or members of the South Bank's non-existent avant-garde. I took a high stool in a corner and waited.

Seven cigarettes and four gin-and-tonics later, at exactly ten minutes past eight, Deborah Black pushed through the door and slalomed her way to the bar.

She hadn't changed. She was nothing more or less than the woman the girl had suggested. A harder model, sure of her gravity and clout, somewhat thickened in the waist; still the dark eyes and meaty mouth; still the Cleopatra cut. Only some difference in her bearing, shoulders thrown a little back, head held with confidence. *Money*. Unmistakable in her clipped order and obliviousness to the waitress's personhood. She sat on a high stool of her own and crossed her legs, me imagining the hiss of electrified nylon. Julia, no doubt, would have been able to cost the clothes, but to me they gave nothing away: maroon suede skirt, black knee-high leather boots, a black blouse and a black suede jacket, draped across her lap. Some difference, too, in her concession to cosmetics. Eyes much made-up and lips a wet burgundy. Matching fingernails, three or four rings, a heavy gate bracelet, silver. I watched her fingers opening her handbag, purse, hand over the note, take the drink, light a cigarette; remembered them wrapped in Alice's hair, felt excitement moving in my bowels. Ten years.

I didn't have much time. This wasn't a woman who waited. This was a woman who was waited *for*. She would finish her drink, her cigarette, then go.

Lighting an eighth cigarette of my own (no roll-ups tonight), I slid from the stool and moved slowly between the drinkers to where she sat at the bar. I knew one thing: that the betrayal would begin with my very first words.

'It's me,' I said.

She turned at the sound of my voice, chin up in reflex confidence, eyes for an instant widening on recognition, then settling. A compressed smile.

'Well, well,' she said. 'How funny. I had a feeling it would be you.'

We found two armchairs separated by a low table. *Bicycle Thieves* had started and now only a handful of patrons remained in the bar.

Small talk out of the question. That, if nothing else, mutually apparent. Her face now being an index of all the surprises she no longer, thanks to money, had, it was easy to tell that Robin turning out to be Dominic had been one. Perhaps the first in a long time. The hair sickles swung when she leaned forward to flick ash. Apart from which movement she sat back in the armchair, legs again crossed, vodka and tonic held with bent wrist close to her mouth as in a satire of seduction.

'Where do you want to start?' I asked her.

'Not with any concern for chronological order,' she said. (Some education, then; not enough to prefer 'chronology'. Intriguing. Would she have been . . . *affected*, by education? The part of her I was interested in?)

'Did a lot of people answer your ad?'

'Of course. Dozens.'

'How many did you arrange to meet?'

'A few. The few that didn't sound like imbeciles.'

'I knew it was you.'

'Mm.'

'Is that possible?'

'Well, here we are, aren't we.'

Looks over the rim of her glass when sipping. Me unsurprised, by then, at how visceral – indeed colonic – the excitement had turned out to be. Naturally. The lower organs, the Devil's ownership of waste, his servants' concomitant scatology. In messy business with Alice, the inversion had been her forced reverence for Deborah's shit. *You say fucking please.* My good Catholic script doctoring: *I am not worthy to receive you, but only say the word . . .* Alice gagging, certainly, but with beneath the revulsion some astonished and inarticulable curiosity.

I shifted in my seat, the memory having taken effect. It was difficult to accept the fact of her, sitting across from me. I tried to take in every detail – the milky throat, the lines in her knuckles, the relaxed muscle of her crossed thigh – but there was no staying away from her eyes and mouth, the history (or at least our bit of it) to which they testified. Of every tree of the garden thou mayest freely eat; but of the tree of the knowledge of good and evil, thou shalt not eat of it.

'You look rich,' I said.

'I am.'

'How come?'

She looked down into her drink. Then back at me. 'My dad.'

'Your dad?'

'Our paths crossed. He's loaded. And guilty.'

It goes without saying, the single page in her handbag had ended. She sipped, looked away, looked back at me. I understood. *It goes without saying that you can have money. As long as it's just money.*

'We have a relationship now,' she said, as if she knew my thoughts. 'He wants to make up for lost time.'

'How Dickensian.'

'I remind him of my mother.'

'Do you like him?'

'He's my father.'

'Yes, but—'

'You can't change the past.'

'But you can make the future brighter.'

'Exactly. Who did you lie to to come here tonight?'

Touché. Along with which, for the first time that day, the full force of what I was doing. Beyond the immediate bustling body of excitement I sensed it, a vast, annihilating space of weariness. Natalie's over-the-shoulder look at me before she stepped off the tube, the message in it: whatever it is, I can handle it. I felt now what I hadn't, quite, felt then, the true mass of what she was asking me to declare. Something the size of a planet, a history, a life.

'Must there be someone?' I said.

She said nothing in reply. Just continued with the stare. Yes, there must.

'My fiancée,' I said.

The slightest smile. She had travelled, got used to money, the world. I assumed much exquisite food and costly drink had been devoured, digested, excreted. Her flesh had the glow of it. I assumed much service had been absorbed. It struck me that tonight was a minor curio for her: me, chance, the Fiancée. Hugely titillating, that, the difference in scale: the wreckage of my long labour at love a mere incident to her, a barely piquant distraction. It would add, of course, to the pleasure of inversion. Perfect for me, for whom the ever-multiplying nuances of sin still spoke (yes, ten years on) of a mighty revelation.

With very precise and careful movements, a Gauloise from a gold case; one offered to me, which I took. Revealed in the gesture − *yes it's real gold lots of my things are all my things are the real things now gold is shit to me* − the objects of wealth acquired, absorbed, devalued, despised and now desired with a robotic contempt. The matching gold lighter, however, proved temperamental; I leaned and lighted her (blasphem-ously) with Kelp's Zippo.

'Tell me about her,' she said.

'It's not necessary.'

'Isn't it?'

I looked into my drink. I felt still and heavy, as if I had achieved my full and proper mass.

'Isn't it?' she repeated. She smiled broadly this time, gen-erously, showing a tiny fleck of the burgundy lipstick on one of her upper incisors.

'You've got lipstick on your teeth,' I said. A momentary satisfaction, seeing her poise flicker. Then she found a white handkerchief in her bag and held it out.

'Wipe it off for me,' she said.

After the initial civic blush of the early days with Natalie, London had receded. Now, crossing Hungerford Bridge with Deborah Black, the city's might and myth bellied again, flared out in extravagance. The buried dead sighed, stirred, relieved their cramp. I put one foot in front of the other, sick and certain in my homecoming.

She insisted on 47A, once I had described it. A triumphal glimpse of the world she had left behind. Perhaps a belated blossoming of irony – though still she hadn't laughed once. My skin hung on me cold. A taxi. The two of us. My clipped instruction to the driver. London with bright and averted eyes passing.

The house was deserted. Even Helen was out. The messages light winked on the machine in the hall. I ignored it. Alone at the bathroom mirror my reflection whispered: 'You haven't done anything yet. There's nothing done yet that can't be undone. Talk to her, drink the wine, put her in a cab. The end.'

In the bare-bulbed bedroom I sat on the bed. Deborah meanwhile poked her nose into the room's nooks and crannies, a glass of Paternina cradled in her left hand with the stem hanging between her middle two fingers. The suede skirt and boots – even I could now see – would have cost her a month's rent at 47A.

'Funny how you're not saying anything,' she said. She had her back to me. She had parted the curtains slightly and was peering out into the darkness.

'I was thinking how ordinary my life must look,' I said.

'Very ordinary,' she said. She released the curtains and turned to face me, black bra in the room's ruthless light now shadowily visible beneath the blouse. 'Money changes everything,' she said.

Our usual struggle for euphemism, for circumvention and gesture. Patently not *every*thing susceptible to money's transformative powers.

'Funny, I mean, that you're not saying anything about

answering the advertisement,' she said. She had one arm wrapped under her breasts, the other right-angled at the elbow, its hand still cradling the body of the glass.

What was there to say? She knew anyway. I knew. She knew. That was the way it had always been. Lovers did not finally meet somewhere, they were in each other all along.

'This place stinks, do you know that?'

She moved towards me. I bowed my head. When I looked up, the maroon skirt filled my vision. I could smell the suede, and her perfume, and the silk of her stockings, and her nail varnish. Very slowly my thumbs crept under the hem of her skirt. Very slowly my hands began to push upwards. Very slowly they approached the stocking tops, the suspenders, the packed heat of the space between skirt and lace-wrapped mons. There should have been disappointment, a literary anticlimax after the years of memory and laboured imagination. There should have been an adult voice saying: This is ridiculous. Stop. Grow up.

Instead a multitude, disordered: *For fuck's sake you Jesus Dummie you leave the Devil to the likes of only your actions not your feelings and make a good confession to only your actions not your feelings nothing just I love you I love you too you'd lose your it's just you'd lose your sense of evil is a child's of humour you'd lose your sense of gesture of gesture of boredom and nothing has changed.*

'I wonder if you've changed.'

Deborah's left hand has just deposited the wineglass on the bedside table (digital alarm, last week's tea dregs, Nat's tented copy of *Cat's Eye*) and her right has found its way into the hair at the back of my head and is exerting a gentle downward force so that my face rises to look up at her.

'Honestly, the things I've seen,' she says.

Money. Opens up new sights. But I can see quite clearly that money hasn't helped with the rage or the despair, whatever their sources; that between them undischarged rage and bottled despair forge boredom, perpetually, irritatedly picking up objects and looking at them without meaning, putting them down again. Picking them up. Finding nothing. Putting them down again. This, I believe, is the world Deborah Black inhabits. She is surrounded by things with meanings and prevented for ever from grasping them. The only way out is . . . The only way out is . . .

The skirt is bunched around her waist, now, its maroon peculiarly vivid and throbbing. Revealed, the pornographically unbankruptable black stockings and panties, the exhaustedly titillating white zones of haunch and thigh. She moves her fingers in my hair, draws me slightly nearer. My cock is gridlocked blood, nonetheless denied erection proper by the fit of my jeans, a condition of highly localized pain, but it's better not to think of the word 'pain' because the presence of Deborah conducts the idea it labels to a place where Natalie is suffering it at our hands.

Deborah reaches round and unzips the skirt, which, when I remove my hands, drops to the floor. She steps over it. Degrees of capitulation, these, for me. Each one unknots something that has been contributing, over the years, to a contained discomfort. I wonder how many there are left. I know full well how many there are left. I tell myself I will allow some but not all of them. Some but not all.

'I shouldn't be doing this,' Deborah says, absurdly in the manner of a lunch-hour secretary who'll be late back to the office.

'I don't care.'

And I don't, because now, after the sweet frictional nothings whispered between lace and silk, the panties are gone, too, and six tropical inches separate her thick-skinned vulva from my face. There's a thin triangle of dark hair over her pubis, but the rest has been meticulously shaved.

'This is her,' Deborah says.

I don't understand at first. Then do. On the mantelpiece, a colour snapshot of Natalie, a close-up taken by me one Sunday afternoon in Regent's Park, the light just right, the amateur's point-and-shoot fluke. She's smiling, looking straight into camera, backed by the brilliant yellow of a laburnum tree. The wind has lifted her hair and slashed it across her, once at her throat and once at the corner of her mouth. 'I look beautiful,' she'd said, seeing it for the first time. Not vanity. Observation – along with surprise and suspicion. 'That would be because you *are* beautiful,' I'd said, at her shoulder, wrapping my arms round her. We had stared at it together in silence, as if it showed an interloping third person, someone who might come between us.

'This is her,' Deborah repeats, having reached over and picked the photograph up.

I don't say anything. I don't look up. Instead I try with what little of my might remains to get to my feet. If I can get to my feet I'll be able to look her in the eye and tell her this was all a mistake, that I've wasted her time, that in fact I'm one of the imbecile ad respondents she should never have bothered arranging to meet. I'll be able to hand her back her underwear and skirt, call her a cab and wave good-bye from the doorstep of 47A.

An experience, this attempt, like trying to make a fist first thing in the morning: a delightful failure. I look up.

Slowly, Deborah turns the photograph round to face me. Quite. I must see. For a moment there's a struggle to keep the real Natalie out of the image, to see the object, not the person. But this, too, is a failure. The phenomenal boundaries dissolve: I'm looking at Natalie.

Immediately apparent the ascendancy of arousal over sadness. Indeed, there's a slight fracture of disappointment that Deborah isn't construing the juxtaposition as an aphrodisiac. Then I see – her glance down at me – that on the contrary she's well aware of how this might be exploited (she might spit on the image, perhaps, wipe her backside with it) but sees, too, that such employment is beneath her boredom. Which is of course the more potent aphrodisiac, the discrepancy in scale I recognized earlier in the bar: that this is a big thing to me, a trifle to Deborah Black. This thought inflates Deborah (who not contemptuously but indifferently tosses the photograph onto the bed) in my imagination, transforms her into a creature of godlike ennui.

Not a further word is exchanged between us until what I've known all along was going to happen happens. Annihilating the years, Deborah and I move into the place beyond words. Her body is older and meatier, with a look and feel of many absorbed unguents. Her mouth seems bigger. A suggestion in her limbs of considerable strength.

The answer machine's red light is a metronomic pulse behind my eyes, an indicator of the world that will not quite recede. My disinterested mathematician is busy with factors and probabilities from that world. Meanwhile, there stand Deborah Black and Dominic Hood, re-embracing, in the ludicrous arena of my bedroom at 47A, with Julia's painting looking on and trapped Natalie on the bed forced to stare out of her frame into the brash heart of the bedroom's shadeless bulb.

We're quickly angry with each other, since the absence of a victim throws us back within the limits of what we can do to each other. Our arms and legs grow impatient, being told by our minds that this could all be so, so much better. But we do what we can. On the bed (Natalie taking our combined weight), on the floor, up against the wall. None of it enough. All reeking of preamble. Much-travelled Deborah, especially, is intermittently disgusted by these parameters. Stale bread, no doubt, after the globe's caviar and truffles. There are moments when I think she's just going to get up and leave. My own irritation comes and goes. I know, too, that our material surroundings are offensive to Deborah. 47A has served its purpose as a reminder of the mundanity with which she no longer need be troubled. On my knees behind her, contemplating (no Logan Street sun, no sleeping Jules) the spread backside and pendant vulva while she stands with back arched and palms flat to the wardrobe, darkly doppelgängered in its strip of mirror, I imagine her costly travels through celebrity mansions and five-star hotels, the perpetual deference from waiters, porters, maids. I consider the slaved-for food that has passed through her gut and turned to shit, and of millions diseased and starving. Very arousing, all this injustice. Very arousing, too, this concentration on her as a digesting animal. All part of the imaginative task (Dominic Hood a good Catholic fantasist to the last) of elevating the body over the soul.

She registers it, the sound of the downstairs door and people on the stairs, a few quietly exchanged sentences. Some slight adjustment of hip and scapulæ tells me she's heard. My disinterested reckoner – lit now by the answer machine's winking red light – has new material to work with. I feel there should be an accompanying sound, a honking klaxon or amplified heartbeat, but there isn't; just the sound of ordinary humans ascending the stairs, talking in murmurs. Just that sound and the silence between myself and Deborah Black, whose pulled-apart buttocks remain above me with their secret brazenly sold to view. We both keep very still.

Doors. The concept burgeons for me with new clarity. Doors open and reveal things, countless times, the world over. People on either side. The door's opening arc that has hitherto yielded familiarity now opens as onto a dream, a version of life in which the familiar components are rearranged, a body with its limbs wrongly attached. One day a door opens onto what you spend the rest of your life wishing you had never seen.

Natalie opens the door and enters the room. The door swings shut, slowly, behind her. Deborah and I (Deborah still with palms pressed, me still on my knees) look at her. Strangely off balance, Natalie tilts back and lets the closed door take her weight. A green shirt of mine hangs on the hook behind her, framing the burgundy hair, hair which, should I bring my nostrils close, would smell of Tesco's shampoo, cigarette smoke, the evening's rain and Indian food. Her understanding and incomprehension are both complete, and fill her in equal measure. Her mouth opens, slightly, but this reflex, this preparation for speech, is infinitely precipitate. There are no words. Perhaps even no feelings.

'What's her name?' Deborah says.

'Natalie,' I say, more excited than ever before in my life. Natalie is breathing loudly through her mouth. Deborah turns and takes three steps across the room towards her. I get to my feet, slowly, flushed, dizzy. My skin tingles as with pins and needles, and my face feels warm with joy.

Deborah looks over her shoulder at me, then back at Natalie, who isn't crying or trembling but who is pressed against the door as if held by a tremendous force, a nuclear wind only she can feel. Only her left hand moves, groping for the door's handle.

Deborah reaches forward, grasps Natalie's chin in her right

hand and shakes it a little, as if testing how well it's attached to the neck. Natalie's eyes remain wide, seeing past everything into nothingness. My body feels full and newly perfected and a great calm is upon me. Divinity beckons. Deborah and I could step into it, so gently.

Deborah returns to her former position at the wardrobe. Still Natalie hasn't moved or spoken. When I move close behind Deborah she arches her back for the denouement. A divinity diametrically opposed to grace. The promise is infinite, a giant and rich reward, a heaped feast of being upon which one can ever gorge and remain empty. Natalie's face discovers a new nakedness of expression and she collapses straight down onto her knees.

'Tell her.'

It is required, of course, that Natalie look at me, *be* looking at me to receive *les fleurs du mal*, the full bouquet like a spray of fresh roses splashed in her face to take her breath away; but she won't, can't look now. Can't. Won't.

'Get out.'

Delivered. She doesn't look back. I see the final, additional blow these two words bestow in a strange, barely visible movement of her neck and shoulders. Her hair hangs forward over her face, and thinking of all the times I've run my fingers through it while she daydreamed or dozed, the last skein of our love is laid somewhere deep in me, drawn down into the serpent's coil and I come, with a feeling of mean, pure beauty, deep in Deborah Black's lonely guts, feeling (she sighs, presses back into me, face turned in over-the-shoulder profile, tongue curled in businesslike martiality) the last moment of euphoria already nipped at, bitten off prematurely by the beak of the ordinary world, which in an instant has turned transcendence into a game-show prize and the rose of fire in my heart to a knot of stone.

I shrivel, quickly, and withdraw, hearing Natalie stumbling down the stairs, the front door slamming. A peculiar tension from Joe's room reaches out, making its humble sympathy known. My own room's air encases me like armour. I sink to my knees, filled with the desolate happiness of having returned to certainty after the doubt stirred by love.

Deborah dresses with brisk precision, saying nothing. This has been too small for her, of course. My limbs are calm, my senses shut, as after (I imagine) the torturous delivery of a stillborn foetus. I see a great many things very clearly. Messages, prescriptions, truths come and go in the air around me, the ephemeral script of a bonfire-night sparkler. One lingers longer than the rest. *Be alone.*

Deborah is weary. The Devil has once again reneged on his promise. Instead our arms and legs and faces are hyper-human, dully sensitive to their limits. These have been *antics*. What, after all, could we have done, here, in the policed world of Dominic Hood and 47A?

For a moment I think I see Kelp holding the sizzling wand, grinning and scribbling away like a madman. Then he's gone. The tail of the message hangs for a second, then vanishes.

Deborah goes to the bedside table and retrieves the Paternina. She takes a hard gulp, swallows, audibly. Then looks at me.

'I never want to see you again,' I say.

CHAPTER SIX

◆

White Magic

The message on the machine said: 'It's me. We went out for dinner instead. Bumped into Joe and Laura.'

I burdened Julia with the job of telling the family – not just that there would be no wedding, but that it was over. *Over.* Julia fought me for information.

'But what the fuck am I supposed to tell them?' she said.

'Tell them whatever you want,' I said. 'Just make sure they understand they'll get nothing from me. Make sure Mum understands. Tell them whatever you want.'

I got a letter from my mother, of course. Among many other things: '*Surely there's nothing that can't be talked through with Nat. You two were so much in love. Are you really going to throw all that away? I don't know what's gone on between you. Julia doesn't tell me anything. Couldn't your father and me be of some help? If you want to come home for a while . . .*' et cetera, ending with '*You know we love you very much and will do anything we can to help. Phone soon, sweetheart. Your loving Mum.*'

Smarter Julia was more direct. 'You fucking moron,' she said. 'What are you *thinking*?'

'Please, Jules.'

'Don't you dare say "Please, Jules" to me, Dominic Hood. What have you done to her? I can't fucking *believe* you people.'

'What people?'

'You people who have *love*, for God's sake, who piss it away like so much . . . like so much . . .' She had phoned Natalie herself, but had not been spoken to. Eventually, she'd gone round to the Finsbury Park studio, to find it empty. She'd written. No reply.

'It smells wrong, Dommie,' Julia said on the phone. 'You're my brother and I love you but the only reason you're giving out this minimalist "I betrayed her" line is because it was really something worse than that, something more than just cheating on her.'

I said nothing.

'Well? Wasn't it?'

'Yes.'

A long pause. 'Something disgusting,' Julia said. Not a question.

'Yes. Something disgusting.'

More silence. I imagined her, teeth clenched.

'Did you hit her?'

Nothing.

'Dominic you fucking tell me you didn't hit her. *Tell* me you—'

'I didn't. Shut up now. Just shut up, okay? I didn't hit her.'

'You can't tell me,' she said. 'That's disgusting enough.'

I couldn't tell her, then.

It's too late, but I can tell you, now.

★

An hour after Natalie's stumbling departure and Deborah's silent one, Joe knocked and put his head round the door. In with it came (from his room) the opening strains of 'Don't Fear the Reaper' and (from him) the scent of marijuana and burped beer.

'You all right?' he asked, eyebrows raised.

'Yeah.'

'What happened, man? Nat said—'

'We had a row. Can't talk now, Joe.'

'Fair enough fair enough fair enough.'

'Not your fault.'

'Didn't know I was dropping you in it, you know?'

'I know. It's okay. Don't worry about it.'

'D'you want a cup of tea?'

'No thanks. I'm fine. It's all okay.'

'Okay. Sorry, anyway.'

Magic – black or white – recedes. The mundane waits like a faithful dog. My room was still my room, the window's view still of the terrace that backed onto ours, the carpet still in places balding, Natalie's face in the photograph still confined to its smile.

I tidied up. Rinsed the glasses and corked the Paternina's remaining third. Changed my sheets and duvet cover. Lit a frangipani incense stick. Finally, had a long shower and got into bed, empty, and humming with exhaustion.

Waited. Wondering.

Knowing, really: long ago I had learned how to move past my own surfeit into new desire. Physically, more than enough time had passed.

So I closed my eyes.

The Devil's in the details, they say. But not in this case. In this case the Devil's in the big picture. What does it matter whether we pulled Natalie's fingernails out or cigarette-burned our initials into her breasts? The details are unimportant. What's important is that we kept her conscious of what we were doing. Of what I was doing. We asked her to tell us what love was worth in the face of our willingness to step into divinity. We asked her, elaborately, the Devil's question.

Afterwards (wiping up; the endurance of the practical necessities and the quiet nobility of the products – Kleenex – to cope with them) I should have been overwhelmed or crippled or sickened with guilt. In fact, I felt a deep calm, the peace of having the truth of me out again. Dominic Francis Hood, intact, in full knowledge of himself. He was a thing that worked against life and love. Very well. Something followed from that: the future was unknown in its practical details but clear in its essence: he would reach the logical conclusion of himself. There would be a time and a place.

Two months later I got an unsigned Manhattan skyline postcard.

The land of opportunity.

That was all. I pinned it up on the wall in the place where Julia's painting used to be.

I'm tempted to juggle with the facts here and say that then, immediately after my second good-bye to Deborah Black, I went into a self-destructive decline. The truth is, however, that the night of carnage at 47A precipitated something altogether less predictable, and less easy to describe. Trivially, I cut my hair very short and took to wearing an immaculate (budget-busting) three-piece suit. Blinding white shirts (ironing, starch), Windsor-knotted paisley ties in red, green, blue, yellow and ivory; black Bally lace-ups which I got shone on the corner of Tottenham Court Road, mornings on my way in to work. I started keeping my fingernails, toenails, ears, navel, nostrils and teeth unnaturally clean. My memory for facts began operating with superhuman efficiency. A little aura of authority formed around me. The Cornerstone lot couldn't quite assimilate the change: incredulity, piss-takes, then uncomfortable silence on the subject. Even David – himself a three-piece and bow-tie man since undergraduate days at Cambridge – eyed me askance, after the first jokes fell flat.

Otherwise, I became economical with my salary. And my language. My professional self focused, became ravenous. I went to everything. Launches, trade fairs, conferences, signings, readings, screenings – anything that would consume time among those who knew me least. Even my authors noticed, not knowing what to make of it; not caring, as long as *the figures* remained healthy. I was becoming, after all, very good at my job. The goodness of a person who knows that only complete surrender to some alien apparatus for living will forestall the real business of his life. Julia's painting was wrapped in a blanket on top of the wardrobe. I drank, I suppose, but not excessively; hangovers too much interfered with my morning pleasures: the cafetière coffee, the tying of my tie, the now unselfconsciously indulged-in tabloids, the espresso and shoe-shine, the superhuman workrate of my first two hours in the office.

I never saw Natalie West again.

Penguin sold the Exeter house and made a bit of money, even after the divvying-up with Tanya.

'I'm coming up to London,' he told me on the phone one

baking Friday afternoon. He had told me the same thing half a dozen times before.

'Yeah, okay,' I said.

'No listen, I'm going to be a teacher.'

'Yeah, okay, Pen.'

'I'm doing a PGCE at UCL. Start September.'

'Obviously you're joking.'

'No, I'm not. I've had it with sales. They're all cunts. I mean, obviously I'm a cunt myself, but not like those cunts.'

I was sitting at my desk at Cornerstone exhaling gigantic swirls of cigarette smoke into a shaft of sunlight so broad and clearly defined it looked fake. The offices were deserted but for a near-catatonic temp at the photocopier and a large bluebottle which waltzed the air, buzzing softly, now and then bumping into the window. On my desk was a letter from Tessa Hammond, Kate's agent. The *Herb Girl* phenomenon was up and running and Tessa was regretting having sold us the rights to the next book for as little as she had. There was nothing she could do, except make polite noises (this letter) about how big the next advance would have to be if we intended to publish Kate a third time. Kate herself had taken off on a six-month round-the-world trip, allegedly to research locations for the next book, in fact just because – *Girl* already in its fifth printing – she knew she could afford it.

'Oi, bollock-brain, are you listening?'

'Sorry, Pen. What?'

'I said it's a one-year course and then I want to get into a private school. Preferably a girls' private school. Preferably with tartan skirts and white knee socks.'

'You really aren't joking, are you?' I said. 'What in Christ's name are you going to teach?'

'Design and technology, stupid. I've got a fucking degree in architecture, in case the entire planet's forgotten.'

'Good God.'

'Yes, sir. The benefit of my expertise.'

'God help them.'

'God help us all, Dummie,' Pen said, heavily. 'God help us all.'

Prostitutes, I discovered, were expensive. Nonetheless by mid-'97 I was seeing one. Inez. Two hundred pounds an hour, half of which went straight to City Angels Escorts. The first visit (a flat in Paddington, owned or leased, I supposed, by the agency) was an attempt to stave off boredom. Or not boredom exactly: it was just that my energy for *things* had begun to seem insatiable. Films, video games, speed-crosswords, web-surfing, squash, cooking, *work*, all with a ferocity and precision no one who had known me in my former incarnation would have believed. And all possible, apparently, on an average of only six hours' sleep a night. Inez was twenty-three, slim, Spanish, and just getting used to *her* new self, having arrived at it after an initial period of being disgusted by what she did. 'I got used to it,' she told me. 'You can get used to all sorts of things.'

We *talked*. We had sex, too, of course (neither the altered states of Deborah and Natalie nor the subsistence couplings of the lost years, but something elusive in between; and curiously I could find no room for her in my fantasies), but what interested me was hearing about her life, the other clients, the agency personnel, her childhood in Madrid, her experiences of London, her family. As the months progressed (once a month was all I could afford on my salary, until I started dipping into the little I'd been saving; thereafter every other month I saw her twice), I tried to get the sex out of the way within the first twenty minutes, so that I could listen and absorb. 'Maybe you should write my biography,' Inez joked.

334

'Maybe I should,' I said. I could have. It became a kind of compulsion, to find out and remember as much about a complete stranger as possible, without compromising the distance between us. A study. I would – occasionally – have preferred to skip the sex altogether; but when I proposed it Inez laughed as at a sinister suggestion best dealt with lightly.

One afternoon, mid-session, we heard a key in the front door, then, incredibly, the door opening. Footsteps approached the bedroom. For a few moments we froze – absurdly, in a sixty-nine, me unable to see much beyond the darkly divided diptych of her rear – then frantically separated just as the bedroom door opened.

A man in his mid-fifties in a good suit entered. Grey at temples and beard. Dark eyes and a complexion closer to Inez's than mine. *Her father. Tracked her down. The reclamation of Inez Maura.*

Having made his entrance, however, he seemed unsure of what to do next.

Quick-off-the-mark Inez (robed, now, belt tied with no-nonsense tightness) stood with her feet planted firm and her arms stiff at her sides. 'What the fuck are you doing here?'

'I had to see you.'

'How did you get in?'

'The other key.'

'What other key? Jesus Christ. Get out. Get *out* of here!'

Not afraid. Good. No need for me to be. I had got my trousers on.

'Who is he, Inez?' I asked her, standing, taking a step between them.

'I had to see you.'

'I told you no. I can't fucking *believe* you. You better get out *right now* before I call the police. I mean it.' She moved to the bedside table's cordless. 'I *mean* it.'

He was in a state, whoever he was. Not her father, I decided. It didn't matter to me. I was in a state myself. A surge of disgust that there was a scheme of things behind this, belonging to him, unknown to me, alien to my own. He stood there with his face deadened and stupid (now that he had arrived, had surrendered to the forces driving him), and through him I got a glimpse of an entire world against which my own was meaningless. Vertigo. Me standing and looking down over the edge of a sickening drop. Into absolute emptiness.

'Please,' he said.

Some large signal of readiness from my muscles, a curious accord or cohesion. To my surprise, a feeling of nearness to joy.

It happened, when it did happen, very fast. Some movement from him towards her – and I went.

Nothing to do with Inez. No chivalry, but terror and disgust. Fear of the dully mysterious forces that had brought him here. It must have looked either comical or ugly, me with arms and legs whirring and flailing like a short-circuiting replicant; an absurdly compressed exchange of kicks and punches before we locked in a stalemate of mutual neck-wringing. Then the rigid, shuffling dance that had us crashing into the flat's furniture, item by item.

'I'm dialling!' Inez boomed. She had the hot face of a furious toddler. 'I'm dialling!'

We had hobbled through the living room and come to a Manichaean impasse in the doorway. His aftershave was expensively complicated, but there was curryish sweat, too. I had known his hands would be strong, that he was desperate enough to drop ten years. There was a wife, grown-up kids; part of his strength came from the rage at what he had done to them to be reduced to this. It was all that sort of shit. It was all that sort of *shit*.

336

The blood deprived of oxygen causes. The pressure on my windpipe was a forceful seduction. *All the months of carefully locked-up.* It wouldn't count if I let him. He had to win fair.

It might have been Inez talking on the phone (not, obviously, to the police, but to City Angels, I supposed, or whatever thuggery they kept within shout), or he might just have come to the end of what he had. Either way he slackened, and I sideways headbutted, and he released. I shoved him out into the thickly carpeted corridor and stood and watched as his face collapsed into a grimace like the Tragedy mask, then righted itself; or rather rearranged itself to display a new and brutal version of his fifty-plus years and the problems that had led him to this, his father, his mother, a universe screaming empty physics – *all that sort of shit* – and he turned and shuffled away.

I sat down, feeling sick, on Inez's leather couch, which gasped as it received me.

'You all right?' she said, handing me a Scotch.

'Fine, love,' I said. I didn't know what to do. It was as if I had seen something. I didn't know what.

'The agency'll refund you, you know,' Inez said.

It was as if I had seen something.

In January 1998 we had a leaving dinner for Joe, Sorrel and myself at 47A. Joe and Laura had bought a one-bedroomed garden flat in Hackney, which, after Joe had finished with the interior and Laura had finished with the garden, would make them enough money to buy a one-bedroomed garden flat not in Hackney. Sorrel was moving into her latest beau's penthouse flat in Swiss Cottage. I, having been promoted in the wake of *The Herb Girl*, was moving into a flat in Camden with Penguin. I didn't like to think about it. It made me anxious. Yet when he had put it to me I had agreed as brightly as if he'd suggested a pint down the pub.

Helen wasn't going anywhere.

'There'll be new people coming in here,' she said. 'I can't face new people.'

'It'll be okay,' I said.

'No,' she said. 'I don't think it will.'

The evening limped into non-event. Laura and Joe got stoned and fell asleep at the dining table. Helen ate nothing, instead chain-smoked and drank like an automaton. Sorrel affected levity through her first four glasses of champagne, then sat on the washing machine swinging her legs, face set in an expression of pinched mirth. She was surprising herself.

'Where'd you say you two were off to?' Helen asked her.

Sorrel had moved on to vodka and tonics, the third of which she downed before answering. 'Capri,' she said. 'His parents have got a villa there. I've never even met them. They'll probably hate me.' A tinkling laugh, and the next glass raised as to an invisible guardian angel.

Later, long after our silent consensus that the leaving dinner was over, I lay in bed listening to Joe and Laura making boisterous love on Joe's octogenarian mattress. *I never want to see you again.*

I got up to pee.

The stairs were in darkness and Sorrel's voice startled me.

'I know what you think,' she said, as I set foot on the landing.

I froze, let my eyes adjust. Her bedroom door was open, an oblong of lighter darkness. She was sitting with her back against the doorframe, knees drawn up to her chin, whatever garment – nightie, T-shirt – pulled over the knees and down to her shins. She got up in drunk increments, tinklingly iced vodka and tonic in her hand.

'I *fuck*ing know what you *think.*' The unbalanced emphases of the inebriated. She swayed, pitched forward, put a hand out to steady herself, missed, and staggered face first into the opposite side of the doorframe. The drunk's singularity of purpose, too: she didn't spill her drink. 'Fark. Hurt my face, now. Dominic?'

'I'm here,' I said, stepping forward with a hand out. She took it, and in a second, arms wrapped round my neck, had hung two thirds of her bodyweight on me.

'Sorrel,' I said.

'Shshsh. *Shshshsh.* I know what you fucking think.'

'I don't think anything. You're just pissed, that's —'

'You want to have sex with me because you think I'm juss a fu— *huc.* Oh blast these hiccups.'

I steered her backwards into her room. To an observer, two imperfectly reanimated corpses trying to remember the waltz.

'See?' Sorrel said as I dropped her onto the bed and, unable to extricate my arms quick enough, came down on top of her. 'It's not exactly swee—*hips* – sweeping me off my—'

'Sorrel, let go of my hair.'

'Why'd you cut all your hair off, eh? Umm? I liked it better when you—*hic* – fuck. *Huc.* When you had all your hair on.'

'Sorrel, please let go of my hair.'

But she wouldn't, without a fight. I had to prise fingers. By the time I was finished, she was sobbing.

'Shshsh,' I said, easing myself up off the bed. 'Shshsh, don't cry. Come on, it's okay. Everything's going to be okay.'

But she grabbed the waitsband of my jeans (all I had on) and wouldn't let go. I sat down on the edge of the bed. 'Sorrel,' I said, 'for God's sake. It's four in the morning.

You're just pissed, that's all. You'll be all right after you've had some sleep. Come on now, stop crying.'

'You lie with me.'

'What?'

'Juss make – *hips* – spoons.'

'This is ridiculous.'

'Please. *Please*.'

'Two minutes,' I said, lying down with full but postponed bladder behind her.

'Thank you.' In a horribly human rasp. 'Thank you.'

Nothing. There she was, warm and soft, slotted in in front of me, smelling of Giorgio of Beverly Hills and belched champagne, hair a silky treasure on the pillow, backside – guarded only by the hem of the T-shirt and the lace of her knickers – a firm yet tender insinuation against my groin. But nothing. The faintest flicker of blood, an isolated pinprick or two, but really just deadness. At best a grudging respect for the irony of it all.

A minute passed. Two. The crying subsided, then stopped, became tremulous breathing.

'I feel sick,' she said at last.

'Are you going to throw up?' I asked, tensing.

She thought about it for a moment, consulting her guts, then exhaled with voice. 'Hououyhhhhh,' she said.

'Hold on,' I said, leaping over her. 'I'll get the bucket.'

I wondered, sour-eyed and dehydrated at the hospital later that morning, whether Helen would ever forgive Sorrel for saving her life in so typically self-absorbed a fashion. The bucket was in the bathroom. So was Helen, steeping, unconscious, in a bath dyed with her own blood.

I had every intention – having waited, filled with memories of my last Casualty wait (*Are you the person who came in*

340

with Gregory Kelp?), for three hours – of getting home from the hospital quickly, having one of my very hot showers and scrupulous shaves, then suiting and booting as usual to get into Cornerstone no later than eleven. That, I'm sure, was my intention when I emerged from the ward into sunlit Goldhawk Road.

Intention or not, it's not what I did. What I did was wander in a daze through west London.

Hours passed. Sunlit street names blazed on their plaques. I squinted, leaned up against a piss-darkened lamppost, felt light-headed, unreliable in my articulations.

In a wood-panelled pub in Notting Hill I ordered a double Laphroaig and a pint of Boddington's. Helen's . . . The trouble with Helen is that . . . I've often thought . . .

Nothing spectacular. The coven of nurses, doctors flapping like white vampire bats, the crash of trolleys, lights, the cranked bed with its past of pain and expiry. Stitches, oxygen, transfusion, me trying to think back to St Dymphna's human biology, *another* laminated transparent man, life-sized this time, showing the circulatory system – *anterior ulnar, basilic, radial, cephalic, median, interosseous, brachial* – a compact little detonation of guilt for never having *given blood*, Helen tubed up and cadaverous but with nonetheless life bleeding back. Nothing spectacular. Penitent Sorrel smelling of toothpaste and puke had struggled in an hour after I'd arrived with Helen in the ambulance, but had had to keep dashing out, the stink of medicine stirring her gorge. Really – *really* – nothing spectacular. Merely that, sitting alone at Helen's bedside, I had noticed that four or five single blond hairs were sweat-stuck across her left eye, and had, without thinking, reached across and brushed them back. My hand had paused, hovered, then gently brushed the rest of her hair away from her face. The act reminded me of childhood, my mother's hand dipping down through the fever, fingertips cool against my face. At which point, belatedly, it came to me that Helen had tried to kill herself, had been brought, courtesy of her life's hollows and empties, to the preference for death. It was just Helen lying there, with her largish head and heavy jaw, jugular pulse visible, hands plain and at rest at her sides, unable to disguise their history of not having been held. All the details of her, and no one to whom every one of them was precious. I thought of all the days and nights I'd left 47A with Helen (alone) in it, on any one of which I could have asked her what she was thinking or what she had dreamed about the night before.

A sudden feeling of being watched. I shuddered, looked over my shoulder. Nothing. My head ached. I lit another Silk Cut. Stood. *The ordinariness of causes.* Then, not sure why I had stood up, went to the bar and ordered another Laphroaig. I found I was smoking very fast, and that without quite being aware of doing so, I had drunk the whisky and walked out into the brilliant streets.

Finding violence (a back burner of consciousness busy with how curious it was that fear drove one in search of violence) was less easy than I thought. Drunk, I wasn't taken seriously. My first attempt – lewdly gurning and blowing kisses to a skinhead and his girlfriend across the room – failed. The skinhead wasn't a skinhead. He was a Buddhist.

'I'm sorry you're so unhappy,' he said, as they brushed past me to the exit.

But London obliged, eventually. Chucking-out time outside a nightclub off Oxford Street, patrons groggy from six hours of chart music, ecstasy, lager and bellowing at each other straggled out like wasps from a smoked nest. Tattooed men and candy-coloured girls. A great deal of amorphous anger anyway, among the men, having not, the bulk of them, pulled – although, ironically, it was a young and voraciously snogging couple who came to my rescue. Deeply and mechanically kissing, both with eyes closed and slow-moving heads, her bottle-blond in white Lycra cocktail dress and silver stilettos, a good two inches taller than him; him with buzz-cut cannonball head, homemade tattoos and a body of densely developed muscle evoking anatomical Latin: *trapezius, Latissimus dorsi, transversalis, Quadratus lumborum.* I imagined, during the moments leading up to my gambit, the two of them making love. Him a pit-bullish rutter, face scrunched as in misery or constipation, furiously bucking, scrabbling to dig down to the place where he was relieved of the pressure the world kept putting on him to be something other than he was, her with eyes shut and legs afloat, fighting off the thought that she wanted nothing but for it to be over and him not to hate her, wondering why she had fought so much with her mother, where her father was.

I tapped him on the shoulder.

'Would you be so good as to tell me what that charming girl is doing with a poxy and fat-headed little twat like you?' I asked him.

Pain hurried consciousness and a raging thirst back in. Voices, before opening my eyes.

'He's awake.'

'He's lost some teeth.'

'That's the least of it.'

'You know, it's amazing, you see someone without their teeth, you think they've been blacked out with biro.'

'Life imitates art.'

'I don't like the look of that eye.'

'I don't like the look of any of it. I don't like the look of *him*. Dommie? Can you hear me?'

Jules and Penguin. A brief grope into the void for my history and identity, then there it was, still intact. Pain was making its fiery presence felt in a dozen different places. Moving anything other than my eyelids, I thought, would only make things worse.

On moving them, however, I found that only the left set worked, the right being plum-sized and gummed shut.

'Sorry,' I said, abstractly. It seemed the appropriate articulation. A white ceiling, faint odour of antiseptic and blocked drains. Hospital.

'Oh God, Dommie, look at the fucking *state* of you.'

I tried sitting up. Got no further than the first muscular contraction.

'Don't move, you pillock,' Pen said. 'Christ almighty, Dum. What is it? Water?'

I nodded, feeble, tearful with thirst. Pen got up and poured me a glass from the bedside jug. I drank it, and two more, then, with sorry-for-itself left eye blinking slowly, sipped a fourth.

'How long have I been here?'

Pen looked at his watch. 'They brought you in last night – well, early this morning. It's just gone two in the afternoon. They'll probably keep you in till tomorrow. Christ, man you should see yourself.'

'Brought me in where?'

'Queen Charlotte's,' Julia said. (Where they had brought – where *I*, in fact – had brought Helen. I wondered if this was her bed. It seemed likely, given God's . . . given His . . .)

'You look like a mugged granny,' Pen said.

'I *feel* okay, by the way,' I said. 'Just in case anyone's ready to move on from aesthetics.'

'Don't you joke about it,' Julia said. 'Don't you dare *joke* about it, Dominic. It's disgusting. You know that, don't you? How absolutely disgusting this is?'

'I know, Jules, I'm sorry.'

'What's the *matter* with you?'

'I don't know.'

'You must know.'

'I don't.'

A pause. Pen sensing himself an inhibitor. 'I'm going to the coffee machine,' he said. 'D'you want one, Julia?'

When he had gone, we fell quiet. Her hand took mine, gently, wove its cool fingers into my hot ones. All the hours and days of our childhood. I could see she was close to tears, only the urgency of solving the problem holding them back.

'I'm sorry, Jules,' I said.

'I want you to stop.'

'I can't.'

'I want you to stop all this.'

'I can't.'

'You have to.'

'I know.'

'You *have* to.'

'I *know*—ow.' Imprudent emphasis: a current of pain from upper jaw to temple. Nonetheless it halted Julia's line.

'What is, actually, wrong with me?' I asked. Then tacked on, 'Medically, I mean.'

She would be thirty-five next month, and was more beautiful than she had ever been. Beauty that showed the soul's wear and tear, the quarrel with desire, the long campaign against the self's isolation. I wondered, briefly, if there wasn't some huge shift awaiting her, a religious conversion, a sexual transformation, murder, love. Wondered, too, what it would do to our relationship if I simply told her. Everything. About myself.

'Three broken ribs,' she said. 'Broken nose, dislocated shoulder, seven stitches in your head, four in your left knee, cuts, abrasions and multiple contusions. I don't even know what contusions *are*.'

'Bruises. Multiple bruises.'

'Your eye. Jesus, Dommie.'

'Can I go home?'

'Don't be stupid.'

'Come on, Jules, that's small potatoes by hospital standards.'

'They're worried about concussion. You'll have to stay till tomorrow at least.'

Visions of my desk at Cornerstone, a revolting flash of my scribbled-in diary.

'David,' I said. 'I need to—'

'I've called him,' she said. 'Told him you were in a car accident. You've got to stop all this, Dommie. *Please*.'

I couldn't look at her, quite, not after hearing again the genuineness of the entreaty, sensing the approach of emotion, the old, patient, fierce love. Instead I looked away, out of the ward's window, which showed only a car park, some tarpaulined building work, a hard-hatted man, one hand on hip, smoking a cigarette, staring down into a hole in the ground.

'Need to pee,' I said, giving her hand a squeeze. 'Now what sort of machinations do you think that'll involve?'

In the week that followed, the first in the Camden flat, I moved unsteadily from room to room in dressing gown and slippers, reintroduced to my body via its chameleon contusions, ribs at the mercy of sneezes, coughs, hiccups, farts, defecation. I felt sorry for my bones but not, much, for myself. Showering was out of the question. Instead the flat's sepia-bottomed tub, filled after the plumbing's half-hour of epilepsy with water as hot as I could stand it, wherein I washed my loins and dabbed, gingerly, with sponge, at my armpits, neck and face. The mirror showed a haggard and tow-haired version of myself. My pair of bad eyelids – the colour of Nigerian lips, initially – opened by degrees, to reveal half the white shot with blood. Upper-front-toothless and stubbled, I gurned to myself in the shaving mirror, impressed by my body's ability to present all the outward appearances of a Cruikshank lunatic.

The ordinariness of causes. A gnawing rat of realism worked at me from within, suggesting psychotherapy, hypnosis, or at the very least some serious thinking about my earliest memories of my mother – to the latter of which I gave some energy. Without discovery. I remembered loving my mother very much, and resting more or less continuously in the belief that she loved me. Long conversations about Clouds and Autumn and Animals and The Sea. Certainly the odd smack on the legs, certainly occasional tears, but nothing *significant.* I was carried, kissed, kept entertained.

Ditto my father. Without a doubt I thought him a demigod, but we were friendly with each other. Shoulder-rides and swinging from his hands. Footie in the back yard, praise for my drawings, his heroic smell of Brylcreem and aftershave.

They were a physical couple. Possibly capitulation to the wiles of Dr Durex had liberated them generally. Giggles from the kitchen – *Shshsh! Get off! Stop that!* – then more giggles, then a silence filled with something they were doing for a moment, then *Now bugger off, will you?* His emergence, smirking, Julia rolling her eyes, me understanding that they had been *snogging.*

I *had* no ordinary causes. Nonetheless that sickening glimpse into the void, physics going indifferently tooth and claw about its business on the long loop from Big Bang to infinite compression, nobody to blame for anything.

At my request David had the half-dozen manuscripts under my care biked over, and I sat with them at the dining table (fugged with painkillers and the leftover pain they failed to kill), grateful at least for the feel or presence of work, even if my professional self knew that in my state very little work of any use was being done. Evenings, Pen and I made quite a pair, him marking, me pretending to edit.

'Do you think this is the way it'll stay?' I asked him. 'Into our old age?'

He didn't look up from his work. 'No,' he said. 'Because unless you change out of that fucking dressing gown soon I'm going to put something in your tea.'

Then, at the end of the week, David came to see me, with, God bless his yellowing teeth, a large bottle of Glenmorangie.

'Christ, Dominic, your poor *eye*.'

'It looks worse than it feels.'

'It was a fight, wasn't it?'

'Yes, I'm afraid it was.'

We would have to discuss this, we both knew, my doing things like getting into fights. We weren't going to discuss it yet. Besides, there was something else worrying him.

'We've got trouble,' he said, after I'd poured, we'd clinked, and he'd taken his first sip.

'Trouble?'

'Kate Durrell. Gone AWOL. In India. Goa, I mean.'

'What?'

'Tessa thinks she might have had some sort of breakdown.'

'You're joking.'

'I wish I was.'

'The book?'

He looked at me, without blinking, mouth very still. Ah.

To date, *The Herb Girl* had sold 300,000 copies. Film rights had gone to Warner for a million six. And the second novel due. We hadn't heard from Kate for months. But we had had regular bulletins from Tessa to the effect that our star was alive and well, living in a hotel in Calangute, and that the book was going, in Tessa's words, splendidly. Certainly the contract's delivery date had come and gone, but there was nothing unusual about that. Apparently there was, in Kate's case, more to it.

'It's killing Tessa to come clean,' David said, after we'd both lit cigarettes. (It was the first time he'd been to the flat, and I could see that the shabbiness unnerved him. He sat in one of the room's two corpulent armchairs with the body language – long legs plaited and elbows pulled in – of a man who feared contamination.) 'But it's gone past the point where she's got any choice. For months Kate refused to say anything to her at all about the book. Then, a couple of weeks ago, she told her she'd written six hundred pages of, in her words, complete dogshit.'

'Fuck.'

David sipped, swallowed, flicked ash. 'Quite,' he said. '*Fuck.*'

'You said Kate had gone AWOL?'

'Not strictly speaking. She's at the academy.'

'What academy?'

'The' – he took a piece of paper from his pocket – 'Vipassana Academy in Dona Maria. Vipassana and Dona Maria. Christ what a mish-mash. Anyway, the people at the hotel told me she'd got sick – "got crazy", was the phrase, in fact — and gone to the academy ashram whatever for refuge.'

'Holy shit,' I said.

David cleared his throat. 'Holy, as you say, shit.'

'What are we going to do?'

It hadn't occurred to me that there was anything *to* do.

'Well, I was thinking,' David said, looking down into his drink, 'that you might go out there and bring her back.'

I wondered — Air India Economy en route to Bombay — whether Julia might have put him up to it. It was certainly within my sister's scope. David had dismissed the suggestion haughtily enough — 'I know it's hard to believe, Dominic, but I do, actually, run this company. I do, actually, from time to time *make decisions*' — but I wasn't wholly convinced. Pen's repeated pronouncement that it would 'do me good' had me suspecting even him of collusion, however peripheral.

Nonetheless (with new false incisors and still-aching ribs) the 747 three weeks later, the harried switch to domestic, the arrivals hall at Dabolim, the first pungent whiff of Goa's night between exit and cab, the breakneck ride to Vasco da Gama, check in at the Maharaja, air-conditioning, smell of jasmine incense and drains, then the blessed plunge into the supergravity of foreign sleep.

Dona Maria, five miles north of Chaudi at the foot of the Sahyadri Hills, population 2,461, living for the most part in rudimentary bungalows or basic apartments but also, at the poorer end, in broken-down barns, huts and shanties, sometimes twelve or sixteen to a couple of rooms. After the academy the town's three main attractions are the Church of the Blessed Sacrament, the Holy Family Convent High

School and the Metropole Hotel, at which last I checked in, bus-shaken, dehydrated and insufficiently ibuprofen'd later that afternoon.

'I'm afraid Miss Durrell has left us.'

'Tell me you're joking.'

'Not at all. She went three days ago.'

'Not the day after I telephoned?'

'Yes, actually, precisely the day after you telephoned.'

'How was she?'

Evening. Reception at the academy. A short, orange-and-maroon-robed young monk with bi-focals and an irrepressible smile. Me, in spite of myself, suspecting him of concealed enlightenment. I was hungry, too, having had nothing since an oily Chaudi bus-station samosa, and now the smell of roasting spices from the kitchen across the yard set my stomach growling.

'She was, I have to say, not very happy,' he said, allowing the Nirvanic beam to subside for a moment. 'Many of our visitors come here in times of trouble, looking for a simple solution. The solution *is* simple, of course, but simplicity requires a tremendous effort. I'm not sure what Miss Durrell was looking for. She seemed very confused.'

'They told me at the hotel she'd gone crazy.'

A ridiculous laugh, a tiny *tee-hee-hee* which nonetheless seemed to bring tears to his eyes. 'They think anyone who moves from the hotel to the academy is crazy,' he said. 'Although,' sobering, 'I do believe Miss Durrell broke a window there.'

'At the Metropole?'

'Yes. She threw her laptop computer through it.'

I exhaled, heavily, desperate for a cigarette. The monk got up and moved to the reception's doorway, as if drawn by the scents from the kitchen. My stomach yowled, loudly.

'Do you have any idea where she might have gone?' I asked, getting to my feet.

He turned to face me again, another expansive grin. 'Yes,' he said. 'She's gone to the convent at the Church of the Blessed Sacrament in town. Would you like to join us for dinner, Mr Hood?'

The concrete exterior of the Church of the Blessed Sacrament had for reasons beyond me been painted a strange dusk colour, something between cobalt, silver and mauve. A hideous building altogether: no arches, no fluting, no stained glass. Rather, a pre-fab look – housing office, down-at-heel clinic, detention centre – with unlatticed windows, blood-red woodwork and a flat-topped tower with the look of having once been taller, subsequently lopped.

The convent attached, however, was a collection of long, low, whitewashed buildings with red rooftiles, pink stone floors and shady, arch-flanked colonnades. Orange, lemon and apple trees, oleander, the ubiquitous bougainvillea and a small, ornate bird bath into which the last awake sparrows flitted and splashed. Very much the air of an easy billet, I thought, the nuns not sticklers.

'I'm afraid Miss Durrell doesn't wish to see anyone.'

A white-habited Filipina nun, sweeping the main colonnade with a birch broom, strokes counterpointed by the rasp of the garden's cicadas. Excessively conscious of mere maleness (without even having *begun* to take my soul's rottenness into account) I had cleared my throat at fifteen paces then asked, as chastely as possible, whether a message might be sent to Kate.

'I understand, Sister,' I said. 'But if you might just tell her that her editor is here, and that he has flown from England specifically to see her?'

'Miss Durrell has been very specific herself,' the nun said, with barely restrained dimples. She was in her thirties, and retained the peculiar naked facial flirtatiousness of the celibate. 'Whether you have flown from England or anywhere else. I'm sorry, but we respect the wishes of our guests.'

Oh, how many fucking rupees has she put in the poor-box? Just tell me. I'll double it.

Of which I'm not sure how much would have made it into articulation had I not at that moment caught sight of Kate herself, coming out of the church and walking across the yard away from me towards the single-storey block of (presumably) cells.

'Kate!'

She stopped in her tracks, turned. Recognized not just me, but the end of something, flight, escape, postponement I saw it in her face. Her soft shoulders, which had tensed at the sound of my voice, dropped again. She put her hands into her pyjama pockets, looked down at the earth beneath her bare feet.

'Shall I call Father Adrian, Miss Durrell?' the nun asked, over my head.

Kate hesitated a moment. Moved her foot a little in the dust. Then shook her head, no.

'Who's Father Adrian?' I asked, having crossed the yard and followed her to a bench under the orange blossoms. 'The holy bouncer?'

She looked terrible. Red-eyed from booze (the reek of which – whisky, I thought – came on her breath), lips cracked, hair scraped back, thick with grease. Her feet were grimy and her fingernails bitten down to the quick. A large, well-executed dressing on her left elbow, about which I thought it prudent to remain silent.

'How are you, Kate?'

'Not good, Dominic.'

'Aren't the nuns treating you well?'

'Have you got a cigarette?'

The sun had sunk behind the hills, leaving a frayed tissue of cloud bloodily stained in its wake. Darkness was gathering in the garden's hollows. A very faint odour of vomit from Kate, too, I decided, in with the whisky; perfectly bearable, given the orange blossom, honeysuckle, incense, old stone and, from somewhere nearby, woodsmoke.

'There's no book,' Kate said, simultaneously breaking my heart and earning my respect for cutting straight to the chase.

'At all?' I asked.

She smoked, calmly, one hand still in the pyjama pocket. 'I started reading,' she said. 'History.' Then a laugh through her nose. 'I was going to write a serious . . .' Dismissive hand gesture. 'I know what people think of me. I read the reviews.'

'Kate,' I said. '*Kate*, for heaven's sake what's the matter with you? You're a *lovely* writer. Plenty of critics said so.'

'Plenty of *glossy magazines* said so,' she said. 'The broadsheets all said sentimental. Sentimental *codswallop*.' She laughed again, blatantly without amusement. 'I don't want to be a lovely writer,' she said. 'I want to be . . .' swallowing, swallowing – couldn't say it. Looked down at the dust on her feet instead.

'Maybe,' I said, quietly, 'you've taken this on too soon? You've got time, Kate.' *The Herb Girl* was still selling. Latest territories to fall Israel, Turkey, Greece, Japan, Brazil. There would be money for Kate (and Tessa, naturally) and money for us.

'There's no rush, you know. I mean, I know we've got delivery dates and whatnot, but—'

'Fuck it,' she said. Silence. Two more white-habited nuns crossed the courtyard, one carrying a stack of laundry. They glanced over at Kate and smiled. She seemed not to see them.

She stood up. 'Come on. Let me show you something.'

I followed her across the yard. The sisters kept two visitors' rooms, which, if unoccupied by nun relatives, could be rented out to pilgrims seeking contemplation. A simple room – one hard, mosquito-netted bed, one little table and chair, one bamboo blind, one coarse brown rug – but Kate had made as much of a mess as one rucksack's contents allowed. Also no laptop, nor any other evidence of writing. No evidence of *reading*, even. Surprisingly unconcealed on the table, a bottle of Teacher's whisky, one third gone.

Kate found two mugs and poured, added *vala pani*, grimly clinked with me, neither of us up to even an ironic toast.

'I think the best thing,' I said, 'might be for you to come home and have a rest for a while.'

She wasn't listening. She was lifting the mattress and scrabbling around underneath. An A4 manila envelope. Not empty.

'Here.'

'What is it?'

'Take it out.'

I put my mug down. (Hardly daring to hope.) Removed from the envelope a manuscript of some three hundred pages.

a novel
by

KATE DURRELL

Say nothing. Say nothing.

'If it ain't broke,' Kate said. 'It's probably what you all wanted, anyway. Christ, I disgust my fucking self.'

She wouldn't be pacified – and drank more the more I tried. At ten o'clock the Filipina nun came and said no visitors after this hour and goodnight sir and you may come again tomorrow and please remember the poor-box in the church and in any case it is not good to agitate the guests in future please.

Having put three hundred rupees in the church's poorbox, I sat for a moment in the pew nearest the door. The Scotch had soothed my ribs, the manuscript my Cornerstone fears, and there was in any case my bad-tempered curiosity about how God would react to my setting foot in his house. Satisfied immediately by the charged silence and the candles' collective expression of pain: they were small, pure, flames of light; I was a rotting servant of darkness. The one Scotch – even Kate's wild measure – though rib-easing, hadn't been quite enough; white-faced Natalie with her back to my bedroom door, left hand searching for the handle. *Get out.* It was the same God, here, of course. What had I expected? One who didn't understand English?

Someone walked past the church door. I hadn't turned quickly enough to see. Just a shadow. Nothing.

I lit a candle for Kelp, turned one last time to the altar, then walked out into the compound.

The cicadas were in full chorus now. Bats flitted, silently. A mosquito bit my neck. Adjoining the church was a small reception room with door open, throwing a long slab of light onto the dust. Beyond I could see a plain wooden table bearing a bowl of greenish plantains and a bright yellow teacup; on the wall a month-to-view holy calendar illustrated with Michelangelo's *The Last Judgement*, and on the floor a leather rucksack of fantastic age and recent travel, the heel of one large sandal poking out of the top. At the rear of the room, another door gave onto, I presumed, the priest's private quarters.

Whim, I told myself, mentally. *Let's have a look at this Father Adrian.*

The rear door open a crack. Beyond it, two male voices. The first, young, I thought, Father Adrian's.

'I'm glad you could come, Father. Are you sure you want to go straight away?'

'If you were in his shoes, would you want me to sit down and have a cup of tea first?'

A pause. The pain of the rebuke. Then Adrian: 'You're right, of course. Forgive me.'

The other was unpacking or packing, the sound of zips, buckles, press-studs. 'No, I'm sorry. There was no need. Will we walk?'

'It's not far. We had the loan of Dr Sutay's car, but the clutch . . . He's up there now with Father Rodriguez. I've got a list of the medications the boy's been given over the last few days.'

'Irrelevant. How's your strength?'

'Sorry, Father, my—'

'Have you eaten, slept?'

'I'm fine.'

'Said mass today?'

'Yes.'

'Good. Now you will make a good and complete confession to me as we walk.'

'Father, I . . .'

'What?'

'Nothing.'

'It's just a confession, Adrian. Haven't killed anyone recently, have you?'

'It's not that.'

'What, then?'

'I'm afraid.'

'Yes.'

A pause. Zipping and press-studding with an air of finality. Then a new kind of stillness. The voice that wasn't Father Adrian's. 'Give me your hand. Now, listen to me. You're a good man and a good priest. This is a battle we can't lose if we have faith. Do you understand what I'm saying to you?'

'I understand.'

'Good. No more talk of fear. Let's go.'

They were coming. I abandoned the door and back-pedalled through the reception room, out into the compound. It had happened so quickly, no time to feel anything. Now, with my long shadow stretched across the slab of light, I felt unbearably hot. I turned and ran in tiptoed, high-stepping strides, to the cover of the trees.

Nothing to go on. A shadow passing a door. A Columbo hunch. Not even that. One lighted candle. Whim. Kelp would have been proud.

I pressed myself against the bole of the apple tree, hardly breathing. *Be very still, until. Be Thomas*, in fact; *concede nothing until you have seen him, in the miraculous flesh*. As yet just a voice. Perhaps a delusional event.

They came out at last.

It was him.

I tailed them to a bungalow set alone on the first low ridge of the hills. Lights in all the windows. A small front garden of dusty palms and tamarind trees. The two priests had gone at a clip, Father Adrian half running to keep up with Malone's long stride. I was – as I had been since the age of twelve or so – very unfit. The front door opened, admitted them, and closed again. I leaned heavily on the garden gate, lungs roasted, trying not to vomit. I turned and looked back into town. A jumble of lights of mixed strength. A dozen or so red fires, twinkling. The main street marked by the Metropole's neon.

Through the gate and into the garden. Tamarind, dogshit, guava, jasmine, a channel of odorous wet earth where a drainpipe had bled. The country's endless permutations of perfume and stink. The dogshit a worry; *guard* dog. But there was nothing for it. I crept to the nearest window and peeped in.

A large and spartan living room, tidy, uninhabited. The first Goan television I'd seen not blaringly on. I crouched and moved along the wall. FERNANDEZ, it said on the front door. The second room at the front of the house was a kitchen, also uninhabited, also tidy, with not only a Babel tower of gleaming *hundi*s but a steam-buckled Sacred Heart next to the doorway that led to the back of the house.

Had the man who at that moment entered the kitchen not had quite so much on his mind he would surely have spotted me gawping. But he was lost in himself, frowning, top dentures biting down on bottom lip, index finger of left hand massaging left temple. Dr Sutay, I inferred from the dangling stethoscope. Short, paunched, bald and much perspiring. He turned to the refrigerator, yanked the door open, grabbed a bottle of *vala pani*, unscrewed, stared into it, then drank almost the whole lot. He poured what was left over the baking dome of his head, rubbed eyes and jowls with pale palms and fingertips, then turned and walked back into the doorway's darkness.

Ducking down I had clipped my bottom jaw on the window ledge and bitten my tongue. Pain, delayed for my scrutiny of the doctor, now arrived, along with the coppery taste of my own blood. *They'll be at the back. The bedrooms are at the back.* I crouched and crept again. Murmur of voices, a woman crying.

Halfway down the bungalow's flank, an open doorway. A narrow corridor separating the kitchen from one of the bedrooms. Two chairs faced each other. In one sat a plump brown woman in her forties (blue and green sari, fleshy midriff), face in hands, rocking herself, gently. In the other, a much-wrinkled old nun from the Blessed Sacrament. She sat forward, fingers gripping the other woman's kneecaps, mouth pursed, breathing loudly, the look of someone trying desperately to communicate without speaking. The sari'd woman rocked and wept, the sister gripped and breathed. Together they looked like a pointless mechanical toy.

Further down the corridor a door opened and two men emerged – brothers, I guessed by their resemblance – both with strong moustaches, white bush shirts and ancient flip-flops. Fifty and thirty, give or take. The older – taller and thicker in the waist – approached the two women.

'They've started,' he said to the weeping woman. The sister maintained her grip on the knees. The midriff bulged and withdrew with the rocking motion.

'Stop it, now. Come on. The old father is here. It'll be all right. It'll be all—'

A sound from the room at the end of the corridor, then, which silenced and momentarily stilled everyone. The woman in the sari dropped her hands from her face (pinched features and eyes raw from crying) and froze, staring, seeing nothing. The nun released the kneecaps and stood up. The younger brother hurried away from the sound and grabbed the older by the elbow.

I crossed the doorway and headed for the back of the house.

Through the open bedroom window at the rear of the house a scene. A bed faces me. In it, tied hand and foot to the four corners is a skinny and big-ribbed boy in his early teens, naked but for a pair of sweat-soaked pyjama bottoms. At the head of the bed is Dr Sutay, still with stethoscope dangling, still with head gleaming from its recent rinse, fists clenched on womanish hips. Next to Dr Sutay, Father Adrian da Souza, a young priest of slight build and side-parted schoolboy hairdo with a full lipped mouth and gentle (frightened at the moment) brown eyes. Presumably shriven en route, he stands with crucifix in one hand, *Rituale Romanum* in the other, perspiring, short-back-and-sides aglisten, licking his lips.

Behind him, with his back to the door, is a good-looking dark-skinned man in his mid-forties – Mr Fernandez, I decide – dressed in faded jeans and a pale blue cheesecloth shirt. A broad, sensual mouth, generous quiff of greying hair and eyes of a light enough brown to give him an elfish look. Barefoot, he stands with his palms pressed against the door. Next to him, hands joined, eyes locked on the boy on the bed is another young priest – Rodriguez, also Goan, with a crew-cut and a prodigiously large Adam's apple. His blacks are shiny at elbow and knee, and he is shaking. Too young for all this. Too young, too afraid.

And of course there is Ignatius Malone, six-four in his desert boots, sandblasted, long-shanked, sea-dog face crenellated and fiery with life. Twenty-three years, I make it. A hundred more lines inscribed round the mouth and eyes. Still the white thatch of hair, thinner now, still the sun-drenched skin, the ferocious eyes, the perennial stubble. A stoop to his shoulders, but still a tower of wiry strength. No cassock but a set of blacks with surplice and violet stole thrown over. The Giacometti limbs move filled with a calm disgust and anger. The others in the room look like Lowry men next to him. The room itself has turmeric yellow walls and a low white ceiling. Black linoleum floor tiles. One rickety desk, chair and wardrobe. Crucifix mounted on one wall, *Return of the Jedi* poster on another.

The skin whitens round the boy's strained ribs. He fills his lungs and repeats the sound the corridor heard only a few moments before, a loud, guttural slew of vowels that have the veins in his neck showing milky blue. His tied legs jiggle and his tied hands open and close. It seems impossible to me that the voice can belong to him. Dr Sutay reaches down and places his hand on the boy's forehead, but at a sign from Malone removes it again.

It seems I haven't been listening. Malone's voice has been a rattle of stones, but as the boy's head rises from the pillow with cloudy eyes and mouth open too wide the rattle resolves itself into words: '. . . and let Thy right hand in power compel him to leave Thy servant Michael' – making † the sign of the cross – 'that he dare no longer hold him captive, whom Thou has vouchsafed to make in Thine image, and hast redeemed in Thy Son who lives and reigns with Thee in the Unity of the Holy Spirit, ever One God, world without end.' A terrible succession of loud farts from the boy, wet gunshots, but Malone goes on: 'I command thee, unclean spirit, and all thy companions possessing this servant of God, that by the Mysteries of the Incarnation, Passion, Resurrection and Ascension of our Lord Jesus Christ, by the sending of the Holy Ghost, and by the coming of the same our Lord to judgement, thou tell me thy name, the day and the hour of thy going.' The smell of expelled gas reaches me at the window. Heaving, I drop down on all fours in the dust. Indescribable (nonetheless one must try) stench: rotting cheese, diarrhoeal shit, bad meat, something joyously putrid. I open my mouth, retch, dryly, vomit nothing, recover, and if truth be told feel the garden's darkness pressing and my hair on end. I return trembling to my position at the window to see Malone standing one hand on hip, the other pointing down at Michael, whose face is proceeding through an extraordinary (muscularly improbable, beyond even poor Alice's range) sequence of grimaces and leers, and who still punctuates the denunciations with the occasional fart. 'And these signs will accompany those who believe,' Malone barks. 'In my name they will drive out demons; they will speak in new tongues; they will pick up snakes with their hands; and when they drink deadly poison it will not hurt them at all; they will lay their hands on the sick, and they will recover. Lord, hear my prayer.'

'And let my cry come unto Thee,' Fathers da Souza and Rodriguez all but bellow.

'The Lord be with you.'

'And also with you.'

'*Je m'appelle Petit-Poppo,*' a toddler voice from Michael's mouth says. '*Embrace moi, mon père, baise moi, baise moi, mon—*'

'Silence,' Malone commands.

'Name's Batter-'em-down Maggie,' another not–Michael woman's voice says, then begins fruitily giggling.

'Silence!'

'*Me llamo Fuerte-Fuego*,' another child's voice says, and is followed by a deep animal growl, unnaturally loud, a special-effect lion roar with reverb and echo, beyond the reach of any human larynx. Mr Fernandez slides down onto his haunches, shivering and with mouth corners down. Rodriguez descends, too, to comfort Fernandez, to comfort himself. Father Adrian's hands grip *Rituale Romanum* and cross as if they are volatile living things which might at any moment struggle from his grasp and go zooming away out of the window. Dr Sutay has taken a pace back from the bed. He runs his left palm from forehead to chin repeatedly, as if trying to remove a membranous veil. My hearing comes and goes; until Malone's voice re-enters, volume suddenly turned up:

'. . . by Whose power Satan fell from Heaven like lightning: with supplication I beseech Thy Holy Name in fear and trembling, that to me, Thy most unworthy servant, granting me pardon of all my faults—'

'You like it, don't you?'

'Thou wilt vouchsafe to give constancy of faith and power, that shielded by the might of Thy Holy Arm, in trust and safety I may approach to attack this cruel devil—'

'We'll fuck you in the ass in New York City you cunt scumbag they know they've told me cocksucker they've—'

'Through Thee, O Jesus Christ, the Lord our God, Who shall come to judge the quick and the dead, and the world by fire, Amen.'

The boy on the bed shakes his head from side to side in vigorous denial. Mouth open, a bass and unbelievable groan comes from what sounds like the belly of a giant ship inside him. Malone advances, crucifix in hand. When he bends to wrap part of the violet stole round the boy's neck, the boy fights the bonds as if electrified; the wrist cords have already broken the skin, and are pink with blood. His knees knock and cleave to each other as if he's dying for a pee. One twist of his body away from Malone reveals that he has shat himself; the white pyjama bottoms are dark and sodden with a copious evacuation and again the smell is overpowering. Dr Sutay pulls a hanky from his pocket and crushes it against his nose. Father Adrian covers his with his hand. Mr Fernandez is shaking his head from side to side, slowly, with collapsed face, as if at the extreme edge of breakdown. Young Rodriguez is kneeling, rosary to lips, eyes shut tight.

Malone lays his right hand across Michael's forehead and with his left brings the crucifix between them.

'Behold the Cross of the Lord, flee ye of the contrary part,' he says, calmly.

'The Lion of the tribe of Judah, the Root of David, has prevailed,' Father Adrian uncovers his mouth to respond.

'Lord, hear my prayer.'

'And let my cry come unto Thee.'

'The Lord be with you.'

'And also with you.'

Convulsions. Michael silent but for a protracted exhalation which somehow continues evenly through his spasms. The room is stuffed with the smell of rot. If I move my face forward a few inches I feel it touch my nose like a gauze. Malone murmurs, hand pressed to the boy's forehead throughout the convulsions. Dr Sutay hovers, hanky still crushed to mouth and nose like a maddening flower. Suddenly Malone's voice rises:

'I exorcize thee, most foul spirit, every coming in of the

enemy, every apparition, every legion; in the Name of our Lord Jesus Christ † be rooted out and be put to flight from this creature of God †. He commands thee—'

Michael, despite tied wrists has risen to an almost sitting position. His mouth moves very rapidly, nonetheless out of sync with what comes out of it, the sound of someone tuning a radio – warbling, whistles, a blast of sitar and tablas, then an American jock 'so the message is smog, smog, sa-*mog*—'

'Who has bid thee cast down from the highest heaven to the lower parts of the earth,' Malone bellows. 'He commands thee, Who has commanded the sea, the winds, and the storms. Hear therefore and fear, Satan—'

'*Noli me tangere! Noli me tangere! Noli me*—'

'Thou injurer of faith, thou enemy of the human race, thou procurer of death, thou destroyer of life, kindler of vices, seducer of men, betrayer of the nations, inciter of envy, origin of avarice, cause of discord—'

'Stick it up your hairs—'

'Why do you stand and resist when you know that Christ the Lord destroys your ways? Fear Him, Who was sacrificed in Isaac, Who was sold in Joseph, was slain in the Lamb, was crucified in man—'

'Use the Force, Luke—'

'Thence triumphed over Hell. Depart therefore in the Name of the Father † and the Son † and the Holy Ghost †, by the sign of the Holy † Cross of Jesus Christ our Lord, Who with the Father, and the same Holy Ghost, lives and reigns ever one God, world without end, Amen. Lord, hear my prayer.'

'And let my cry come unto Thee!' Father Adrian shouts.

'The Lord be with you.'

'And with thy spirit.'

Michael falls back, breathing heavily. Malone's knees go through a series of ticks and clicks as he kneels. Father Adrian kneels, too. Only the good doctor remains standing – and in fact rounds the bed, stethoscoped, hanky-sniffing, bends and listens with head cocked to the patient's heart. Not happy with what he hears, he moves to untie a wrist, but Malone's giant brown hand shoots across to intercept him.

'This is ridiculous,' Dr Sutay says over Malone's still babbling voice (' . . . look upon this Thy servant, Michael, who is grievously vexed with the wiles of an unclean spirit, whom the old adversary, the ancient enemy of the earth, encompasses with dread . . .'). 'This is *thoroughly* ridiculous,' the doctor repeats, not because the utterance represents what he at this moment thinks, but because the habit of his profession and idiom demand it. 'Mr Fernandez, please, for heaven's sake . . .'

Michael is hyperventilating.

'Mr Fernandez, I must insist, I really must.'

'I adjure thee, old serpent!' Malone growls, jumping to his feet and yanking the doctor away from the bed. 'Not in my infirmity but by the power of the Holy Ghost that thou go out of this servant of God, Michael, whom the Almighty God hath made in His own image. Yield therefore not to me but to the minister of Christ. For His power presses upon thee Who subdued thee beneath His Cross. Tremble at His arm, which, after the groanings of hell were subdued, led forth souls into the light.'

My joints hurt from the long-held crouch. The bedroom's stench feels familiar. Inside me there's a great effort being made to cover up what has been put there. You like it, don't you? Now glowing like a branded rune. The Devil did voices.

I turn away, slither down onto my buttocks, facing the

garden's darkness and the lush skirt of the rising hills. The air is an odorous continuum, heavy enough to lean on. I think – it seems – nothing in particular, but sense that time is compressed, that what feels like seconds is in fact minutes, that what proceeds in the room behind me is both impossible and utterly unsurprising.

No telling how long it goes on; I've passed into a cloudy version of consciousness, peripherally aware of voices above and behind me. 'And think not that I am to be despised since thou knowest that I, too, am a great sinner . . . God commands thee. The majesty of Christ commands thee. God the Father commands thee. God the Son commands thee. God the Holy Spirit commands thee. The sacrament of the Cross commands thee. The faith of the Holy Apostles commands thee. The blood of the Martyrs commands thee.' Thoroughly, *thoroughly* – and indeed all quite inevitable and unsurprising. The stillness of the Fernandez garden is like the stillness of the woods when I watched Burke's repellent body blurting its blood bubble onto the stone. Past joins present in a humdrum and extraordinary handshake. I've curved away these years, curved away and returned. Thoroughly ridiculous and insisting on its inevitability, this business in the room behind me. Thoroughly . . .

Sutay is perched on the desk edge biting bottom lip with brilliant upper dentures. The *Return of the Jedi* poster adheres to the wall now by only its lower left drawing pin, and revealed behind it are several poorly executed (but manifestly efficacious) symbols and ciphers of black magic. Mr Fernandez and crew-cut Rodriguez are on their knees, Fernandez with tears streaming, Rodriguez with eyes and mouth tightly closed in fear (I know) of bodily infiltration: ears, nostrils, mouth, anus – all devil's portals; if he could seal himself he would. Father Adrian is on his feet, his schoolboy face pouchy under the eyes now, as if from gloved blows. Michael lies very still, eyes closed, but as Malone's commands rain down on him his mouth opens and an enormous coiling black turd is tubed out of it, moving with the quiver and curl of piped icing. His body moves in very slight rhythmic convulsions (as in the dregs of orgasm) as the turd continues outwards into stinking coils on his bare chest. Malone's voice steadies, reverts to simple authority: '. . . now therefore depart †, depart thou seducer. The wilderness is thy abode. The serpent is the place of thy habitation: be humbled and be overthrown. There is no time now for delay. For behold the Lord the Ruler approaches closely upon thee, and His fire shall glow before Him, and shall go before Him; and shall burn up His enemies on every side. If thou hast deceived man at God thou cannot scoff. One expels thee from Whose sight nothing is hidden. He casts thee out to Whose power all things are subject. He shuts thee out Who hast prepared for thee and for thine angels everlasting hell; out of Whose mouth the sharp swords shall go out, when He shall come to judge the quick and the dead, and the World by fire. Amen'

The ejected turd, if measured end to end, would be many feet long, and its odour surpasses everything that has gone before. Sutay charges forward and gathers it up in a towel. One final, bass groan leaves Michael's body (my ears pop) and he coughs, opens his eyes and looks at the people in the room around him.

'Dada?' he says, in the correct voice, as Malone waves Fernandez forward. 'Dada? What happened? Who tied up my hands and feet?'

Mr Fernandez is suspicious (and who can blame him?), concerned no doubt that this is the demon's last ruse, this perfect impersonation of his son's voice and unpossessed demeanour, but Malone urges – all but drags – him forward, muttering: 'We pray Thee, O Almighty God, that the spirit of wickedness may have no more power over this Thy servant, Michael, but that he may flee away, and never return.'

There is no doubt that Michael *has* returned. Mr Fernandez kneels and unties him. Half laughing, half crying, embraces and kisses the bemused boy, who, as reality returns, is embarrassed to find himself the centre of this strange audience's attention. Father Adrian is weeping and grinning, *Rituale Romanum* clutched to his breast. Rodriguez is still emphatically down on his knees in white-knuckled prayer with eyes closed and lips quivering. 'And let us fear no evil,' Malone says, straightening. 'For the Lord is with us, Who lives and reigns with Thee, in the Unity of the Holy Ghost, ever one God, world without end.'

'Amen,' Father Adrian da Souza says, all but shaking with laughter. Dr Sutay has deposited the turd-snake on the desk and returned to the bedside. Prising Fernandez gently away, he begins checking the boy's vital signs – but I notice that this time he glances first at Malone for permission. Michael, sobbing a little now, lies back and lets medicine have its way.

Malone points to the unsavoury bundle on the desk. 'Take that outside and burn it,' he says. Rodriguez opens his eyes and looks at Father Adrian. Father Adrian looks at the floor.

'Both of you do it now,' Malone orders. 'It's nothing to be afraid of, just filth. And like the rest of his filth it will be consumed in fire. It's all right. Go on, do it now.'

Young Father Adrian carries it at arm's length with nose averted, Rodriguez behind him, one hand on his shoulder, like a blind man being led. Malone takes a single stride over to the chair and sits down in profile to me. He leans forward, legs apart, elbows on knees, fingers interlocked – an unpriestly posture, what with the surplice gaping like a bawd's skirt. He looks tired and wide awake, somewhat a young man in an octogenarian's skin. For the longest time, he doesn't blink. He's not seeing what's going on around him. The real work is elsewhere, in the past, in the future, not here. This was nothing. Straightforward as chicken pox. They're afraid of him, he knows; doesn't bother softening himself. I wonder how many times he's done this, how many times he will do this again.

From the shadows of the garden's fringe I watched Fathers da Souza and Rodriguez burn the odious bundle. They poured on kerosene and it went quickly, with a soft *woof*. Their two faces shone in the buckling light. They looked purged them selves. What they had just witnessed had left them precise of movement, sparing of speech. Rodriguez, I could tell, hadn't believed until tonight, not really. Da Souza a different matter. Now there was space for him to grow into a being of spiritual clout. I could see in his firelit face that it was coming to him, that he was a soldier in a war, that Lucifer really had fallen and taken legions down with him, really was doomed to lose in the end. It came to him, I observed, all this, as he stood, one hand in pocket, staring into the flames.

They stayed to eat. After wailing Mrs Fernandez and the moustached brothers had assimilated the miracle of Michael speaking in his own voice and behaving himself, the group reconvened in the living room for samosas, pakoras, dahl, puris, lamb biriani and half a dozen sambals, all splendidly laid out on a low table and tucked into as if nothing extraordinary had happened. The aged sister from the Blessed Sacrament listened with screwed up face while Michael explained (some subconscious residue) the plot of *Alien*, which he had seen recently on pirate video. The handsome brothers drank Tiger beer and talked animatedly of another brother's success in exporting carom boards to Covent Garden market, London, England. Dr Sutay scratched his chest hair and palmed the dome of his head, chatting, yes, but with one eye on Michael, knowing (I knew) that his tests would show everything normal, and that here was dammit another round lost to the hocus-pocus, the mumbo-jumbo, the witch doctors of the Holy Roman Catholic Church.

Malone, meanwhile (in a pair of brown-tinted spectacles I hadn't seen before), ate very little, just enough for politeness. This I put down to what I imagined was a slow, irreversible trajectory away from the grosser functions of the body. Another ten years, if the Devil spared him, and he would become slightly translucent, a vessel for light. He sat slightly apart, the others having as if by silent consensus drawn away from him. He was used to it, loved them no less. I wondered what he would dream that night, whether the strength of his faith had erased the need for dreams. I wondered whether he would remember me.

Which curiosity could have been satisfied there and then. I could have knocked, told them I was an old friend of the father's from England, that I had heard a rumour he was here. Sheer novelty would have got me an audience.

But I wanted him alone. Too many questions, me not sure I was ready for the answers. Nor for the horror of him not remembering me.

I left them. Mindful that a local demon had been recently evicted and would be on the prowl for a new home, I put long-unuttered prayers in my mouth, crept from the Fernandezes' garden, and began the long jog down to the cooking fires and dog-yelps of Dona Maria below.

◆

'Listen,' Holly said. 'You fucking listen to me now. I'm going to tell you.'

'Come on Holly, love—'

'Shut up. Shut *up*.'

The end of a perfect evening.

I met her after her day shift at McLusky's had ended. We walked back, dawdling, up baking Broadway. She tried on a white sundress in Canal Jeans and, after an absurd teenage wrangle (with hissing voices and clamped teeth and blushing) at the till, let me buy it for her.

Encouraged, I took her to dinner at Lucky Chen's, followed by silly-looking yet nonetheless potent cocktails at a nearby bar, then on – both of us seduced by the evening's expanding spontaneity – to a nightclub called XVI on Houston and First, where we drank and adopted a pose of anthropological curiosity about the Young, and drank further, and for the first time since knowing each other danced, Holly with shocking sexuality (eyes closed, arms raised, hips and backside effortlessly miming transport), me with the spasticity excusable only by drunkenness and decrepitude, and still without saying much to each other found ourselves through into the small hours, both suddenly terrified at what having had such a good time might mean. After which I lost sight of her for at least an hour, and eventually found her curled up in a booth downstairs with wrecked make-up and tears and snot on her face and a rigidity of body that seemed a kind of punitive reaction to the corporeal fluidity of the dance floor.

A fierce struggle to get her into the cab and home, her spitting obscenities and the cab driver not sure, then eventually the mercy of our street and the clattering ascent of the stairs until finally thank God the door shut behind us and me only at that moment with a first opportunity to notice my own nausea and racing pulse.

For a long time after the initial threat of confession she lay on her side on the bed silently shaking and crying. I turned out all the lights and lay down next to her, not touching.

'I had a little girl,' she said.

What else had I thought? Hadn't I thought it would be a child? Wouldn't it have taken something unimaginable to turn her into this version of herself, to invert all that strength and life? Hadn't I (I asked myself in the dark, smelling on her perfume, cigarette smoke, the club's dry ice) *supposed* it, the abortion, the miscarriage, the death?

'You don't have to tell me,' I said. 'You don't have to tell me anything.'

'I killed her.'

A strong surge of presence from the outside, then, the city, the continent, the planet, the old, patient, rheumatic world that had seen everything, to whom no death was special. It shrank us. The same sort of diminution as . . . as . . .

'I had her young. I didn't want her, at first. I was on my own. I had a council flat. I came home one night, drunk. Hadn't been out for a long time. I paid the babysitter.'

The great and merciless banality was that time went on, regardless, if one remained alive. And if it went on in the wake of loss or suffering, deformity or death, one mutated to accommodate it. If one remained alive. As I had done. As Holly had. I had a particular feeling, lying next to her, a precise sense of the portion of pain she had been allotted. Now visible, retrospectively, in all her movements: the way she carried her bag; made a cup of tea; blew her nose; walked up stairs; looked at her watch; kissed me; turned away when she came. A portion of pain so great as to leave no bit of her unafflicted.

'I went in to look at her. She was asleep. First time I'd really felt she was mine. Maybe just because I was drunk. I had this thought that I'd get into bed with her. Be there when she woke up in the morning. Give her a surprise.'

Her voice a flat rasp, scored by the hours of cigarettes and drink, by bawling over the club's throb. I put my hand on her.

'Don't.'

Removed it.

All the building's unjudgemental noises: the air-conditioning, a door downstairs slamming; someone's flush. Outside, a police siren whooped, twice, then fell silent. No extra help from things if, with death available, one decided to remain alive. No concession to survivors if survival was a choice.

'I went to the bathroom and threw up,' Holly said. 'Passed out. When I woke up I was outside on a stretcher, and the fire-engine lights were flashing on the houses. All the neighbours had come out to see.'

I had her young. How young? How long carrying this?

'It was a cigarette. My cigarette. I must have left it upstairs. Or dropped it and not noticed. It's funny. You still smoke. You'd think . . . You'd think that having killed someone . . .'

Nothing else, then, until the first shift in the sky's light.

'Her name was Lilly,' she said. 'It was her birthday today. She would have been ten years old.'

◆

'Father Malone has gone, I'm afraid.'

'What?'

'He left early this morning for Bombay.'

'*Fuck*. Sorry.'

'That's quite all right. Why don't you come and have some lemonade in the garden?'

The night before, I had returned light-headed to my room at the Metropole, showered in the hotel's end-of-the-day strands of freezing water, combed my hair for the first time in two weeks, cut my finger- and toenails, collapsed on my bed and fallen immediately into a deep sleep. No dreams. The sleep, after what I'd seen at the Fernandezes', was as picked clean as a Texan sky. I had woken with a child's feeling of Christmassy excitement, of being torturously close to the long-promised gifts. Also a feeling of reduced gravity, as if I'd lost weight in the night. Morning *chai* and Goa's raving sunlight; further weight loss after an emphatic bowel movement; then the short walk, dodging beeping Tempos and burping Vespas, to the Church of the Blessed Sacrament.

'Father Malone never stays put for very long,' Father Adrian da Souza said, over the lemonade. We were at a little wooden table in the garden, the iced jug and two glasses having been brought by a young and beaming boy of jet-black eyes and slept-on hair. Young Father Adrian sat legs stretched out, ankles crossed, hands deep in trouser pockets. He had the quietly powerful look of a woman who has recently discovered herself pregnant. From his body's easy gravity last night's ordeal might have been twenty hours of rich sleep.

'I was there last night,' I said.

An interrupted lemonade sip. 'Sorry?'

'At the Fernandez house. I saw everything.'

Sip. Swallow. Glass down. All implications assimilated. 'Oh?'

'I followed you from here. I saw the exorcism. I mean, what else can you call it?'

'What else is there to call it?'

'You don't deny it?'

'For what purpose?'

He had grown already, a plethora of former fears shrunk to negligibility; some of Malone had rubbed off or penetrated him. (The language of impregnation and fecundity insisted. If he had clasped his hands protectively over his tiny belly it wouldn't have been inapt.) He had become a priest in the service of God. In the service of *God*. He smiled. *Dreamboat*, the nuns would say, not thinking of the Holy Spirit at all. *Those dimples*. The post-annunciation Mary I imagined similarly corporeally enriched.

'I know Father Malone from when I was small,' I said. 'I wanted him to . . .' Tailed off, trying, inwardly, to understand why I had been prevented from seeing him again. The Christmassy jitters had settled. A kind of humility or hunger for the future in its place. 'What do you think happened last night?' I said.

He looked at me a moment longer, holding the dreamy smile, then took another gulp of the lemonade. 'I think you know, don't you?' he said.

'When I was small,' I said, 'something happened between Father Malone and myself. He did something extraordinary, something that made me believe he had . . . magical powers.'

'Magic,' Father Adrian said, 'is just a word the world uses to talk about what it can't explain. But what happened last night can be explained. The explanation is that faith in God triumphs over evil. What other explanation is required?'

I said nothing; experienced instead an inner reflex of self-consultation. Which revealed (the brand now a thing of iron), *You like it, don't you?* It was there, solid and cold. I could hold on to it. Let everything else buckle and diffuse.

'I can't believe he's gone without my seeing him,' I said. 'I wanted him to hear my confession.'

For a moment or two we sat silently, looking into the sky. The sun was shrinking our palm-shade. Already Father Adrian's shoes and trouser cuffs blazed.

He lowered his eyes. 'Perhaps I could help?' he said.

He wasn't very interested. In the face of which, I found I could tell him. Deborah, Alice, the childhood peccadilloes, all the years of mental filth.

'There would be reasons,' he said. 'There would be reasons for this.'

Half our palm-shade annihilated, now. Cicadas, bluebottles, sometimes the whir of small birds; once, in my peripheral vision, a dusty black cat slinking out from the bougainvillea, regarding us for a few moments, then slipping back into the bushes. I *had* struggled, when it had come to it, not to utter the words but to find them. *I have, Father, the disease of cruelty*, I had said, in the end. Then we had exchanged a look, me asking with my eyes, *Do you understand?* Him, after a gentle, distracted consultation with the new power, answering with his, *Yes, I understand.*

'Reasons beyond the Devil?' I asked him now. 'Beyond temptation?'

More consultation. The sin was of little interest to him. More fascinating by far was the store of power that told him how to respond to it. Suddenly he smiled down at his folded hands.

'My brother would say so,' he said. 'He's a psychiatrist in Poona.'

'For Deborah,' I said, opening, opening, 'for my friend – the girl from then – for her, maybe. Something had happened to her. I'm sure something had happened to her.'

'She had been damaged?'

'I think so. I don't know. Anyway, I hadn't been. Nothing

had happened to me. Nothing had happened to me except that even in childhood I seemed to come awake to something. To choose it, freely. I don't believe she did.'

'We're not always the best judges of what has happened to us.'

The black cat emerged again, crossed the yard, slipped into the church porch.

'You're going to say this is just a reaction to last night,' I said, 'but I did used to wonder whether she wasn't – whether both of us weren't in some way possessed.'

He didn't respond, seeing the boy approaching. I lit a duty-free Silk Cut. The boy arrived – slept-on hair now slicked down and side-parted (he looked much as I imagined Father Adrian himself had looked as a child) – to collect the empty glasses and jug.

When he had gone, Father Adrian shook his head in mild dismissal. 'The criteria for possession are very specific,' he said. 'I don't think the behaviour you're describing would meet them.'

'I know,' I said. 'It wasn't anything like last night. And yet, there was something.'

He waited, head on one side, not looking at me.

'One enters a state of transport,' I said.

'Transport?'

'A state of' (*almost* balking) 'beatification. As in aesthetic rapture. A state approaching divinity, I would say. That's the Devil's promise, isn't it? I only stopped because I was afraid. Of the earthly consequences. Of getting caught. And somewhat from fear of God.'

'She wasn't afraid of the consequences, then, this girlfriend?'

Deborah, I could tell, had stuck.

'I don't know,' I said. 'I never knew what was going on inside her. Except when we . . .'

Didn't finish that. Looked down. Then around, for something to place against the shame. The garden's colour events like contained explosions: laburnum; mango; Indian coral. Blossom scents, but laced with disinfectant, dung, somewhere eggs frying.

'There was a woman I fell in love with,' I said. 'I waited for love. To see if it would make a difference.'

'But it didn't.'

'No. I knew that the more I loved her, the more pleasure I'd get from seeing her suffer.'

He remained silent, with a slight frown and one single twitch or pucker of the full lips.

Then suddenly he looked up, bored with me, alert to the vast new territories the power would allow him to travel into. He unclasped his hands and sat up straight. A small bell rang in the convent. A lone droplet of sweat crept down my left cheek, reminding me of every hot-faced childhood tear. I kept still.

Father Adrian shook himself a little, brought his hands together on the now sunlit table. 'I'm not Father Malone,' he said. 'But I can tell you what I think you should do.'

A week and much author-talking-down-from-the-ledge later I flew home from Bombay with Kate, *The Tamarind Tree*, a thudding hangover, and a brand-new lease of Faith. Kate upgraded me to join her in first class.

'How about if I never write anything again?' she said.

'Okay,' I said. 'But for now how about you try to get some rest?'

'Well, it would probably depend on the desk officer,' I was told over the phone, back in London. 'It shouldn't, but that's more than likely what it would come down to.'

A Friday afternoon in my office at Cornerstone. Rain so heavy it slithered down the panes in membranous sheets. There had been, earlier, a thunderstorm, the splintering and booming of which had precipitated, finally, my call. Cornerstone's lawyer had put me in touch with a criminal-law acquaintance, Edmund Tate, Esquire, to whom I had pitched the problem fictionally: one of our authors has this story, you see, about someone who, years after the crime, feels compelled to confess.

I had worried at the surely threadbare nature of the approach – *Well, Doctor, I've got this friend, you see, and he's got this rash* – but Tate's titillation at being called in to sort out a novelistic problem occluded what would otherwise have been exposed.

'I see,' I said.

'The police would have to be convinced a) that the claim was genuine, and b) that there was at least a reasonable chance of securing a prosecution. You'd be surprised how many people walk into their local stations claiming to have done all sorts of things.'

'Yes?'

'Oh yes. Anyway, how old is the girl?'

I'd left Deborah – or whoever would have appeared in the pitch as her fictional correlate – out of the story, so I knew he meant Alice. 'Sixteen,' I said.

'Story set when?'

'Early Eighties.'

'Sixteen age of consent then. But not mentally compe-tent, you say?'

'No, not mentally competent.'

'Tricky. In any case they'd need her to corroborate the alleged criminal's story. Is she traceable? Would she testify? They'd need her to testify.'

'Christ, I don't know.'

'First off, they'd have to find her. Then get her to testify. How many years on you say?'

'At least a dozen. Fifteen.'

I heard him take a sip of something. 'So basically you've got a character who walks into a police station one day and says he molested a mentally impaired sixteen-year-old girl fifteen years ago and would they like to do anything about it?'

'Exactly.'

'Chances are they'd tell him to fuck off out of it, if they believed him. Even if they took him into custody they'd have to contact the alleged victim to get the story checked. Which would mean finding her. Is she findable?'

'The plot requires it.'

'Then it would be down to her corroborative testimony. Does that help?'

'Yes, yes, this is all marvellous.'

Off the phone, I sat back with cigarette and much-needed Glenfiddich, feet up, considering. *Is she findable?* A good question. Eastfield the obvious starting point. Was there any reason why she wouldn't still be there?

I sipped. Looked at the phone. And the other number which, thanks to Father Adrian's instructions, I would, eventually, need to call.

Number called, services engaged, there was nothing to do but wait. Or rather not nothing: I went (again, as directed by Father Adrian) to confession every week, mass every Sunday, said Malone's rosary every night before sleep. Not a word about any of it to Penguin or Jules. I had to range far afield for a priest of the old school until at last I found Father Ahearn at the Church of the Holy Martyrs, a flaking East

End parish between Stratford and Leyton. Flatulent Cork soak he was, to be sure, but not all the fire in his belly was gas and grog.

'These are the abominations of that filthy bastard,' he hissed, 80 per cent proof through the grille; all foulness of mouth excused if employed in execration of the Devil. I confessed the still regular masturbation, sparing none of the detail. 'The perverted antics of that shit-eating father of lies. You know this, don't you?'

'Yes, Father.'

'You know this is a war for your immortal soul, don't you?'

'Yes.'

'Yes? Then stop being such a feckin gutless streak o' piss and *fight* like the dog you are! Are ye the dog for a fight or not?'

'I am, Father.'

'Wha? Who's that whisperin'?'

'I *am*, Father!'

'Well that's more like it. Now. For your penance, you'll . . .' Thence off into a bitter and welcome cocktail of prayers, abstinences and devotions, without fail ending: 'And you will *not* open the door to these impure thoughts and deeds again, junderstand me now? Nor will you take a drink to your lips for two weeks solid. Not a drop, mind. Clear?'

'Clear.'

'For 'tis in the weakened state that the Devil finds us ready to his hand. You know this, don't you, you miserable dog?'

A pause. The wardrobish smell of the confessional. My knees aching.

'Father, I wanted to ask you something.'

'Ask away, then.'

'Is it possible to still feel guilty after you've confessed and been forgiven?'

A long silence. The sound, eventually, of him scratching what I guessed was his stubble. Gravelly sigh. 'For two reasons,' he said, at last. 'Either you've lost your faith in God's holy sacraments, or you've not fulfilled your penance.' Then, tagged on: 'And many's the miserable cur of a sinner guilty o' both.'

It may have been coincidence (if you like) that that was the very evening I got the call I'd been waiting for.

'Alice Beale,' I was told. 'Torquay. Got her own council flat. Mrs Lingard died three years back. Leukaemia.'

'She lives on her own?'

'Apparently. You got a pen?'

I wrote down the address.

'Not a very interesting job for you, then. I'm sorry.'

Fiction-steeped, I'd expected him to say something appropriate to his genre. *Listen, chief, it's a hundred a day whether it's interesting or not.*

He said, however: 'I'll send you an invoice. Let me know if there's anything else.'

The following Saturday, I took the train from Paddington.

It was – in observance of the laws of aesthetic perversity – a beautiful day of high blue skies and stratus clouds, prodigal sunshine and a light spring breeze. I was blessed with a quiet carriage. Any of the usual annoyances – screaming baby, salt-of-the-earth grandma, toddler with running puzzle-book commentary – would have driven me to murder. I felt nothing in particular, knowing the next few hours could change my life, perhaps even ruin it. If anything a dull peace, the consolation of understanding that one's fate is in someone

else's hands, the ego's curious dead-slow or shut-down manifest in a physical relaxation bordering on numbness. I
noticed bits, as the train rolled through Oxfordshire,
Berkshire, Wiltshire, Somerset, forced into imagist vivid-
ness by my state, I supposed: a blue and yellow tricycle on a
short-cropped green lawn; a decrepit grey horse in profile,
staring as if into eternity; a hollow tree with a rusty bike
frame thrust into it; a Tesco carrier bag caught on a hedge.
I drank a cup of coffee, strong, with lots of sugar and milk.
My face glowed hot without warning. I pressed it against the
window. A brilliant field of rape. I fell asleep.

The sudden noise and smell of the outside world shocked
me when I changed trains at Exeter, but I was back on board
before it had fully reasserted itself. I slept again, and in fact
nearly missed Torquay, but came to just in time. I grabbed my
bag and staggered out, blinking and creased, onto the platform.

Here was my street map. There was the black and white
street. Here were the other streets coming into being with
each step. Here was the estate. Here was the council block,
the lobby, the lift, the graffiti, the door, phone-booth red
with stainless-steel letterbox and spy hole. A dog inside
barked when I rang the bell.

'Do you know who I am?'

Two seconds for full recognition, then her face set in
blankness. 'Yeah.'

'Would you mind if I came in and talked to you for a few
minutes?'

'What for?'

'Just to talk to you for a moment.'

I looked down at my feet crossing the threshold. Vampires
can't come in unless you. The hallway. Brown industrial

carpet, white walls. A chest of drawers with a red telephone on it, Monet's water lilies reproduced and blu-tacked above. A mac on a hanger. Smell of dog and burned toast.

She had turned out broad shouldered. All the freckles I remembered. Now her hair was jaw-length, with a short fringe. Like Deborah's. She had learned physical composure, an economy of movement the sixteen-year-old never had; either that or it was an extension of the rigidity that had taken possession of her face. She walked quickly in small steps into the lounge. By the time I had shut the door behind me and followed her (she hadn't actually said, 'Come in', just turned her back on me), she was sitting on a pink velour couch with her knees drawn up to her chest. Red woollen sweater, faded jeans and thick yellow socks. A large, long-haired German Shepherd sat alert alongside her, growled, steadily, as I sat down, stopped when she gave it a shake. My mouth was dry.

'I've come to tell you I'm sorry.'

She looked at me – mild curiosity – then out of the window, then back at me. Silence. Then, brightly, back to the window. 'I don't know what you're on about.'

'Nothing I can say, obviously, can make up for anything,' I said. 'But that's only part of the reason I came to see you.'

If the dog was uncannily tuned into his mistress's moods my presence wasn't leaving her as cold as she gave out, because the low growl started up again. The animal shifted its weight from its left front paw to its right, then back again. I wondered if she was contemplating setting it on me. That would have been one solution: let the animal rip my face off. The dog was aware that this was an option, and manifestly favoured it. But she gave it another nudge and said: 'Lie down, Mannie. Lie down.' Very fluidly the dog obeyed, put its head across her and nuzzled, so that she dropped her knees and let the long snout into her lap. She smiled, wrapped a hand loosely round the golden muzzle and gave it a shake.

'I wanted to ask you, if you'd like, I'll go to the police and tell them what I did.'

'That's bloody ages ago. What you on about, anyroad?'

'What we – what I did.'

'There's no point goin' on about daft games.'

'I thought that if you wanted, I could—'

'It were abuse.'

Her voice startled me more than what she said; a tonal shift suggesting the availability of a completely different personality. It were abuse. I thought: the cells renew themselves every seven years. This is not the same hair we yanked. These are not the same wrists. This is not the same face we spat in, these not the eyes from which we licked tears. This is not the skin, the flesh, the blood, the bone. But this is the same person. The soul is not renewed. The consciousness is not renewed. The memory is not renewed. This is the same person. It were abuse.

'Yes,' I said. 'It was. It was a terrible thing I did. A terrible, wrong and wicked thing.'

'I'm not stupid any more, you know.'

'No.'

'I'm not in care. This is my flat.'

'Yes, I can see. Do you like living here?'

'You don't aff talk like I'm an idiot or summat.'

'No, no. No. Sorry. I'm sorry if it seemed that way.'

'You'd go to jail. Why've you come here now?'

'I'm not sure. I think because ever since those times I've felt . . . I've felt that what we . . . I mean what I—'

'Why've you come here now? Is she here as well?'

'No. No, she's not here. I don't know about her. Probably

they'd find her if we went and told them. The police, I mean. They'd find her, eventually.'

Some noise beyond the human auditory range drew a single bark out of the dog, which made me jump with comical violence. She saw. I thought for a moment she was going to laugh. I almost laughed myself. She didn't laugh. 'I don't know why you've come here,' she said. 'How'd you know where I live?'

'I hired someone to find out. A private detective.'

'What?'

'A private detective.'

'Like on telly?'

'Yes.'

She didn't like that. Therefore nor did the dog. He began growling.

'Mannie, shush. What did you tell him?'

'He didn't know — I mean, I didn't tell him anything. Honestly. Nothing. I just told him I was trying to find you. I swear.'

She looked out of the window again. We were on the sixth floor. Clouds — blinding white, with soft grey underbellies — had drifted in off the sea. It was still bright (the light touched her ginger eyelashes), but there would be rain within the hour, the doubly depressing dullness of the wet seaside day. She lowered her eyes, still facing the window but not looking out. The dog turned its head slightly and looked at me. I wished (*half* genuinely) that she would set it on me and have done with it. I'd seen a police-dog demonstration, once, as a child. A handler dressed up as a crook with a rag-wrapped arm the dog flew at on command. I was impressed by the animal's transition from intelligence to savagery. I had said to my mother: 'I don't like it. I don't like it.' (I don't like it, she'd said. We *know*, Deborah had said, fondling me.)

'I can't ever take back what I did,' I said. 'I know that.'

'Anyway I've got go to work in a minute.'

'It's just that I wanted to tell you . . . I mean I know—'

'You must be soft in the head. You must be *daft*.'

'I know it must seem useless. Wrong, even. But I spoke to a lawyer and he—'

'You dint go the police, did you?'

'No. No, I—'

'You've got nowt to tell *them* about *me*.'

'I didn't go to the police. I just spoke to a lawyer. I didn't use names or anything. I just said *supposing*. He said the police would—'

'I'm not going to any police. They were only daft games, anyroad.'

'What I did was—'

'I've got go to work now.'

I closed my mouth, tried to keep it closed. I had no idea what she was thinking. She kept her eyes low. One hand still fondled the dog's chin.

'Is your' – articulation and incredulity formed simultaneously – 'is your life all right?'

Her other hand rested on the arm of the couch. Its index finger flicked back and forth over the velour, making a soft scratching sound with its nail. She got up, shoving the dog aside (it leaped to the floor) and went into a small kitchen adjoining the lounge. Sound of matches, the light, the first drag and satisfied exhalation. I wanted a cigarette myself. She stood leaning in the doorway, one arm wrapped round her middle, the other holding the cigarette close to her mouth. She rested one foot on top of the other. The dog, as if on telepathic command, came and sat directly in front of me, staring.

'Is your dog going to attack me?'

'He would if I told him to, or screamed or made a fuss.'

'It was criminal. It was . . . I committed a horrible crime against you. If you want to, we can go to the police. I'll tell them what happened. If you tell them it's true, I'll be charged, prosecuted, and probably go to jail.'

'Prob'ly get leddoff. Anyway shuddup about it.'

'If you were willing to corroborate, if you were willing to tell them, they'd charge me. I think they'd have to.'

'This is schewpid. You've got go now. I don't know why you've come.'

'Please, I just wanted to—'

'I'm not havin' it int papers an all that. I'd lose me flat. I've got a *job*, you know.'

'Have you? What is it?'

'In Queen's Park greenhouse. I know all about plants. Maggie sorted it.'

'Who's Maggie?'

'Me link worker.'

'That's good. Are they tropical plants?'

'There's one with bananas.' The dog began to growl. The dog sensed us drifting from relevance. 'Anyroad, you've got go. Mannie, be quiet.'

It was a struggle in her between curiosity, annoyance and fear. I thought: If I get this wrong she'll scream at me to get out and the dog will rip my face off.

'I'll go, of course, if you want.' I took a business card from my pocket and left it on the arm of the chair. I stood up. 'But I want you to know that if you change your mind—'

'That's all yonks ago. I'm not talkin to any police.'

'No. No, I see that. But it wouldn't have to be the police. You could talk to your link worker if you wanted.'

'What *for*?'

'To get them – to get the authorities to punish me. To get

them to lock me up. If you told Maggie about it. If you want, *I'll* talk to Maggie—'

'Don't you dare!' Sudden and very loud barking from the dog, up on all fours, stepping closer. 'Mannie. *Mannie*, lie down. Mannie. *Lie down.*'

The dog didn't take his eyes off me. There was a profound understanding between us, me and this dog.

'You've got go now,' she said. 'Mannie, stay. Good boy.'

She followed me out into the hall, soft-footed in her thick socks. Last command notwithstanding, Mannie came padding quickly after, poked his head out alongside her knees.

The landing smelled of chip fat and urine. 'The card I left,' I said. 'I've put my home address on the back. I'm sorry for everything. I just wanted you to know that I hate myself for what I did.'

'Were there anyone else?'

She meant did we do it to anyone else.

'No. No one else.'

'Just me coz I were schewpid.'

'I'm sorry. I wish I could help put it right – I mean I know it can't be put right . . .'

'You don't say nowt to Maggie. Promise.'

'I promise, of course. I'll leave you alone. But if you decide—'

'An not police, neither. Promise.'

'I promise, if that's what you want.'

'You *promise*.'

'I promise. I swear.'

Tears welled and fell down my cheeks. My mouth moved, emptily; the ugly faces people pulled, crying. It was as if I had only just noticed her, standing in the doorway with her weight on one leg, one foot on top of the other; as if I had only just realized who she was. It wasn't pity, just a feeling of all the space between us. The uselessness of saying anything. How all of this still reeked, whether I liked it or not, of being about *me*.

She observed the spectacle of my tears and wobbling face with obvious discomfort.

'Sorry,' I said. 'Sorry, sorry.'

'Don't come here again.'

'I won't.'

A crammed silence while I waited for the lift. A single bark from Mannie which bounced off the landing's vandalized concrete.

'Tecks ages, that lift.'

'Take care of yourself.'

'You don't say nowt. And don't come round again.'

'If you ever need anything . . . money – God, I know that's stupid, vile – anything . . . But I promise I'll never bother you again. Sorry for coming here. For everything.'

The lift arrived and the doors opened. She wanted to see me get into it. She wanted to see me going away.

We looked at each other for the first time just as the doors were closing.

'Sorry,' I said.

She stared.

The summer of 1998 was also the summer Joe and Laura got married. There was a handwritten addendum inside the formal invitation: 'Please note, it says Dominic + Guest, coz I *know* there'll be a bird on the scene – but Laura says if she's blonde with big tits she's not letting her in on principle. Hope you can make it. (I'm a bit thin on the rellies and Laura's got about ten thousand Irish.) Cheers, anyway, Joe.'

I read the note with the morning mail at Cornerstone,

and only at the very last minute stopped myself from ticking the 'NO I CAN'T ATTEND' box. Something, some glance of sunlight on the pocket clip of my fountain pen, some twitch of this light like the sparkler writing that night in the bedroom of 47A, some glint or fragment – ah what's the point of denying it at this stage of the story? – some visible flicker of *Kelp* sent my tick into the affirmative box instead. I thought: Ridiculous. Thoroughly ridiculous.

There wasn't 'a bird' on the scene, blonde or otherwise, so I took Pen, who required much persuading into one of my old suits. I had evolved out of the pinstripes into pale and baggy, Forties-style ensembles which Julia rescued from charity shops and had re-lined in sumptuous golds, reds, greens and purples. (You'll look like Mickey Rourke in *Angel Heart*, she had told me, which comparison I hadn't appreciated.) It became a hobby of hers, finding these pale suits for me. At the time of the wedding I had half a dozen, and some forty Oxfam ties.

'How come you look cool and I look a complete nangle-berry?' Pen asked me before we left for the train station.

'That would be because I am cool and you are a complete nangleberry,' I said.

We stood side by side looking at ourselves in the long mirror on the back of the bathroom door, dizzy from the unusually high concentration of aftershave and deodorant in the small space.

'Is this sort of suit even fashionable?'

'It's classic,' I told him. 'Fashion doesn't enter into it.'

'I look like a fucking homosexual gents' tailor,' he said. 'Dear Christ, Dummie why did I let you talk me into this?'

Sorrel's invitation must have been forwarded, because her reply came in an airmail envelope with messily affixed Greek stamps. Joe showed me the note that came with it: 'Dear Joe

& Laura, *very* sorry I can't make it, but I know you'll have a lovely English summer's day for the wedding. I'm on Poros with Marcus at the moment, teaching English, believe it or not. Yes, me! Marcus thinks I've gone soft in the head. Anyway, loads of luv and have a wonderful day. Say hi to the others if they're there. I miss England *loads*! Luv again, Sorrel xxx.'

'Who's Marcus?' Joe asked me.

'Christ knows,' I said. 'It was Guy or Gordon or Giles or something she went off to Capri with, wasn't it?'

'No return address,' Joe said.

'No.'

'What do you make of that?'

'The fear that one of us might show up looking for free bed and board.'

'Poor Sorrel,' Joe said. Then added: 'You know, I'd've shagged the *arse* off Sorrel.'

Laura's Irish crew peopled the church (in a village just outside Bath, weather, as predicted by Sorrel, fine) both corporeally, with ruddy flesh and exotic hats, and spiritually, surrounded by a sort of baby's breath of lapsed and boozy Catholicism. Joe, with hair and beard trimmed and glimmering, looked like Jesus in a suit. Laura didn't come up even to his shoulder. She stood beside him like a small white flower, letting the words of her vows out quietly and carefully, as if a mispronunciation or slip would bring the church crashing down around them. Unsurprising to me – massgoer, sacrament-swallower, rosary-sayer – that the age and weight of the ritual transformed lanky Joe and his tiny bride into archetypes: husband and wife. The odd moment when Laura had made her entrance: until then it had all been sunshine in the churchyard and lipsticked women in improbable hats and men with their hands in their pockets. Until the moment Laura came in, accompanied by the organist's palsied Wedding March, against all reasonable cynicism arresting us – suddenly – and we took on our roles as witnesses to a holy rite. Of course people cried at weddings. Not the obvious weepers (Mum and Dad watching their offspring's loyalty transferred like a slow-motion baton change), but the peripherals, the second cousins, the flatmates, the cleaning ladies, because just for a moment the ritual revealed life as something magical and sacred and old.

I cried, too, you'll be justifiably nauseated to hear. Not only from feeling part of a mythic enactment, but because I thought of Natalie. *Will you marry me?* I closed my eyes and let the ruthless image in: Natalie's face under a veil, her eyes when it's lifted seeing me, recognizing me as her husband. I would have felt it, too, that she was my wife. *Are you sure you loved this woman?* Father Adrian hadn't asked, but had looked it, after I'd told him about Natalie. I wondered (opening my eyes, keeping my face averted from fidgeting and collar-yanking Pen) whether I had. A great part of me was certainly desperate to conclude that I hadn't, but ultimately there could be no doubt: Love's proof was the Devil's need to ask it his question.

Creeping horror came again, there in the church, as Laura arrived next to Joe at the altar. Natalie would have it – what I had done to her – for the rest of her life. I might as well have wrecked half her face with an iron.

Queasy, I covered my mouth with my hand. Pen looked at me: What the fuck? I shook my head, violently, heaved, swallowed a lump of vomit, jammed my teeth together, slowly got myself under control. There was nothing else for it. I was compelled to let the sickness and disgust settle on me like vampires. I remained still throughout the ceremony, swallowing, emptily.

'Who's the blonde bird talking to Joe?' Penguin asked me at the reception, having sidled up to the bar and extracted me from vacuous conversation with a minor auntie or in-law. I followed his gaze. It took me a few moments because she'd lost a bit of weight and I'd never seen her dressed up.

'Jesus Christ, that's Helen.'

'Helen who?'

'From 47A. Fucking hell.'

'Fucking hell what?'

'She looks different.'

'I think you should introduce me.'

'The one who tried to kill herself, Pen.'

'Yeah? So?'

'I'm just saying.'

'Just saying what?'

'I'm just saying, she's got issues.'

'We've all got issues, Dummie, for fuck's sake. I lived with *Tanya* for four years. Now get us over there.'

I hadn't seen Helen since the hospital. Her mother had come and taken her home, then returned a week later to pick up her things and clear the outstanding rent. She'd told us nothing. She'd blamed us for not knowing that Helen was going to attempt suicide. Mistakenly. She should have blamed us for knowing and doing nothing about it.

'It's good to see you,' I said. I'd left Pen at the bar, though I was aware of him watching us. Joe had been 'borrowed', as the event's stars always are, by Laura's mother. Helen and I were alone.

'You, too,' she said. 'I wasn't going to come.'

'Neither was I. Changed my mind at the last minute. You look . . .'

'I go up and down. Don't kid yourself.'

'I didn't mean—'

'It's a condition. I go to see doctors.'

'Look, forget that. I'm sorry. It's just good to see you . . .'

'Alive?'

'Well, yeah, actually. Alive.'

'Anti-depressants.'

'Can you get me some?'

'It's not hard. Just go and see your GP. Tell him you feel lousy all the time. He'll sort you out.'

'I can top that,' I said. 'I go to confession every week.'

'Bollocks.'

'I don't know why I've just told you. No one else knows. Seriously – so not a word.'

'Christ, and I thought *I* was doolally.'

'Just think of it as an anti-depressant.'

'Does it work?' she asked, taking a minute sip from her champagne flute.

'It keeps me on the straight and narrow.'

She smiled. It really *was* good to see her alive. Over the next ten minutes (Pen shooting me silent queries) she filled me in on life since near-death. She had gone home to her parents' in Reading to recuperate, and had spent six months in her childhood bedroom in a state of misery bordering on catatonia. ('Lost fucking *stones* then.') Then her father had had a heart attack and slight stroke.

'Shamed me, I suppose,' she said. 'Think the old bugger did it on purpose. He's been suspiciously well since, apart from the left side of his mouth's a bit lazy.'

Intentional or not, it got Helen out of bed and, by degrees, back into the land of the living. 'So now I'm working for Reading council,' she said. '*Gardening*, if you can believe that. Actually, I love it. No books. No money, either, obviously, but it's nice to be outside in this weather. And I've taken up painting.'

Still a deal of trouble there, one could see. Three or four tiny grey veins visible in her forehead where there had been none to see before, and some of the hairs one took at first glance for blond were actually white. But there was wryness, too, and some disgusted determination not to give in. Unsteady, battered, but resolved on seeing it through.

She looked queerly grown-up in her navy-blue suit and matching high heels. I remembered moving the sweat-damp hairs off her face in the hospital long ago. I remembered thinking that no one held her details precious. I remembered the fountain-pen flash, the Kelplight sparkling suddenly in the Cornerstone office gloom, and found myself struggling to keep a straight face as I said: 'Listen, Helen, there's someone I want you to meet.'

I marked my thirty-fourth birthday in October with a solitary trip out to the west coast of Wales, where I stood on a narrow and glistening beach between two outflung spurs of black rock and watched the sun go down into the sea – with co-operative or perhaps satirical drama – in flakes of blood red, copper, pink and gold. Thereafter the water the colour of mercury. I stood a long time in the dusk, listening to the surf's repetitive rasp, wondering what, if anything, I was feeling. The one year of Father Adrian's prescribed duties had stretched into three, and much comfort I'd had from them: the forgotten pain of kneeling; the rosary's hypnosis; the church smells of candle wax and flowers, incense, worn wood, stone. Comfort, yes – and the battle with the Devil went on – but what else? *D'you know how you realize you're old?* Pen had asked, years ago in Exeter. *You realize you're old when you realize that inside you still feel young.*

Stars appeared, by degrees. I took out the hip-flask, drank a silent rum toast to Kelp, wherever he was, then turned and headed back into the village.

Kelp's instinct, light-carried from the afterlife, had been sound, of course. By Christmas that year Pen and Helen were an item. It must have been frustrating for him – Kelp, I mean – watching the living blundering, missing the obvious connections. It must have driven him to break the rule (surely there was one) that the dead must on no account interfere with the lives of the living. I watched Penguin and Helen coming towards me in Hyde Park hand in hand and thought: Bugger must've got a disembodied knuckle-rap for this mischief.

'You know what the weirdest thing about it is?' Pen asked me, back in Begshall on Boxing Day.

'What?'

We were in – of course – the Coopers' Arms, which had been somewhat tarted up: carpets, booths, a *menu*, no Galaxian, hardly any teenagers. The current landlord wore a tie. The pub dog had gone, too – presumably, to meet his maker.

'The weird thing is that I know she's not . . . The weird thing is that, you know, compared to Tanya . . .'

We weren't on halves of mild or Guinness any more. We were on double Glenfiddichs. 'Pen,' I said. 'It's not weird. It's nothing mysterious. It's just that there's more to attraction than looks.'

'Yeah, yeah, but that's not the weird thing. The weird thing is that something happens to her . . . something happens when we're having sex.'

'Oh God, what?'

Penguin performed a tension-removing gesture with his

head and neck, then lit a roll-up with the silver lighter Helen had given him for Christmas.

'The other night, right?' he said. 'Actually it first happened weeks ago – in fact, maybe the second or third time we slept together. Anyway the point is, sometimes, when we're having sex, I'll see her face from just such an angle . . . It's like a look she gives me. I mean, don't get me wrong; even without this the sex is very nice, you know, really *very* nice. But there are these occasions – the other night was one of them – when we'll be doing it – it's not a *positional* thing, you understand; I mean I just need to get a *glimpse* of her face . . .'

'Pen, what *happens* when you get these glimpses of her face?'

He sat back and exhaled a long cone of smoke. Considered for a moment. Then leaned forward, conspiratorially. 'She becomes the most beautiful woman I've ever fucking seen,' he said. 'Now what in the name of Miriam Stoppard do you make of *that*, Nigel?'

Not a bad Christmas that year. No snow, but the Hoods reunited at Logan Street for the first time in what seemed a very long time. Julia and I with our astonished parents in the back pew at St Joe's midnight mass, both if the truth be told slightly drunk from hip-flasks but nonetheless in tune, proudly, for the carols. Me on the edge of fatuous tears for much of the service, swallowing, blinking. My mother noticed, and put it, thank God, down to inebriation, for which I got a mild scolding once we were out in the frosty night.

Julia was to drive the two of us back to London in a recently purchased Mini Cooper S. Come time for the farewells we were grateful for each other's company. My mother and father looked small in the Logan Street doorway, him with his arm round her. Old, too, for the first time –

though I had noticed her shoving his hand away from her breasts, still with the old delighted exasperation. The street itself looked tiny and dark. I thought of those summers that had stretched ahead like a great, open space of years, sky blue and hot, empty of all but promise.

Julia managed not to cry until we'd pulled away. Among many other things success had allowed her to ask herself how she'd come by it. Thus the re-evaluation of her childhood, their encouragement – most significantly, their willingness to take seriously the notion that making art was what she wanted to *do* with her life. They had, simply, believed in her.

'Come on, Jules, don't.'

'It's not the leaving,' she said, then sniffed. 'It's that they . . . It's that the world's left them behind. Our world, I mean. They know there's nothing they could do now if something went wrong. They know we've left them behind. Mum said to me . . .' But she couldn't go on for a minute. I gave her a tissue from the glove box. 'Mum said to me . . I'd gone into the kitchen to get something, you know, and she was standing there with the tea things, not doing anything, with tears – with tears in her eyes, and when I said to her: "What, Ma?" she said: "You and your brother, you know, are the best things I've ever done. I look at the two of you, and I can't believe . . ."'

We drove for a while in silence. Begshall receded, gave way to the moors, motorway traffic, rain. Sometime in the past, she had stopped asking about what had happened with Natalie. I wanted to tell her that she reminded me of her, that Natalie had reminded me of *her*.

'I'm going to make a lot of money this coming year, Dommie,' she said at last.

'Yeah?'

'Yeah. Really a lot.'

'That's good. That's great – isn't it?'

Whatever it was, she would come to it. I started looking through the CDs: Roberta Flack, Mahler, the Doors, Janis Joplin, Stravinsky, the Velvet Underground, Dylan, Prokofiev, Carole King.

'There's something else,' she said, indicating and pulling out to pass an articulated lorry, the wheels of which suddenly loomed up whirring silver and black in the rain. 'If I make money, I mean.'

'What?'

We overtook, pulled back into the left lane. Huge wet green fields sloped away from the road. Friesians stood with heroic heads bent to the flooded grass. 'If it works out that way,' Julia said, 'I'm going to have a baby.'

In the New Year, I wrote to Father Adrian. We had kept up a trickle of correspondence, wholesome chit-chat ('The garden is full of blossom just now as I write. Sister Philomena is blessed with the greenest of thumbs') for the most part, with occasional circumspect references ('I'm keeping to my practice, though sometimes I feel very far away from God') to our dialogue in the garden. Neither of us mentioned Malone, the Fernandez bungalow, the sausage of filth that had appeared out of Michael's mouth. We didn't have to mention it. The fact of our correspondence proved it had happened.

The letter I wrote in January of 1999 was different.

'I've come to a strange place in my life,' I wrote.

I've done everything you told me to do. I've kept to my penance in every detail, without fail, and I've done at last what I believe it's been in my power to do to make peace with the past. But perhaps my faith hasn't been strong enough, because I don't feel clean. Nor do I feel, much of the time, that God is listening. Not that I blame Him, obviously. I'm still tempted, still fail. I know this in itself is nothing — we lose battles but the war goes on — but there is the nagging feeling that I'm missing something elemental. I have felt remorse. My confessions have been sincere. But I'm beginning to feel . . . I don't know how to say this. I'm beginning to feel foolish.

I would very much like to see Father Malone. Do you know where he is? There are things I need to ask him, things about what happened between us years ago when I was a child. I've felt that our lives — mine and Father Malone's, I mean — have been linked in some way, which I know, obviously, sounds and probably is ridiculous, but still, there are things I need to ask him. I know he travels a great deal, but do you know where I could reach him? Or where I might begin the search?

I hope, as always, that this letter finds you and the sisters in good health and joyous faith.

Regards,

Dominic.

I waited. March and April came and went. Millennially anxious David had a group of eggheads visit Cornerstone to explain what might happen to our computers come midnight 31 December. We coddled Kate, sent *The Tamarind Tree* current down the commercial circuit, geared up for the preposterous success we knew the repeat formula was going to be. I got a note, allegedly from Clifford Gill himself, in fact from one of his secretaries, saying well done for spotting talent and buying it and David says you've been marvellous and don't think these things go unnoticed and when are you next across the Pond and so on. Clifford himself, I imagined, lying on a warm rock somewhere in the sun, being expensively fellated by a human being young enough to be his grandchild, ignorant of my existence.

I began to wonder how long it would be before Pen moved out to set up home with Helen, with whom he was in love.

'You've told her that?'

'What?'

 That you love her?'

'Fucking hell.'

'Well, it's important.'

'Yes, arse-finger, I've told her.'

'In those exact words?'

'Yes, in those exact words.'

'You've said: "I love you, Helen"?'

'What's the *matter* with you?'

'And she said the same thing to you?'

'Eh?'

'What did she say to you when you said: "I love you"?'

'Keep your voice down for fuck's sake.'

We were in a breakfast café on Portobello Road on a sunny Saturday morning. Helen was meeting us for market shopping. Or, rather, meeting Pen. I was going to David's in Notting Hill for his birthday lunch.

'Sorry,' I whispered. 'What did she say when you told her that you loved her?'

'She said: "Oh my God."'

'Why?'

'And then cried.'

'Ah.'

'What do you mean, "Ah"?'

'No no. I mean, she was surprised.'

'I don't know if she was surprised, but I got laid six ways to Sunday.'

'So you're in love with each other.'

'Look, can we change the subject?'

'Why don't you two have a baby?'

'Why don't you kiss my hoop?'

'No, seriously.'

'Yeah, okay.'

'No, *seriously*.'

He stopped eating and put his knife and fork down. 'What *is* the matter with you?' he said.

'I don't know. I'm just happy for you.'

He took a sip of tea and returned to his utensils. 'I think you're going soft in the head,' he said. 'Why don't you go and see a prostitute or something?'

June passed, and still no reply from Dona Maria. I wrote another letter in July. I had stopped going to mass. I hadn't been to confession since I saw Ahearn in February. I had stopped saying the rosary. When I tried to pray I felt on the ether a weight of impatience; God's, I supposed. The last visits had revealed something scornful in the Holy Martyrs Communion silences. Further, I lost more battles, a *lot* more. I ran the torture reels (Natalie, Deborah) with a kind of stunned delight at my own and the Devil's stubbornness. With, afterwards, predictably dismal feelings of sickness. Most of the time I took on as much work as I could, to drain myself of energy which would otherwise have been imaginatively ill-spent.

Then at the very end of August I got a reply from Father Adrian.

Dear Dominic

Many apologies for the delay – six months! – in my reply, but I've been visiting my family in Poona. My father, who had been unwell for some time, passed away in April. I was there with him in his last hours and was able to administer the Last Rites and send his soul to God in a state of grace, for which I'm thankful. My return was delayed: I stood in at St Xavier's in Poona for Father Mendez (who was also very ill), until his recovery by the grace of God. I know Father Rodriguez intended to forward my mail, but he's had a busy time himself – and to make a long story short, I didn't see your letters until I got back here halfway through July.

Now, as to the content of the letters.

It grieves me to hear that you're feeling so far away from God. I'm so glad that you fulfilled your penance, and I'm sure that your attempts to repair past faults were sincere.

Please excuse this feeble letter. I hardly know what to say. I can only tell you what I know to be true, that God loves you. You must continue your relationship with Him. It's a hard love, sometimes. The more He loves you the higher His expectations, therefore the harder your trials. Don't forget that even Our Lord Jesus Christ thought His Father had forsaken Him in His agony: Eloi, Eloi, lama sabachthani?

I know you are strong, and I know that your faith will hold you fast. Read the Scripture every day. Practise charity. Receive the Sacraments. You will come close to Him. I know this in my heart.

It is difficult to speak of Father Malone. Again, I hardly know the words to use. I know what an inspiring figure he has been, to you, and of course to myself and many others, but you must brace yourself for a shock. Father Malone has left the Church.

A great loss it is to all of us, and I pray daily that he will be reconciled. I don't fully understand the sequence of events that led to his crisis.

It happened in America, in New York. He was there – how shall I say this? – he was there on his usual business. You understand? This was almost a year ago now. But something happened. Something — it isn't permitted to speak of the details like this, in a letter. I'm sorry. I know how hard this news will be for you. The story only reached me recently, from an American Jesuit who was visiting Father Mendez at St Xavier's when I was there. Perhaps it's not true? I've written to Rome to enquire, but so far nothing.

I'm so sorry, Dominic, to be the bearer of bad news, especially at a time when you're feeling low. But I felt it would be wrong to keep it from you. I don't think you should see him just now, until we know the facts. That's my advice. And yet I feel compelled to help you in this, even against my reason. I don't know where Father Malone is. All I can give you is the address of the American, Father Gozzano, in New York. Perhaps he'll know?

Keep up your spirit, my friend! Don't forget what we were a part of, together, that night.

Again my apologies for the delay in my reply. Stay in touch — and God bless you.

Adrian.

I rolled a cigarette, poured myself a large (filing cabinet — I was at my Cornerstone desk) Scotch, and sat back in my chair. It was a warm and sunless afternoon, office windows open. While I sat, letter in one trembling hand, half-eaten sandwich in the other, rain began to fall, gently at first, then in berry-sized droplets that burst in *tups* on the sill.

They'll fuck you in the ass in New York, cunt.

I put down the letter and picked up the phone.

'No, no, no, no, *no*,' David said. 'Categorically no. Out of the question, Dominic. There's *Frankfurt* coming up, for heaven's sake.'

He meant the book fair in October, at which we'd be talking up *The Tamarind Tree* to European publishers. We were in his office the following day. No rain this afternoon; just brash sunlight picking out not only his curling fag-smoke but also the spiralling motes disturbed by my entrance. David sat in his armchair (leather, oxblood, leaking snow-white stuffing) with one attenuated leg wrapped round the other, a hefty manuscript on his lap and a blue felt-tip in his left hand.

'You don't understand,' I said. 'It's the equivalent of a family illness. Think of it as compassionate leave.'

'Your family's in London and that ghastly whatsit Begshall.'

'David,' I said, 'I've got to go. I'll give my notice in if necessary.'

'Are you out of your mind?'

'Perhaps. I'm sorry.'

'But, Dominic, *Frankfurt*.'

'I can't help it, David, I'm sorry. If you knew . . .'

'Yes?'

'I can't explain. My whole life's been leading up to this.'

'Don't for God's sake be so dramatic, will you?'

'It's someone who saved my life.'

'Are you serious?'

'Yes.'

'Someone actually saved your life?'

'Yes.'

'Who?'

'A priest.'

'Good God.'

'Bizarre it may seem. Nonetheless the truth. Now he needs help. Now I believe he needs my help.'

David unwound his legs and unbalanced the manuscript,

a hundred or so pages of which slithered to the Turkish rug at his feet. 'Damn and bollock blast,' he hissed, laboriously extricating himself from the armchair's uncanny pull. Ignoring the scattered pages he crossed to the desk where he *whumped* the remainder of the manuscript down. 'Dominic,' he sighed, 'this is all ridiculous. Thoroughly ridiculous.' (*Thoroughly* . . .) 'Can't you at least wait until after the book fair? I mean you'd owe me a month's notice anyway.'

'David, I'm leaving immediately.'

Which made him genuinely angry. 'For Christ's sake, Dominic,' he said, putting his long fists on his hips. 'That's completely impossible. I'll bloody sue you for breach of contract. After all we've done here together?'

'David, I know how bad—'

'I'm not having it. It's bloody ridiculous. You can work a month's notice at least. In fact, I'm not sure it isn't six weeks in the new contract. And where are my bastard cigarettes?'

They had slipped down behind the armchair's cushion, from whence I fished them out and handed them to him 'David, calm yourself,' I said as he lit up afresh off the previous butt.

'Calm myself?' he said, whipping his spectacles off and putting them on again immediately. 'Calm myself? I can't believe you. You're ill. You're having some sort of—'

'David, if you don't let me go now I'll force you to. I'll go down the corridor and stick my cock in Lysette's ear and you'll have to sack me. Either way, I'm going.'

His left hand darted up and began vigorously massaging his right trapezoid. Then just as abruptly stopped.

'Why are you doing this to me? I want you to *work* here.'

'I *want* to work here, you know that. This is an emergency.'

He took his glasses off again, slowly this time, with defeat, and slouched back to the armchair. He didn't sit in it, just stood and stared down at the manuscript pages on the floor.

'Is it truly, *truly* an emergency, Dominic?' he said. 'I mean, don't bugger me about here. Tell me the truth. Do you really have to go?'

I thought of what Gozzano had said on the phone.

'Yes, David,' I said. 'I really have to go.'

That night I sat with Pen in the flat's little back garden. It had been overgrown when we'd moved in, but under Helen's direction Pen had cleared and replanted. Pen had become an old lady about flowers; he'd put in fuchsias, hibiscus, petunias, lilac, primroses, and cared for them with a tenderness (inanity, I said) which was patently an extension of his feelings for Helen. *Sublimated paternity*, I'd further suggested, eliciting his stock two fingers and curled upper lip.

Halfway through our second bottle of Tesco's chianti I told him the story of Ignatius Malone. All of it, from St Edmund's medical room to Father Adrian's letter two days before.

'You're joking.'

'No, Pen, I swear on my mother's life.'

It was dark, humid and still, the two of us flickeringly illumined by the half-dozen lit wicks in a single candle the thickness of a human thigh, which sat on a little folding table next to us. A Miles Davis CD had been playing when we started drinking, but had finished not long after I began my narrative. Pen's questions and interjections had dwindled as I'd talked. Now I was hoarse. The fridge in the kitchen shuddered, rattling its bottles of San Miguel.

'Are you fucking *serious*? You *saw* this thing come out of the kid's mouth?'

I had known this would be the bit that stuck. Not Burke's resurrection.

'Yeah, I did.'

'Fuck off.'

'Pen, I'm telling you. I saw it.'

He scratched his head, vigorously. 'The thing about the other kid – what was his name?'

'Burke. Callum Burke.'

'Yeah. That could've been anything.'

'I've wondered.'

'And that was the fucker . . .? This same bastard?'

'The same bastard.'

'Jesus Christ.'

Some moments required for the revolution of all this in his head. 'I can't fucking believe you never told us any of this.'

'I know, I know.'

'I mean this *exorcism* thing . . .'

'I wouldn't blame you if you didn't believe me.'

'That's not the point. The point is you should have fuck ing told me about the exorcism thing. Christ, I'd have started going to church again at least. I mean, fucking *hell*. If what you're saying is true . . . I mean what about . . . I mean how come it didn't make you start going back to church?'

'It did.'

'What?'

'I was going every Sunday until this year. And confession.'

'Why didn't you *tell* me?'

'I don't know.'

'I mean, I could have been hit by a car or something.'

We stayed up long into the night, talking. I didn't tell him about Deborah. I didn't tell him about Alice.

I did tell him that I was leaving for New York in three days.

'Oh great,' he said. 'Fucking fantastic. What about the rent?'

A protracted and painful session with David had got me a month's unpaid leave, at the end of which period, if I didn't return, I was out. Money – my sad little savings account – set some parameters, sufficient to cover next month's rent, buy my air ticket and scrabble along in New York for a while as long as I wasn't fussy about where I stayed and what I ate.

'You'll need looking after,' Julia said. 'It's just as well I'm over there myself next week.'

Which, obviously, I hadn't bargained for. (*Meeting the New York publishers and agents,* I'd said. *David usually goes, but he thinks it's time I did.*) Julia had swallowed it without resistance – but what good was an alibi if she was going to be *there*?

'Why?'

'Your employer, actually, has requested the pleasure of my company.'

'*David?* What are you talking about?'

'Your *overall* employer,' she said, then rolled her eyes when it was patent that the information wasn't going to elicit anything other than my look of lobotomy. 'Jesus, Dommie. Clifford *Gill*. It's his seventieth birthday party. You can be my date.'

'No no no no no,' I said.

'Yes yes yes yes *yes*. You should've been invited anyway, you being the Cornerstone star and all. It's perfect. I'm staying with Lydia Bond. Do you know her?'

'No.'

'We're showing together next month at Clifford's. Where are you staying?'

'I can't remember.'

'Do you want me to see if Lydia—'

'No no no. No.'

'Well, look, I'm only trying to be helpful. Christ, I thought – stupid fucking *me* – that you might've been glad of my company. Obviously—'

'Jules, shush, will you?'

'What in God's name is the matter with you?'

'Nothing. Nothing. Sorry. Yes, it'll be good to spend some time with you, and no, I don't need your friend to put me up, thanks anyway. Give me the number where you're staying.'

I travelled light. One hold-all, one Mickey Rourke in *Angel Heart* suit, one rosary, formerly the property of Father Ignatius Malone, erstwhile globetrotter, resurrectionist, caster out of devils.

CHAPTER SEVEN

◆

The Second Miracle

A Manhattan is a cocktail consisting of four parts whisky, one part vermouth and a dash of bitters. Manhattan is an island at the north end of New York Bay between the Hudson, East and Harlem rivers. Administratively part of New York City, a major financial, cultural and commercial centre. Population 1,487,536 (1990). Area 47 square kilometres.

Dictionary definitions calm my nerves. Drink and city, however, mingled en route, so that, arriving, I was stupidly surprised to taste neither whisky nor vermouth in the atmosphere – although five paces out of the terminal at JFK I was sure I could detect a whiff of bitters (a dash, as Cornerstone's *Collins* had said) interpreted by edgy and dehydrated me as the smell of trouble.

Ninety degrees and raining. Summer rain at dusk dropping in oily pellets through the reek of traffic and waste. Coming in by cab from Queens I watched the lit skyline loom up like a giant and complex deity and felt what every European feels, confronted by something so televisually familiar: that I had been here – many times, in loves, deaths, songs, crimes and disasters – before.

I checked in at the Studio Hotel on 26th Street and Broadway, the establishment's moniker unearned, since it had no connection, obvious or obscure, to the appurtenances of either music or film. But it did have a fat owner-receptionist with a tanned and porous face set in the expression a two-year-old might display just prior to starting bawling. A sweat-heavy Hawaiian shirt with short sleeves and stressed buttons hugged his tureen gut and twin dugs, and a cigar the diameter of a baby's wrist smouldered foully in a tinfoil ashtray close at hand.

I referred to my reservation.

'We don't take reservations.'

'I telephoned from London last week and reserved a room.' Which I had, having consulted the *Shoestring Budget Guide to New York*.

'I don't care if you telephoned from Timbukfuckintu, pal. We don't take reservations here. You wanna make a reservation, call the freakin Waldorf.'

We looked at each other for a few moments.

'Do you have a room available at the moment, for tonight?'

'Sure.'

A few more moments. (One of the last places of its kind, even I, virgin to the city, could tell.) He lifted the baby's-wrist cigar to his mouth and wetly sucked, *pup, pup, pup*.

'Great,' I said. 'Cash in advance okay?'

Sixth floor, seventy-five a night, no icebox, no phone, no room service. A senile elevator stinking of Chinese food and sweat hoisted me to my room, a gloomy oblong with sagging ceiling the colour of old blood and a sour-smelling bed. My window overlooked the wet street. Opposite, a parking garage neon blinked. Two Hispanic busboys shared a cigarette at a diner's delivery entrance. Rain-jewelled cars and cabs purred, growled, hissed and honked. I stood watching, disbelieving, in the way one is always disbelieving when the business of airports and passports and currencies and cabs has been dealt with and suddenly one realizes – smack – that the journey is over, and my God here one is in a foreign country.

Father Vincenzo Gozzano had been unequivocal: *Don't come here.*

Here I was.

◆

'It's a warning,' I said.

Kelp's ghost has been arriving later, recently. This time just after six a.m. He had appeared at the bedroom window, half in and half out of the air-conditioning unit, with chunks of Manhattan's dawn light showing through him. I lay (low down on the bed, with my head close to Holly's soft flank), watching him with the detatchment it's been possible to develop over the months. Curiously, it was the detatchment that led me to my ominous conclusion, just after – with fading grin and tiredness-bright eyes – he faded.

'What?' Holly said.

'A warning. To get away from here. To leave.'

'I have to go to work.'

'No, listen to me, Holly. Listen. I thought it *was* just him telling me to leave you. It's his thing – it used to be his thing: Some are born to leave, some achieve leaving . . .' I saw her face. 'I'm sorry,' I said. 'I know. I know this sounds mad. Maybe I'm wrong. Forget it.'

'I've got to go.'
'I know.'
'We have to talk.'
'I know.'
'I'll see you later.'

◆

The church of the Holy Name was on 13th Street, between First and Second Avenues. Gozzano was small and muscular with hard black eyes and a dark thatch of unprofessionally cut hair. Forty, or thereabouts, with a thin, sensual mouth and some acne scarring about the brown forehead and cheeks.

'I can't help you,' he said. 'It was stupid of you to come. I told you on the phone.'

We sat (him on an upturned bucket, me on the back doorstep) with God be praised ice-cold bottles of Sam Adams in a small walled garden at the back of the church, where, sans dog collar and with rolled-up sleeves revealing deep brown flexors, he had been weeding a border. Very slight Italian traces in the accent. He sounded exhausted.

'You can help me,' I said, his terseness infectious. 'You might choose not to, but you can help me.'

'You're a reporter.'

'No. I'm an editor. I'm not looking for a story.'

'An editor not looking for a story. Very good.'

'Look,' I said. 'You know where he is. Is he here?'

No response.

'All I'm asking you to do is ask him if he'll see me. Tell him Dominic Hood from St Edmund's in Begshall twenty-four years ago. Tell him I was there in Goa when he exorcized the Fernandez boy.'

'What do you mean, you were there?' No flinch at the word 'exorcized'.

'I watched from outside the bedroom window,' I said. 'If I'd wanted a story that would have been more than enough, I promise you.'

'I can't help you,' he said, and took a long pull at the Sam Adams, trachea highlighted in the sun. Then the lips wiped, a brief glance at the floor, and back at me. 'Not because I choose not to, Mr Hood, but because I actually can't. I don't know where Father Malone is.'

'I don't believe you.'

He laughed in one quiet snort: I'm supposed to care? The unflinching eyes had seen things, had been in the front line. I wondered what he had shared with Malone.

'Sorry,' I said.

The long-lashed eyes closed, slowly, then opened again. 'He was here with us for a short time,' he conceded. 'Now he's gone. I don't know where.'

Soft drone of bees in the lilac nearby. I hadn't slept well at the Studio Hotel. Doors had creaked open and slammed closed all night, the sound of a pointless firing mechanism. Now the sun was directly above the garden and my eyeballs hurt from the light.

'What happened, Father?' I said. 'Do you know what happened?'

'Yes, I know.'

'Would you tell me?'

He closed his eyes for a moment and let his shoulders slump. Very tired. A finite amount of energy with which to hold me off.

'You've come a long way to find a dead end,' he said. 'I'm sorry. Tell me what your relationship was to Father Malone. Give me something. *Quid pro quo.*'

418

'So it's true the Church never gives anything away for free?'

'The sacraments are free. Salvation is free. Should we start charging for those?'

I was, let it be admitted, attracted to him. Bizarre new twist. The jet-lag and sun-daze allowed it, however, without much fuss; but I did wonder, with only mild concern, what was happening to me. How attracted? Sexually? Yes, but with the feeling that it was in lieu of some other relationship; a ham-handed language for a refined idea. I imagined myself telling Pen: 'I think I fancied this priest, but it was only because I believed in the quality of his soul.' Imagining Pen's face in reaction, I had to stop myself from laughing.

'Father Malone helped me, once,' I said. 'When I was small. He did something that altered the course of my life, which I know sounds melodramatic. I don't even know if he'd remember me. It's just that ever since then what he did has stayed with me. It's been a source of faith.'

'You've seen and believed,' Gozzano said. 'Lucky for you. But I doubt Father Malone would remember you.'

'He'd remember what he did.'

'Which is to remain mysterious, I see.'

'It would injure my credibility.'

At which – recognizing the Church's own rationale – he smiled acknowledgement.

'I heard from Father da Souza that Malone had left the Church and I couldn't believe it.'

'It's true.'

'How can it be?'

'Because faith can be tested and found wanting.'

I knew what he – the disinterested intellectual, not the priest – was thinking: that this was the danger of charismatic leaders. Charismatic leaders were not God. Faith had to be faith in God, all else being ephemera. Whatever had happened to Malone had riven him, Gozzano, too. Sleeplessness had left orbit shadows and stripped an already spartan idiom to its bones. As if in confirmation of which he brought his free hand up and with thumb and forefinger pressed the point between his eyes for relief. Then dropped that and took another pull at the Sam Adams.

'Are you seriously telling me that Father Ignatius Malone has lost his faith in God?'

'No. In himself as a priest.'

'I don't understand.'

'No.'

'Can't you tell me? I mean it's a fucking long way from London. Sorry.'

Redundant apology. The profanity hadn't even registered. Exhaling heavily, he looked away from me to where the bees waltzed in and out of the lilac. No question of what his duty as a priest of the Roman Catholic Church was. The novelty of my three-thousand-mile journey notwithstanding, he must send me, none the wiser, on my way.

'You're only troubled because you trust me,' I said.

He breathed through his perspiring nose. 'Not troubled,' he said. 'Tired. How was it you came to encounter Father Malone in Goa?'

'Accident,' I said.

'Not that you believe it was an accident.'

My turn to look away into the flowers, which didn't help at all, with the light stirring the colour into an eye-itching swarm. 'Come on,' I said. 'If I say it was fate you'll tell me we're free. If I say it was an accident you'll tell me God's got a plan.'

He made a dismissive gesture with his left hand. I was insulting his intelligence.

'Listen,' I said. 'There's no reason for you to tell me any-thing. If you don't trust me just tell me and I'll fuck off. I'm well aware that if you do tell me you'll be failing in your priestly duty. But I swear my motives aren't cynical. I wanted . . . If there was any way I could help Father Malone . . .'

He looked up at me. 'Help him?' he said. 'Or get help from him?'

I closed and opened my eyes, slowly. The sun and the single beer had dizzied me. Limbs jet-lagged and dreaming. All the garden's details rarefied. Gozzano sat on the upturned bucket with feet apart and elbows resting on his knees, rolling the now empty Sam Adams between his palms. Then he stood up.

'There's no way you can help him,' he said. 'But come with me.'

Into the Hadean subway. A train under Broadway to 60th Street. At a deli on the corner Gozzano bought a three dollar bunch of irises.

'Your first time?' He meant New York. We had walked for five minutes, and beyond knowing that we were still heading uptown I was without bearings.

'That obvious, is it?'

The heat throbbed. At crosswalks car grilles breathed against our shins. Vents in the asphalt released steam and the subway's burned-metal stink. The exposed limbs and midriffs of black people glowed with the warmth of polished mahogany.

'In here.'

We had turned into a quiet street of expensive apartment buildings. Halfway down the block, a church of pale stone fronted by a small yard of flowerbeds and shale, with a yew tree in each corner and a dark, waxy hedge running at shoulder height round its perimeter. I followed him through the gate and round the shadowed side of the church, beyond which we emerged into a small graveyard. A hundred or so graves, unsystematically spaced, some new and marked by mawkish stones (doves, lambs, weeping angels), others old and plain. The grass long, speckled with daisies and butter-cups, a few little apple trees for shade. Difficult to believe the city contained such places. Nonetheless, here it was.

The thought – suddenly – that Malone was dead. That was why there was nothing I could do. It was over. He was gone.

But Gozzano could have told me that Downtown and saved us both the hike.

At a new grave with a simple stone of white marble Gozzano stopped and deposited the irises in one of the receptacles. A great many other flowers there already, arranged with care. He crossed himself, said a silent prayer, crossed again, then dragged his hand down over his face as if to wipe away tiredness. I looked down at the inscription.

VALENTINA HUNTER

BELOVED DAUGHTER OF JOHN AND GRACIELLA
BORN MARCH 14TH, 1986
DIED DECEMBER 9TH, 1998

ETERNAL REST

'I don't understand,' I said.

I had been staring at the dates, thinking, Jesus Christ, twelve years old – the parents, the abominable inversion of outliving the child; how get beyond it? – and was shocked, when I turned to Gozzano, to see his face wet with tears.

Two, three, four, five hurried out from his ducts as I stood gawping. No other indication of grief. The beautiful mouth remained composed. It looked like not grief but a chemical or mechanical reaction. I put my fingertips to his elbow. 'What?' I said. 'What is it?'

He turned away for a moment, bowed his head, then hurriedly wiped his face with his hand. I was going through my pockets for a tissue or hanky, knowing I didn't have one, merely to create the sense that I was at least trying to do something useful. He turned back to me, face blank.

'I don't understand,' I repeated, as gently as I could.

'There was an exorcism,' he said. 'The girl died.'

Valentina Hunter was Gozzano's niece, the daughter of his sister, Graciella.

'You've read the statistics,' he said. 'Seen the movies, I imagine. Most cases are treatable within the frameworks of physiological or psychiatric medicine. This wasn't one of them.'

We sat now in an over air-conditioned sports bar somewhere in the Seventies on the Upper West Side with doubles of Johnnie Walker Black Label on the rocks and a corner booth to ourselves. Red-brick walls and a highly polished floor of blond wood. He'd removed the dog collar. 'Other customers don't like it.' He needn't have bothered, the place being empty. A middle-aged bartender in the black and white stripes of an American football referee leaned on his elbows at the bar, languidly chewing peanuts and gazing at a wildlife photography magazine. The jukebox was silent, though its neon tubing flickered and pulsed. We sat facing each other, the smoke from my cigarette at first going straight up then veering violently left into a current of conditioned air.

'In Goa,' he said. 'How long did it last?'

I thought back to the Fernandezes' bungalow, my vigil at the window. 'Difficult to say,' I said. 'Maybe an hour or two?'

'Valentina was in a state of possession for two and a half months,' he said. 'She'd been troubled for at least a year before that.'

'I don't understand,' I said – aware, irritatedly, that it was becoming my litany. 'Didn't the doctors . . .? Didn't she go to a hospital?'

'They looked for tumours, brain lesions, chemical imbalances, motor neurone disorders, drug-abuse. My sister . . . The police investigated my sister and her husband. A psychiatric examiner at the hospital concluded Valentina had been sexually abused. All nonsense, of course. They called it everything from epilepsy to Tourette's. Schizophrenia. They gave her hypnotherapy, anti-depressants, tranquillizers.'

'Did you know what was going on?'

'They kept me out of it. My sister and I aren't close. Hadn't been for many years. I had no idea anything was wrong until October last year. Then Graciella called me. I try to rationalize what happened by thinking that it's brought me close to my sister again.' He paused. 'Then it disgusts me that such thinking is possible.'

It hadn't taken long. Malone had been on sabbatical at the Jesuit seminary in New York, writing the series of lectures he was scheduled to give in the United States the following autumn.

'I've never seen anything like it,' Gozzano said. 'Except, naturally, in the movies.'

'Tell me.'

'I can't.'

'What did you see?'

424

'I saw a child destroyed. I saw a living body fall by degrees into corruption and death.'

'You had no doubts it was a genuine possession?'

Again the joyless snort. 'The first time I went to see Valentina,' he said, 'she told me in detail the dream I had had the night before. She spoke in the voice of Father Rossi, my teacher at the seminary in Bologna, dead ten years. She called me Gozzi, his name for me. But that was nothing.'

The whisky had settled me, but also foregrounded my slight sexual titillation at the collarless brown throat and wisps of dark upper-chest hair. I thought: These feelings are to distract me.

'There were many other things. Sins I had committed as a child no one knew about. She opened her mouth and a scratchy recording of the conversation I'd had on the phone with Father Malone came out. At times she didn't look like Valentina at all. Once, her voice – Valentina's own voice – came through saying there was something sticking in her back. When we lifted her, her back looked completely normal, but it felt as if there was . . . I felt wings folded there. Things made of bone and like leather – but there was nothing to be seen.'

I kept still at this, letting the words hang.

'Yes, yes, I know,' he said, taking my silence for objection. 'I know. One does not believe in these things. But what do you want? There they are.' His eyes were wide, red-edged from the recent tears. I imagined him as a small boy in Bologna, sitting on a warm step, looking up and sensing God's weight in the empty blue sky.

'How many voices?'

'Dozens. Always.'

'My name is legion,' I said.

'Yes. The exorcism lasted weeks.'

'*Weeks?*'

'Father Malone and I barely slept. We moved Valentina into the infirmary at the seminary. Voices disappeared one by one.'

I looked across the bar and out of the window, where Manhattan's traffic played havoc with the sunlight. Buildings still stood, people still walked, checked their windowed reflections, stopped, hailed cabs on tiptoe. Time still passed, seconds, minutes, hours, days.

'It was wearying beyond belief. The effort to hold to . . . As soon as you begin to doubt your authority . . . It's a matter of faith, of course, in the end. Always.' He pressed his palm to his forehead then forced his fingers through the dark thatch of hair. I thought of Malone, the long limbs and glamorous face, prematurely aged. *Lots of them have white hair*, Julia had said. I wondered, in the wake of this latest confrontation, how he looked now.

'I'm sorry,' I said. 'It was your niece. I didn't take it in, that she was your niece. I can't imagine how you feel . . .'

'There are no words for what I feel. I'm not sure there *are* feelings, even now, months afterwards.'

'How did she die?' I hadn't meant to ask so abruptly.

He took a slow sip, looking at me, unblinking, as if we had switched to a telepathic mode.

'Why am I telling you this?' he said at last. I didn't reply. He swallowed a large mouthful of Scotch. I watched the ice slip up and rest against his top lip. Eyes closed for the whisky's descent, then opened again to stare at me.

'I watched Father Malone age in front of my eyes,' he said. 'I watched Valentina taken from us by whatever was inside her. At a moment when she seemed to be sleeping, my sister began stroking her hair. She had beautiful hair, fine, silky.

The first stroke of my sister's fingers pulled the hair away from the scalp. Then Valentina opened her eyes and started to laugh. Her own hands came up and she pulled the rest of her hair out. It came out easily. Easily.'

'But the voices one by one went away,' I said, steering away again from the gory particulars.

'Yes. We were exhausted. You can't imagine it.'

'I can't imagine what I saw in Goa going on for weeks, no.'

'The body can stand only so much. The body is material. We had her tied down. I was sure Father Malone's strength would give out. He struggled, sometimes, with the words of the rite. You can't imagine the tiredness – not just physical, I mean, but the weariness of soul, the constant blasphemies, the stench, the screams, the excretions, my sister forced to watch her daughter tortured.'

Bells, faintly, rang in me. How not? Words are words, hung about with our own connotations, histories, acts.

'Father Malone broke out in a rash which bled. After three weeks he confided in me that he had not been able to see out of his right eye for several days, and that he was afraid for his left – not for himself, for his ability to do his work.'

I thought back to the Fernandezes' bungalow. The room's packed energy. The contemptuous authority with which Malone had pulled Dr Sutay's arm away from the boy.

'But she died,' Gozzano said, with an abruptness to match mine of a moment before. 'The last voice she spoke in was different. Quiet. Although her lips were moving.'

'What did it say?'

A pause – the same as the one in Pen's attic when Kelp had told the story of his mother's table-tapping and Charlotte Anne. (Charlatan. The dismal pun arrived, twenty years late.) *What did it say?* Pen had asked, in his small voice.

Gozzano leaned back in the booth. A layer of earnestness or pain had evaporated, replaced by some willed wryness. It was obvious from the sudden shift in his posture that he thought he had indulged himself, undeservedly, in telling me all this. Ashamed of himself.

'When the last voice spoke it said: "It's not her I'm taking, Father. It's you." Valentina died of a heart attack. Coroner's verdict.'

We looked at each other in silence for a few moments. The bartender remote-controlled the television's volume up, baseball crowd and dyspeptic commentator fading in. Gozzano fished in his pocket and took out his collar. He was done. He had failed. It was time to go.

'There's no danger in your having told me any of this,' I said, truthfully.

We stood at the entrance to a subway station. Crowds and sunlight loud and brilliant after the quiet and cool of the bar. He was going underground, I, armed with his directions, was going to walk.

'I believe you,' he said. 'Nonetheless.'

'I promise you, Father, it's safe.'

'I know. How long are you in New York?'

As long as it takes. There is nothing else.

'I'm not sure,' I said. 'I'd still like to see Father Malone – more than ever, actually. Do you think he's left the city? Left the United States, perhaps?'

Gozzano shrugged. 'It's a good place to stay if you want to destroy yourself,' he said. 'Maybe he's still here. I'm looking for him myself. The police, of course, don't regard him as a missing person because there's nowhere, officially, he's supposed to be.'

'Maybe I'll hire a private detective,' I said. 'It wouldn't be the first time.'

We didn't shake hands, but exchanged a final look that made me wonder whether the attraction hadn't been mutual. He looked as rich as a liqueur standing there in the subway's maw; visible, I thought, the dregs of dogged energy. I wondered whether he would ever be able to justify the loss of his niece, whether the ride would ever be worth the price of the ticket – and as if he'd read my mind he said, before turning to descend: 'I used to think suffering was training for death. I used to think it was God's way of loosening the bond between the spirit and the flesh, so that when death came the spirit would be free to travel home. Now that strikes me as . . . Now there's just a hole, where the thinking about suffering used to be.'

Then he was gone, swallowed by the darkness and the busily living crowds.

My fat-gutted cigar smoker was partnered by a thirty-something lupine Irishman of a stubbled seediness much in keeping with his place of work. Long jaw, long eyelashes and long, dirty fingers. He slunk, low-shouldered, perennial joint lip-stuck and dangling, and spoke in a register lower than that for which his larynx was made.

'Where'd y'eat lass noite?'

'Veselka. In the East Village.'

Derisive nasal blast, then: 'Fock'n East Village. S'all anniebody wants here. Fock'n East *Village*.'

Bad times, it was to be inferred, had been had in the East Village. Disappointments in love.

Out of boredom, perhaps, he gave me many unsolicited recommendations for bars and eateries which, on the one or two occasions I tried them, turned out to be stinking dives lived in by drug addicts and criminals.

For three days I pounded the streets in the heat, asking at

churches, hospitals, police precincts, libraries, shelters, even bars and restaurants. Nothing, of course.

★

'You look odd,' Julia said.

'What do you mean, "odd"?'

'Like you're on something. Tranks. What's the matter with you?'

'Nothing. It's this goddamned heat.'

'It's *drinking* in this goddamned heat.'

'Who are you, Mother Teresa?'

'I'm just saying. You look funny and I don't like it.'

'Duly noted. You look like a goddamned piece of fruit yourself.'

We were on the roof of Lydia Bond's apartment building on Bowery and Great Jones looking straight up Third Avenue. Lydia had gone down for ice, leaving us a moment alone. The heat was a weight on us; even lifting the beers to our lips an effort. We had agreed our goddamneds needed practice.

'Anyway, I don't know about this thing,' I said.

'What thing?'

'This thing. Clifford Gill's party.'

'There'll be girls there.'

'Very funny.'

'Yes, well, what are you these days? Celibate? Homosexual?'

'Look just because you're here to get impregnated—'

'I'm *not* here to get impregnated.'

'Aren't you?'

'No.'

'Oh.'

'I'm too old now. Painted into sterility. Anyway, it'll be fine. You'll enjoy yourself. Besides, the great man himself

430

would never forgive me if he found out one of his Cornerstones was here and didn't get to meet him.'

'Well, I'm none too goddamned sure about that, Toots,' I said.

Lydia's pivotal show (ten years ago) had been a single installation called 'The Doctor Will See You Now', which featured a wall of one hundred alternating door handles and formaldehyde jars, each jar containing a dully preserved post-mastectomy breast. Clifford had made her a deal of money over the five years that followed and she had invested cannily, in real estate. 'So cannily,' Julia had told me, 'that she hasn't made a piece of work for the last two years. It's my project to get her back out into it.' Lydia was aware of this agenda and had manifestly mixed feelings about it. Doubt, I could see, had crept in. Success had led her to the place from whence it felt necessarily obscene or bankrupt to take herself at all seriously. 'Which would be okay' (Julia again) 'if she could channel it into work. But she can't. She's a serious person. Too serious for the airy, sold-out posture. If she doesn't do some proper work soon, there's going to be a psychic fracture.' A diagnosis I was inclined to credit, having observed during the afternoon Lydia's rate of alcohol consumption, periods of furious nail-biting, and chain-smoked Winstons.

We picked up her boyfriend, Pete, on the way to Clifford's.

'I don't like the sound of it,' he said, of our intended destination. 'The last party Lydia made me go to I came home in a dress. I don't remember what happened.'

Pete, thin-faced and black-eyed with goatee and girlish cheekbones played piano in a band called the Mystical Toupees, whose music (definitely ironic, definitely to be taken with a pinch of salt) he described as a fusion of Pearl Jam and Pennies From Heaven. Their first CD, *Karmic Mousse*, had just been released, and was not, Pete said with a mixture of melancholy and contented resignation, going anywhere near the Billboard 100.

'I'm planning to drink quite a bit tonight, Dominic,' he said to me, accepting one of my proffered American Spirits. 'I'd be honoured if you'd join me.'

'Oh he's your man for that,' Julia said for me, having seen that my mind was on something else.

Clifford had 'places', the Tribeca loft being one of them. The size of a football pitch and densely populated by the time we arrived just after ten, Dominic Hood in ivory Mickey Rourke in *Angel Heart* number, Jules in a backless purple dress with leg-showing front slash, Lydia in black leather trousers and white halter-top, Pete in pin-striped flares and a green silk shirt. Two hundred people at least, many women in spaghetti-strap dresses showing sleek scapulae and complex complexions, many men in exquisite suits and at-ease body language, all exuding the air of absorbed wealth, a blend of climates (judiciously dipped into, year round), service-industry polyglotism. Artists, too, dotted the room (a blue hairdo, yellow tinted spectacles, a torn pair of jeans, a pink backpack), several of whom had been made wealthier than they had imagined they would be by Clifford Gill (or Clifford Gill types), and who were unsure, in these green days, how to feel about it.

Clifford Gill himself looked – as was to be expected in a man of his inestimable wealth – very well. Six foot two, large-framed, with leonine head and Buffalo Bill hair, he moved among his guests armed with brandy balloon,

Monte Cristo and smile of generous, brilliant scepticism. He had achieved that state enjoyed by the money-blessed in which enemies are kept as pets, close by, to keep the flagging human interest piqued. The eyes – dark, large, long-lashed even at seventy – looked through or perhaps beyond their objects, to places or states of being out of the reach (it had turned out) even of fantastical wealth. One would not have been surprised to discover his investments in teleportation research, cryogenics, astral projection, virtual realities, interplanetary travel; money and appetite had mapped this world too quickly. Surely there must be others?

'I can't quite believe I'm in the middle of this,' I bellowed at Julia over the music's throb. Large video screens were throughout, showing incongruously assembled footage – *The Texas Chainsaw Massacre*, the Jackson Five, soft pornography, Reagan's inauguration, Ali and Frazier.

'This lot *live* like this,' she shouted back. 'It's terrible, but you bloody well know you could get used to it.'

'I'm used to it already,' I said, heading to the bar in Pete's wake.

Drunkenness and pointless mingling over the four hours that followed (wherein I managed to avoid Julia's proposed introduction), punctuated by predictable moments of self-confrontation in the bathrooms, after the last of which I vomited, then staggered back out into the hall, where Pete – who appeared to have drunk himself sober – intercepted me.

'Hey,' he said. 'Terrible party.'

'Yeah, well, at least you're not wearing a frock,' I said. Over Pete's shoulder I saw Clifford turn to greet someone, a dark-haired woman in a short black dress. With her back to me she walked into a slow embrace with him. I watched his arms come round her – one rested a split second on her backside then flicked away, the other snaked up and pressed between her shoulder-blades.

'A what?' Pete said.

'A frock. A dress.'

'Oh, yeah, right.'

They kissed, briefly. I read his lips saying, Let me get you a drink.

'You okay?' Pete said.

'What?'

'I mean you look a bit fuckin green, man, if you don't mind my saying so.'

'Just chundered. Barfed.'

'Oh. Okay. Cool. Lydia says you're gonna stay at her place with Julia for a few days, right?'

'Did she? She hasn't said anything to me. Still, my hotel's vile.'

'Studio, yeah, I know it. Fuckin hole. Well I'll see you there, then, sooner or later, okay?'

We shook hands, then he went to find Lydia.

I stood looking and felt (or imagined I felt) the party's noise receding. She still had her back to me, elbows in hands, weight on one leg. As I moved towards her, Clifford returned with a drink and – over *her* shoulder – caught sight of and seemed to recognize me. (I found out later that the look was for someone else, another art dealer, in fact, *behind* me, who had just arrived.) Misreading his smile and raised eyebrows, I stepped up just as he seemed to finish announcing me to the woman in the black dress, who turned, slowly, to face me.

For a few moments we looked at each other. The art dealer had been waylaid in my wake. Now Clifford found himself confronted by someone he had never seen before.

Deborah Black came to our rescue. 'Dominic Hood,' she said (as Clifford, relieved, affably bored, extended his hand). 'Have you met my father?'

◆

Earlier this evening Holly stood me up.

We had arranged to meet at Bona Fides at eight. I was there, she never arrived. I called McLusky's. Left two hours ago. I called the apartment. Got the machine. Imagination's sluice opened a crack and let the first dirty trickle of horrible explanations through. As I walked with aching lungs back towards the apartment I felt the crack widening.

But knew a moment before fitting the key in the lock (a faint sound of throat-clearing and page-turning from within) that she was there, safe.

'What happened?' I said.

'I got sidetracked.'

'What?'

She held up the journal. 'Sidetracked *reading*.'

All the room's objects now very attentive. Even the street lowered its voice.

'I see.'

'Is it true?'

'How much have you read?'

'About half. Why, does it get *less* true?'

'It's true,' I said. 'It's all true. It's my story.'

Alcohol's gravity drew me to the kitchen counter, where a two-thirds-full bottle of Jack Daniel's glowed with consolation. Didn't bother with ice. Just two fat fingers, quaffed in one. Better. A Zippo'd American Spirit, two deep drags, better still. Humility and calm, two of my three watchwords with Holly, the other being, as we had both been recently made aware, tenderness.

She sat with the journal open in her lap, her own cigarette smouldering on the desk beside her.

'What does this mean?' I asked her.

She stared at me, then down at the floor for a while. Then finally back at me. She looked very tired. More than anything else I would have liked to put my arms round her, feel her shape up close to mine.

However.

'It means you keep a little distance from me,' she said. 'It means I read the rest of it.'

'It isn't finished,' I said.

'Then I read what there is.'

She took a drag, looked down again at the page. I poured her a drink identical to mine, walked it over to her. The apartment's objects were thinking it might be all right to breathe again. She took the glass, sipped.

'I think you should go out now,' she said.

◆

The day after the party, Deborah left for a week in Fiji with Clifford Gill.

I got back to the Studio at a quarter to five in the morning and slept until noon the next day.

'Back home, then, is it?' the wolfish Irishman said, when I checked out.

'No, actually, I'm staying with a friend.'

'Got lucky lass noite, then, did ya?'

'Yeah, you could say that.'

'Not wunna dem fock'n mad Village bitches?'

'No.'

'Ah, well.' Then, after he had made out a handwritten receipt. 'She got annie mates, then?'

'What?'

'Dis bord. You an hor, me an hor mate . . .'

I took a taxi to Lydia's and wished the journey could have been longer. The cab was brand-new and flawlessly driven by a bearded Rastafarian in a monumental leather hat. I would have been happy to remain slumped in the back seat all day, crawling through the skyscraping matrix absolved of the responsibility for making sense and taking action, now that the search for Ignatius Malone had been made to lead me nicely back to my beloved Deborah Black. It was a relief, finally, to see that the plan had been there all along. It was a relief to know at last my part, my pantaloon role in the play. It was a relief like the beaten heavyweight's swoon into sleep to know that it was over, the training, the track, the heavy bag, the *fight*. That cab ride was peace, the first numbing shot of surrender.

But it was over too soon. Out of the cab. Quick glare and flash of sun on Lydia's stoop, then the buzz, the hello, the door's electric fart or groan, and I was in, with humans to deal with, conversations to make, questions to fend off.

The week passed surreally. Having invented 'meetings' with half a dozen publishers I walked, purposelessly, all over the island, killing time, drinking, seeing nothing. The night before Deborah was due back, Julia tried to get it out of me.

'Nothing,' I said.

'Don't say "nothing", Dommie, you cretin. It's me.'

'I met someone at that Clifford Gill thing.'

'Yeah, so did I.'

'Umm?'

'Never mind. Who did you meet?'

No point, now, in not telling her. 'Someone from Begshall, believe it or not.'

'A girl from *Begshall*?'

'Yes.'

'Fucking hell. That's pretty incredible, Dommie.'

'Yes, it is.'

'What happened?'

'Nothing. She's in Fiji till tomorrow.'

'Fiji? Blimey. What's she doing in Fiji?'

'I've no idea.'

'But you'll see her when she gets back.'

'I don't know.'

'Oh come *on*. Why wouldn't you?'

'She brings out the worst in me. Or I do in her. Something like that.'

At which Jules snorted and made a dismissive gesture.

The Devil, as has long been averred, takes care of his own. Lydia and Pete were driving Julia to JFK, then heading up to Vermont to take advantage of Lydia's parental home for a week while Mom and Dad vacationed in New Mexico. Some brief and disingenuous protestations from me before accepting Lydia's suggestion that I stay (for my bogus 'one more week') and loft-sit in her absence. 'Besides,' Lydia said. 'I'd appreciate it if you fed my fish and watered my plants.'

In the late afternoon after they had all left ('Don't do anything stupid, Dommie,' Julia had said on the stoop between kisses) I walked to the Church of the Holy Name. Gozzano wasn't there, only two Hispanic cleaning ladies, to whom I eventually managed to communicate that I was leaving a telephone number and address for *el Cura*, Padre Gozzano, he would know why, and could they make sure he got it?

I stayed to pray, too, though when it came to it I just knelt with my eyes open, feeling the place filled with an implacable Presence; its question (traces of which had been trying to find expression in me through the months with Ahearn) blazed in the stained glass and candle flames: What are the practices of Faith when the Faith itself remains untested?

After twenty minutes I got up and left, without genuflection, without even crossing myself.

'No, I need to sleep. I'm jet-lagged.'

'When, then?'

'I don't know. Call me in twenty-four hours. I'm exhausted.'

How many details? How many facts?

An eighth-floor apartment on the Upper East Side overlooking Central Park. Carpet the colour of Polynesian sand and sparse, costly furnishings in dark wood or ivory leather. Nothing in the bedroom besides bed and walk-in wardrobe.

'Most people are afraid of money,' Deborah said. 'They treat it like something with its own intelligence, which might not do as it's told. The first thing to learn about money is contempt for its stupidity and obedience.'

Her accent (and, presumably, her mind) now a thing of multiple nuances, like the skins of the women at Clifford's — her father's — party; flakes and flavourings of a dozen countries chipped in for its mystery. She blinked and moved slowly, eased by the possession of new languages. I thought of her in the room at 47A, how exquisite it had been to see her take hold of Natalie's jaw, how my response to the gesture – arousal – had let me into a place of great familiarity and emptiness.

I sat on the edge of one of the lounge's leather couches. The apartment smelled of clean furniture, flowers (pansies, lilies, irises and white roses were vased in abundance), a version of marijuana I'd never encountered before, and, occasionally, her lemony perfume. She stood, just-showered, wet-haired in a thick white bathrobe. Muslin drapes filtered the sunlight at the window behind her. She had given me a large Scotch. Iced water for herself.

'Clifford Gill,' I said. 'It's a joke, presumably.'

'Presumably,' she said. 'Can't you see the resemblance?'

'How long have you known?'

'I've always known. My mother's legacy. The one thing she left me. Knowing's one thing, however, proving another.'

'Not that you've needed to.'

Which she ignored, sipping her water.

'How long have you been living here?'

'Since I saw you in London.'

Cue for a mutually testing look: did we remember it the same way?

'I never saw her again.'

'No.'

We only came into each other's consciousness momentarily. The room contained invisible angles and corners, cutting us off. It was very quiet, the apartment's conditioned air gentle. For what seemed a very long time neither of us said anything.

'I've missed you,' I said.

Different, that afternoon. Every minute squared the number of things we didn't bother saying to each other. Silence – our old element – expanded, crept round the room's unseen obstructions, heightened then obliterated altogether our sense of time passing, until eventually any word would, as in the old days, have jarred or clattered. I remember bits: Deborah lighting a Gauloise, the crackle of the flame sucked through the first millimetres of tobacco and paper; her unmade-up eyes smaller than of yore, pouchy from too much sleep; a view from the window of the avenue below, cars in bright colours through the leaves of the plane trees; me opening the wardrobe-sized refrigerator and finding it empty but for a handful of yellow apricots and a bottle of Perrier; me walking into the bedroom minutes or days after her and finding her lying on her back with ankles crossed and eyes closed; tugging the soft knot of the towelling robe; her body again, different and the same.

There were fragmentary acknowledgements, half-admissions that yes, here we were; but still we revered silence as if any uttered word would murder us. Language would in any case have dulled us down to something merely unlikely and extraordinary – and we wanted (didn't we?) more than that. We were almost bored. Not, as at 47A, by the consequential limitations, but by the distance still to travel beyond merely fucking each other.

Silence extended post-coitally. She sat up and swung her legs over the edge of the bed. I regarded the strong-boned back with its thin meat and hint of ribs, the downy neck, the now rough-chopped androgyne hairdo. The bedroom window, also muslin-draped, softened what would otherwise have been a blinding lozenge of Manhattan light. We were at the start of the end of something. She got up, slipped back into her robe, and walked out of the room.

When, fifteen minutes later, dressed (skin peculiarly alive to my clothes' light friction), I stood at the apartment door looking back at her sitting without any postural art on the couch, and said: 'We'll see each other again,' the sudden presence of language was brutal and ugly.

'Yes,' she said.

Lies to Lydia and Pete on their return from Vermont the next day. Thanks very much, yes a *lovely* time, *so* grateful, fish transferred their loyalty, still that was fish for you, yes yes yes ever so. No I didn't need a lift to the airport, yes I'd give Julia a big kiss, cheers, cheers . . .

They waved me off from the stoop. To the cab driver it must have seemed an inordinately gushy farewell considering the destination I gave him, namely, of course, the Studio Hotel.

Fat-gut made a great show of being both disgusted and unsurprised to see me, as if he had predicted (had he, he would have been right) that some hamartia would drag me back. On the other hand he was willing to concede higher powers at work when he looked and saw that the room I had occupied the week before had been vacated that morning. This elicited a few wet *pup pup pup*s on the turd-sized cigar and a corrugation of the sweat-lacquered brow. He looked at me blankly when I slid the seventy-five across the desk.

'A hundred,' he said. 'In advance.'

'What do you mean, "a hundred"?' I said, redundantly.

'Room's a hundred a night, cash in advance.'

'What, it's gone up twenty-five dollars since last week?'

'Yeah. So?'

He had my respect, so naked the misanthropy. It wasn't even greed.

My old room greeted me with its history of illicit couplings and botched abortions, overdoses, handjobs, murders, breakdowns and boredom. I didn't bother unpacking. Just dumped the holdall in a corner and lay down on the voluble bed.

'I need money,' I said to Deborah.

We sat in a bar restaurant called Poinsettia not far from her apartment. Had I been able to bring myself to think of Natalie I would have thought (as I can now): Natalie would have hated this place. All its space and crystal, its primped and gelled wait staff, its endorsement of the decadent palate and jaded gut. Had I been able to think in that way. But there was, in Deborah's company, only the one way I could think of Natalie Jane West.

'How much do you need?' Deborah said.

'That depends.'

'On?'

'On how long I'm staying here.'

'How long do you want to stay here?'

'That depends. On how long you want me to stay here.'

'That depends,' she said, not smiling, never smiling.

I raised my eyebrows in enquiry.

'On what you might want to do here.'

Her claret fingernails rested either side of a tall glass of iced water. She had dressed boyishly; black silk blouse and tight trousers of tan suede. I had noticed a new capacity for total stillness in her. For perhaps a full minute we remained silent, her looking to her left, me transfixed by the declivity where her clavicles met. I knew what she meant, I thought. Felt the first tricklings of excitement and dread.

Eventually she turned her small, cold, rich face to me.

'Do I understand you?' I asked.

But she didn't answer.

★

In the days that followed we barely spoke. We met whenever Deborah said she wanted to meet. We met for sex, and for the shared intuition. It was all we had ever had, and it was all we had now. There was, it was plain, another life to which I was not privy. We didn't discuss Clifford Gill, nor the relationship that might endure between them. She gave me cash when we met. Brand-new bills. Handed them to me either just before or just after. Lying awake on my verminous Studio bed I'd try to imagine Penguin's reaction if I picked up the phone to tell him that a rich woman was paying me for sex. Which cognitive dissonance — it being virtually beyond me to think of Penguin at all — made my nicotine headache worse. On the postcard I had written: 'Dear Pen, staying another couple of weeks, Love, Dummie.' Dropping it into the mailbox, I had doubted his existence. Deborah, meanwhile, gave me a pager, then a mobile phone.

There are questions. Chiefly: What did I think I was doing? I had lost my job. The month's grace had been and gone. I hadn't even phoned David to tell him I wasn't coming back. The credit card was full. But for Deborah's crisp handouts I was broke. I was living in a scabrous hotel with one bag of clothes and one rosary. I had stopped asking after Malone. I was waiting for what Deborah knew.

The land of opportunity.

So I waited, not knowing what I would do. Not *not* knowing, either.

Summer ruptured and rotted the city in daily increments. Sunburned derelicts lay about, weeping, muttering, venting geysers of incoherent rage; dogs' tongues came out and stayed out, lewdly; garbage trucks ingested Manhattan's waste with agonizing languor; Madison Avenue women plucked at the underarms of their blouses and dabbed their throats with hankies; the sky held in absolute turquoise stasis. All torpid, all inevitable. Nights, the streets breathed easier, grew humble and reflective.

I waited.

Then some consequences found me. A message at the desk to call Julia Hood, immediately, with reversed charges if necessary.

'What the fuck are you playing at?'

'I decided to stay on.'

'At that disgusting hotel?'

'At that cheap hotel.'

'You told Lydia you were leaving for the airport.'

'A lie.'

Pause. The Atlantic Ocean. Then she said: 'What are you doing, Dommie?'

At which I almost lost my temper, screamed down the phone, *Leave me the fuck alone and let me go to hell in peace will you?*

'I'm involved with someone,' I said.

'The girl from Begshall?'

'The girl from Begshall.'

'What about your job?'

'Jules . . .'

'Jules nothing.' Another long pause. Then she said: 'Cornerstone called me.'

'Oh God.'

'I spoke to David.'

'Oh God.'

'Dominic, he can't believe you.'

'Yeah, well.'

'Yeah well, yeah well. Fucking *hell*, Dommie. What are you *living* on?'

'Look, Jules, for fuck's sake I'll get another job when I come home. I've got money.'

'Where from?'

'Never mind where from – Jesus. Look do me a favour will you? Stay out of my fucking life. I know you're trying to look out for me, but . . . I'm in the middle of something here that I can't . . . I'm involved. *Involved.*'

'Yes, well, that's all very fucking New York of you but Penguin's doing his fucking nut. There's the rent, you know. What's he supposed to do?'

I told her I'd send Pen a money order. I told her I was all right. Nothing dangerous or illegal.

'Yes, well, I told Lydia you were still there.'

'Oh *great.*'

'I told her you were back in that *bloody* hotel and she *still* had the generosity to suggest that you stayed at her place.'

'I can't do that.'

'I *know* you can't, idiot, but have you got any idea how sweet it is of her to offer?'

'I'll call her and thank her.'

'Take her out to dinner, you miserable bastard.'

'Okay.'

'I mean it.'

'*Okay.*'

'And for God's sake ring Mum and Dad, will you?'

'I will.'

'I'm getting sick and tired of telling them you're all right. Especially since you're obviously *not* all right.'

I was exhausted when I got off the phone. So exhausted that I almost didn't answer the mobile when it rang.

'Are you in or out?' Deborah said.

I was kissing her navel, a pause in oral descent; her voice startled me. I did, actually, jump, slightly, though she'd spoken softly. The temptation was to say, 'What?' I resisted, however, and instead hovered over her midriff, looking up between her breasts. Her head was propped on two white pillows. I had kissed the lipstick off her mouth; now it was naked, and the richer for it.

'Don't stop,' she said. 'Are you in or out?'

I hesitated. I knew what she meant. I thought I knew what she meant. I knew what she meant. I kissed her belly, gently nipped, felt its quiver and flinch. I kissed lower, skirted the pubis, dropped into the gully of her crotch and carefully closed my lips around her clitoris. She knew that I understood her. She would be spared having to repeat it. Knowing which, she was content to let me consider it in silence.

It. Consider. Our familiar need for euphemism. I didn't consider at all. I knew my answer. Had known my answer from the moment the question left her mouth. Had always known my answer.

'Who else is involved?' I asked, between the pornographic licks children give their ice-creams.

She rolled onto her side, away from me, reached down and spread her buttocks.

'No one.'

'Clifford.'

No answer.

I went through the motions despite being much removed from my own tumescence (my tongue traced labial calyx and corolla, worried her clitoris, grazed her perineum, dipped extravagantly into her anus); for the first time my excitement seemed less than hers, which, despite or perhaps because of the haul into language, was rising.

'Have you done it before?' I asked, and dipped again, deeper. She sighed, heavily and protractedly. Reached down for me, grabbed my hair and tugged. I slid up behind her and wrapped my arms round her, shocked somewhat to see her face shut and frowning. 'Have you done it before?' I repeated.

But she wouldn't answer. I knew, suddenly, many things. Trivially, locally, that we would hold back, this time, remain in this state of reaching out. Postponed consummation was required. A fee, a fraction of the Devil's guerdon (in advance, pal); coming now would detract from the weight we could bring to it. It. It. Finally It. The thing unsurpassable that would change the world. I knew that our references to it would always be made through this body of smoke, this smoke of the body conjured between us to mask the vulgarity of logistics, the vulgarity of *planning*. Without the body's smoke it was all vulgar charts and numbers and trajectories. I knew I would be allowed either my past or my future, never both. I knew, I knew . . .

'You'll come with me.'

'Yes.'

'You want to.'

'Yes.'

You'll come with me. Yes. Thus the big bargains made, with little words, these monosyllables the tiny tips of ice-mountains flaring down thousands of feet beneath the surface. I was both at blood-clouded ease and in great agitation because the prosaic mind – mighty, insistent, anxious – wouldn't quite sleep, *would* poke its nose in with questions about the how and the where and the who and the when (but not the why, of course; that was not a question for the good prosaic mind); nor would my memory succumb properly to the drug, but shot splinters through to the surface, vivid shards of Kelp's grinning face in white-gold and brilliant green, my father's smacked lips after the first sip of the noon Teacher's, Penguin's sleeping body after the night with monkey-nosed Jill, Julia's fingers in my hair, those countless childhood times of her shshsh, Dommie, everything's all right.

I grabbed Deborah's chin and forced her face round to look at me. When her eyes opened I saw what an appalling *heave* was required for her to come back from her own brink. But she, like me, knew she must (the Devil's children know their father's laws), this time. Of course she knew that. Wasn't that how *I* knew, because I had picked it up from her?

'I'm in.'

Which again begged irony since, saying it, I eased my cock slowly and still in grave danger of ejaculation out of her anus and let it rest instead flush and undischarged against her sacrum, while our breathing subsided and the reality of the humming and white-lit apartment returned in painful increments. Irony begged but denied.

I dressed quickly. She lay on the bed, observing, breathing deeply. When I was at the door, she said: 'Shall we take a trip in a few days?'

We were, apparently, lovers, young, with money and all the time in the world.

'Yes,' I said. 'That sounds good.'

In the days that followed I found myself able to move about quite naturally as a tourist. I went to the Metropolitan Museum of Art. Watched roller-bladers on the rink in Central Park. Ate healthily at sensibly priced restaurants in the East and West Villages. I went to see movie after movie, the theatres' air-conditioning a sensual delight. I even went to the top of the Empire State Building. I bought a Yankees baseball cap and a pair of sunglasses. I smiled at shop assistants and reciprocated their hope that I'd have a nice day.

I don't remember how many days passed before the

sacred mobile rang. When it did, and I had with a surge of adrenalin answered it, Deborah and I spoke for ten minutes about what I had seen at the Guggenheim that day, and about my daily improving relationship with Fat-gut and his Irish partner. Everything that passed between us now was in accordance with an intuited set of laws and prescriptions. I was lying on my bed smoking an American Spirit and watching Jay Leno on the Studio's standard-issue snow and flicker set. (I had by that time developed a love for American television, the more dedicated to trivializing existence the better.) Leno muted, on, superficially, we chatted. It was by far the longest exchange since we'd met here.

Then, after recommending Veniero's patisserie for desserts and sweet treats beyond Manhattan compare, she said: 'Tomorrow we might be able to go into the country.'

'Yeah?'

'Yes. Maybe even sooner. I'll call you.'

'Okay.'

'See you later.'

'Bye.'

Language is innocent. Money is innocent. The knife, the car, the house, all innocent.

I switched the television off, got up and went to my room's one window. It seemed a long time ago I'd introduced myself to its view: the facing brownstones, the parking garage's blinking neon, the candy-striped diner, the solitary mailbox like an armoured dwarf, the pickled bum who sauntered and held forth but never left the block. A long time ago. There had, I remembered, been rain the night I arrived, a storm in the small hours. Now the sun was going down on another headsplitting day of heat and light.

In the bathroom I splashed cold water on my face, but it wasn't enough. I had to get out.

'Where you goin', fuckhead?' Fat-gut rasped, when the fetid lift had delivered me into the lobby.

'Yeah yeah yeah,' I said. 'Fuck off.'

'Yeah, next time you bring home booze you better bring home some pussy, too, or I'm gonna fuck *your* skinny ass.' I gave him the vee and got almost to the door when he suddenly barked: 'Hey! Fuck, I forgot. There's a message for you. Mick took it. Now where the fuck . . .?'

I walked back across the lobby. Dizzy, I leaned on the desk while he hunted.

'Fuckin' Irishman never . . . I told him I got a freakin' *system* for—Ah, got it.'

He straightened first himself then a greasy slip on which a message had been scrawled. I don't know whether it would have had more impact if he had been courteous enough to hand it to me to read myself. In any case he didn't. He growled it out with the cigar still wedged in the corner of his mouth.

'Call Gozzano. Gozzano says he's got nooz.' He lowered the slip and looked at me with his habitual expression of acute constipation. 'Who da fuck is Gozzano?' he said.

A strange cab ride to the Church of the Holy Name. Sun down, the city's lights mercurial. My head lolled on the back seat. I suffered half-dreams and startings, was buzzed around by a swarm of television jingles and advertising images. My driver's look in the rear-view: You got the fare, chief? Yeah, I got the fare. Don't throw up in my cab. I won't, I promise. Time didn't quite stop, but deviated from its normal behaviour, meandering through the twilight and neon, taking little side roads and rests, pooling unpredictably at the crosswalks where headlit humans came suddenly near, stark and intimate, bright and distinct as exotic birds. Someone's yellow vest. A scarlet thatch of hair. Two legs in black and gold stripes, striding with the gait of a stiltwalker. I remember (ludicrous, *ludicrous*) wiping tears away. I wasn't thinking of Malone. I wasn't thinking of Deborah and our upcoming trip into the country. I wasn't, I believe, thinking at all – but was accompanied by my childhood. I sat next to it like an amnesiac next to his unknown family.

'He's not well,' Gozzano said. 'He's been living on the street. He took a beating. The chaplain at Beth Israel recognized him.'

'Beth Israel?'

'A hospital. I don't know if he's awake. He's been sleeping, on and off, for the last two days.'

We sat one behind the other in the pews, him in profile, me glancing between him and the candlelit altar, above which a crucified Christ was flanked by the Virgin Mary (serpent daintily trampled underfoot) and the tabernacle, draped in iridescent green. The altar front had a bland sub-Leonardo relief of the Last Supper, fat-breasted dove spreading its wings above Jesus's head. Take this, all of you, and eat it, for this is My body, which will be given up for you.

'I was surprised to get your message,' I said.

The black eyes stared at the floor for a few moments. The pitted skin glowed in the candlelight. A jaw peppering of coagulated blood from a dull razor. The waxy hair in need of a wash. The argument with God continued, I supposed. Exhaustion stretched behind him in a wake littered with prayers, imprecations, novenas, rosaries. It was consuming him, this battle – or purifying him.

I cleared my throat. 'Father?'

'I wasn't going to call,' he said, his voice hoarse. 'I had decided not to, after our last meeting. But it wouldn't go away, the thought that I should. I asked God.'

'And He told you to tell me?'

Gozzano smiled and blinked, slowly, in pain, not amusement. 'No,' he said. 'God is silent. I have had no sense of His presence – of His existence – since Valentina's death.'

I knew there was nothing more important to him than this, but I struggled to pay attention. If I lay down in the pew, I thought, I would fall immediately into a deep sleep.

'So I made the decision without God,' he said. 'What else is one to do?'

The priest's living quarters consisted of a small lounge, a kitchen, a bathroom and a bedroom, all sparsely furnished and immaculately clean. The bedroom window looked out onto the garden, cheering what would otherwise have been a singularly joyless cell.

'I'll be just next door,' Gozzano said.

For a few moments I stood back from the creature in the single bed, listening to the phlegmy rattle of its breathing Then I went to the plastic bedside chair and sat down.

He was very changed. The cables from jaw to collarbone hung slack in two shrivelled dewlaps. The face was sunken and crazily, prodigally wrinkled. One eye was opaque white, the other milkily veiled. The skin of the hands, formerly the colour of black tea, bordered on translucency, barely covering a revel of veins and capillaries. The whole nail of the ring finger was off. It seemed as if his jaw had receded – as with the removal of dentures – but between the rimed lips I saw his own tall and tarnished teeth, though several were missing. Only the remains of the white Beckett thatch testified to his identity, that and the hawkish, long-nostrilled nose.

He lay in the crisp bed propped up on several pillows, wearing thin blue pyjamas, the jacket very short in the sleeves – Gozzano's, I inferred.

'Who's there?'

However shocked at the changed appearance, the changed voice shocked more. Gone resonance, depth, certainty. Here instead an old-lady falsetto. 'Who's there?' he repeated.

'Father, you won't remember me,' I began.

'Tell Vincenzo I want to go now.'

'Father, please, listen for a moment. My name—'

'What? Who is that?'

'My name is Dominic Hood. We met many years ago at St Edmund's Primary School in Begshall. Do you remember?'

'I don't remember. Where's Vincenzo?'

'I know what happened to Valentina,' I said. 'I know she died.'

He turned his head to me and I looked into the wrecked eyes.

'Can you see me, Father Malone?'

'Who are you?'

'I'm nobody, nobody important. It's just that I remember you from many years ago because you did something extraordinary for me. Then I saw you again in Goa. I saw you, that night at the Fernandezes'.'

'I don't know you,' he said. He had lifted his head slightly. I saw what a strain it was for him.

'Please don't be alarmed, Father.'

'I'm not your father.'

'I know you think you failed with Valentina.'

'I killed her.'

'No, you didn't.'

'You don't . . . Who are you? Where's Vincenzo? Are you here to take my life?'

'No, no, please, Father, don't upset yourself.'

'If you are I'm ready.'

'I just wanted to talk to you. When I was ten years old . . . One day, Father, when I was ten years old, you came on a visit to St Edmund's Primary School in Begshall, your own old school, they said it was, though I found that hard to believe. You remember Miss Warburton?'

He rested his head back on the pillow and began, to my horror, crying. The wasted hands came up to cover his face. I looked around the room. A box of Kleenex on the chest of drawers. A glass of water and a half-empty jug. I got up and fetched him a tissue, tried to get his hands away from his face, but he resisted. I let them be. Instead placed my own hand on the mighty forehead (the winds, sands and ocean sprays of the world had . . .) while he snivelled and mewled.

'Listen to me,' I said, quietly now. 'All I want you to do is listen to me for a few moments and see if you can help me remember something from long ago. Then I'll leave you in peace, all right?' The grown-up's melodious tone for the anxious child. I felt sick to hear myself – and sickened further when, between sniffs, he said in a tiny voice:

'All right.'

I looked up and saw Gozzano standing in the doorway, watching. We looked at each other, said nothing. I leaned close to Malone, smelling old-man skin, a Beechams powder drink on his breath, the starched sheet, Vicks chest rub.

'Twenty-four years ago, when I was ten, you came to my school in Begshall, in Lancashire, in England. Miss Warburton was my teacher – as she said she was yours, though as I say, I found that hard to—'

'Vincenzo?'

'Yes?'

'What time is it?'

'Just after ten-thirty p.m., Father.'

'In my class there was a boy called Callum Burke,' I continued. 'Callum and I were enemies.'

Malone sat up and made groping movements as if to get out of bed. Gozzano rushed over. 'Ignatius, no, no, no. You must rest. Come along, now.'

'I must go.'

'No, no, you must not. You're not well, my friend, and I am looking after you.'

A look askance from Gozzano. I said: 'Just a few minutes. Please. *Please*, Father.'

We both looked down at the man in the bed. His face was wet and a slug of snot had crept from one nostril. Gozzano took the tissue from my hand and wiped it away, then laid his hand along Malone's cheek. 'Shall we hear this young man's story, Father,' he said, 'just to pass the time a little?' But Malone didn't answer. The one opaque eye (it looked as if someone had plucked the original out and replaced it with a cue ball) was almost closed. The other eye flickered, incapable of focus.

'One day,' I said, taking his hand – onion-skinned, gothically knuckled – in mine, as he with saurian deliberation tongue-moistened his cracked lips, 'Callum and I were fighting, you see, and I chased him out of the school and across the playing fields and into the wood. I chased him for a long time between the trees and the flowers, Father, but in the end . . . in the end, because I was chasing him, he fell into a ditch.'

I had faltered because I had caught a whiff of shit – unmistakable. Malone lay very still, one crescent of the white eyeball visible, the other still twitching. His fingers had tightened on my hand and I'd withdrawn it. Now he held the sheet up close to his lips as if employing a giant napkin. His mouth moved, slightly. When I moved close I could hear him whispering Latin.

'I'll get something,' Gozzano said. 'I'm sorry, Dominic, you'd better go and wait for me in the other room.'

'Callum Burke fell into a ditch lined with stone slabs, Father. He cracked his skull and died. He was dead. I sat on the edge and watched a puddle of blood form round his face.'

'Dominic, enough.'

'But you came and sent me to look along the path for your rosary, Father.'

'Dominic stop at—'

'And there was no rosary on the path, because it was in your pocket, but when I came to find you Callum was alive, large as life walking at your side, Father, alive again. Alive, you see, after having been dead. Now how was that possible, Father Malone? You tell me, will you? I've waited a long time to see you.'

Gozzano had come round to my side of the bed and taken my arm. Gentle pressure, easing me away from the bed. I resisted.

'He doesn't understand you,' Gozzano said. 'He doesn't remember.'

'Father?' I said. Malone didn't respond. Tremendous physical strength in Gozzano waiting for an opportunity to spend itself. It would, I knew, do him good; it would let him claim something back, to fight me, something small in recompense for his niece, and Malone, and his suffering, and God's silence, it would give him something euphoric to do with his limbs. I very nearly co-operated, feeling my fists clenching and my knees atingle, but Malone threw the sheet off and got out of bed. Before Gozzano could grab him he had stumbled into the chest of drawers and gone down hard on all fours, gasping. The pyjama bottoms, dark with wet, stinking shit, were absurdly short in the legs, too, and revealed Malone's withered and varicosed calves when he knelt. His feet were calloused, yellow-tinged.

I covered my face with my hands. Uncovered. Malone had gone down into a foetal position (the same sequence – it flashed to me – as mine on the day of Burke's assault with cricket bat). Gozzano was trying to get him upright. 'Ignatius, come on, get up and let's get you to the bathroom. Come on,' then suddenly, '*Fucking move yourself, for Christ's sake.*'

Dominic Hood, meanwhile, observed, blood gone heavy.

'Help me get him to the bathroom,' Gozzano said. He had one of Malone's mantis arms round his neck and had hauled him up onto one knee. Malone's other arm looked dead, stroked. The dark and big-boned head ducked and dipped, as if nodding in gentle agreement with something. 'Help me, will you?' Gozzano said, but he had managed to get the old man to his feet and was walking him to the door. Malone in minty blue pyjamas leaking excrement, snivelling again, moved alongside him like a giant and delicate puppet.

'I don't remember,' he said, quietly, to Gozzano – the amnesiac's honest aside to his lawyer. 'You know, I forget . . .'

I put my hand in my pocket and pulled out the rosary. *This* rosary, Father Malone, I had intended to say, producing it, theatrically. This rosary I have in my hand. Don't you remember?

I thought of turning down the sheet and dropping it into a shit stain. But didn't. I hung it around Christ's neck, on the crucifix, above the bed.

There was a storm the evening I said my third and final goodbye to my beloved Deborah Black. Indeed, there were storms all the day and all the night. Not quite a random detail, I think, Devil or no Devil.

I don't remember the journey from the church back to the Studio Hotel. Only that the small hours found me sitting not on the bed but on the floor in the corner under the window with exhausted limbs and drunk face flashed upon by the parking garage's autistic neon, listening to Manhattan's rain and the first stirrings of distant thunder.

'Time to go.'

Three a.m. The mobile. Deborah.

'Now?'

'Yes, now. I'll pick you up outside the hotel. Half an hour.'

Ordinary words again. I showered, quickly and clumsily, alternating hot and cold water (an alleged cure for jet-lag I'd read in one of teen Pen's shop-lifted Harold Robbinses), brushed my teeth, changed into clean clothes, drank a pint of the Studio's dubious tap water then took the lift down to the lobby, where, lullabyed by CNN, the Irishman was dozing on duty. I crept past, slipped out onto the stoop. The rain's static and time filling with fragments – the snack you can pay no eat-between-meals attention to that man as on a darkling behind the curtain plane stick it up your for mash get no abstract reason – until there was the dark car (black, American, conspiratorial) with my beloved at the wheel, her face a pale oval behind the rain-speckled glass of the driver's window.

I tried to kiss her when I got in, tried to force myself to grasp it all in the appropriate way, but she backed and got her hand between us, not angrily, but as if disappointed by the crassness or vulgarity of the idea, a nuance of the Devil's proscriptions I'd missed. There was the one giant vulgarity towards which we were heading, of course, but it was permissible only if all its antecedents were decorous and restrained.

'Where are we going?'

But she shook her head at that, too, irritated. 'Don't talk to me,' she said, quietly, as we pulled away from the hotel. 'I don't drive very often. I need to concentrate. I don't want to have an accident. You've been drinking.'

'Is it *verboten*?'

'This isn't a game, you know.'

'Shut up and concentrate, then.'

'Maybe this is a mistake.'

'Just fucking drive, Deborah, for fuck's sake. Just drive.'

Which – no doubt because I had never spoken like that to her before – had the astonishing effect of making her shut up and drive.

I managed to keep awake until we were out of the city with, I suppose, some fairy-tale or crime-novelishly inherited idea that I must keep track so that I could find my way back, or construct an appropriate alibi, or God only knew what. Moot, in any case, because when we crossed the George Washington Bridge, heading into more rain and the first cobalt scabs of daylight, I closed my eyes (with the intention of easing the bourbon's sting) and fell immediately into a deep sleep.

I didn't dream. Or if I did, didn't remember it. I woke (hung over, with sour guts and a plough blade buried behind my eyes) to American thunder, dehydration and the sight of Deborah at the wheel, driving with a look of tranquil absence I'd never seen on her before, as if the miles from New York had mesmerized her. She glanced at me, blankly, then turned back to the road.

I sat up and looked out: a sky of bruised and voluble

clouds; summer fields pea green and waxy; conifers in huddled congregations; a premature darkness.

We passed through small, clean towns, all much the same:
the scatter of white houses and the single drag, abandoned in
the rain. Here and there Dutch barns in confectioners'
colours. Pennsylvania. I imagined myself looking down at
North America from the stratosphere: a wrinkled and
strangely breathing homunculus on the face of the waters.
One godlike glance east would show me England's blanched
and crenulated coast . . .

Deborah pulled the car into a gas station, deserted but for
its solitary attendant and one young couple at the edge of the
steaming asphalt, putting air in the tyres of their Volkswagen
van. The boy, in combat trousers and a pink vest, was tanned
and leanly muscled, with a head of roughly chopped black
hair and a Celtic tattoo circling his upper arm. He crouched
at the tyre, frowning. The girl stood bent, holding a faded
denim jacket over them against the rain. I could see nothing
of her but a pair of turquoise hotpants and two short golden
legs ending in white laceless baseball boots.

For a moment, after she'd switched the engine off,
Deborah sat still, staring at the couple through the rain-
struck windscreen. Then she blinked and came to, unclipped
her seatbelt, found her shoes and slipped them on.

'Stay here,' she said. She got out of the car and hurried to
the kiosk.

I unbuckled and reached across to the driver's doorwell for
a spied plastic bottle of tepid Evian, drank all that was left,
then lay down across the seats, head in the still-warm impres-
sion left by Deborah's backside and thighs. Rain
Tommy-gunned the saloon. *My whole life's been leading up to
this*, I'd said to David. I'd meant Malone. Thought I'd meant
Malone. No. Of course. This. Not just this trajectory – the

phone call, the miles, the articulate silences between us – but this particular constellation of details: the day's chain of storms; the gas station bearing all the colours of America's myth; the taste of plastic and old water; the car's smell of vinyl and fuel; my cheek in the ghost of her body heat.

Without any motive I was aware of, I reached forward and sprang the catch that opened the driver's glove box. Three items: a pack of complimentary mints; a map of Manhattan; a handgun.

It looked like the guns of my imagination, I suppose, like screen guns, though on picking it up I discovered the unexpected gravity and chill, its mass and pent kick, its chambered consequences, its one succinct and disinterested solution. One's hand understood, immediately, with acute déjà vu.

When Deborah returned (having touched up her makeup) I was back in the passenger seat, shoes off, flexing my toes. A whiff of the lemony perfume came in with her. The short dash between kiosk and car had blotched her black silk blouse with rain. Either the thought that I might have looked in the glove box hadn't occurred to her, or it had and she was indifferent to it. I put my hand on her knee – but again the impatient look – so I left her to starting the engine, swinging the car across the forecourt, easing us back out onto the iridescent road.

Half an hour later we stopped again in a lay-by overhung with dripping plane trees. Deborah punched a number on her mobile phone.

'We're not far. No. As before. Twenty minutes, maybe. *Bien.*'

The roads narrowed. Between towns the houses were bigger, privately wooded or sprawlingly lawned. Now Deborah was awake. She smoked a Gauloise in fierce, precise increments. I watched the slight movements of her hands and thighs. A source of rich pleasure to me, that the car's weight and power was entirely dependent on her small body and measureless will.

The road forked and Deborah took the left, plunging us into a tunnel of shadow beneath overarching trees. The route climbed gently through wet and glistening woodland; then pale gateposts on the right, a drive lined with mulberry bushes and silver birches, a clearing, and a large white detached house built in a hollow of the hill. In the dull storm light the building was surreally distinct. They'd picked it for its isolation. They. Them. Whoever they were. Deborah's and my (and, presumably, Clifford's) silent partners, the fix-its, the facilitators, the voices on the other end of the line.

Deborah killed the engine and sat for a moment in silence looking at the house. I imagined it having been hurled down from the sky. It defined this spot like a gravid and brilliant icon. All the windows were dark. It had had families, and would again: well-off American adults with strong-boned teenagers and anxious young; it would host troubled Thanksgivings and harmless sex, poisonous quarrels, Dad's bathroom epiphanies and Mom's early-morning griefs; it would rattle with friendly possessions and absorb decades of ordinary, unarticulated love.

But not yet.

Rain came down hard and lightning went over the hills in a bluish shiver. One one thousand two one thousand three one thousand four one thousand then thunder like a giant tree starting to fall, then a sudden stop, then the completed crash and rumble.

'I'm incredibly thirsty,' I said.

Deborah moved in a hiss of silk and nylon to straddle me, without a word. More than the sudden weight of her on my lap, it was the way in which she had abandoned the driver's seat – a place, a role, a set of instruments, a means that had brought about the desired end and therefore was no longer required – that tightened my scrotum, released the first blood-innuendos. More arousing than the dark stocking tops and magnolia thighs revealed by my hands' single slide up her dress was her blank pragmatism: the car had brought us here; it could be temporarily forgotten; we could begin.

Thunder mumbled and the rain thinned to a mist. Her big mouth tasted of the recent cigarette and the ghost of the gas station's freshen-up. She kissed me unequivocally, licking my teeth, biting my lips, receiving my tongue with feints and flickers. For a moment she was physically very close – the citric perfume and floury scent of cosmetics – then she was gone, through the passenger door and out into the heat. The land's smell rushed in, resinous and mulchy. I sat for a moment waiting for my pulse to settle. Deborah walked round the steaming bonnet and opened the driver's door. I watched while she took the gun from the glove box and dropped it into her bag.

'Come on,' she said.

By the time we got to the back door the rain had eased, then suddenly come down again, with new bulletins of thunder. Large drops fell and burst on the porch. I followed her inside.

The house was furnished comfortably but without con-viction, a place to be visited and made use of without sentiment. An airy kitchen with scrubbed pine worktops, a terracotta floor, copper light fittings and a gigantic fridge which, when opened, displayed to my surprise fruit, French bread, cold meats and cheeses, rows of Dos Equis, Pepsi, Perrier, and a dozen bottles of wine. I took a Pepsi and swallowed as much of it at one go as my parched throat would allow, amused at my own surprise: naturally the fridge was stocked; if they'd thought it out this far, why would they fall short of refreshments?

I joined Deborah on the couch in the lounge. The veil of blood had lifted a little for both of us, unsatisfactorily (disturbed by the rain on the back porch, the fumble with the keys, the snap and hiss of the Pepsi, the presence of magazines and newspapers – today's, on inspection – on the bay window's seat), and now we must do what we could to draw it down around us again. Therefore on the couch we kissed like ravenous automata, fondled and squeezed each other with a kind of bored urgency until, after multiple false starts and dead ends, we had what we needed: that throbbing intimation of a profound wisdom – a deification – waiting on the other side of what we were about to do. I was bothered by the mechanics of organization. I was bothered by the click-scratch of connection to someone on the other end of the phone – by the *Bien*.

No talking, naturally. Yes, I freed her breasts from blouse and bra, yes, moistened their tips with my tongue, felt her cool fingers round my cock, felt her face's heat, saw the eyes gone dead and close, heard the little sounds of bad-tempered arousal on her lips, but all that was only a means to a rare and particular end: a shared and dreadful apotheosis. Yes, we rubbed and squeezed each other, carefully, pressure and friction and reciprocated looks of yes, yes we *are* calculated to lead us on to the level which would demand the next thing, and the next and the next and the many nexts until there would be no next things.

She stopped me and kissed me long and deeply with a little groan of restrained indulgence; I started to feel it, then, the downward pull into a lower level of being, a steadily pulling promise, surprised to find that divinity was the shape concealed beneath the skin of the beast.

We disengaged. Deborah got up and straightened her clothing. We grinned at each other, as if our faces were not in our own control. It was like – *so* like – that state of giddiness partaken of by Dominic Hood, Kelly Saunders, Stew Fletcher and poor Elaine in the warped and dawdling minutes leading up to the first struck match. (Stick it up your hairs, as Stew would have said. Any objection?) That state of giddiness in which the boundaries of our selves threatened dissolution. A final fusion would be required if we were to do the work in hand. Certainly *I* required it. Certainly I wasn't up to it alone. Certainly it had always been me and someone larger. Certainly it had always, even before I'd encountered her, been me and my beloved Deborah Black.

Picking up her handbag, she turned and went into the hall. I followed her.

At the door that led down to the basement we paused and kissed again, gracelessly. I snaked a hand up her short dress and into her panties – but for the first time since she'd picked me up at the hotel felt a flicker of doubt. Something was missing. That presence which, with Alice, had thickened the ether. I had a brief, vivid memory of myself dropping the postcard to Pen into the mailbox. A feeling flitted into and out of me: that there was a great wave of inappropriate laughter welling up inside me. It came and went like a butterfly, this feeling, then disappeared.

No. As before. Twenty minutes, maybe. *Bien.*

Deborah took the key from its hook and unlocked the door to the basement. It swung open soundlessly to reveal a flight of a dozen or so steps going down beneath the house. She flicked a switch just inside the doorway and four bare bulbs burst into vulgar light. The stairs were covered, untidily, in black plastic sheets. Again the sudden sense of bottled laughter, the thought that if I let it out, it would overwhelm me.

And still that something (what if not the Devil?) missing. I stood at the top of the stairs, sniffed and listened for him, but the ether was empty. Even the storm (which I had assumed was his stroke of self or genre parody) seemed to be abating.

Nonetheless, down the stairs.

The room was lined with the same black plastic throughout, walls, ceiling, floor. I took in a large couch and two armchairs, a red sports bag in one corner, and against the wall to my left an eight-by-four steel container, padlocked. It was only after these that I noticed the hook and cable suspended from the ceiling and the two hooks coming up through the plastic, bolted to the floor.

Deborah put the handbag down on the couch and moved across to the container. She placed her hands flush against its lid, as if trying to determine its contents clairvoyantly. I moved close behind her, cupped her breasts and licked her ear. She rubbed her backside against me, turned her head for me to suck her curled tongue.

Another key in the padlock. Breathing heavily, I stepped up beside Deborah and helped her lift the container's lid. Tumescence equivocated, burgeoning and waning. I lifted Deborah's skirt with the intention of pulling her panties off, but stopped at the sound of something moving in the container.

Together, we drew back what looked like a painter's spattered tarp to reveal what lay beneath.

Deborah spoke very calmly to her. 'This is a gun. Can you feel it? If you co-operate, you won't be hurt. Do you understand?

It's very important you don't attempt to resist. Nod your head if you understand me. Good. Now, we're going to get you up from here, and it'll be necessary for just a short time to attach your wrists above your head. I know you don't know what's going on, and that this is frightening for you, but you must trust me. If you want to leave here unharmed, it's vital that you don't struggle. Do you understand?'

The girl looked about twenty, maybe twenty-five – hard to tell past the blindfold and tape. (There would come a time when we would take the blindfold off. It had been necessary up to this point, but now it was just a prop; its removal would be another calibration of our conviction.) She was thin, with red elbows and bitten nails. The gap between the waistband of her faded jeans and cropped purple T-shirt showed a skinny white belly with a shallow – indeed Elainish – whorl of a navel. Her hands were cuffed and her bare feet hobbled. I helped Deborah attach her to the hooks, an upright position that left the girl not quite flat-footed, but not quite on tiptoe either, revealing the faint blue matrix of veins beneath the skin of her midriff and lower ribs.

We backed and sat together on the couch to look at the girl. She was sobbing and mumbling behind the tape, but not struggling at all. I had a curious, acute sense of all the land and sea between myself and England: the rucked Allegheny Mountains and heaped Appalachians, the Dutch-tamed fields with their smithereens of Shawnee dead, unglamorous New Jersey looking across at Manhattan's imperious heights, then the meaty Atlantic and its joyless sweep all the way to Cornwall with its tiny collection of ghosts and bones. The land of Kelp's death. It brought a kind of vertigo, this vision, and I watched dizzily, as if from a great height, as Deborah undid my flies, tugged out my

468

half-erect cock, bent, slipped first just the glans into her mouth, then followed through and took it deep in one slow pass.

It wasn't fear that held me back. Certainly not fear of consequences. I had no doubt that sufficient precautions had been taken, sufficient money spent. This was, after all, a consumer item – albeit for an exclusive club of consumers – and if Deborah knew anything she knew how to spend money. But something distracted me. Tumescence waxed and waned. At moments I came very near to the state needed to proceed, then some indistinct portion of consciousness would get in the way. For the time being this flirtation with myself was pleasurable, but some anxiety lay close behind it.

Very loud was the silence of the unearthly realm, bare of either God or the Devil. The girl on the cable was absolutely alone. Her cries would go unheard, we would lap up her tears, string out pain for days, weeks, months without fear of interruption. I had no doubt that we might do what we willed, proceed into the great arena. I had no doubt at all.

With barely veiled impatience Deborah got to her feet. She left the gun on the arm of the couch and crossed to the sluggishly wriggling girl. I followed, protruding cock still bobbing absurdly between flaccidity and erection. Together we stood close to her, knowing she could feel the warm radius of our bodies. I undid Deborah's skirt. It dropped to the floor and she stepped out of it. I pulled down her panties and she repeated the careful step, leaving only shoes and blouse, the uniform of indulgence and impunity. Letting the tip of my cock enter her from behind, I reached round and filled my hands with her breasts, kissing and licking her right ear while she spoke again to the girl:

'Listen to me carefully. You're not leaving this place.' (The girl's mumbling increased; she shifted her weight from foot to foot.) 'No one knows you're here. No one is coming to rescue you. You're all alone. I don't know whether you believe in God, but this is where you find out whether God believes in you.' She stopped, and with a movement of her hips against mine made it clear that silence, now, from me, was unacceptable.

Therefore I opened my mouth and out came words. 'The time you've got left is going to be spent in pain,' I said. 'Terrible pain.' (The girl writhed, attempting to hook herself away from us; a long groan from behind the tape. My cock slipped out of Deborah's cunt. I had a strange feeling, as if dozens of long-tensed muscles throughout my body were one by one beginning to relax.) Nonetheless I continued: 'Soon, all you'll want is to die. But you won't, not for a long, long time. The pain will be unbearable, and you'll be forced to bear it again and again and again. Your purpose between now and the end will be to suffer. Do you understand? It's only your suffering we want.'

I thought, with Cartesian clarity and distinctness: No one is going to stop us.

It arrived, this thought, with silent inevitability, and with it the beginning of another feeling like the earlier temptation to inappropriate laughter.

Deborah moved behind the girl and licked her neck, at which the girl flinched and roared behind the tape as if she'd been burned. Deborah laughed, quietly, reaching round and lifting the purple T-shirt up over the diaphragm, the palpitating ribs, the small, braless breasts. I watched as the girl twisted and groaned, as if some combination of these sounds and movements could free her; but of course there was nowhere for her to go.

At which I found that I had backed away and sat down on the couch. I felt very heavy, minutely conscious of the weight of my body and the unique space it occupied. Deborah was moving her fingertips over the girl's pale flesh, as if searching for a hidden mark. I looked down to see that my cock had softened completely. I put it back inside my trousers and zipped up my flies. After a moment, I picked the gun up and examined it. Deborah had gone over to the sports bag and was down on her bare haunches rummaging in it, a finicky artisan searching for a particular tool. The girl was sobbing, now, steadily. I found the safety catch and adjusted it. (I thought: You come to America, eventually you handle or are confronted by a gun.) I looked at the girl again, wondering if she did believe in God, and whether, having understood her position, she was calling upon Him to come to her rescue.

The feeling of heaviness passed, and was replaced by one of absurd lightness. Walking across the rucked plastic, I was convinced that only the gun's weight in my hand prevented me from floating up to the ceiling.

I stood next to the girl. I could smell her: sweat, urine, old denim, greasy hair. Sour breath came through her raw nostrils. Snot had been forced out of her nose and now slid over the tape that sealed her mouth. The innumerable details of her coalesced to form an overwhelmingly distinct particular: a person, this person, here, now – her. I wondered what her name was and what books she'd read. I considered that when she died the tally of her body's life would be complete: so many nail-clippings, so many haircuts, so many tears, laughs, sneezes, coughs, farts, blinks, hiccups. So many thousand dreams and wakings. So many thousand kisses. The earlier thought returned: No one is going to stop us. For the last time I hesitated, attending to the unseen for any sign of a presence. But it was empty. There were three of us in the room: the girl on the cable, Deborah Black, and me. That was all.

Deborah, who had been absorbed in her search through the sports bag, rose and turned to see me holding the gun.

Right up until the words left my mouth I had no clear idea of what I was going to say. Then the words were in me – and out:

'Tell me a joke,' I said.

She had a long plaited leather crop in her hand. Seeing her look surprised, it occurred to me that it was the first time I'd seen her look surprised. *That* surprised.

'What?'

'Tell me something funny. Anything.' The empty air reached tentacles into my mouth and one by one pulled these words out, each one inevitable and fresh.

Deborah stared at me for a moment, then took a step forward.

'Don't move,' I said. 'Just tell me anything, anything that's ever really made you piss yourself laughing. Anything at all.'

'What are you talking about?'

The hanging girl had gone quiet but for the occasional sob. Deborah and I now stared at each other. Neither of us spoke. Dominic Hood very convinced that if he let go of the gun he would float up and bump softly against the ceiling. I looked away from Deborah for a moment and thought: This room is ridiculous. When I looked back at her in her shoes and blouse I knew that with only a slight effort I would be able to see her as ridiculous as well. Myself, standing there holding a gun, the most ridiculous of all. I almost burst out laughing. I could feel it, the great welter of reasons for yielding to laughter rising behind me like a glittering ocean wave. I knew I mustn't give in to it yet. If I gave in to it now I'd be incapable of doing what needed to be done. But it wasn't easy. The temptation was all but overwhelming, and the more I realized how important it was not to start laughing just yet the more difficult it became to resist.

Nonetheless I raised the gun again and pointed it at Deborah. 'Get dressed,' I said.

She stared at me. We had had a great deal of practice in the art of looking at each other and knowing without speaking what each other was thinking. Despite which, she said: 'Don't be stupid.'

I moved the gun to the right and pulled the trigger.

The loudest indoor noise I'd ever heard. A hole in the wall behind Deborah breathing wisps of plaster dust. My hand and wrist feeling like they'd been stomped on by a hoof. In my peripheral vision, the girl, starting, violently. Under the boom of the shot her gagged scream. Then silence returning, the air emptying.

Deborah put the crop on the floor. I kicked her panties and skirt to her and held the gun on her as she put them on.

'I'm sorry,' I heard myself saying. 'It's not quite in me to do this, apparently.'

CHAPTER EIGHT

The Old Medicine

Deborah drove. I sat in the back with the girl's gagged and blindfolded head in my lap and the gun in my hand. 'Forget what we said,' I told her. 'We're not going to hurt you. Don't worry.' She trembled, though she'd managed to stop whimpering once the car was in motion. Her head was a warm boulder in my lap. I stroked her hair and told her it was going to be all right if she just kept calm and didn't try anything mad. Obviously she didn't believe me. She'd heard that line before, after all.

Firing the gun had emptied my own skull of all but practical considerations. (Beyond them, however, still laughter poised in a giant, ultramarine, glittering wave, beyond the breaking of which was some vast space of air and freshness I had an intimation I might finally be allowed to enter.) Considerations such as: we'd have to release her before we ran out of gas. We'd have to make sure where we dropped her wouldn't readily connect with where we'd held her.

We'd have to make absolutely sure she didn't see us. I'd have to decide what to do about Deborah.

We drove for forty-five minutes. 'Where, exactly, am I driving?' Deborah had asked. 'Just in the opposite direction from where we started,' I'd told her. She drove west.

The weather remained dull, warm and rainy. Deborah steered in silence, aureoled in a dead fury. On a small road, a mile short of a place called Blue Spring, we stopped in a tiny lay-by overhung on both sides by dripping beech trees.

'How much money have you got in your purse?' I asked Deborah.

She looked, her face very still and slightly flushed. 'Four hundred and something.'

'Give it to me. You've got credit cards for gas, haven't you?'

She just looked at me.

'Okay,' I said. 'Now you're both going to have to help me.'

Under the gun's shaky direction I got Deborah to remove the leg-cuffs and guide our girl some thirty or forty paces into the woods that bordered the road. It was cooler under the wet trees, with a delicious smell of humus and rain. I had a job keeping the girl quiet. She was sure we were going to shoot her. 'We're *not* going to hurt you,' I kept saying. 'We're going to let you *go*.' But (who can blame her?) she sobbed and stumbled. Deborah held her elbow to prevent her from tripping and falling. Had anyone witnessed our progress I would have had some difficulty convincing them that despite driving two women at gunpoint through the undergrowth I was in fact doing both of them a favour. I glimpsed myself in the dock, feeble truth my only answer to the prosecutor's facetious cross-examination: 'Ah, so let me get this straight, Mr Hood. Your intention was to *release* the victim?'

I stopped perhaps twenty paces in. Deborah stared at me. It was still raining.

'Okay, now listen,' I said to the girl. 'This is what we're going to do. My friend is going to take the handcuffs off. You keep your eyes closed, and count to fifty, slowly. We'll have the gun pointed at you. We're not going to hurt you. It was a mistake. We're letting you go. But you have to give us that count of fifty. Understand?'

Sniffing, disbelief, nodding anyway. My stomach rumbled, loudly. I stuffed most of the bills into her pocket. 'There's three hundred dollars in your pocket and the road is directly behind you as you're standing now,' I said. 'When you get to the road turn left and go a mile or so and you'll come to a town called Blue Spring. Do you understand? Now remember: don't move until you've counted to fifty.'

Deborah stood with her arms folded and her weight on one leg, like a headmistress listening to an unlikely alibi.

'One more thing,' I said to the girl. She flinched and put her shoulders up as I stepped closer. 'Shshsh. Don't be afraid. Listen. One question. Tell me the truth. Has anyone, since you were taken, interfered with you, sexually?'

Deborah snorted, patently contemptuous of the idea. She shook her head when I looked at her, wearied by my naivety. No, imbecile, that's not how it works.

'Have they?' I repeated to the girl. 'Tell me the truth. I need to know.'

The girl hesitated, trying to guess what the right answer was, regardless of what the honest answer was. I could all but hear the calculations.

'Your answer won't make any difference to us letting you go. Just tell me the truth. Please.'

'This is ridiculous,' Deborah said.

Lowering her shoulders (if I'm going to die anyway I

476

might as well tell the truth), the girl shook her blindfolded head. No.

'Okay,' I said. 'Unlock the cuffs. Do it.'

I don't imagine she counted to fifty. I wouldn't have. In any case we were out of sight and away in seconds – not towards Blue Spring but east, towards the freeway, towards New York.

What should I have done about Deborah? Shopped her? Shot her in the head? Explained the choice between practising evil and keeping a sense of humour? Fucked her one last time, for the road, *on* the road?

It was a strange ride back to Manhattan, silent again, but not this time in any search for euphemism or code. I believe I wanted to feel sad, but couldn't. Felt instead either numb or hysterical, holding the gun between my knees.

She was balanced, I thought, between rage and disgust, neck flushed, small face set in glassy blankness. But however unbearable this was for her, this not tearing me apart, it permitted the same aversion of consciousness that had been necessary to get us down into the basement in the first place.

Meanwhile the rain hammered down around us as our funereal car ploughed back to Manhattan, Deborah bringing all her energy to bear on saying nothing, on keeping herself turned away, me slumped and happily exhausted, giggling now and then like a simpleton.

I should have shot her, I suppose. Back there in the Pennsylvania woods. One, in the back of the head. Rid the world of, et cetera.

Well, maybe I should and maybe I shouldn't. But since I wouldn't have shot myself, too, I couldn't face it. I couldn't face *knowing* her any more, either.

'You'd better keep the gun,' she said, having drawn up,

incredibly, at the Studio Hotel. I turned in my seat and studied her profile. She was such a beautiful, small-faced woman. Completely alone.

'That would be a threat, then, would it?' I said. 'What are you going to do? Send one of your father's goons after me?'

She sat with her hands on the steering wheel and the engine running. She didn't know what to say. If I'd handed her the gun there at that moment it's just possible that she would have pointed it at my head and pulled the trigger. Not for revenge, but as a way of ending her own appalling freedom. But I didn't hand it to her. I put it in my pocket. 'Well, I'll keep it,' I said.

I felt sorry for her because she was so torn between the need to speak and the need to stay silent. To speak would be to discharge rage. To stay silent would be to remain far enough away from herself to make even rage redundant. I wondered, looking at her small, white, dark-eyed face, what she would do when she got back to her apartment. I couldn't imagine. I had come to the end of being able to imagine her. I wasn't interested any more. I thought: How sad to have lost Natalie for this.

The last storm had peeled the air and brought out a thinner, nastier version of the city's odour, but it was bearable, even comforting at that moment. I slammed the passenger door and rounded the bonnet to the sidewalk. I could see beyond the stoop to where, in the nicotine-coloured lobby, Fat-gut stood in paunchy profile to the world with his head cocked in reverie, elbows gripped in plantain fingers, cigar protruding like a tumour. I went to the driver's window and indicated she should roll it down, which she did, electrically. It hummed, quietly, as it descended between us.

'I'm sorry,' I said. 'I'm not big enough to be of any help to you. I think this is the last time we'll see each other, don't you?'

I didn't know what was coming. I thought perhaps she was going to spit in my face. I was conscious of the light in the lobby at the top of the stoop behind me. I thought of all the miles we'd just travelled together, and how odd that we should be saying goodbye after so much silence. I did feel, just for a moment, sad.

'You fucking idiot,' she said.

I stood, hands on knees, as the window hummed up between us. She didn't look back at me. She indicated, got a gap, then pulled away. I sat down on the hotel's bottom step and lit an American Spirit.

And though for the first time since leaving London I missed them all I knew I couldn't go back. Instead, with absolutely the last money I had in my pocket, I took Lydia and Pete to dinner two days later.

'So the situation is this,' Pete said. We were at a restaurant, Mango Hub, Pete's choice, in the East Village. 'The situation is that you don't want to go home but you're broke and you don't want to borrow any money, right?'

'Well, yes, pretty much. I don't see any way round it.'

'Would you do anything to stay here? Any kind of work, I mean?'

'Anything I could do, I suppose, yes. Anything I was actually capable of.' (I had to shut myself down somewhat, dealing with the good, innocuous exchanges being riddled with mines.)

'There's Buddy's,' Pete said, looking at Lydia, then back at me. 'I mean, if you're really willing to do anything.'

'And you can stay at my place till you get on your feet a little,' Lydia said.

'He won't get on his feet working at Buddy's,' Pete said. 'That's the trouble with Buddy's. Buddy sits on his fat ass and you don't get on your feet.'

'Well, just till he finds something better,' Lydia said.

They both looked at me. 'You'd better tell me who Buddy is when he's at home,' I said.

Buddy was a fat evil dwarf-man from Brooklyn who ran a café just off Union Square. He had a basin haircut and a baggy face the colour of porridge, a cherubic mouth and two fat pouches under his eyes. All his employees were illegal workers (in my time Abdul, Siobhan, Islam, Raoul, Roberto and Buntu) on five dollars an hour. Workers, it turned out, were allowed a half-sandwich, a Coke and twenty minutes for lunch. If you didn't like it, hey, fuck you. Workers could be dismissed without notice or pay. If you didn't like it, hey, fuck you. There was a long list of these things ending in hey, fuck yous. It was perfect for me. I did a month of six-day weeks and lost a stone and a half. I wasn't even much of an inconvenience to Lydia, since I was only ever at her apartment to sleep. After an embarrassing and torturous struggle I persuaded her to let me give her thirty dollars a week (which, it subsequently transpired, she saved in a jar and gave back to me when I moved out) for the couch. I spent my free time eking out Bloody Marys at the Cutlass (a filthy alcoholics' bar on Second Avenue) or sitting in Washington Square Park, or just wandering around the city, browsing, browsing, never buying.

Then, at Lydia's suggestion (my own brain in the wake of Deborah's departure was good for not much more than receiving Buddy's brayed instructions, alcohol and sensory impressions) I put the ads in. Proofreading, research, editing, *improve the quality of your writing*. Not an instant success, but

I gradually began to get by, discovering in the process the near illiteracy of educated America.

A friend of Pete's was dumped by his girl and needed someone to share the rent. He, Ruben (Jewish father, Norwegian mother, thin, blue-eyed, with a face like a kestrel and blond, wispy, shoulder-length hair, struggling pianist with another band, Kneecap), slept in a bedroom the size of a fishtank guardian angeled by Debbie Harry and Harpo Marx while I took the living-room couch watched over by Iggy Pop and William Shatner, with folding chintz screens for privacy. 'I knew she was gonna dump me,' he admitted. 'But a fuckin *banker*, man? I mean, that's like finding out she was really a *guy*.' So I acquired a drinking partner for sessions at the Cutlass, where the barmaid, a hefty and brown-lipsticked biker with the largest uncosmeticized breasts I had ever seen, leaned on the heels of her hands and looked down at us over the bar, tutting and shaking her head with maternal weariness.

'Hey, guess what,' Julia said on the phone.

'What?'

'Are you sitting down?'

'Yes, I'm sitting down,' I lied. 'What is it?'

'I'm having a baby.'

I had just got back from my shift at Buddy's and was in fact standing just inside the door. I was exhausted.

'Say that again,' I said. 'I thought for a moment you said you were having a baby.'

'I'm having a baby,' Julia repeated. 'I'm having a baby and I'm three and a half months gone and I'm too old and everybody's already made a huge bloody deal about it, so please just take it in your stride, will you?'

I sat down on my bed-couch and lit a cigarette. 'Jesus Christ,' I said.

'Yeah yeah yeah. Look, just say you're happy for me.'

'I'm happy for you. When . . . I mean, how . . .?'

'In about six months. In the usual manner. Don't ask for details. Pot luck. He doesn't and won't know anything about it. Ships in the New York night. That's all the account you're getting. You and everyone else, for that matter.'

'Holy holy holy,' I said.

'Anyway, there you are. Now. What are you playing at, exactly?'

Penguin had done the sensible thing and moved Helen into the Camden flat. A Kelp-mission accomplished. *The Tamarind Tree* had been optioned by Miramax. Julia had sold the West Kensington flat and bought a house with a big garden in Crouch End.

'So are you going to tell me what you're doing or not?' I heard her blow on and then sip a hot drink. 'What happened with your involvement?'

'We're no longer involved,' I said. 'A necessary firework, now finished. That's all the account *you're* getting.'

'Fine,' Julia said. 'But how are you existing? I mean you're illegal, aren't you? You're not coming home for Christmas, I assume. Or the bloody obscene millennium.'

No, I wasn't. Christmas came and went (a movie Christmas, with snow, ding-donging Santas, four-dollars-an-hour elves, brilliant window displays and the Poor, staggering around blimpish with ragged layers wishing they had never been born) without my taking part in it.

Millennial New Year was rougher. I should have stayed indoors. *Would* have stayed indoors, I believe, had Lydia not insisted on my coming to her party. *Is Clifford Gill going to be there?* I had asked. *Not unless he's in a fucking good disguise,* Lydia had said. So I went.

I had wondered, periodically, whether I ought not to be expecting Deborah's retribution – the sniper's noon bullet, the balaclava'd night raid, the dawn hit-and-run – but had found it difficult to live in fear. Still, halfway through the countdown to midnight at Lydia's (a hundred or so people crammed into her loft to camouflage with desperate celebration their horror not at a thousand years having passed, but just those which constituted their own lives so far), I was hit (like them), by the full force of having been alive for the whole of my life, a third of which, at the most optimistic estimate, had already gone. Kelp had been dead for eighteen years. I was, whether I liked it or not, a man. God and the Devil had been driven out by the girl on the cable with, on either side of her like the two thieves, two truths: no one made you do it; no one came to the rescue. I had seen it, beyond argument, in her bared belly and taped mouth, in the cuffed wrists and the blindfold, in my own prevaricating member. It was a strange and naked world and we were each of us wrapped in more or less layers of dreadful freedom. Malone was in a monastery in Italy, a place in the mountains where they took care of priests God had seen fit to test beyond their strength. I stood among Lydia's guests and considered all the pieces that refused to fit: Burke's blood-uttering head in the ditch of stones. Michael Fernandez's evicted turdsnake coiled and inert on his chest. Fifty-six dead and us not among them. These things refused to submit – but what was one to do with them?

One mustn't rely on these things, I thought, while the crowd went *five . . . four . . . three . . .* It's not that one mustn't believe in them, it's just that one cannot, should not . . . *two . . .* rely on them, and so far I've lived my whole life . . . *one, Happy New Year!* And popopopopopopop went a hundred party poppers and *beeeeeeepaaaaarp* went dozens of car horns on Third Avenue and *yeaaahh* went the guests and *shshshsh* went the city and the old earth underneath it all with no one paying attention.

The first New Year I had no one it made sense to throw my arms round. So I didn't. For a surreal moment I just stood there in a bubble of silence despite the roar, jostled by the embracing bodies of the guests, alone, until with horror and relief I saw Ruben (she's *gone*, man, ah, Jesus, she's fucking *gone*) flailing towards me in tears and with crumpled mouth and thought: I wish Pen were here, complaining about something. But Ruben was upon me, mumbling incoherently and I suspected drooling into my Mickey Rourke in *Angel Heart* lapel, and there was nothing to do but accept him and hold him upright and tell him I knew, I knew, and everything was going to be all right and fuck it anyway let's get another drink for Christ's sake.

But we were caught up by this time in a slurred and bellowed rendition of 'Auld Lang Syne', which as it had until then and has ever since and will I don't doubt for the rest of my life served as the pure distillation of all my own and the world's aching sorrow and survival, and reduced me within three notes to near-hysterical tears, as Ruben and I clung to each other unsatisfactorily in the middle of the mob's hastily formed circle. Too many old acquaintances, too much forgot . . .

A bad moment, but it passed. January, February, March and April went by (no microelectronic meltdown, no survivalist new order, just the planet's ancient indifference to our petty modes and measurements) with me soldiering on at Buddy's. But the bits and pieces of proofing and coaching meant I could cut back to three twelve-hour shifts instead of six. I wrote, too, freelancing as Ruben Gould, who banked the cheques ('checks' here) minus more or less what it would cost him in tax, then handed me the rest in cash. *Shark Fishing Monthly, The Curator, The Roman Catholic Voice, Books & Pictures, Peak Magazine, Street Skate, The Smoker* – standards low and money variable, but vastly preferable to hacking veg at Buddy's.

Ruben was a brick. 'Ruben,' I said to him, 'you, my friend are a fucking *brick*.' 'No sweat, Nick. No sweat what ever.' I got used to being called Nick.

I caught Gozzano before he left for Italy. He was going back to Bologna, where his mother was ill – dying, I knew from his face. We sat in the little back garden as before. Scarlet poppies had come up in the borders.

'They look like the flames of the Holy Spirit,' I said. 'Or so my sister says.'

'A writer?'

'A painter. A pregnant painter. Out of wedlock, too.'

Eliciting the dismissive gesture formerly seen in response to the free will and God's plan koan. We were drinking not Sam Adams but homemade lemonade, courtesy of one of the Holy Name's Hispanic cleaning ladies.

'You're not coming back, are you?' I asked. He still looked tired, but cleanly so. The ghastly patina I'd seen before had passed from him.

He looked up at the blue spring sky. 'There's a quality of light in Italy you don't get anywhere else in the world,' he said. 'If you've grown up in it then move away you feel as if there's always something wrong with your eyesight.'

'I didn't realize Jesuits were at such liberty to come and go.'

'They're not.'

'Meaning?'

He looked away, pitted face glowing in the non-Italian

light. 'I'm no kind of priest at the moment,' he said. 'Perhaps never will be again. The horrifying thing about that is the relief it brings. It's the relief that makes me suspicious.'

We shook hands in the vestibule, and he gave me a small hardback book with a black cloth cover and its title embossed in silver. *Weapons in a Real War: The Sacraments, Evil, and Equivocation in the Modern Catholic Church* by Fr Ignatius Malone. 'Out of print,' Gozzano told me. 'I thought you might like to have one.'

It was a beautiful day, even in so ugly a place. I realized I hadn't been to mass at Easter. Wondered how Gozzano had felt at Communion, wondered if he'd made it through the Athanasian creed: *I believe in One God, the Father, the Almighty, Maker of heaven and earth, of all that is seen and unseen . . .*

Meanwhile spring sunlight on the asphalt, garbage cans, wretched dandelions. Across the street in a wire-fenced schoolyard half a dozen black teenagers were playing basket-ball. With Gozzano's hand in mine I wondered what had happened to the attraction. Impossible to tell whether it, specifically, had gone, or had merely subsided along with all other libidinal activity in the post-Deborah world.

'You're staying, yourself?' he asked.

'I can't go home just now,' I said. 'The opposite of your condition, actually.'

There's no home like place. There's no home-like place. There's *no* homelike place . . .

Then, in September, against my better judgement and in ignorance of who or what I might become in doing it, I started seeing Holly.

◆

'Well, at least I know why you've been so nice to me.'

We sat facing each other on the fire escape, perhaps half an hour before dawn. Someone had let a fire hydrant off in the street below. A lovely smell of evaporating street water drifted up to us.

She had showered while I'd made coffee. Ten minutes out on a mid-July fire escape and her hair was dry. Her face looked small and scrubbed. Sawn-off denims and a white vest. There was already a line of sweat along her clavicle. Her feet were still and golden, the toenails white-varnished. I hadn't known, quite, in the way that one doesn't, what I felt for her, until now, it having come to leaving. I was stupidly surprised by the complex ambush of emotion. What in the old world I would have supposed to be love.

'I should go,' I said.

She drew on her Marlboro, exhaled, nibbled a nail. 'Yes,' she said.

'I've got my ticket,' I said. I had bought it, forced myself not to hope.

She looked at me and I saw that she knew that even that had been an expression of hope, a daring of the gods to prove me wrong.

'I can't,' she said.

'I know.'

A UPS van rattled and shuddered past below us, then the street went quiet again.

'How do you know I'm not going to the cops?' she said. Not angrily. With genuine curiosity.

'I don't,' I said.

She stared at me, trying, I knew, to see it all. Some kind of residue.

'I can't,' she said again. She didn't mean the cops. She meant me. 'If you stayed . . . You should go.'

She leaned her head back against the rail, looking up at the variegated sky. For a long while she said nothing. Then: 'I need to go away for a while. Some big place. Arizona, maybe. Texas. I don't know.'

Which was as much of a concession to herself as she was going to allow, or allow me to hear.

'It'll do you good to get away from this place,' I said.

She lowered her head and looked at me. 'Still worried about warnings from the dead?'

I hadn't meant that, just that going away would help with getting the taste of me out. But I did, now that she'd mentioned it, wonder if she would be safe.

'It's okay to believe in these things,' I said. 'Maybe not okay to rely on them, though.'

'You have to go now.'

'I know.'

'I don't want to see you any more.'

'I've left numbers on the thing. I'll be at Lydia's if you . . .'

Slow, pained blinking. Her face turned in profile. Angry at the nearness of tears.

'You should go now. Go on. Please go now.'

A week later, having lived and worked illegally in the United States for the better part of two years, I took a red-eye from John F. Kennedy airport to Heathrow, London, England.

'Holy Mary, Mother of God,' Pen said, when he opened the door.

'Wrong,' I said.

'Holy Christ.'

'Wrong again.'

'Who is it?' Helen called from the lounge.

Pen just stood there with his mouth open and his shirt

488

half out of his trousers. I hadn't told anyone I was coming. 'I don't believe it,' he said. I kissed him on the lips. He needed a shave, and his breath was louche with whisky. 'I don't believe it,' he repeated. Helen appeared in the hallway. 'It's bloody Dummie,' Pen said. 'It's bloody Dominic Hood.'

I didn't recognize the Camden flat. It was clean. The curtains matched. There were rugs. Books. Things.

'Christ why not turn into fucking *adults* all of a sudden,' I said. 'I leave you alone for five minutes—'

'Shut up shut up shut up shut up,' Pen said. 'Tell us everything. Tell us everything, for God's sake.'

As the evening unspooled via booze and cigarettes I reclined by degrees until I found I was lying on my back on the carpet telling (some, naturally, of) my tale to the ceiling's stucco rosette. When I next looked up Pen and Helen were curled up together on the couch, whispering.

'You fell asleep,' Helen said.

'Talking gibberish and fell asleep,' Pen said.

'It's jet-lag,' I said. 'Sorry.'

'It's Scotch,' Helen said. 'I've got to go to bed, Sunday or no Sunday tomorrow.'

They made an awful fuss of me, the pair of them. The sofa-bed was unfolded and fitted out with crisp linen and a hefty quilt. A large glass of iced water and two Nurofen within reach. Helen even produced the last toothbrush I'd had before leaving for New York, which Penguin had refused (he denied this now) to throw away.

When Helen went into the bathroom Pen looked at me, warily, and said: 'You all right?'

'Don't I look all right?'

'You look like you've been through the mill, if you want the truth.'

'I don't know whether it's the mill,' I said. 'But I've been through something. You don't know the half of it.'

'Yeah, well, I'd like the half of it sometime. I mean, what *happened* to you, for fuck's sake?'

'One day,' I said. 'One of these days, Pen, I'll tell you the whole rotten story. *You* two are all right, obviously.'

'Yeah yeah yeah. You know.'

'Yeah, I do know. Helen loves you.'

'It's because I'm fantastic in bed.'

'It's because she feels sorry for you.'

He turned the lights off, one by one. In the darkness, as he crossed the floor to the bedroom, I said: 'Pen?'

'What?'

'I've missed you.'

He thought about it for a moment, then said: 'I've missed you, too.' Then, after a further pause: 'I just wish you weren't such a raging homosexual.'

Laura and Joe were back in London, proximity to Laura's parents in Bath having not helped. On the other hand, a windfall from a dead uncle had helped Laura set up on her own, doing garden clearance and bottom-of-the-market design, with Helen as second in command.

'I don't suppose you're looking for a pair of hands, are you?' I asked at breakfast, broke, in need of employment, useless.

Helen looked at Pen, who shrugged. 'Well, as a matter of fact,' she said, 'we might well be. Laura's going to be taking a bit of time off next month. She's pregnant.'

I looked at Pen. 'Size of fucking Jupiter,' he said. 'Christ knows how they're going to get it out.'

Julia's daughter, my niece, Valerie Maude Hood, whom I'd never met, had a lot of dark, shiny hair that fell in ringlets around her cheeks and large eyes the colour of prunes. She frowned a lot, and Julia warned that if she hadn't learned the art of keeping her mouth closed by the time she started school people would think she was retarded.

'She's a bit of a tart with blokes, I'm afraid,' Julia explained. Within five minutes of my arrival, Valerie had climbed onto my lap and twice licked my face. 'A trait I can assure you she doesn't get from me.'

The new house in Crouch End was big enough for me to stay without getting on Julia's nerves, and when my sister saw that Valerie was willing to be looked after by me, she would have paid for me to move in permanently. She had taken a year off work and described the withdrawal symptoms as *homicidal urges*. I relished having absolutely no free time whatsoever.

'It's for you,' Julia said, handing me the phone one night a few weeks after my arrival. Then with a flash of eyes, 'Some *woman.*'

'Hello?'

'It's Holly.'

Silence. Still, I wagered, transatlantic. All the heart's sleeping idiocies and manic hopes bolt upright.

'Don't say anything,' she said. 'Just listen.'

'Okay.'

'Your friend. Was it true?'

'My friend?'

'Kelp. Did he really . . . Do you really think he was trying to tell you to get out?'

'I don't know, Holl. Christ, I've missed—'

'No, don't say anything. Don't say anything about that. Promise.'

'Okay. Okay, I promise.'

'It doesn't matter, anyway. I'd already booked my ticket. I'm leaving tonight.'

'Where?'

'New Mexico. Anyway, it doesn't matter. I just wanted to . . . I don't know—'

'What do you mean, you'd already booked your ticket?' I said. 'Already before what?'

A pause. Longing. Love. Excitement. Hope. Magic. Loss.

'Before I saw him,' she said. Then she hung up.

I had no reason to consider the date when, with throbbing fingers, shallow breathing and the eventual dull realization that the line was dead, I hung up the phone. But like many other people, I've had reason to remember it since. McLusky's, like other places in that part of town, isn't there now.

By Christmas (the world within weeks having made light of all loud assertions that the world was now a completely different place) Valerie still hadn't mastered the art of keeping her mouth closed and Julia (hosting our parents that year) still insisted it was a mark of retardation.

'I wish you wouldn't say things like that,' my mother said.

'Maybe it's because we keep dropping her on her head,' Julia mused, at which my mother got up and took Valerie from her, as if Julia might otherwise have dropped the child on her head there and then.

'Remember when I dropped our friend on his head?' my dad said. 'Our friend' was (always had been) me.

'What are you talking about?' I said.

My mother shuddered.

'You dropped me on my head? When, for God's sake?'

'You were very small,' my dad said, after a visibly satisfying sip of Jules's Chivas Regal. 'Less than a year old, I think. I was throwing you up in the air and catching you, but I dropped you.'

'Jesus Christ.'

'You just went through my hands. Funniest bloody thing. Bounced straight off the bed and landed right on your nut on the floor. I didn't tell your mother about it till about a month later, after I'd watched you for signs of . . . Well, after I knew you were all right.'

My mother, with Valerie on her hip, went towards the kitchen to check the bird. My father chuckled, took another sip, returned his attention to the *TV Times*.

Julia looked at me. 'Which explains a great deal,' she said, knowing not whereof she spoke.

Which is all hunky dory, but what about . . .? Well, one means what about the . . .? One knows it's a delicate question and all. But still, one has . . .

Peace. I know my duties. I'll try. Something did change after that day in Pennsylvania. What changed was nothing more or less than that I began to find my fantasies . . . I hesitate . . . *vacuous*. Nothing – or at least not the thing they promised – followed from them. All along the Devil's work had smuggled in the intimation that it led to something big. *Big*. As far back as I can remember, all the way back to Deborah and Eastfield evenings with Alice, beyond that to the first primitive handjobs, further back still to *They made tapes*, to the *Weird Crimes* head-holder, to Kelly and Elaine (may her antipodean fortunes favour her, poor thing), as far back, yea, even as I, Dominic Francis Hood can go, the Devil's whisper was that his work must yield a profound revelation, a mighty and subversive truth, a vision so monstrous that one's humanity must evolve into divinity to encompass it. And yet, when it came down to it, the only thing the work revealed was that it was done by human hands, a truth neither mighty nor revelatory, but banal. 'The lie that knowledge follows from evil,' says Father Ignatius Malone in his *Weapons in a Real War*, 'is a superbly cunning – indeed a *diabolically* cunning – lie, but no less a lie for all its dark majesty. A giant, unholy, fabulous, seductive and tantalizing Grail of a lie; but still, in the end, a lie.' *And since we don't like the taste of it in our own mouths*, my margin note says, *we've a Father of Lies to tell it for us.*

But I mustn't get carried away. It hasn't been an overnight renaissance. Sometimes, just for old times' sake, I'll have an experimental go. I'll lie back and think of . . . Well, you know the material. Every now and then I'll put myself to the test.

Generally, it doesn't work out. Generally, the flesh is willing but the spirit is weak. Oh, how *wanting* that spirit is found to be. Generally, the whole thing collapses, struts kicked out by the memory of Pen bouncing up and down in the back of the Volkswagen, or Jim and Jake in the Brig, or raggedy Ange and monumental Tony. Generally, I prefer to keep my entitlement the best memories I have. Generally, it comes a cropper when I think of Kelp, and Holly's postcard from New Mexico.

> Dear Dominic
> I'm coming back to London next summer. Which doesn't mean anything.
> Holly.

There remains, I suppose, only one thing to be told.

Pen and Helen had their wedding in February.

'Thought we'd better get on with it,' Pen said.

'Get on with what?'

'All this marriage and kids stuff.'

'Is Helen pregnant?'

'What the fuck are you talking about?'

'I just wondered—'

'Of course she's not pregnant. Jesus Christ, *is* she?'

'*I* don't know, do I? What the fuck are you asking me for?'

'Well you started it. Holy God, Dummie, I'm getting married today and you're telling me my wife's already pregnant. She'd probably tell everyone before she told me, too. She's like that, you know.'

'Well, why don't you *get* her pregnant, now that we're on the subject?'

'Oh yeah, very funny.'

'What, can't you manage it? I mean you haven't got much time, you know.'

'I bloody *will* get her pregnant if you don't watch your mouth. Then we'll see who's laughing, eh? *Then* we'll see, won't we? Yes, we will, Nigel.'

A moment came, at the reception that evening, when I had to leave the celebration and step outside for a few moments alone with a roll-up and a well-iced Glenfiddich. I believe I've had such moments at every party I've ever attended – close to the great, revelling force of living flesh and blood, close to it, but just a little separate, to test the degree to which I can stand myself, to test (sounds grandiose, I know, but come on, we've travelled a long way together) my ability to go on living in the knowledge that I'm going to lose everything in the end, even myself, even my life.

So I stepped outside into the Windmill's car park. It was dark, piercingly cold, and very clear. I shivered. I could hear the music and babble of voices in the room above.

A car door opened and closed somewhere nearby. A woman in a long, warm winter coat came towards me, walking slowly, boot heels *tuk-tukking* on the tarmac's frost.

'Dominic.'

I started to think: how did she know where to . . .? Then stopped, because of course she would know. Kelp got it from her, after all.

She looked much older, but very well. Her hair was grey, cut short like a boy's. Once I recognized her, I wasn't surprised to see her. I was just surprised that she had survived.

'We wanted to invite you,' I said. 'We wanted . . . No one had an address for you.'

'I wouldn't have come,' she said, and smiled. Something had happened to her. Her eyes were bright, tired but awake. I thought: I wonder what Kelp would have looked like as a grown-up? As an old man?

'Shall we go inside?' I said. 'I just stepped out for a . . . Let's go inside. It's freezing.'

'I'm not staying,' she said. 'I just wanted to give you a message.'

I looked at her. Had I had a different life, there were all sorts of things I might have said to her. As it was, I said: 'Are you all right?'

She grinned, then, and for the first time I saw the old resemblance to her son: his smile, bright as a knife. 'Haunted,' she said – and believe it or not we both laughed.

'Penguin would love to see you,' I said. The cold was biting. An effort to keep my teeth from chattering.

'Give him my best wishes,' she said. 'He doesn't need them, but give them anyway.'

'I will. Of course I will.'

'His best wishes, too. He would have given them himself, but we – there are certain limitations.' She grinned again, and I thought I understood. Not her car door opening and closing after all. Well, I thought, you can believe in these things. It's just not best to rely on them.

'He said to say to you: "Give my love to the opsimath."'

I didn't ask her to repeat it. I didn't bother telling her I'd have to look it up. He probably *wanted* me to have to look it up. It was typical of him.

After she'd gone, I turned and went back to the living.

◆

The Opsimath

Time will tell, they say. They're right. Time *will* tell. That's what time does, arch-blabbermouth that it is. One day, Time will have told all, and that will be the end, off with the last light and down into terminal and dreamless sleep. Perhaps not even time for a species to say goodnight.

In the meantime, however, there is the business of being alive and trying to get better. In the meantime, for example, there is spring.

'We must work in the garden,' Helen said to me this afternoon, when we had stretched lunch – cheese and pickle sandwiches, hot tea, a Twix – as long as was seemly under the bespectacled and slightly strabismal eye of our current client, an accountant who has recently acquired a live-in lady much younger than himself and who has decided that *the time has come* (like me he is fond of portent) to get his back garden in order.

We must work in the garden. It's the only bit of Voltaire we know, but as a post-lunchtime rallying cry it gets the job done. Serves as gentle reprimand, too, when I'm caught leaning on my spade staring into what looks like space but is in fact the ether of memory or desire. 'We must *work* in the garden,' Helen whispers, with precise emphasis. She knows me, that I require the odd soft prod.

I wonder much what has become of Jim and Jake, Nancy and Jill, Tony and Ange, Natalie Jane West, Linda, Sorrel, Kelly Stew Fletcher, Elaine Sharples, Ruben Gould, Callum Burke, Vincenzo Gozzano, the Fernandezes, Father Adrian da Souza and crapulous Father Ahearn. In my spade-leaning moments the optimist in me toys with the idea of tracking some of them down. But the notion dissolves. I've read and seen enough to know that the thing to do with such memories is treasure them. Go looking for their presents and futures and you'll get trouble, disappointment at best; at worst . . . Well. It's best to let the notion dissolve. I force myself to remember Natalie, and when I do, I wish with a feeling like a cold blade laid against my skin that she has found her way to happiness, in spite of me.

I often wonder what has become of Deborah Black. But when I do I come up against sadness like a wall of raw earth.

I've had no news of Ignatius Malone, and am expecting none.

Other reveries are harder to shake. We're twenty-two days from the start of official British summer time. Nothing since the postcard. Nor any sense that I deserve anything. Just the reflex of hope without entitlement. There is Julia's painting, me on the couch, the white-dressed woman looking out of the window behind me, disturbed brush-strokes at our heads and feet. Time will tell. And whatever the story, I will have no trouble believing it.

In the meantime, there is the business of living and trying

to get better. In the meantime there is my old friend Penguin, and my sister Julia, and my mother and father, and Valerie's growing vocabulary, and the green grass of Kelp's grave, and the knowledge that certain things are not quite, apparently, in me. In the meantime there is the great empty space left by God and the Devil; within it the opportunity to listen to the curious sounds of human approximation. In the meantime there are, stubbornly, stains of magic, creases of the bizarre. In the meantime, as wise Helen will surely have cause to keep reminding me, we must work in the garden.